Sign up for our newsletter to hear
about new and upcoming releases.

www.ylva-publishing.com

Amy!
I hope you enjoy the book
C. Mills

OTHER BOOKS BY CHARLOTTE MILLS

Body of Work
Payback

CHARLOTTE MILLS

FAIR GAME.

DEDICATION

To C, thank you for not letting me off the hook.

ACKNOWLEDGMENTS

Thank you to Astrid and everyone at Ylva Publishing for their support with this project. To Miranda Miller for her guidance and assistance through the editing process; sequels can be tricky creatures. To Michelle Aguilar for pulling me into line once again.

CHAPTER 1

He crept up the stairwell, his trainers making only soft thuds on the concrete steps as he edged closer to the top. Sleep would have claimed Morris hours ago, but there was no reason to draw attention to himself. Besides, he knew little about the sleep patterns of the old woman in the next-door flat. He didn't like taking unnecessary risks.

He pulled the key he'd fabricated from his pocket, hoping the time spent earlier would pay off. The caretaker had been oblivious to his actions when he'd stopped by Morris's flat the other day. It was amazing what you could do with a lighter and a piece of sticky tape.

The sharp edges of the metal scraped against his skin: in his haste, he had bent the key out of shape.

"Shit!" He clapped his hand over his mouth.

He pressed the key against the wall to flatten it. Sweat clung to the inside of his latex gloves as he took hold of the padlock. Slipping the key into the slot, he held his breath and wiggled the thin metal. His jaw ached as he crushed his teeth together, fearing he would have to resort to plan B—the heavy bolt cutters in his rucksack. He rolled his shoulders as he tried again, jiggling the thin metal. He felt it twist to breaking point under his firm grip.

The padlock snapped open seconds later, preventing any further negative thoughts. He pulled off the lock, removing the key to flatten it again, this time against the door frame. He already had plans to remove the evidence as soon as it had taken effect. He opened the door. Darkness and warm air greeted him. The orange glow from the streetlights below provided some ambient light, but the surface of the roof was lost in the darkness. He stepped out into the moist air and slipped the padlock between the door and the frame to prevent it from closing on him.

He scanned the roof for the ventilation point he needed and moved towards his target, then pulled the required tool from his rucksack. After removing the screws, some WD-40 along the joint seam eased the release as he pulled off the mounted ventilation turbine. The sharp, scratching squeal stopped him. He remained crouched on the roof, gazing across at the only possible onlookers. Why the fuck couldn't Morris have lived in the other block? He studied each of the third- and fourth-floor windows. Due to the design of the block, only people in two flats could see him. Each window appeared dark; some had blinds or curtains visible, but most of the top-floor windows were black holes against the timber panelling. He clenched his jaw, still angry that his preparation had taken longer than he'd planned. Experiments could be unpredictable; he knew that now. There hadn't been anyone living there two months ago. Now some stupid woman had moved in, creating more complications for him.

Satisfied there was no one watching, he added more release agent. The turbine came off with little resistance. He placed his torch in the ventilation shaft before turning it on. There was the length of wood he'd placed in the shaft earlier. He switched the torch off, placing it next to his rucksack, and slipped on the face mask he'd pulled from his pocket.

The chemical scent of the mask filled his lungs. He removed the large plastic box from his rucksack and placed it carefully on the roof. He'd spent weeks culturing this specimen in the incubator, so he couldn't afford at this stage to damage it. This had to be the only source they would find in the flat. It needed to look like an unfortunate accident, an element of chance that had created this invisible killer. Except he hadn't left it to chance at all; Morris was already showing signs of flu.

He'd been smart in his choice of bacteria. Legionella wasn't common, but it did happen. With the location he had chosen, it was unlikely that anyone else would be affected. To stand any chance of inheriting whatever fortune Morris had hidden away in that dump of a flat, he needed to be totally unconnected to any of this.

He retrieved the fast food container from his bag. The right environment was needed for it to flourish—or at least to look like it had. Lowering it into position at the bottom of the ventilation shaft, he retrieved the wire and placed it into his bag.

After uncoiling the fishing wire he'd already tied to the metal, he popped the lid. In his experiments, the rusty surface had proven a good medium for the bacteria. He stretched his arms and teased the metal from its watery box. Standing, he carefully lowered the metal plate down the shaft. He fed the fishing line between his fingers, waiting until it settled on a solid surface before grabbing the torch to check its progress.

Content that it had reached its final resting place in the food container, he settled it flat. Morris would get weaker and weaker now, and soon he would struggle to breathe. Morris already had a slight fever, he'd seen it earlier when he dropped off some shopping.

Only a little longer would push him over the edge. Morris had to suffer, and he wanted to watch every minute of it. He'd quickly shelved his hit-and-run idea; Morris didn't deserve to go that swiftly. A warmth filled his chest as he pictured himself telling Morris exactly what he had done, just before the end. Morris needed to see the pain that he himself had felt for so many years.

He snipped the fishing wire and coiled it around his hand before pocketing it. He only needed to add the bacteria-laden water; then he could sit back and watch it unfold.

CHAPTER 2

LEXI RYAN STRETCHED OUT ACROSS the bed, expecting to clash with part of Helen's body at some point, only to be thwarted. Had it all been a dream? She rested on her elbows as she quickly scanned the dimly lit room for anything that would point to Helen's presence. Once her gaze landed on a familiar black coat on the chair in the corner of her bedroom, relief flooded her. For so many nights, she'd dreamt of Helen in this bed. She couldn't face waking up to disappointment again.

It was hard to believe that almost two months had passed since they had met up again. Lately, she'd relapsed into acting like a teenager—living for the weekends when Helen visited. She smiled to herself as she thought about their first meeting all those months ago in Warner. Despite their rocky introduction, they seemed to bring out the best in one another, at least in Lexi's eyes. Impersonating a police officer may not have been the best idea, but her choices were limited at the time. In the end, she'd assisted in apprehending a serial arsonist and a hit-and-run murderer during her stint as DC Kate Wolfe, hadn't she? Although it still didn't make up for the fact that she had also taken a life during her time there.

Richard Jarvis had attempted to grab a knife as he'd barrelled towards her before falling and cracking his head on the floor, but the circumstances made little difference to her. Was he even a victim? Hadn't her sister been the real victim—not to mention all the other children he'd abused during his sick life?

No matter how much she sugar-coated it, the harsh truth was that if she hadn't been there, it would never have happened. Her desire to inflict revenge and face her sister's sexual abuser had been too strong. She could have persecuted him for months before exposing him if she'd put her mind to it; instead she had gone for shock tactics.

In her panic, as he scrambled towards her, she'd missed the knife entirely. She could never have fought him off—he had been too well built. Her limbs twitched at the thought of having to fight for her life. It could have ended so differently. What if she'd been the one dead on the kitchen floor? Would he have called the police? Would he have got away with it? What about her mother? Who would have been left to look after her then?

Her decision to escape Warner with her freedom had been her only option. But leaving Helen behind was one of the most difficult things she'd ever done. Their last conversation, unsurprisingly, wasn't a great success. She had, after all, cheated her way into Helen's heart. Time was all she could offer. Let the dust settle between them. This gave Helen the upper hand. She could have arrested Lexi if she'd wanted. She had known exactly where Lexi would be in two months' time.

Lexi had almost talked herself out of going, convinced Helen wouldn't be there. The unease in the pit of her stomach when she saw Helen walking towards her on the pier had been like a murmuration of starlings moving around in her stomach. But confessing her feelings had been liberating, and two months of solitude had only clarified her desire for Helen. The fact that they were reciprocated was remarkable.

Helen was the most stunning person she had ever met, let alone dated. Smart, sexy, and with a sense of humour. Not to mention her insatiable sexual appetite, which was currently the reason for the ache in Lexi's body as she stretched again.

This time, Helen had arrived prepared to stay more permanently, especially if she accepted the offer on her house. Would Helen move closer, to Bristol even? Surely that would depend on what job she chose to do. Lexi didn't dare broach that subject yet. She was still processing the news that Helen had left the police force. It had seemed to be a job that fit her perfectly, at least at first. But the personal tragedy of her stepmother dying, not to mention the pressures of the job and the harrowing cases she had worked on in the past, had taken their toll.

After their first night together in that pokey little cottage in Warner, Lexi knew that she would either go to prison for the murder and unlawful disposal of Richard Jarvis or never see the inside of a cell. There was no grey area with Helen. You were either under her protection or you were her target. Lexi was grateful to not be the latter. Detective Chief Inspector Helen Taylor was tenacious at her job. Ex-DCI Taylor now, of course. Was that something else Lexi had to take responsibility for?

She squinted at the clock in the near darkness. It was almost two a.m. What was Helen doing up? She swung her legs over the side of the bed. A chill from the open window made her pull on her dressing gown before she ambled through her flat. She trailed her fingertips along the wall as she peered into the dark sitting room. No Helen shape was visible. As she stood in the kitchen archway, a silhouetted figure outlined against the large window came into view. From Lexi's position, it was impossible to see which way Helen faced. The glow escaping from the streetlights below provided only a slight orange incandescence.

Leaning against the wall, the narrow room put her at barely an arm's length from Helen. She fumbled for the light switch. On closer scrutiny, she saw that Helen faced the window. She showed no reaction to Lexi's approach. Once again, Lexi was glad she had a top-floor flat. There was nothing else the same height for miles around, which to her meant little need for curtains and the freedom to walk around naked whenever she wanted. Unfortunately, the dark material surrounding Helen told her she had yet to embrace this concept.

"Here you are! You know, Thomas Edison's inventions did make it to these parts."

"No. Don't!" Helen said.

But it was too late. The blinding flash filled the room. Helen shaded her eyes.

"What? Why?"

She shut off the lights and stumbled over to where Helen stood. Her authoritative tone reminded Lexi of the position this woman once held.

Lexi squinted, and flashing blurry lights filled her vision. She had to wait a few seconds for her eyes to readjust to the darkness, but even with her shadowy vision, she could see that Helen had ducked.

Helen moved her hand from her eyes; she'd managed to shield them just in time. Once she stood again, her focus back on the roof adjacent to the kitchen, she scanned the area for the figure she'd seen moving around. From the distance and movement, it was impossible to say whether it was a man or a woman. The flashlight they'd been using was still on the ground where they'd left it.

"I've been watching someone on the roof over there." There was no need to point; only the roof was visible from the window. The adjacent building was a storey lower, which made the roof almost level with Lexi's flat. Helen estimated the distance between the buildings to be around ten metres.

She moved closer to the window. Lexi bumped shoulders with her. Helen wasn't sure if it was the result of the darkness or Lexi's annoyance.

As she watched the dimly lit flat roof framed by the kitchen window, Helen struggled to make sense of the dark, blocky shapes. The glow from the street-level lighting made the roof darker. So far, on each of the occasions she had stayed at this flat, she'd paid no notice to her surroundings, her focus on Lexi and little else. But the screeching she'd heard earlier had grabbed her attention.

"If roof people are going to be a regular occurrence, I'll have to curb my nudity, or at least get some nets."

Lexi's fingers searched for hers. They slid home as she clutched at Helen's hand. *Nets, really?* She couldn't see that happening anytime soon.

"What's he doing? Funny time to be adjusting an aerial. Isn't that how that puppet guy Rod Hull died?"

A smile pulled at Helen's lips. She'd truly missed Lexi's wit. "I think it was the fall that killed him." She stood behind Lexi, wrapping an arm around her waist. "I'm impressed you even know who he is."

She slipped her hand under a loosely tied sash, disappointed that Lexi had bothered to dress, even though she had done the same. She deposited a kiss on Lexi's cheek, her eyes still fixed on the roof beyond. The flashlight stayed on the ground. Had they seen the flash from the kitchen light? Were they hiding, biding their time, waiting for them to go back to bed?

"I blame Emu. All those years with Rod's hand up his jaxi, the temptation to give him a nudge must have been too much for him," Lexi said.

Helen continued to scan the roof for any kind of movement. Nothing. "I think you might have scared him off."

"Good. I'm just getting used to this flat. I don't need any bloody perverts hanging around."

"Umm." Helen gripped Lexi a little tighter. People didn't creep around in the dark unless they had to, which meant the person was probably doing something they shouldn't.

"You're so suspicious of everyone. You probably think Jessica Fletcher is a serial killer."

"You laugh, but she *is* the common denominator every time." Helen was secretly impressed by Lexi's premillennium references. She liked how Lexi knew that anything after that would be lost on her. It wasn't so much the six-year age difference between them; it was more the fact that twenty years on the police force had restricted her familiarity with TV and popular culture unless it was crime related.

Lexi twisted in her arms to face her. "What are you doing up, anyway?"

Her face was in shadow, but Helen could hear the concern in Lexi's voice. "Couldn't sleep." She yawned, making her out to be a total liar.

"Okay." Lexi took her hand. "Back to bed."

She led the way back to her bedroom. Once inside, Lexi released Helen's hand and switched on a small lamp.

Helen scanned the view from the window. The absence of any rooftop beyond prevented her from snapping off the dim light.

"Are you regretting your decision to stay here?"

There were several feet between them, but with those words the distance didn't feel just physical. "What? Why would you ask me that?" Helen saw the worry in Lexi's eyes. She stepped closer and rested her hands on Lexi's waist. "I'm here because I want to be. I want to be with you."

The fine, wavy lines were still visible on Lexi's forehead. "You're not up worrying about it?"

Helen struggled to prevent a grin. "No. My sleep patterns are a bit screwed up. I've started taking afternoon naps—"

"Like an old lady." A smile finally appeared on Lexi's face, and her shoulders rose at least an inch.

"I don't remember you complaining earlier." Helen replied.

"Well, that was earlier. I've slept since then. I might need reminding."

"I see."

Helen raised an eyebrow as she pulled at the sash of Lexi's dressing gown, slowly loosening the bow. When she glimpsed what lay inside, her body stirred once again, a gentle throb between her thighs. She slipped her hands inside the gown, and they roamed over Lexi's firm flesh, the fingers finding warm breasts, hardened nipples. A glance up revealed that Lexi's lips had parted. Trailing a hand up to Lexi's neck, Helen brought their lips together. She made the kiss deliberately slow, then edged her tongue along Lexi's lips before slowly pushing inside. She knew how to drive Lexi crazy.

Lexi grabbed at her T-shirt.

Helen pulled back. "I love you. You have to trust me."

"I do. It's just the ground has shifted a lot for you lately with your stepmother's death and with leaving your job." Lexi smoothed the front of her shirt. "I love you. I can help. I want to help."

"I know you do. It'll take me a little time to adjust, that's all."

That was certainly true; Helen hadn't been unemployed since leaving school. Even then, she had joined the police cadets while she was at college, biding her time till she reached her eighteenth birthday. For the first time in over twenty years, she had nothing pressing on her mind, no crime sprees to crack, and no plans in place for her future. Her stepmother had been the one constant in life beyond her job. It still surprised her that Julia had had the presence of mind to prepare for it. The property and money she'd kindly left her would see Helen through until she had something in place. Right now, she had no clue where that would take her.

Helen stepped closer. She trailed kisses down the side of Lexi's face, stopping near her ear long enough to whisper. "I only want to be right here with you."

Lexi's response was immediate: her hands latched onto Helen's hips and pulled her closer.

The dressing gown slipped easily from Lexi's shoulders as Helen backed her towards the bed. She locked eyes with her as Lexi settled back onto the sheets. Helen pulled off her own T-shirt and underwear and dropped them onto the floor. She loved seeing the desire in Lexi's eyes as she knelt on the bed and covered Lexi's body with her own. Lexi reached for her. Her kiss was insistent, one that battled her for authority, but Helen wasn't about to give up her position of power so easily.

She pulled away from Lexi's lips but pressed her hot centre against Lexi's hip, releasing a groan at the contact. Ignoring her own desires for now, Helen trailed kisses down Lexi's neck and caressed the soft skin with her fingers. Lexi's body arched into her.

Helen ran her tongue around the hardened nipple, sucking it into her mouth. As the bud brushed against her tongue, she knew exactly what she wanted to do. She caressed Lexi's body and moved further south, tracing the line of her ribs with soft kisses as her fingers circled protruding hip bones.

She settled between those thighs as Lexi brought her knees up along either side of Helen's head and raised her hips slightly. Using her fingers to part Lexi's smooth lips, Helen found the jewel beneath. She couldn't resist blowing a cooling breath over the hot surface.

At Lexi's sharp gasp, Helen looked up into those darkened brown eyes above parted lips before returning to her focus. She flattened her tongue and dragged it from Lexi's entrance to her clit, receiving a groan of approval that made her repeat the action several times before she closed her mouth around the hardening clit. She placed a firm hand on Lexi's stomach in an effort to rein in her lunging hips, then used her tongue to bombard the bundle of nerves.

Her own arousal surged as Lexi's groans and panting increased. The jolt in Lexi's stiffened body told her to increase the pressure. Only moments later, Lexi came hard against her mouth. Her legs collapsed against the bed.

Helen climbed up Lexi's panting body. Lexi's hand circled her neck, guiding their lips together for an urgent kiss, then held Helen in place while she devoured her mouth, as if removing every trace of the juices that coated her lips. Helen settled a leg on either side of Lexi's thigh. Her clit throbbed at the close contact. As she moved her hips against Lexi's body, the intense pleasure flowed through her like a warm shiver.

Lexi slipped a hand between them, and Helen raised herself. Lexi's fingers eased between her lips and pushed inside, filling her as they nudged her G-spot. Straddling Lexi's thigh. Helen focused on her movements as she rode Lexi's fingers, plunging them deep inside her with every drive. Heat radiated from her body as she edged closer and closer to release.

Lexi sat up and stretched her arm around Helen's waist, a support as Helen continued to thrust herself onto Lexi's fingers. Kisses peppered

Helen's chest before Lexi's warm lips latched onto her right nipple, tugging at the sensitive bud and sending Helen over the edge. The quake ripped through her body. Lexi softly kissed her cheek as Helen slowly regained control of her limbs.

"I love you," Helen whispered against Lexi's shoulder.

CHAPTER 3

"God, where did the last couple of days go?" Lexi rubbed her face, not yet ready for the day ahead. She rolled over, burying herself against Helen's back, the warmth of her body making it even more difficult to even consider getting up.

"Maybe you should phone in sick."

"What?" Lexi looked up, breathing in the floral scent from Helen's hair. "Who are you, and where is the real Helen Taylor? Have the pod people taken you?"

Helen faced her, smiling. She was obviously enjoying her newfound freedom, to the point of purposely wrong-footing Lexi on a number of occasions over the last couple of days. She very much doubted Helen had taken a day off sick in her life, let alone faked it. When they'd first met, Helen worked around sixty hours a week. She imagined that schedule was slowing down compared to when she was an overworked police officer in Manchester. Right now she was stationary, in more ways than one. This time she decided to ignore it.

Helen's smile faded. "I have to go back to Warner at some point over the weekend."

"You do? Why?" She moved her hand across Helen's body, holding her firmly. She had been looking forward to spending the weekend together.

"The people who are buying my house are cash buyers. They're pushing for a quick sale, so I need to go and clear out the furniture I want to keep."

Panic rose in her throat. "You're coming back, though, right?"

A frown appeared on Helen's face. "Of course. Don't you want me to?"

She held Helen's gaze. "You'd bloody better." Her hand gripped Helen's torso a little tighter before she gently grazed her lips over the bare shoulder in front of her.

"Should only be for a couple of days. I need to sort out a few things, pick up some more clothes."

It sounded permanent, giving Lexi more confidence. "Maybe I could come with you, help out."

Helen glanced at her for a moment, a serious expression on her sleepy face. "Is that wise? What if someone sees you?"

Lexi turned to lie on her back. She knew Helen was right, but she didn't have to like it. Impersonating a police officer in a small town, then leaving the officer's dead body to be found in a house fire pretty much burnt her bridges on returning to Warner anytime soon. "What are you going to do today?"

"I don't know. Do you need me to do anything?

"Nope." This change to instant domesticity had been a little weird at first, but she was certainly growing accustomed to the benefits. She turned on her side again. Stretching out an arm, she wrapped it around Helen's waist, pulling their bodies closer. "I do have Netflix." She grinned at Helen. "Do you know what that is?"

She managed to scramble to her feet to escape the slap that was coming her way. Escaping the bedroom, she quickly headed for the kitchen, offering to make some tea as she left the room.

Lexi stood in the kitchen, waiting for the kettle to boil. She'd probably viewed this man-made landscape countless times since moving in two months ago. Having not seen anyone on the adjacent roof in all that time, she struggled to understand why someone would be clambering around in the middle of the night now. She wandered into the sitting room. Opening a cupboard, she dug around for something that might occupy Helen for at least some of the day.

The kettle clicked off, focusing her attention on her own day. Even though she'd only worked at the internet firm Shield Securities for a few months, it was the perfect job for a geeky hacker. From mostly "grey hat" to "white hat" in one job change—not bad. No doubt she'd spend most of the rest of the day running more checks on the new encryption software they were working on. As she returned to the kitchen, she checked the clock on the wall. She only had twenty minutes before she had to leave for work.

Tea made, Lexi walked back to the bedroom. She deposited a kiss on Helen's lips before she took her tea into the bathroom. Once she was showered and refreshed, Lexi moved back to the bedroom to dress, ready to leave. "There's a couple of good documentaries on Netflix, *Making a Murderer* and there's a drama about the Unabomber. I'm sure you'll find something to watch."

"If only I knew how to use a remote control; it's been so long."

As Helen lay in her bed, an eyebrow raised in challenge. She rose to it. "Don't tell me—you used to change channels by clapping your hands when you were a child." She recalled her uncle David's old-fashioned TV with the unceremoniously named "clacker" remote control. "My uncle had one that used sound waves to change the channel, the remote looked a bit like a dog thingy they use for clicker training. I used to constantly annoy my sister by clapping to turn off her favourite programmes whenever we went to his house."

"Is this kind of ageist attack going to be a regular occurrence, do you think?"

It was only a six-year age gap, but Lexi couldn't help exaggerating. From what she knew of Helen so far, there were few floors to pick up on. She had to start somewhere. "Probably. And it's not so much ageist as Ludditeist." Lexi caught Helen's grin as she stepped closer and took a seat on the side of the bed next to her reclining figure. She leant forward, placing a soft kiss on Helen's lips, then pulled back, she turned her body to pull open the bedside drawer. Her hand rummaged for the item she sought in the small space. "Here's your key for the flat. I've written the door code down for you too in case you want to go out. Help yourself to anything you want. I should be back around six."

"Don't work too hard." Helen said with a little too much glee in her voice.

Lexi spun around when she got to the doorway, filled with jealousy that Helen had another lazy day ahead of her. "I've left you something on the kitchen table you might find interesting if you get super bored."

Lexi strolled into the open-plan office, coffee in hand. She could hear two of her colleagues griping about Gordon Lingard. To be fair, he was the perfect target—an IT manager without a great deal of expertise in IT. He was merely a people manager, a shepherd of the office environment, nothing more. And the boss was always a perfect target.

"I'm telling you, it's classic Putt's Law: he knows nothing about what we actually do every day." Roman continued to mumble as he took his seat in front of his computer.

Lingard bashing had become a regular talking point in the office.

"More like the *Dilbert* principle if you ask me," Lewis offered from across the room.

"What's that?" Lexi asked as she neared her desk. Had they really taken the time to create yet another label for their inadequate boss? They had way too much time on their hands.

Lewis perched on the edge of his desk, facing Lexi. "It's where the least competent people are promoted to middle management in a company in order to limit the damage they're capable of doing."

"Okay." Lexi shrugged, hoping for more information.

"In Lingard's case, it's more like who you know, not what you know. He used to be one of us out here in the pit." Lewis raised his arm as if surveying the land of the office. "But where one of us would be dropped like a hen in a fox house if we fucked up, he was promoted further up the chain in less than a year of being here."

"How do you know all this?" Lexi sat forward in her chair.

"A friend of mine used to work here before me said Lingard didn't have a clue, and that his uncle on the management board got him the job. But he fucked up one too many times. They had to find him a new job where he could do less damage. They cleared out every one of the coders and programmers like us, and started with a clean slate."

"Dropped out of college, didn't even finish his degree," John chipped in.

"No shit!" Lexi flopped back into her seat. At least that explained why they disliked him so much.

"At least you graduated, Ryan," John offered.

"And you have some experience, even a little brush with the boys in blue." Roman turned towards them.

To an outsider, they probably sounded like they hated each other, but Lexi had acclimatised to their harsh conversations. They were only minor blowouts. No grudges were ever held for long. "You checked me out?" she asked, purposely sounding incredulous. The jab about the police was unwelcome, regardless of her juvenile status at the time of her arrest. She'd made sure that would never happen again. Still, she was annoyed. She thought she'd fitted in pretty well considering what she was running from in Warner. Her team obviously didn't take any chances on new colleagues anymore.

"Like you haven't done the same to us."

Shit. Lexi pursed her lips. "Maybe a little," she lied. She knew pretty much every detail of their lives. It had been too tempting to pass up when she'd first started there. "Do you really leave that webcam on every day to watch your dog?"

Lewis's face reddened with embarrassment as Roman sniggered at her words, which only seemed to annoy Lewis more.

"He gets depressed. I need to keep an eye on him. At least I don't set booby traps to spy on my own mother," he fired back, his eyes locked on Roman's head.

The guilt Lexi felt soon dissipated. "What?" She laughed; this was getting juicy now.

"He has a motion-sensitive camera that clicks on when someone goes in his room," John clarified.

"Thank you, Jean-Claude."

Lexi grinned. The moment she'd first seen John's unfortunate actual Christian name on her screen, she'd figured his parents were big fans of the action movie star.

"Yeah, well, at least I don't still live with my mother," John replied, sounding defensive.

"Why wouldn't I? She cooks, cleans, washes my clothes. You're the crazy ones." Roman blindly waved his hand around the office.

He really was a sexist pig in so many ways. The office fell into silence as everyone settled in at their workstations. Lexi was grateful the spat had ended; they had to work together after all. Not that any of them appeared to carry any resentment. They seemed to have the collective conscience of psychopaths. Apart from Lewis. The way he cared for his dog's mental state was kind of sweet.

"Where were you last week, anyway?" John changed the subject.

"I worked from home on Friday." Largely due to Helen's surprise visit on Thursday night. Not that she actually did any work. It was a good job Lingard was a shit boss. "I was helping a friend. They're moving in for a while." *At least I hope she is.*

"Man or woman?" Roman didn't even look up from his screen.

"What?" The question confused her.

"Man or woman, your friend who's moved in?"

"Woman."

"Ryan, Ryan, Ryan. When will you see that men are the future?"

Lexi smiled to herself. Roman had a super-sized superiority complex too. *Men might be in your future but not mine.* "When will you understand, Roman? A woman brought you into the world, and this one can just as easily take you out."

"Burnt," Lewis called from across the room.

Lexi settled at her desk. She tapped at the keyboard, bringing up the Bitblocker programme she'd been working on before taking time off. She felt bad if she had been the instigator of that little blowout. She couldn't be sure. She picked up her bag, rummaging around till her fingers found what she was looking for, then stood, quietly making her way across the room. "Hey." She hovered next to Lewis's desk, waiting for him to look up. "Sorry about your dog." She placed a Ruffle bar on his desk, subtly pushing it towards him like it was contraband.

Lewis smiled at her. "Don't worry about it. I used to be able to bring him to work with me, but Lingard won't let me anymore. So I like to keep an eye on him when he's on his own."

Lexi had always wanted a dog as a child. She wondered what Helen would think about that little addition to their home. *Whoa, one thing at a time. She's only just got here. Give her a chance to settle in.*

She scolded herself all the way back to her desk.

Curiosity eventually got the better of Helen, and she dragged herself from the comfort of Lexi's bed. She was unable to be quite as free and easy as Lexi and dressed in a T-shirt and shorts she found in a drawer opposite the bed.

She wandered into the kitchen to make a cup of tea, leaning back against the worktop she saw the binoculars Lexi had left for her on the kitchen table. Why hadn't she produced these earlier? Helen plucked them from the table as she stepped towards the window, training them on the adjacent roof. She searched the area where she thought the torch had been—nothing. Whoever had been out there had had ample time to tidy up. Helen thought back to what she'd seen two nights ago, tried to picture exactly where the figure had been moving around. In the daylight, it seemed so different. There were several ventilation turbines and large grey boxes. She supposed they could be air conditioning and electrical units for the building. The only way onto the roof seemed to be via a door on the right-hand side. The large, blocky shape must have been a stairwell next to the lift shaft. With only a low ridge around the outside, it would be easy to fall.

She could take a look around the roof of the building she was in. They looked to be the same design, only one floor different. Maybe then she could figure out what the man was doing up there in the first place.

Jesus, she wasn't a copper anymore. Whatever the man did in his own time wasn't any of her business, was it?

Placing the binoculars back on the table, Helen tried distracting herself by making a sandwich. She moved to the sitting room to make herself at home in front of Lexi's large wall-mounted TV. After several failed attempts, she eventually got Netflix up and running. Settling for Lexi's first recommendation, she sat back and relaxed.

The jangle of keys woke Helen from her hazy nap. She wiped at her mouth in case she'd been drooling again. She adjusted her slumped position on the sofa to sit up a little straighter, moving the blanket to cover her lower half. She crossed her legs at the ankle as they stretched out onto the coffee table in front of her. The TV was still on. She couldn't be sure how much she'd missed of the latest episode of this particularly frustrating programme; she was in a Netflix fog.

Footsteps quickly followed as Lexi strolled into the room. "Hey. How was your day?"

"How have you not smashed up your TV watching this?" Helen immediately replied as the arrogant police officer reappeared on the screen.

"What?" Lexi removed her messenger bag. She craned her neck towards the flat-screen TV fixed to the wall opposite the sofa. "What are you watching?"

"*Making a Murderer,*" Helen said with annoyance, considering Lexi had suggested it before leaving for work this morning.

"Oh. Yeah. Maybe not one for you, considering your background."

Lexi removed her jacket and threw it over the armchair. She pulled off her work ID, dropping it on top of her jacket.

"How was *your* day?" she offered as she caught sight of the ID hanging from the black lanyard. "You shouldn't really wear that outside of work. Everyone can see who you are."

"Huh." Lexi's face scrunched up and looked confused until she seemed to have spotted the object of Helen's distaste. "Yes, Guv," she said with a grin and made her way closer. She knelt on the sofa next to Helen. Their bodies brushed together. Helen raised an eyebrow, following Lexi's every move.

Reaching for Helen, she placed a soft kiss on her lips. "So, any more roof action to report?"

"Nope. Nothing. And thank you for the binoculars. Good day?" she asked again. She still hadn't received an answer.

Lexi settled next to her. "Not bad. So, what exactly have you got on under that blanket?"

"That's for me to know and you to find out."

"Really?" Lexi quickly snaked a hand underneath the blanket, her hand finding Helen's thigh and quickly moving higher, skirting the hem of her shorts as she leaned closer. Her lips created a warm sensation in Helen's stomach as they trailed up her neck, slowly making their way towards hers. Helen parted her lips almost immediately, welcoming the intimacy as fingertips moved up the inside of her thigh. The mild rumble emanating from Helen's stomach halted Lexi's fingers at the crease at the top of her thigh.

"Hungry?" Lexi offered with a grin.

"Starving." She'd barely bothered with her lunch; lounging around gave her little appetite. But now that she was awake, she was ravenous.

"I picked up a pizza on my way home."

"Sounds good."

Lexi climbed off the sofa. She faced Helen as she pulled her to her feet. Helen followed close behind as Lexi led the way through the flat.

"It's not homemade, I'm afraid. But what it lacks in quality, it makes up for in quantity." Lexi pulled the large sloppy joe from a shopping bag on the kitchen table.

Helen swallowed down her guilt for not pushing harder to cook for them tonight. Her vague offer when she'd texted Lexi earlier had been met with a *Got it covered no problem* reply. "I think you might need a bigger oven," she said eyeing the pizza's enormous size.

"We just need to be a bit creative, that's all."

Her stomach grumbled again as she watched Lexi fold up the edges a little so it would fit into the oven. Glancing at the instructions, she saw the cooking time. "Fourteen minutes on gas mark seven."

"Fuck! Fourteen minutes, I'm so hungry." Lexi grabbed up the egg timer, wrenching the top section to the required time before thumping it back on the worktop. "Wine?"

Instead of answering, Helen posed a suggestion of her own. "I'm sure I can think of something to occupy your mind for the next fourteen minutes."

Lexi grinned. "Trust me, my mind is already filled with the things I'm going to do to you as soon as my basic needs are met."

"I see." Helen stepped closer. She pressed Lexi against the cabinets and work surface, her hands circling her hips as she nuzzled up against her neck. The familiar flowery scent, mixed with sun-warmed skin, filled her lungs as a gentle heat began between her thighs. Lexi's hand cupped the side of her face, she drew back to look into Lexi's darkened brown eyes for a moment before leaning forward to capture her lips. Helen let her hand fall between them as her fingers traced the seam of Lexi's trousers below the zipper. When Lexi's lips parted, she continued to draw lazy circles on the front of her clothing. Helen knew exactly how to distract her.

"Okay. Okay. Ground rules." Lexi held her at arm's length. "No touching below the waist until we've eaten."

"What?" Helen missed the contact, forcing reluctant concession. "I'd forgotten how militant you can be about food." But Lexi continued to hold her at bay. "Okay." Helen finally relented with a grin. But she wasn't about to let Lexi off the hook quite so easily.

Helen kept her hands firmly around Lexi's waist this time as she pressed Lexi back against the worktop again. She slipped a knee between her thighs and struggled to keep the grin from her lips as Lexi pulled back and looked at her again with an accusing air.

"What? You said 'no hands.'"

With her appetite sated for the time being, Helen placed her empty plate on the coffee table in front of them.

"There's more if you're still hungry." Lexi placed her plate alongside Helen's. Pushing them both further back, she then stretched out her legs, propping her sock-covered feet onto the edge of the table.

"Not for me, thanks." She pulled Lexi's hand into her lap, stroking the back of it with her thumb. It was all the encouragement Lexi needed as she turned on her side, snuggling up to Helen.

"You're quiet. What's on your mind?" Lexi asked.

Huh. Had she been that obvious? Before she could put her words in order, Lexi beat her to it.

"The roof guy?"

"Well, we don't know whether it was a man or woman, do we?" *Yet.* "Whoever was out there has removed all traces of whatever they were doing."

"Which was what?" Lexi asked without changing position.

"I'm not sure yet."

"*Yet.* You know you're retired—right?"

"I do." Helen pulled away enough to look Lexi in the eye. "It's just— there was definitely something going on out there." It was too suspicious. If it was so innocent, why were they doing whatever they were doing in the dead of night?

Lexi regarded her, a slight amused-looking grin tugging at her lips. "What?"

"Still always on duty," Lexi said with a chuckle.

Ignoring the remark, she asked her question. "Do you know how to get onto your roof?"

"Why?" Lexi frowned at her.

"I want to take a look around, see if I can figure out what they were doing out there."

"There's a caretaker guy you could ask, I met him when I first moved in. I've got his number somewhere."

"Thanks." That would be a last resort; for all she knew it was him out there that night. Helen pulled Lexi closer as her gaze travelled back to the TV screen.

CHAPTER 4

Half-dressed, Lexi sat on the edge of the bed, drinking the last of her tea. She observed as Helen stretched out her long limbs under the covers. It was Friday already, which meant Helen was heading back to Warner.

"So I'll see you in a couple of days." She knew Helen was naked, yet she resisted the urge to slip her hand under the duvet. If she started something, she knew she wouldn't be able to stop.

Helen still appeared sleepy, relaxed. "Umm, shouldn't take too long. I need to clear out the last of the furniture from the house, put it in storage till I get a job, I guess."

There had been no mention of Helen getting her own place. Lexi let it go. The last thing she wanted was for Helen to move out. "I wish I could come with you."

Helen frowned. "Sorry. Not a good idea."

"I know, too risky," Lexi agreed although she'd changed her appearance during her time as DC Kate Wolfe. Dyeing her hair back to its original colour had been her first task after leaving Warner; however growing out the cut would take a little longer. Returning to the scene of the crime was indeed too dangerous. She quickly changed the subject. "What sort of job, a PI?"

"A what?"

"A PI. You could be like *The Equalizer*, saving damsels in distress," Lexi offered with a cheeky grin.

"Damsels in distress! How do you even know about that programme?"

"I sit in front of a computer all day. I get to research lots of things." Lexi drank the last of her tea.

"I see." Helen rolled on her side to face her. "Now, if you'd said *The Gentle Touch,* I might have kissed you."

Lexi placed her mug on the side table. "*The Gentle Touch*, what's that? It doesn't even sound like a cop show."

Helen's smile broadened as she adjusted her position in bed. "Now, I've heard it's perfectly fine to hinder people when they are in the process of getting ready for work."

Lexi turned to see a familiar glint appear in Helen's eyes. "Is that right?" The words had barely left Lexi's lips before she was tossed onto her back. The weight of Helen's body on top of hers was more than welcome.

Lexi arrived at work an hour later, grateful for the small refectory that was on site. She could hear Roman's voice in her head as she ordered a large coffee. *They're probably experimenting on us, captive audience.* He was nothing if not paranoid.

As she approached her desk, she could see several of her team huddled around one of Roman's computer screens.

"Hey, Ryan," Lewis offered as he twisted to look at her. "Watch this, and tell me what you see." He pointed to the screen.

Lexi took a large gulp from her coffee. Her small group of colleagues were, as she had told herself during the first week in the job, people she would probably cross the road to avoid in any other situation. But in the six weeks she'd worked at Shield Securities, she had to admit that they'd turned out to be some of the friendliest people she'd ever worked with. Not including Helen Taylor, of course. Sure, their so-called office resembled a business start-up rumpus room at times. But they worked as a team with a common purpose—when they weren't putting one over on each other. They might not be the most socially acceptable people on the planet, but from what she'd observed so far, Lingard didn't care what they did as long as they got their work done on time.

Lexi took her position next to Lewis. She waited for Roman to start the video again.

The image of a chubby puppy with his head stuck in a bin lid appeared on the screen. She was about to ask what it was she was meant to be seeing when a bare-breasted woman flashed onto the screen, a bottle of beer clasped in her hand. It was only a millisecond, but it was definitely there. *This is what the fuss was all about. Typical.* Despite her familiarity with the female form, she still felt the heat rise in her cheeks. It wasn't exactly the first sexual reference she'd encountered in this job. She had a feeling her colleagues generally saw her as an ex-hacker and not a woman at all.

"It's subliminal messaging. I'm telling you, that's what it is." Roman announced.

"If that's true, why can't you see it? Everyone else can accept you," John gave the still-seated Roman a manly pat on the shoulder.

Lexi considered making a guess, but thought better of it. She was still relatively new and didn't want to upset the apple cart for the second time in a week. Roman's brain obviously wasn't wired like everyone else's in the room.

"Okay, Ryan. What do you see?" John asked.

"Half-naked woman." At one time, she might have been embarrassed to admit it, but after interacting with these generally asexual individuals, there was no fear of harassment. "Or women, I should say; there's another one."

"What?" John and Lewis almost said in unison as they moved to scrutinise the screen behind her.

They weren't just nerds, they were horny nerds. Lexi stepped back to enjoy the frisson of excitement she had inspired at the idea that they had missed a chance at seeing another naked woman up close, who didn't even exist. She was pretty sure that if she asked for a show of hands right now, asking which of them had actually had sex with another person in the last month—or year, for that matter—there wouldn't exactly be a forest in front of her.

"What? Where?" Roman met her eyes. "You can't trust her. She's drinking the company Kool-Aid."

Lexi laughed. Roman was probably the most suspicious person she'd ever met. He never consumed anything from the refectory or water cooler, convinced it was impregnated with some cocktail of mind-controlling drugs.

Lexi took her seat, tapping on her keyboard to log in. She heard the dull tones of Gordon Lingard getting closer. That was odd. He generally preferred to manage their bear pit from a distance. Lexi was fully expecting to be chewed out for taking time off last week. Instead, when she peeked above her screens, she saw he had another person in tow behind his tall frame—a young woman, her blonde hair swinging behind her as she tried to keep up with Gordon's unnaturally long strides. She could hear him babbling on about the team. He was giving her the rundown on all of them.

"Morning, morning." Gordon stopped in the space separating her desk from Roman's. His bald head glistened as he waited in silence, presumably so all eyes could look at him. "This is Shelby Larson. She'll be joining us from next week."

Lexi reluctantly made eye contact as she discreetly closed the window she'd opened to search for *The Gentle Touch*. She hoped Helen didn't plan on physically modelling herself on Maggie Forbes; she doubted a perm would suit her at all.

"So, Lexi, could you show Shelby around, get her acquainted with the basics for when she starts next week."

"Uh, sure." Lexi stepped out from behind her desk. *Why me?* She studied her colleagues, each one of them unable to make eye contact with the blonde. *Okay. Now it makes sense.* "Shelby, this is Roman." She pointed to her colleague seated nearest to her, his eyes still glued to the screen inches from his face, a barely audible grunt emanating from his mouth. "And that's Lewis and John." They both attempted to make eye contact but failed miserably although Lewis did manage to glance at her chest while John attempted a wave that failed to physically materialise and transformed into a camp salute.

"Hi." Shelby offered weakly.

Still annoyed she hadn't received the same kind of stunned welcome when she'd started, Lexi looked back at Shelby. Her youthful lean frame, slender features, high cheekbones, and pale complexion gave her a slightly Swedish appearance. Lexi blew out an understanding breath before turning on her heels. "Let's start out here, shall we?"

Lexi waited till they were out of earshot before speaking again. "Sorry about that. They're a bit stunted. They don't get out much."

Shelby made no comment, as if it passed over her head entirely.

"I thought there might be some younger people working here." Shelby finally broke the silence as they slowly walked along the corridor.

Jesus, how old does she think we all are? Who was she kidding? IT was indeed a young person's game, but luckily there was no substitute for experience. "Oh." She tried to keep the disappointment from her voice. "Have you worked somewhere like this before?" By the sounds of it, Gordon had bluffed her into joining the company. He was a good front man; she had to give him that. He just knew nothing about what they actually did all day. Lexi was pretty sure Lingard knew nothing about the various "high-interaction honeypots" they'd set up to draw hackers in and study their moves once inside the fake networks.

"No. Freelance, mainly writing code for different software firms."

Lexi nodded. She found that hard to believe, considering the team she was joining. They were largely hackers with a different-coloured hat on. "Okay, these are the toilets. There are showers in there too, if you're planning on cycling or running into work." Wasn't that what young people did these days—run themselves ragged before even starting work, then slot in a hot yoga session during lunch or something equally ridiculous?

Shelby's eyebrows rose in surprise before knotting together in disgust. Lexi continued down the corridor. *Maybe not.* "Lifts." Lexi waved her hand to the left as they passed. "The stairs are here." Pushing open the door, she led the way down to the ground floor to point out the most important feature. "Here is the cafeteria. The coffee's pretty good. Closes at seven, if you're pulling an all-nighter. Although there's a machine just around the corner."

"Great."

Lexi wasn't convinced by her reply. With that perfect complexion, she probably only drank defrosted glacier water. Pointing across to the opposite end of the foyer, she added, "The security desk over there is where we all have to swipe to get in. I expect Gordon will sort you out with a pass when you start."

"Does that happen often?"

She must have seen the confusion on Lexi's face as she continued. "All-nighters." Shelby explained.

"Uh, no. Well, I mean, I've only been here a couple of months myself, and I've only been called in after-hours once, for an attempted security breach."

"Where did you work before you came here?"

"London." Lexi was running dry on things to point out, being pretty new herself. She had no tips to pass on at this stage. "Let's head back up." She led the way back into the stairwell and breathed a sigh of relief when Shelby didn't question her further.

"Have you…?" Shelby's tone dropped several octaves, echoing in the tall space, "ever been in trouble with the police? For hacking, I mean?"

"I err. How old are you?" Lexi deflected, scrutinising the young woman. She hated talking about her humiliating arrest, for hacking into her school grading system, amongst other places, a minor lapse in judgement.

"Eighteen."

Jesus! Lexi could remember being almost as annoying at that age, but never quite as developed as this young woman was. Shouldn't she be holed up in her bedroom, hacking into the FBI database or something? "Have you?" Lexi questioned.

"No. Well, almost. I don't intend on getting caught up like that again."

Is Gordon aware of this snippet of information, I wonder? "It's kind of a rite of passage for some of us." Lexi was careful not to indicate whether she had been in trouble. As they arrived at the main office, she smiled, hoping her reply would quench Shelby's curiosity and end her interrogation. "So this is where we all work. The desk over there is free, so you can set up over there when you start." Lexi was secretly glad it was a distance away from hers.

"Okay, thanks. Gordon says you're working on some new encryption software at the moment."

Gordon had a very loose tongue. What was he thinking, talking about their work so freely? "Uh yeah? We're running some in-depth tests on auto-encryption and developing a threat model." Lexi purposely avoided any detailed talk about the current issues they were having with the encryption key. IT, or rather online security, could be a dirty business, and highly competitive. Helen's suspicious nature was certainly rubbing off on her—not to mention Roman's guarded outlook.

Truthfully, Lexi could see from her current position in the office that none of her colleagues were actually working on the encryption job, their minds still firmly occupied with the subliminal messaging video from earlier.

"Okay. Well, I should probably get back to it. I'll take you to Gordon's office." Lexi crossed the large space, stepping around the foosball table as she led the way to Gordon's plush office at the far end of the room. The blacked-out windows were a testament to the fact that Lingard didn't want to know what they did most of the time.

"Whereabouts do you live?" Shelby asked.

"Err." Lexi stalled for a moment; there was something off about this young woman. "Not too far away."

"What area?" she persisted.

Was she fishing for information? Shelby's questions seemed to be more about her than the job she was starting in a couple of days.

"I'm living in the city centre at the moment, but I'm not sure about it." Shelby offered as if an afterthought.

"Oh." Lexi quickened her pace, immediately knocking on Gordon's door to draw an end to the awkward conversation. "I'll see you next week," she said before walking away.

* * *

He waited for the staff to leave for lunch before discreetly locking himself in the workshop. He could have purchased a bump key, but he didn't want anything he needed for this to be traceable back to him. Why would he, when he had all the facilities he needed close at hand? That stupid bitch had forced his hand; now he had another mess to tidy up.

He placed the key next to the only free vice in the workshop. Anger rose within his chest as he surveyed the scene around him. Grabbing the nearest thing to hand, he threw the ball peen hammer at the wall, catching the notice board that lined the far wall. Several items were dislodged, increasing his frustration. "Fucking twats."

It was as if everyone had just stepped out for a minute, but the reality was they had moved on to their next session, leaving all the crap for someone else to tidy up. Namely him. Bastards. He was surrounded by mindless lazy fucking bastards who thought they were too good to tidy up after themselves. He'd bring it up at the next staff meeting, again. Even though it wouldn't make any difference; it never did.

He rested his hands flat on the workbench as he took a calming breath. He needed to focus. Struggling to ignore the chaos around him, he moved to the shadow board to grab a micrometre. He returned to the bench. Using a fine Sharpie, he marked out the five points he needed, spacing them out evenly along the key blade. He secured the key in the metal vice. Selecting a number of needle files, he began filing down what was now excess metal on his spare back door key. This was his way out; it had to be; he couldn't wait much longer. His hand gripped the handle of the file a little too tightly, and his muscles complained. Stepping back from the bench, he took a breath. That bitch had seen him on the roof—he was sure of it. He wasn't about to let her get in his way.

———————— •••• ————————

He plugged in the wireless jammer, waiting for all the lights to flick on before he got out of his van. He was later than he'd planned, held up at work again. He'd watched the flat on and off over the last couple of days. He was confident it would be empty, at least for another hour or so till she got home. He pressed the buzzer to make sure her friend was still away, and there was no reply.

He let himself into the foyer, making his way over to the mail boxes. There was no name for Flat 4A. He moved with confidence to the top floor, aware that no one ever noticed him. They never did. Even his father had said he had a forgetful face. His father. That was a joke.

Bump key in hand, he thought back to the various YouTube videos he'd watched as he slipped the thick rubber washer over the blade of the key. He slotted it into the lock up to the washer. He imagined the pins inside the lock lifting up as the points of the bump key moved into position. He turned it to the right, then jiggled it a little before turning it back straight in the lock. He rattled the key again and pulled a rubber-ended screwdriver from his pocket. Tapping the end of the key, he continued to manipulate it, tried turning it to open the door. Nothing.

Aware of the noise he was making, he let go of the key. He stepped back, waiting for any reaction. Silence surrounded him. He stepped towards the door again. He repeated the stages under his breath as he worked. Finally, holding his ear close to the lock, he heard the pins snap up. He tapped the end, and as he turned the key, the door popped open.

He quickly pulled out the key, pushed the door open, and stepped inside. The coarse doormat scraped at his shoes as he closed the door. He stood like a statue as he took in the ambience of the flat. It looked barely lived in compared to Morris's. He struggled to breathe if he visited Morris for too long; his place was so full of crap, piled high along every wall.

The main room he stepped into was excessively tidy, every surface clear of debris. He opened drawers, finding only odds and ends, nothing personal. Nothing with a name on it. He spotted the metal drawers on the far side of the room, locked. He hadn't come prepared for that. Stupid.

He moved back to the hallway. Picking up the phone from its cradle, he checked to see if the number was attached. Nothing again. He dialled the pay-as-you-go mobile he'd stolen a few weeks ago. One of the brats had misplaced it in the lab—the opportunity was too good to pass up. Aware that the mobile was on silent, he wanted a record of the number, in case he needed it in future.

He continued through the flat. The bedrooms were the same, no photos, and tidy. Nothing personal hiding in the drawers. Only one bedroom was being used. The other housed a few empty boxes, no bed. Her friend that he'd seen earlier in the week must be sleeping on the sofa, although the excessive tidiness left no evidence. His jaw clenched and he let a frustrated breath filter out. Finding nothing made him more anxious. If she had decided to stick her nose in, he needed to have some leverage. Right now he had nothing.

He entered the kitchen. Taking in the view across to the other building, she could see into Morris's flat so easily, not to mention the roof. He saw the binoculars sitting on the edge of the windowsill. "Fuck!" His mind raced to what else she could have seen over the last few weeks. He picked the binoculars up held the weight in his hand, he dared to glance through them. He aimed them straight at Morris's flat. The endless piled up crap in the sitting room came into sharp view. White heat flowed through his body as he clenched the binoculars in a vice-like grip. He closed his eyes as he pulled them away from his face. He released one hand immediately burying it in his hair, fisting it he pulled until tears filled his eyes. He had to deal with this, soon. He spun around to leave, he placed the binoculars down on the worktop as he left the room. He slammed the front door. Along the corridor he kicked the fire door open, he left via the back of the building to avoid contact with any residents.

CHAPTER 5

Grateful to finally be home, Lexi twisted the key, bringing subdued light into her dark hallway. She entered, greeted by an unfamiliar musky smell as she walked towards her bedroom, eager to get changed. The bitter smell seemed to follow her through the flat. She dropped her bag on the floor and started to undress. Her gaze casually scanned the room; it looked different. Her feet stilled as she pulled her shirt over her head, not wanting to waste time with the buttons. Still holding it in her hands, she studied the room in more detail—the items around her. The wardrobe door was slightly ajar. One of the drawers in the chest was protruding slightly, a tuft of a garment preventing it from fully closing. It seemed untidy and unfamiliar to Lexi. She had always been tidy. Reluctantly at first, when she was a child, but now she relished the clarity and comfort it gave her.

Lexi thought back to the order she'd seen at Helen's house. Helen was very tidy, more so than Lexi, possibly due to the fact she spent less time there than at the police station.

She dropped the shirt on the bed and quietly moved through the rest of the rooms, looking for anything else out of place, her mind dismissing the idea that someone could have broken in. The front door was locked, and for a start, you needed a code to even get into the lobby. And why would a robber pick her flat anyway? It was farthest away from the entrance. An opportunist would go to the first and easiest target.

Nothing was missing. She dismissed the panicky thought. It made no sense.

Still, she continued her tour of the flat, following the indefinable scent. The sitting room looked normal. Was that even the right word? The TV was still attached to the wall. She moved to the small metal filing cabinet on the opposite side of the room. Pulling on the top drawer, she was relieved to find it still locked. It held general paperwork, banking information, various contracts for her flat and job. She pulled the keys from her pocket, checking it anyway. She listened for the metallic sound of the bolt flipping across, allowing her to open the drawer. Everything looked untouched, the folders hanging in the right order.

She opened the second drawer. There were a couple of old laptops stacked on top of one another, a few webcams, and cables stuffed down the sides. Her current laptop was in her work bag as always. Every one of them was encrypted anyway; they would be useless to your average opportunist. She closed the drawer, turning the key before removing it, and stood up, surveying the room again before moving into the kitchen.

What about one of her work colleagues? She quickly pushed that idea aside; she couldn't see one of them getting into her flat. They'd already checked her out, so why bother now? But the image of Shelby Larson flashed through her mind. She had been fishing for information earlier. Would she really be that bold? Besides, she hadn't even told Shelby where she lived.

She tried to think like Roman. As she'd witnessed over the last couple of months, he was a problem-solving master. He could reason out most of their networking or programming issues with—what did he call it?— abductive or deductive reasoning. Unfortunately his paranoia often got the better of him, hence why he still lived at home.

But maybe he was right. To be fair, she wasn't exactly used to living with someone. There was bound to be a period of adjustment. They'd spent time at each other's places before, but not like this. Helen had moved in, or, at least, Lexi hoped she would at some point.

She was being stupid. Helen was probably looking for something before she left. Nothing more than that.

Her eyes roamed around the kitchen as she stood by the table. The binoculars, they were gone. She'd seen them tucked away on the windowsill this morning, the same place where they had been for the last few days. Helen had put them there so that they were in easy reach to spy on the adjacent roof. She turned, scanning the shelving, the table—nothing.

Her eyes finally settled on them. They were on the other side of the room, on the worktop near the doorway, as if someone had put them down before leaving the room.

Roman's daily dose of suspicion was rubbing off on her. She walked back into the bedroom and pulled out her phone, dialling quickly.

Helen caught her breath as she sat in the driver's seat of the hire van. Maybe she should have let Lexi come with her after all. It certainly would have made moving so much stuff a little less strenuous.

The sound of her phone vibrating on the seat next to her pulled her from her thoughts. She smiled as she saw the caller ID. "Hey."

"Hi. When are you coming back?"

Helen heard the tension in Lexi's voice. "Tomorrow, hopefully, if I can get everything sorted. What's up? Are you okay?"

"Uh, yeah. I think so. I just...."

The hesitation Helen heard concerned her; it didn't sound like Lexi. She was normally so confident, bolshie even. "What's going on?"

"There was a funny smell when I came home, like—I don't know, it's probably nothing."

"What kind of smell?" Helen frowned. *Gas leak*, was her first thought, but she'd smelt nothing before she'd left this morning.

"A bit like…like cheap aftershave or something."

"What?" Confusion filled Helen's tired brain, matching her body.

"I know it's stupid. I'm being stupid. It's fine. Don't worry about it."

"Are you sure? I can come back now if you need me." Helen checked her watch, mentally calculating the time it would take her to get back to Bristol.

"No. it's fine. I'm fine." Over the line, Lexi blew out a breath. "I'm fine, really."

"Okay. But call me if you change your mind." Helen gripped the steering wheel with her free hand. She hated the anxious tone in Lexi's words. Why did she have to be so far away? "I'll call you later when I get back to Warner."

Saturday came and went with another phone call from Helen letting Lexi know she would be returning on Monday after she'd dropped off the hire van. There had been more to do than she had first realised. Getting access to Julia's storage locker had required permission from her solicitor, delaying her plans. Left to her own devices, Lexi spent the time clearing out space in her flat for Helen's belongings, an *if you build it, they will come* moment. Maybe if she created some space for her, Helen would see it as a more permanent arrangement.

A phone call from her mother took her mind off things for a while. Somehow, she'd managed to screw up her computer again. As usual, Val Ryan was adamant she only used it to watch crazy cat videos. Her browsing history had told a different story, like the dating sites Lexi had found the last time she'd checked it.

Lexi certainly wasn't opposed to her mother's happiness. Of all people, she deserved some at last. Her concern centred around her mother's continued alcohol consumption, something that had kept her at arm's length for a number of years. Still, she'd had to promise to visit soon to sort the problem out before she could get her off the phone.

With no further weird smells or anything else to report, Lexi tried to dismiss Friday's events from her mind. She decided to concentrate on Helen's imminent return instead. Unfortunately, spending the weekend alone was probably not the best idea.

She moved from room to room, meticulously checking each of the windows to make sure one of them left ajar hadn't allowed a pungent scent to congregate, something she had been guilty of with the spell of recent warm weather. Every time she tried to place the smell, she struggled to associate it with anything in her flat or Helen.

Which left only one option—and a terrifying thought.

He'd seen the car several times on his journey home, always parked in the same spot on the edge of the retail park or the side street in Kingswood. They could almost have done a car share. He knew exactly where to find it, and its age made it easy to break into.

He pulled down his cap as he scanned the area around him, then crossed the strip of grass that separated the side footpath from the edge of the car park. His fingers clenched the carrier bag in his hands as he quickly slipped between the VW and the car parked parallel to it. He crouched down, and the handle of the spikey tool slipped into his hand from the sleeve of his jacket. He immediately jammed the sharp tool into the space between the lock and the bodywork. The point punctured the rusty metal as he twisted it. His breathing increased as he created a jagged hole. Flipping up the handle with his free hand, he removed the tool, and the door released. He got into the foot well, closing the door. Ducking down, he caught his breath.

Confident he hadn't been spotted, he pulled the small drill from the bag. He shuffled his body, forcing the driver's seat all the way back as he settled near the ignition key slot. Whoever the driver was, they were short. He emptied the bag of its contents onto the floor of the passenger's side foot well, then secured the drill bit he'd selected. He was folded up like a deck chair in the tight space, but he had little option.

With the bit placed three-quarters of the way from the bottom of the key slot, he began drilling. He tried to picture what was happening inside. He saw the line of lock pins slowly being destroyed as his arm ached from the pressure. He pulled out the drill momentarily to remove the waste, then pushed it back in again. In his mind, he pictured the broken pieces of the lock falling into place and forced the drill harder. He grinned as it finally reached the key's marked-off depth. He replaced the drill for a slotted screwdriver. Frowning He struggled to insert it, let alone turn it.

"Fucking shit!" He grabbed the hammer from the foot well to try and force it in, but his own body and the tight space prevented him from getting a good swing. "Shit!" His breathing was becoming rapid again. Blood pulsed in his ears. He threw the hammer into the foot well as he slumped back against the door. He closed his eyes, focusing on his breathing. A film of cool sweat covered his forehead. His hands trembled. He twisted his body, forcing his shaking hands into his pockets. He was weak with nausea. His right hand brushed against the spikey tool. The sharp end scraped against his skin. He knew what he had to do.

His fingers tightened around the handle. He held his breath and pushed the point slowly through his coat and jeans into his thigh, welcoming the sharp pain that spread up his leg. His mouth gaped as air flooded his lungs. There was no yelp of pain, only relief as his breathing finally slowed.

As soon as he removed the tool from his thigh, it fell to the floor. His mind focused on the letters that marked him there. Pain seared through him as his fingers pressed along the surface, tracing the word he'd carved into his skin after the disappointment of being in her flat. This was meant to be his solution, a plan that was originally meant for Morris until he'd decided it was too kind. Now he had a new target.

His vision gradually returned as he focused on the rear-view mirror above. The cool blue sky beyond gave away nothing of the warmth outside. He'd come prepared for option B; he just wasn't confident it would work. If it didn't, he could kiss his so-called plan goodbye.

Anger surfaced once more as he yanked the screwdriver from the ignition. He turned the tool in his hand and used it to prise off the plastic casing around the steering column. He threw the cover into the foot well with everything else, then focused on the chaos of exposed wires. His back ached as he pulled out the bundle of red and brown wires. He dragged them towards the light to make sure he had the right ones. Satisfied, he stretched for the wire cutters and latex gloves. He pulled them over his hands before he cut through the first two wires, then stripped the ends and twisted the wires together. A spark of gratification surfaced when he craned his neck upward. The dash lit up. He pushed the joined wires to one side, focusing on the next one.

He blew out a breath as he cut through the wire, then dropped the cutters as he twisted the end, careful not to let it touch anything else. Hesitating for a moment, he touched the wires together. A few seconds later, the engine was brought to life.

After adjusting his position in the driver's seat, he pulled out a roll of electrical tape from his pocket to wrap the ends of the joined wires. Turning the steering wheel was a relief: no steering lock.

He pulled away, glancing back at the retail park. Nothing, no one had seen him. He came to a stop in a remote car park on the edge of the city and scanned the area before casually getting out to change the number plates for ones he'd prepared earlier. The last thing he needed was to get pulled over before he'd had his chance to deal with that nosey bitch.

CHAPTER 6

LEXI HAD A SPRING IN her step like a teenager cutting school as she headed down the road to her flat. She'd left work almost an hour early, not her usual MO on a Monday but necessary. She'd been a little spooked all weekend, which had made her miss Helen more than she'd expected considering they'd spent the last few months apart. Helen would probably be home already, her offer to cook a mouth-watering prospect, given the meals they'd shared in Warner. As she ambled along the road towards the four-storey apartment block, she wondered what exactly Helen would be cooking up in her kitchen. Curry or spag boll, maybe?

Lexi had liked the road her flat was located on the moment she saw it. She liked the way the trees erupted out of the pavement on both sides of the street. It was as if they had sprouted overnight like beanstalks, breaking through the layers of tarmac. They provided some much-needed greenery as she gazed out of her windows, the top foliage breaking up the blocky residential area. The car park out front looked full. Upon closer inspection as she slowed, she could see a couple of the spaces had been coned off, preventing their use.

"Bloody caretaker," she mumbled as she reversed back past the entrance to a space she'd seen earlier.

Lexi carefully slotted her Mini into the tight space. She pressed her key fob to lock her car and walked back along the road. Her messenger bag swinging on her shoulder, she strolled diagonally across the road.

The sharp whine of tyres of a vehicle taking off drew her attention. She looked around to see the front end of a car speeding towards her, and realised she was stuck halfway across the nearside of the road. It made no effort to slow down. She was stunned for a moment. What the fuck was going on? Couldn't they see her standing there? Cars were parked bumper-to-bumper behind her. She glanced back at the car. The sun visor prevented her from seeing the driver clearly. She needed to get to the other side of the road. A space by the entrance was her only option. The large tree next to it would protect her if she could get to it. She pumped her legs to keep up with the momentum of her torso. Her bag clattered against her back with every step.

Lexi managed to duck behind the large tree as the car approached her. The offside of the car caught the edge of the tree as it swerved past. Christ. Whoever was driving, they were aiming straight for her. She lost her footing on the uneven pavement as the crunch of metal made her lurch forward. Lexi fell, scraping her hands across the ground as she dropped into an uncomfortable pile.

The sound of something being tossed along the road made her look up, fearful that whoever it was hadn't given up. She scanned the road. Between two parked cars, she caught sight of a wing mirror bouncing along the tarmac. Her mind barely registered the sound of the car in the distance. It was already around the corner. They had no intention of stopping, which only confirmed her suspicions: she was the target. But why? What had she done?

"Jesus! Are you okay? I'm calling an ambulance. Stay right there."

A woman's shrill voice broke through the silent din in Lexi's head. She jumped. As she came to, all she could hear was her own frantic breathing.

Footsteps approached. A large woman loomed over her. Lexi eyed her, unable to find the words to reply.

"Don't move." The woman held a phone to her ear.

It was the same piercing voice from a moment ago. Lexi tried to sit up, ignoring the woman's pleas. She had no immediate pain. Relief filtered through her.

But her hands had started to burn red hot. As she turned them over, she saw the grit mixing with the blood peeking through her torn skin. She quickly flipped them back over and swallowed hard, the sight of her own blood turning her stomach. The last time she'd gotten hurt was in Warner when she nearly fainted in the street. She swallowed back the bile that threatened and pulled at the strap of her shoulder bag, dragging it towards her. She prayed the padding in her bag had protected the laptop. The woman was talking again, into the phone this time.

Lexi ignored the light-headedness swamping her brain. She tried to get to her feet and reached for the tree as support to get herself upright. She winced as the rough bark scraped against her frayed skin. Her knee was a little sore but nothing more.

She found her voice and tried to talk. "I—I'm fine really." Her voice shook a little; she tried again. "Please, I don't need an ambulance."

The woman looked at her, her mouth agape as she pulled the phone from her face. With one hand on her hip, her robust figure resembled a sturdy teapot.

"Please," Lexi repeated, "I need to get inside."

The woman seemed dubious as she studied her up and down. "Are you sure, lovie? It's no trouble."

Lexi nodded as tears began to sting the back of her eyes. She had been the target. Had she cut someone off on the drive home? She couldn't recall anything obvious. She tried to turn and walk to the entrance of her building, but her knee made her stagger a little.

"Wait a sec. We're in the same building. I'll help you."

Lexi twisted around to see the woman step away and grab a shopping trolley. She pulled it abruptly behind her, then stopped shoulder to shoulder with Lexi. She was a little shorter, making her a good height to lean on, although Lexi didn't really feel comfortable doing it. But she needed the help.

"Come on, lean on me. Let's get you home."

Lexi reluctantly draped an arm over the woman's shoulder, and they ambled towards the entrance. "We're in the same building?" Lexi half questioned. She'd barely seen anyone in the block of flats since she'd moved in. "I'm sorry. I don't even know your name."

"Well, that's not surprising these days; don't know most of the ones in our building. I saw you move in a while back. Like to know what's going on. Curtain twitcher, my Eddie used to call me. He used to love catching me. 'Lillian,' he'd shout, 'get away from that bloody curtain!' Used to scare the life out of me. Must have looked like I was signalling the bloody resistance the way the curtains moved then."

"Eddie?"

"My husband, died a few years ago. That's when I moved here."

"I'm sorry."

The woman didn't respond. An ache began in Lexi's knee as she waited for the woman to tap in the entrance code. "I'm Lilly," she said as she typed it in. "Lilly Murdoch." She pulled her trolley inside. "I'm in number 1B, just there." She deposited the trolley by her front door with one hand while still managing to prop Lexi up.

"Lexi. I'm in Flat 4A on the top floor."

Lilly nodded towards the far left of the lobby. "Let's take the lift."

A cold sensation fell across Lexi, like a shadow in the midday sun as the door closed on the lift. Had someone followed her from Warner? Did they know what she'd done?

───────·••·───────

Helen popped the cork on the wine as the front door opened. "Hey. Just in time. You must have some kind of wine radar."

The murmuring of an unfamiliar voice drew her into the hallway. Maybe Lexi had brought a colleague home, although, in truth, she hoped not.

An old woman held on to Lexi's arm, steadying her as they entered the hallway.

"Lex! What happened? Are you okay?" Lexi looked dazed. Helen had seen that look before when someone had tried to stick a knife in her. "Are you hurt?" The queasy sensation of guilt rising in Helen's stomach wiped out her appetite as she waited for Lexi's reply. It had been her fault last time Lexi got hurt, protecting her from a knife-wielding tramp, an unstable man Helen had stupidly turned her back on. Helen considered herself lucky that Lexi had escaped with only a minor head wound that day.

"I'm not sure. I don't think so."

"Some bloody maniac outside tried to run her over!"

"What?" Helen took the messenger bag dangling from Lexi's shoulder. She placed it on her own before taking Lexi's hand. It felt gritty. She turned it over, seeing the grazed, broken skin. When Helen looked back up, she saw fear in the large brown eyes staring back at her. She took hold of Lexi's upper arm and led them both towards the sofa. Helen knelt on the seat. She lowered Lexi down gently. The action was made all the more awkward with the other woman still holding on to Lexi.

Helen leant over, cupping the side of Lexi's face. She visually scanned her for obvious injuries before focusing back on anxious eyes. "Lex, can you tell me what happened?" She kept her tone soft.

"I'm not really sure. I was crossing the road outside. This car came out of nowhere."

"It didn't stop?" Helen clarified. Her eyes inadvertently took in the rest of Lexi's body again. The sickness rising in her stomach was all too familiar. How did this woman get into so many scrapes?

"He hit the tree and carried straight on round the corner!" the woman replied for Lexi. She was still standing next to the sofa.

Helen met her gaze. "He—you saw the driver?"

"Well, no. Not clearly."

"You didn't see the driver." Helen queried. Her frustration began to rise. She resisted the urge to challenge the woman further; she had helped Lexi.

"Not really. I think he had a hat on, maybe sunglasses. It all happened so quickly."

The woman was getting a little flustered. Helen needed to take a step back. She was panicking her. "Okay. Thank you for your help, Mrs—?"

Helen had plans to talk to her again at some point, to see if she remembered any more about the car. But for now, she just wanted to talk to Lexi, take care of her. She discreetly edged closer to the woman, a hand reaching for her back in an effort to urge her to leave. Thankfully, she took the hint, allowing Helen to move her towards the hallway.

"Mrs Murdoch," the woman replied. "Lilly. I live in 1B. I was coming back from the shops when I saw Lexi falling over. I've never seen anything like it. It was like they were aiming right for her."

Helen glanced back at Lexi. She was so small and pale on the sofa. She made a mental note of Lilly Murdoch's flat number. She'd leave it a day or two, give her time to think about what she saw, but Helen wanted to ask one more question. "Could you tell what colour the car was?" She didn't want to get her hopes up that the woman could identify the make and model.

"Blue, I think. Yes. Dark blue."

Lilly's reply gave her hope she might have seen more than she realised. "Thank you for all your help. I'll let you know how she gets on."

"I'd like that."

"I'm Helen, by the way. Helen Taylor."

"Nice to meet you, Helen."

As soon as she closed the door, Helen rushed back to the sofa. She could see tears surfacing in Lexi's eyes. She knelt on the sofa again. Their thighs touched as she pulled Lexi in for a makeshift hug. It was horribly one-sided. Pulling back, she saw Lexi's hands hanging lifelessly in her lap. Right. Lexi had an aversion to blood.

She cupped the side of her face, softly kissing her lips, relieved to see that some of the colour had returned to her cheeks. Her gaze flickered up to the thin red scar at Lexi's hairline. It had faded over the last few months, but it was still a reminder of how differently it could have gone that day in Warner. Tears began to fill her own eyes, threatening to escape. "I nearly lost you again." Helen whispered before she could stop herself.

"Hey. I'm okay."

Lexi's voice seemed a little more familiar now that they were alone. Helen leant forward. Cupping Lexi's face again, she softly pressed her lips to her cheeks. "Where does it hurt?"

"I…I don't know?"

Lexi's state of shock made Lilly's words ring in her head: *it's like they were aiming straight at her.*

Lexi was a more than capable person. She'd proved that in the short time they'd worked together. Was someone really gunning for her? And more importantly, why?

"I'm sorry." Helen held Lexi's gaze. "You know I'd never let anything happen to you." She stroked the cooled skin on Lexi's cheek. "I should have come back sooner. I knew you were freaked out the other day on the phone."

"What?" Lexi's face was expressionless.

"When you called me."

"It was nothing."

Helen ignored her plea. It had been something at the time. She had been able to tell by the tone of Lexi's voice. She should have listened to her gut. She needed to get the locks changed and quickly. With these two things happening so close together, she couldn't take any chances.

Lexi was avoiding looking at her hands. Helen suddenly knew what her first job would be. "Let me clean up those. I'll be back in a minute."

Helen got to her feet and headed for the kitchen before realising she'd need some supplies. "Do you have a first-aid kit?" she called back from the hallway.

"Err, in…in the bathroom on the shelf."

She returned with a bowl of warm water and a towel and knelt next to Lexi, the small first-aid box tightly tucked under her arm. After placing the bowl on Lexi's lap, she added some antiseptic to the water. "Let's soak your hands in here for a bit." There was no resistance as she lifted Lexi's hands. Helen threw the towel over her shoulder like a chef.

Her mind was working overtime. It was hard for her to accept that someone knew what had happened to Richard Jarvis. The missing person's case was still open. If anything had come up, one of her ex-colleagues would have phoned her straight away to get her take on it. A dark thought entered her mind: could it be linked to her own past? Someone she'd put away that wanted to punish her through Lexi? No one knew she was even there; she'd barely left the flat except to go back to Warner. The more she thought about it, the less sense it made. Had someone followed Lexi back from work?

"You think it's related to the other day," Lexi said.

"I don't know." Helen hesitated, not wanting to say more, but she knew Lexi would read between the lines. "Did you hit your head or anything else?"

"No, I don't think so, just my knee when I fell; but it's okay." Lexi tried to lift her right leg but winced, stopping in mid-movement.

Helen kneeled on the floor. She removed Lexi's shoes, then pulled up her trouser leg to inspect Lexi's knee. It was red with a darkening hue, but no broken skin. "You'll have quite a bruise there, I think." She deposited a gentle kiss on the damaged knee. When Helen met Lexi's gaze, those eyes were clouded with obvious thought. She was about to question it when Lexi volunteered.

"What if it's someone who knows me, knows what I did to Jarvis?"

"What? No way. Lex, it can't be that. No one knows but us."

"A coincidence, then."

But Helen heard the incredulity in Lexi's voice. She stood briefly before she pulled the coffee table closer, then took a seat as she placed the towel across her own knees. She removed one of Lexi's hands from the bowl of warm water and inspected the red, raw palm. She carefully patted it dry, grateful the grit had removed itself.

"What should we do?"

Lexi's aura of calm returned. Helen considered her questions carefully. She needed information while it was still fresh in Lexi's mind. "Can you take me through what happened?"

"I...I skipped work a bit early; I wanted to see you."

Helen smiled as the ends of Lexi's mouth quirked up at her own admission.

"I drove back, parked up. The car park was full, so I had to park on the street. I was thinking about you, what you'd be cooking. As I crossed the road to get to the entrance, I heard a car speed away behind me somewhere. I turned to see it."

Helen reached for Lexi's other hand and glanced up at her, urging her to continue.

"It hit the tree—wing mirror came off. It carried on, going around the corner."

Helen tried to picture the layout of the front of the building. Trees pretty much lined both sides of the street, as did cars most of the time. "The tree that marks the entrance to the car park?" She glanced up to see Lexi nod. It was the only explanation for the car to get that close to the trees. Even then, it would have to swerve towards it—and Lexi.

Satisfied that Lexi's other hand was grit free, she dabbed it dry before beginning her questions. "What sort of car was it?"

"It was a VW, I think. I remember the big logo on the front. Not sure what type, model. Maybe a Polo. It was old looking."

"Colour?" Helen had to ask, to see if it matched up with Lilly's description.

"Dark blue."

Helen nodded. There was no hesitation. "I know it all happened really fast, but did you see who was driving?"

Lexi shook her head. "Too dark. He had some kind of hat on, I think, and sunglasses."

"Did you tell Lilly what you saw?" Helen gently prodded.

"No."

Their accounts tallied so far. "Take me through your journey home tonight."

"I left work a little early, like I said. I had to take a different route to avoid the roadworks near the ring road, so the traffic was quite heavy."

"Anything unusual apart from that?" Helen chose her next words carefully. "No one leaning on their horn?"

"Not that I can remember."

If Helen had still been in the job, she would have simply called in a favour to get a copy of the CCTV tracking Lexi's journey home. Now she only had Lexi's recollection to rely on. She studied Lexi's trembling hands in her lap as they clasped together. This was a woman she had grown to care for and love more than anything else in her life. "Okay." Helen held her hands firmly as she pressed them to her lips. She'd seen a couple of cases of road rage in her time; it never ceased to amaze her the irrational anger and pain people inflicted on each other. But there was just one problem with the road rage idea: how had they beaten Lexi home to park on the street? Wouldn't she have noticed if she was being followed? As terrible as it sounded, she hoped that was all this was. Any other explanation came with a string of problems.

"Let's get the rest of you cleaned up."

Helen left Lexi soaking in the bath. She made a quick call, arranging for a locksmith to call by in the next hour. If someone had gotten into the flat as Lexi had feared, and now this... She couldn't take the risk of the two events being linked or a coincidence. She needed to be vigilant from now on. If someone really was after Lexi, she needed to be prepared, and providing security in their home was the first step.

Next, she called in a favour with an old colleague, Detective Sargent Pete Laker. She needed to know if any dark blue Volkswagen cars had been stolen in the last day or two. She prayed there would be no matches to her description. She wanted to be able to satisfy Lexi's worry and her own. It had crossed her mind that she could enlist Lexi's help in obtaining any CCTV in the area at the time of the accident, but that was a last resort. She didn't want to involve Lexi unless she had to. Helen planned to keep her on the right side of the law from now on.

CHAPTER 7

LEXI SAT AT THE KITCHEN table, removing the old front-door key from her key ring, grateful once again that Helen had taken the initiative and changed the lock. She hadn't been in a fit state after the events of yesterday. The shock had mostly worn off. Now she was angry and scared in equal measures. Helen had spent most of the night until the early hours of this morning trying to convince her that she had nothing to worry about from her time in Warner. It was hard to think of anything else, considering she'd nearly gone the way of "Sandy the ex-biscuit heir—turned tramp," a case that had seemed so straightforward compared to this one. Was this even a case? She'd been convinced that the Warner incident was the only reason she was being targeted, but in truth, if that wasn't the case, Lexi still had no idea who would want to harm her. Of course, friends and family of unconfirmed paedophiles have the right to be equally aggrieved after a death, but officially he was still missing. The evidence she'd seen on Jarvis was compelling, not to mention her own sister's account of the abuse. The one thing she did know was that the sickening guilt that lived in the pit of her stomach was changing, evolving—into what, she couldn't say yet.

Surely if someone knew what she'd done, the first thing they would do was expose the body to kick-start an investigation. It didn't make any sense. The fact that the driver wore a hat and sunglasses worried her the most. Did that mean she knew them, or at least might recognise them from some facet of her life? Or was it a simple disguise? Maybe she had it all wrong and she wasn't a target after all; that she was simply in the wrong place at the wrong time. Lexi struggled to hold on to that thought as footsteps came into the kitchen.

Noticing Helen was already dressed, Lexi wondered what her plans were. "What are you doing up?" Lexi picked up the new key with magnetic circles on the shaft and eyed it with suspicion.

"The locksmith said it was one of the best locks around, unpickable by most."

"By most?" Lexi grinned, sounding a bit more like herself. "So, what are your plans for today?" She knew Helen had made several discreet phone calls since the incident.

Helen poured a glass of orange juice. "First, I thought I'd make sure you got to work okay."

"What? There's no need, I'll be fine, really." Helen was obviously ignoring her pleas as she gulped the entire glass of juice before putting the glass in the sink. Helen had already tried to talk Lexi into having the day off, but unfortunately Lexi only had till the end of the week to finish the project she was working on. She couldn't afford to take time off right now.

"Then maybe look for a job," Helen continued.

"I see." Lexi tried to hide her surprise. She'd thought Helen would take it easy for a while longer; she should have known better. A workaholic needed a regular fix. "What sort of thing are you looking for?" Lexi had her own ideas on this subject, but she knew Helen would dismiss them right off the bat as she had done before. Lexi smiled as Helen took a seat at the table opposite her.

"I don't know. Maybe I'll become a computer boffin, get a job at your place."

They both knew it wasn't an option. Lexi had witnessed Helen's avoidance of technology, and one-finger typing.

"You should become a private investigator. You know you'd be good at it with your background." Lexi had seen the cogs turning in Helen's head from the moment Lilly had helped her through the door; it was in her DNA.

"I don't think so. That's not me anymore."

They both knew it wasn't true, but Lexi saw no value in pressing the subject. She looked at the clock. It was a discussion for another time—she had to leave for work.

Lexi gathered her stuff together. As she got to her feet, the pain in her knee made her flinch when she straightened her leg. "Well, if you're really stuck, I did see a job for a security guard at the technology park on their intranet the other day."

Helen frowned. "Really."

"They always seem to be needing more of them. They treat it like Fort Knox or something."

Helen got to her feet.

Lexi paused. "What are you doing?"

"I'm walking you to your car."

"Okay!"

Lexi tried not to smile as they left the flat. They were silent in the lift. Helen looked preoccupied as she reached for Lexi's hand. At the intimacy, she stepped closer, placing a chaste kiss on Helen's lips. "Thank you."

A response came in the form of a familiar arched eyebrow, followed by a lopsided grin.

They walked across the foyer, leaving the security of the building. Lexi nervously glanced around, scanning the area for anything suspicious. To her relief, the road was quiet. Only a couple of cars remained parked along the opposite side.

Lexi had felt safer during her short spell as a fake police officer. It had somehow given her a sense of invincibility. Wrestling knife-wielding idiots and chasing down arsonists seemed pretty safe to her right now, especially with Helen at her side.

"Where are you parked?"

Helen's words pulled her from her thoughts. Lexi scanned the row of parking slots. "Over there." She nodded towards her Mini Cooper.

"Can you remember where the VW came from? Was it parked up?"

Lexi tried to think back to those few moments after leaving her car. "I don't know." She stood in the road, and looked back at the tree. The scars of the collision were evident in the deep scratches on the bark. Her eyes scanned the road, then the gutter. "The wing mirror's gone."

"I picked it up last night after the locks were changed."

Lexi had no idea Helen had even left the flat last night. She glanced in the direction the car had come from, pointing in the same direction. "I turned when I heard the tyres squeal as they pulled away. He was in the road at that point, heading right at me." Lexi heard the wobble in her voice. She swallowed back the fear that sped up her heart.

"Okay, that's enough for now."

Helen's placating manner annoyed her. "Please don't use those words on me." Lexi clenched her jaw as she glared at the faint rubber tyre marks on the road. She couldn't help but see the similarities with the hit-and-run in Warner. Could it really be a coincidence? Helen's fingers moved against hers, getting her attention.

"Sorry. Slipped back into old habits there."

Helen's tone was like a balm on a graze. Lexi relented, letting her walk them the short distance to her car. She was once again thankful for her presence. Lexi pulled the keys from her pocket and unlocked her Mini. She flashed back to the moment yesterday evening when she'd locked her car. The car park had been packed with vehicles, which was why she'd ended up so far away from the flat. Still, she couldn't recall the blue VW parking up after she had. "I think it was parked up when I got here. I didn't hear it pull up behind me."

"Okay. Good. Text me when you get to work." Helen kissed her on the lips. Staying close, she spoke softly. "Call me if you need me, or not."

———————————————

Helen watched Lexi drive off. With the road clear, she scanned the street for any CCTV masts—nothing. She wanted a clear image of the car, and of the driver. She walked around the corner in the direction the VW had headed. The residential road joined onto a larger street with a few shops and takeaways.

Bingo! The car had to have been caught somewhere. Helen's eyes skipped from one street light to the next. On the third one along, she saw a CCTV camera fixed about two feet down from the drooping light. Making a note of the street name and location of the camera, she headed back to the flat. She still had one more thing to check on.

Helen knocked on Lilly's door. She heard movement beyond almost immediately. Several locks were released, and the familiar sound of a chain being removed echoed in the foyer before the door opened.

"Hi, Mrs Murdoch. Do you remember me from yesterday?" Helen offered, noticing the elderly woman was already up and dressed, her cardigan tightly buttoned despite the warm weather outside.

"Of course, dear. And it's Lilly. Come on in." Lilly moved to one side, allowing Helen to enter the flat.

Helen remembered Lexi's words about Lilly moving here after her husband's death and, more importantly, about her potential for being the eyes and ears of the area.

"How is Lexi this morning?"

"Much better, thanks." Helen took in the surrounding of the overstuffed flat. Downsizing obviously wasn't one of her strong points. "Have you lived here long?" Her gaze fell upon walls covered with shelving that contained plates and animal ornaments.

"Two years or more. Tea?"

"Thank you." Normally, she'd decline the offer when she was on the job, but it wasn't like she had anywhere to rush off to anymore. She followed Lilly through the flat into the kitchen. It seemed smaller than Lexi's. In fact, the whole place did, now that she thought about it. It was so cramped with furniture, she felt restricted moving around the confined space. No doubt it had been built that way to make room for the large foyer at the front of the building. Helen kept her arms close to her sides to prevent crashing into anything.

"I saw part of the registration, you know." Lilly had her back to Helen as she filled the kettle at the sink.

"I'm sorry?" she said over the noise as she stared at the zig-zag stripes on Lilly's cardigan, her hopes marginally raised. "What's that, Lilly?"

"I saw part of the registration. Not all of it, but some of it—the end bit, I think."

"Really?" The make and colour of the vehicle, alongside the part of the registration, would make it a lot easier to trace. "Can you tell me what it was?"

"I wrote it down last night when I came back to my flat." Lilly turned around. She pulled a small piece of folded paper from her cardigan pocket, offering it to Helen.

Helen took the piece of paper, unfolding it, scanning the lettering—ABL. "You think these were the last three letters of the number plate?"

"Yes. I think there was a four in it too, but I'm not sure where."

"Okay. Thanks." Helen stuffed the paper into her jeans pocket. At least she had a reason to call her contact in the police. Maybe they could narrow it down to a few vehicles with any luck.

Lilly poured boiling water into the teapot. "Are you going to call the police? Lexi wouldn't let me yesterday."

"Sounds like Lex." Helen grinned. "I do have a friend in the police. I'll give them a call. Lexi was sure the car was a VW Polo, so they should be able to locate it pretty quickly." Grateful as she was to Lilly for taking note of the car's registration, experience told her it was probably stolen and burnt out by now. But it was worth a try.

"Good. People shouldn't be able to get away with that kind of thing. Could have killed her."

"I know." Helen swallowed hard to try and get rid of that thought. "So you must know the area pretty well. What's it like? I've never lived this far south before." She hoped the old woman wouldn't see through her blundering attempt to change the subject.

"Oh, it's..." Lilly's eyes narrowed before turning to drop teabags into the teapot, sitting next to two prepared cups and saucers. "Pretty quiet, really. Don't get many students out here—too far from the city centre."

"Do you know if the CCTV for the building works?" Helen asked.

"If you can call it that. Karl's called out the technician umpteen times the last couple of months. Some kind of interference keeps causing it to freeze or something."

Helen resisted the urge to smile. She was definitely talking to the right person. "Karl?"

"He's the caretaker." Lilly held her hands out wide. "Big guy, hard to miss." She stirred the tea before putting the lid back on the teapot. "He's not around that much anymore. They keep cutting his hours. He covers both Gallagher and Longwell."

Helen nodded. She couldn't recall crossing paths with Big Karl yet. "What about crime? Is there much in the area?" She wanted a rough picture. She needed to know if yesterday's event was totally out of the ordinary or a run-of-the-mill act by an idiot joyrider.

Lilly studied her for a moment before answering. "Are you pumping me for information? Am I like a CI?"

Helen chuckled. This woman watched far too many American cop shows. "Not unless you're a secret criminal mastermind. Are you?"

Lilly threw her head back sharply as she filled the room with laughter. Helen found herself liking this charming old lady despite the predicament she was in.

When she returned to the flat, Helen pulled out her phone to call her ex-colleague. "Hey, Pete. I've got a little more info for you on that car from last night."

"Okay, let's have it."

Pete's gruff, clipped manner was no different now from when they'd worked together. He rarely expanded on the essentials unless pushed. Maybe that explained the DS rank he'd held for the last ten years or more. Nevertheless, she hoped Pete was taking it seriously. She wondered if she would do the same if the boot were on the other foot and an old colleague had called her out of the blue for help. "You got a pen?" She immediately regretted her tone.

"Yep. Shoot."

Helen was grateful he hadn't taken offence as she continued. "So, according to the witness, the car was a VW Polo, old, dark blue." She heard a commotion in the background, forcing her to raise her voice to be heard. "I've got part of the reg." She tried to sound upbeat, even though she knew in her heart of hearts it would probably be a waste of time.

"Okay."

Helen could tell by Pete's vacant tone that his attention was drawn by something going on around him. "Last three letters are *ABL*." She held back what Lilly had said about the other number, not wanting to give him unreliable information.

"I'll keep an eye out for any reported vehicles that match. I'll let you know if I find anything."

"Thanks." It was the best Helen could hope for considering she was out of the loop now—a civilian. It was the first time she'd regretted her decision to retire. She felt truly helpless to protect the person she cared for most in the world. "Pete, is Hanham a high-crime area?" After talking to Lilly, something told her this wasn't simply a joyrider. There was a bigger picture here; she just couldn't see it yet. What worried her most was escalation.

Whomever they were, if their goal was to hurt or even kill Lexi, they had yet to succeed.

"Err, I wouldn't say so. There are far worse areas, like Whitchurch Hill or Brandon Park, with much higher crime rates in Bristol."

Helen ended the call. She thought about what Lexi had said earlier about the security job. It would be a perfect opportunity to be able to keep an eye on her. She opened her laptop and searched for Shield Securities, all the while trampling down the classic cliché—washed-up copper taking a job as a security guard. Instead, she kept telling herself she was doing it for one reason only, to keep Lexi safe from any nefarious types.

It appeared Shield Securities was one of several companies based at the technology business park. She found the jobs page. The security guard job was tucked between two cleaning jobs. The job spec seemed okay. She was pretty sure she could manage it. A telephone number was listed for any enquiries about the post. They seemed desperate, with no lengthy application process required.

She was swiftly put through to a Hillary North, head of Human Resources. After a bit of small talk regarding her background, she was invited in for a more in-depth conversation at three p.m.

* * *

Helen arrived at the business park early. She was surprised by its size. No wonder they always needed security guards. After several attempts to find Reception, she was escorted to a waiting area outside Hillary North's office. The young secretary acknowledged her presence, immediately picking up the phone, and announced her arrival to the person on the other end. Moments later, a door opened, and a mature woman dressed in a black business suit stood in the doorway.

"Helen Taylor?"

Helen walked over to the woman. Her light brown hair was neatly piled on top of her head. The woman's fringe hovered above her eyebrows. Her skin was pale and clear except for slightly wrinkled pink cheeks that revealed her age.

"I'm Hillary North. Please come in, take a seat. I'm so glad you could come in today." Hillary waved an arm in the direction of the office she'd come from.

"Glad you could see me on such short notice."

Hillary smiled. "Somebody cancelled earlier. I couldn't believe my luck when you called, and an ex-police officer no less."

Any importance Helen had felt at being seen straight away was crumbling before her eyes. She took the offered seat and swallowed her pride as she waited for Hillary to sit behind her large wooden desk. "I've only recently moved to the area from Cheshire."

"You said earlier you were a detective chief inspector when you left the police."

"Yes. It took me a while, but I was a DCI for almost seven years."

"So what made you leave the police?"

Helen considered her next words carefully. "My stepmother was taken seriously ill. She died recently, and I decided I needed a little more out of life. That wasn't going to happen in the police force." She decided to try for the heartstrings, hoping it would satisfy the woman's curiosity.

Hillary's nod was subtle, but Helen picked it up. She reached for the phone on her desk. "I'll get George to give you a tour."

Helen was steered into the outer office twenty minutes later, having been suitably grilled to the point where she wondered if Hillary had ever considered a job as a detective.

Hillary led her towards the gaggle of seats she'd occupied earlier. Helen assumed they were waiting for George to turn up. "We'll obviously need to do some background checks. Until you're cleared, we'd need you to work in the less sensitive areas of the site."

"Right." Helen nodded.

"When would you be able to start?"

Is that it? Is she offering me the job? "When do you need me?" Helen tried to sound upbeat about the prospect of being a security guard on a business park.

"Tomorrow. Eight a.m. I've got someone off long-term sick at the moment, so it would really help me out."

They *were* desperate. "Uh, sure, no problem." At least she'd be around to keep an eye on Lexi. And it wasn't permanent. Helen desperately clung to that hopeful thought.

The interview, tour of the site, and organising of the uniform took almost two hours. As she left Hillary's department offices, Helen pulled out her phone to call Lexi. With her concern for Lexi's safety her main priority, she hadn't stopped to think how Lexi would feel working so closely together. Not that they hadn't done so in the past, and it had been her idea earlier. She genuinely hoped it wouldn't fuck everything up.

After breaking her news, she arranged to meet Lexi at the front entrance for a few minutes.

New uniform in hand, Helen waited outside. Through the large glass panels, she saw Lexi emerge from behind a door in the foyer. Another figure trailed behind her, a young blonde woman. Even as the blonde made her way over to the canteen area, her focus was firmly on Lexi, following her every move.

"Hey," Lexi greeted as she exited the building.

To her relief, Lexi looked happy, the annoyance of this morning long forgotten. "Who's that?" Helen nodded back towards the building.

"Oh. That's Shelby. She's new. Started this week. Gordon asked me to look after her for a while."

"I see." Helen could feel the woman's eyes on both of them. "What's she like?"

"Okay." Lexi lowered her voice, bowing her head. "Bit weird, actually. Asks lots of questions, and not necessarily about the job."

Helen's interest spiked. "What sort of questions?"

"Stuff about being in trouble with the police for hacking, where I live, what I do outside of work."

Helen shrugged. "She's probably trying to settle in, that's all." *Or hit on you?* She decided to keep that last thought to herself.

"Maybe. Although I caught her going through Roman's desk this morning."

Helen's interest piqued again. "How did she explain that?"

"Said she was looking for a marker pen, but she must have walked past a pot-full on John's desk to get to Roman's."

Helen raised her eyebrows. Another oddity in Lexi's life to investigate. At least she'd be in the right place to do that. "Did you tell your boss?"

"No. He already thinks we're all paranoid freaks. Anyway, enough of that." Lexi stepped closer, a grin plastered on her face. "So you got a job. A security guard, no less."

"It's temporary." At least until Lexi's safety was no longer an issue.

Lexi reached out to touch the uniform Helen had tucked under her arm. "We should celebrate. I could cook later." Lexi's hand moved lower, slipping around her waist.

"Or," Helen said with a grin. "*I* could cook."

"Even better." Lexi glanced at the time on her phone. "I have to finish running a few system checks. I'll be about an hour, tops." Bending closer, she deposited a kiss on Helen's cheek. "See you at home."

CHAPTER 8

HE PARKED ON THE STREET near the flats, away from the streetlight, in virtual darkness. He watched the dog walker turn the corner and out of sight at the end of the street before he switched on the jammer. He'd managed to extend its range, giving him more discretion in his arrival. Karl wouldn't figure it out for ages, if ever. The last time he had spoken to him, he was still talking about the foil back plasterboard they'd used in the refit causing all the CCTV interference.

He was only doing this because of that bitch, in case his last warning hadn't had the desired effect. He didn't even know her name yet, but he would soon. When she'd left this morning, another woman had been in tow. Was she living there now? Had she brought in reinforcements? There was something about that other woman too, the way she crept around Longwell House. She'd grabbed the wing mirror. Was she collecting evidence? He didn't like it. Why did everything he try always fuck up? From the look of things, she hadn't even called the police; most people did when someone tried to run them over. He could feel a shitstorm up ahead. Maybe they had something else in mind, if they ever found out who the culprit was. He had to make sure that didn't happen.

Why was he such a useless wretch? He couldn't even intimidate someone successfully. He had no choice now; he had to make his plan work. Unsure of what she'd seen that night, he knew he couldn't take the risk, especially after seeing the view she had from her flat. He needed this to be over. If she put it all together further down the line, she could screw him over.

He quickly tapped in the security code. Entering the lobby, he walked straight across the space. He stepped into the corridor that led to the back of the building and pressed his back against the wall, waiting. The metal of the nail bar hidden in his sleeve had warmed as it pressed into his skin. The building was quiet. His panicky breathing drowned out the soft hum of the lighting above.

He shifted around the corner. Holding up the nail bar, he forced the claw into the tight gap, prying the small door open. He thought it was empty for a moment as his eyes adjusted to the darkness. He slipped his hand inside. His gloved fingers brushed over something, gripping it he pulled it into the light.

———————— •••• ————————

Helen dressed in her new uniform. She caught Lexi's eye as she sat on the edge of the bed, drinking from her mug of tea.

Lexi tilted her head to one side. "Is it like being back on the job again, putting on that uniform?"

"Not nearly as exciting. A lot of walking around and checking of security badges, I expect." Not to mention keeping an unobtrusive eye on Lexi.

Lexi placed her mug on the side table as she stood, heading towards her. "Well, I for one, think you look incredibly hot in uniform."

"Good to know." As she finished buttoning her shirt, Helen smiled as Lexi slipped her arms around her waist. As warm lips travelled up her neck, moving closer to her mouth, she suspected this was an attempt at payback for the other day. She was helpless to stop her body's natural response. Unfortunately, Lexi knew exactly how to push Helen's buttons, and she mercilessly teased her. In an effort to gain control, Helen cupped the side of Lexi's face and guided their lips together, pushing her tongue between Lexi's parted lips. Her other hand moved down to caress Lexi's bare bottom. Lexi had taken to wearing a T-shirt, as opposed to being stark naked in the mornings. She still refused to wear any bottoms, convinced any roof dweller wouldn't be able to see her lower half through the windows.

Helen grinned at Lexi's eagerness as she backed her towards their unmade bed and flopped down on the mattress, taking Helen with her. Helen continued the ruse as she slipped her hand underneath the hem of Lexi's T-shirt. The soft skin was warm against the pads of her fingers. She could so easily get carried away.

She pulled back from Lexi's full lips, pausing just long enough to speak. "Are you trying to make me late on my first day?"

"Me? I don't know what you mean. I'm just reacting to the uniform."

Helen almost laughed at the look of innocence on the face only inches below her own. "Really." She leaned down to kiss Lexi again, more gently this time. "I love you," she whispered in Lexi's ear before climbing off the bed. Once on her feet, she caught Lexi's lopsided grin before she headed for the front door.

"Maybe I'll see you at work." Lexi shouted.

"Maybe you will."

Helen jogged down the last few steps, crossing the foyer towards the front door. The sound of murmuring drew her attention back towards the building. She noticed two people huddled around the mailboxes to the left of the foyer.

"2B, 3B, and 4A," one said.

Lexi's flat was 4A. Helen halted her approach to the front door. She fiddled with her keys to buy herself a few seconds. The raised voices were obviously frustrated and angry about something—she wasn't sure what. Turning on her heels, she headed towards them. They shuffled through their mail while continuing their conversation. Lexi had given her a mailbox key. Finding it on her keyring, she scanned the boxes, looking for the right one.

"4A." Helen said under her breath as she made a show of looking for it, key in hand.

"4A, yours, has been broken into like mine."

"Sorry," Helen replied as her gaze fell onto the slightly bent small metal door that housed the mail for Lexi's apartment. "Oh. What the...?"

"Tell me about it." The larger of the two figures, a young male around twenty-five years old with designer stubble, waved what she assumed were the contents of his mailbox in her direction.

Helen's chest tightened. No way was this another coincidence. "Has this happened before?"

The younger man shrugged.

"Don't think so, not that *I* can remember, anyway." The older man eyed the younger one, who was too engrossed in his junk mail to respond.

"Isn't there a caretaker or something?" Helen asked, recalling Lilly's words. She scanned the walls of the foyer in the hope of finding contact details. She studied the random selection of damaged mailboxes again. Only three out of twelve. There was no obvious pattern; they were in no kind of line at all, diagonal or otherwise. It was suspiciously arbitrary. As if someone was trying to distract from their real target—4A.

"I'll call him. Probably take him a few days to fix it," the older man said.

The mailbox for 4A was at shoulder height. Helen used her key to pry open the sprained door. She cocked her head to peer inside. The dim light in the foyer didn't help. She could just make out two envelopes inside. Aware that at least one other victim had fondled his disturbed rejected mail, she used the very tips of her thumb and forefinger to remove the letters. Helen gripped them tightly, keen to avoid the stares from the two men for her peculiar actions. She smiled and turned to leave.

Chances were that the culprit wore gloves if they were as determined as Helen was beginning to think. But she couldn't dismiss the possibility of latent prints on the envelopes. With her free hand she unlocked her car and rummaged in the boot, finding an unused evidence bag. With the two envelopes inside, she tore off the strip sealing the bag. Holding the bag up, she studied the envelopes—circulars or junk mail by the look of them. One was addressed to Lexi, the other to a Miss K. Harris; old tenant, she figured. She'd need to show them to Lexi to be sure. Wanting to secure the evidence, she pulled back the boot cover, sliding the bag underneath and pushing the cover back in place. Helen knew all too well from experience that cases of stalking or intimidation were notoriously difficult to prove. She would need to gather as much evidence as she could.

Helen had no idea if anything was missing or when Lexi had last checked the mailbox. She knew from their previous conversations that Lexi preferred to be paperless in most of her correspondence and rarely checked the box. She settled in her car as she considered the reasons for breaking into the mailbox. Beyond the obvious of stealing personal information like credit card details, she was stumped, especially as Lexi barely used it. Whoever broke in obviously didn't know that piece of information.

The fact that they had chosen to break open the mailbox put a slightly different spin on Lexi's concern that somebody had been in the flat the other day. The mailbox lock was much simpler to pick, if you were so inclined. Or were they merely trying to ramp up the intimidation? They wanted Lexi to know she was being targeted. They wanted her running scared, but from what?

As Helen drove to work, she felt justified in her decision to take the security job. It was her duty to keep Lexi safe, no matter what.

———————

Helen spent her first morning orientating herself with the site. As she made her way across the car park to the next building on her route, she passed by the rows of parked cars. She took the time to glance at the interiors as she went, making sure the side windows were intact. Towards the edge of the car park where a series of young trees had been planted, she spotted the shadow of a figure in the front of a vehicle. Concern for the occupant made her zig-zag around several cars as she moved towards the dark blue SUV. She could make out the shape of a woman slumped against the steering wheel. Asleep or dead from heart attack. Surely not a dead body on her first day.

As she walked to the driver's window, she was relieved to see the woman's hands move slightly as they clenched the steering wheel.

Helen tapped on the window with her knuckle, not wanting to startle the woman if she was merely taking a moment. Nothing. She knocked harder, knowing full well the dull thud of her knocking would be increased in the confines of the car. The woman jumped in surprise, her eyes wide. Helen got her first look at her. The reflections on the window only gave her a limited view. As the woman tilted her head, Helen saw that mascara had left deep tracks down her cheeks. Her eyes were red-rimmed. Her bottom lip quivered as she gaped back in visible surprise. Hysterical was better than dead.

Helen used her forefinger to draw circles in the air, giving the woman the universal symbol to wind down her window. Without the distraction of reflections, Helen realised the distraught woman was familiar. Human Resources. Yesterday she'd interviewed Helen. Although Helen couldn't remember her name; she'd met so many new faces that morning.

"Oh, it's you." The woman sniffed loudly, trying to wipe away her tears, obviously embarrassed as she sat back in her seat. "Am I in trouble?"

Helen scanned the length of the lanyard, finding the ID card. She managed to make out the surname *North*. "No, of course not. I saw you in your car, and I wanted to make sure you were all right." Helen noted the wedding ring being twisted back into place on her left hand.

"Oh." The woman pulled a tissue from her sleeve. She yanked the rear-view mirror in her direction before dabbing at her eyes, trying to rectify the damage.

It looked like an uphill struggle. Helen could recall the numerous times that she, as the designated female officer, had had to comfort distraught victims or family members. Death seemed to unnaturally age surviving family members. "Are you all right, Mrs North?" Helen asked, knowing full well it was a stupid question, but she had to ask. She figured the woman would either offload or clam up, the latter being preferable. She hadn't taken this job to get wrapped up in some office drama. She wasn't that bored.

"I…I, well, I'm just being stupid. Bit of a falling out, that's all."

Domestic. Helen nodded. "I only have two bits of advice: it takes a bigger person to apologise, and never go to bed on an argument."

"You're not married."

"No."

"Boyfriend?"

Helen hesitated for a moment. She wasn't going to mention Lexi by name. "Girlfriend."

"Oh. Well, at least you don't have to worry about a shithead of a husband having an affair!"

Helen was about to protest her ridiculous statement when she saw the renewed distress in Mrs North's eyes. "I'm sorry." She waited a few moments for the woman to regain her composure before trying to lighten the mood. "For a moment there, I thought I'd found a dead body on my first day."

"Sorry."

North sounded genuine, relaxing Helen's mind a little. "Wouldn't be the first."

North froze for a moment before turning to look at her. "Oh, that's right. You were a police officer, weren't you? I remember now."

Helen nodded. "Retired a few months ago."

"You know, *you* could find out for certain if my husband was having an affair. I could take him to the fucking cleaners."

"No, I don't think I could. I've never done that kind of work." Right about now would be a perfect moment for the earth to open up and swallow Helen whole.

"Come off it. You were a police officer for how many years? You could follow him and find out what he's doing, who he's meeting. I'll pay you."

"I already have a job, Mrs North."

"I know, but this would only take you a couple of hours."

"You really should talk to your husband." Helen took a step back, hoping to end this discussion. "I should get on with my rounds." Helen backed away as she continued across the car park, hoping Hillary North would quickly forget their conversation. Helen had enough on her plate right now with someone trying to persecute Lexi; she didn't need this shit too.

From looking around, it seemed Lexi was safe here, safer than at home, evidently. An outsider would find it difficult to get close to her without being challenged or at least seen on numerous cameras.

With her shift finally over, Helen left the building and headed for her car. Her current security clearance had resulted in her walking about ten miles of the perimeter today and very little else. Her feet were killing her. As she rounded the corner of the building, she passed a semi-circular bench. North was sat in the middle, her eyes red. She'd been crying again.

"Hey." Helen took a breath before sitting next to her. She wanted to make sure she was okay to drive before she let her go.

North's hands shook as they fiddled with a mobile phone. Helen noticed the large crack running across the screen as she turned it over.

"He's going away again, some conference on solar panels in Bath." North sobbed.

"I'm sorry." It was an empty gesture in many ways; Helen didn't even know this woman. "Can I ask why you're so sure he's having an affair?"

North twisted her body to look at her, a flicker of hope in her eyes. *Shit.* She was getting sucked in.

"I called him on his mobile while he was at work the other day, and a woman answered. She sounded so young, I asked who she was, but he must have grabbed the phone off her."

"How did he explain that?"

"Said she was some new apprentice—that he'd left his phone in the conference room and she picked it up." Hillary wiped at an escaping tear.

Suspicious but not damming. "Most work places have apprentices now."

North wiped at her nose. "He's never talked about them before. He's worked there for ten years. It's a small company, all men, from what he's told me in the past."

If she'd had her old work coat on, Helen could have provided North with a fresh tissue. Damn these empty pockets. "Anything else?" Helen asked, figuring there had been more to arouse North's suspicion.

Hillary played with her tissue. "He's started locking his phone with his fingerprint. He never used to do that, just in the last few months."

Okay, so that was a bit suspicious. "Where does he work?" Maybe he was simply being email security conscious.

"At Eco-House. It's a green energy consultancy firm. It's not big."

Hardly top secret. Helen let out a deep breath. "When's he going away?"

"Friday. Will you help me?"

"Let me think about it." Helen stood, satisfied North was safe to drive. "I'll let you know tomorrow." There was an angle here. She needed a moment to think it through.

Hillary fished around in her jacket pocket. "Here, take my card. Call me when you've made your decision."

Helen reluctantly took the card. It was sounding like a foregone conclusion already.

She parked up outside Lexi's apartment block, mentally rolling her eyes at the thought of telling Lexi about North offering her another job, let alone the fact that she was considering it. First she'd caved by getting the security guard job, and now she was going to be doing private investigations on the side. Lexi was fast becoming "Mystic Meg."

Helen had already made her decision as soon as she'd mulled over the benefits of what it could bring. She had to strike a deal with North. She pulled the business card from her pocket and dialled the mobile number. It was picked up on the second ring.

"Hi, Mrs North. It's Helen Taylor." She waited a beat before continuing. "I was thinking about your problem on my drive home—"

"You're going to help me."

"I will *if* you can do something for me."

"Name it."

The positivity in North's voice gave Helen hope as she made her request. "I need you to put me on day shifts—only for a while."

A heavy breath travelled down the phone. "What? Why? How am I going to sort that out? They'll think I'm giving you special treatment because you're new. Or worse, because you're a wo—"

"I don't care what they think." Why did North even care? She was older than Helen. Had she struggled in her own job role as Helen had in the past? She would happily accept the burden for making the request. It wasn't how she usually operated, but she didn't have a choice right now. "Believe me, I wouldn't ask if it wasn't important. I'm trying to look after someone. I can't be there for them if I'm on the night shift."

"Are they ill?"

Helen considered lying, wondering if it would make North come through for her. She took the gamble. "Sort of. I need to be around for them, that's all." Protecting Lexi was her priority, no matter what.

North took an audible deep breath, releasing it directly into the phone again. "Let me look into it. I'll get back to you tomorrow."

Helen grinned at North's obvious bluster. She was pretty sure she had enough clout to arrange this minor request, especially if she wanted to know what her husband was really up to.

"Holy shit! Are you fucking kidding me? Hillary North tried to hire you to see if her husband was cheating on her?" Lexi leant against the door frame. "Fuck."

The woman had barely even acknowledged Lexi's existence since she started there, but on her first day, Helen got taken into her confidence. Lexi couldn't help but be slightly aggrieved. What was she—merely a geek employed to keep the wheels turning? A faceless geek amongst many others?

"I know," Helen mumbled as she pulled off her jumper.

Lexi watched Helen strip off her uniform. She hung her trousers by a belt loop on a hook. Her white shirt quickly followed. "Are you going to take it?"

Removing her final layers, Helen spun around to look at Lexi, shrugging as she grabbed a towel from the rail.

"Well, I did say you should be a PI." Lexi tried not to gloat.

Helen eyed her sharply as she stepped into the shower. "Don't even say it!"

CHAPTER 9

FRIDAY CAME AROUND FAR TOO quickly for Helen. Thankfully, Hillary North had come good on her request. Helen was on day shifts until further notice, which also meant she had a job to do this evening. She closed the front door and immediately began stripping off her uniform on the way to the bathroom. As she got into the shower, she heard the front door close. She smiled to herself. Lexi must have been hot on her heels the entire way back from the technology park. Due to their slightly different shift patterns, they had agreed to take separate cars, but Lexi must have skipped out early again.

"Hey." Lexi's voice echoed in the hallway.

"In here," Helen called from the shower. Footsteps headed in her direction. Peeking out of the shower, she watched as Lexi appeared in the doorway.

"So, you're out on surveillance tonight, then."

"I am," Helen replied. She waited for the other shoe to drop. Lexi had been dropping hints about joining her from the moment Hillary had asked for her help. She regarded Lexi as she began to undress, her clothes falling to an untidy pile on the floor.

"Want some company?" Lexi offered.

Helen stepped back. "Sure." Wait a minute. This was it; the shoe was dropping. She quickly shuffled forward, barring Lexi's entrance. "Whoa, are we talking about the shower or tonight?"

"Both."

With Lexi's grin, Helen realised her suspicions were correct. "I'm not sure that's a good idea."

"Come on. I promise I'll be good." Lexi flinched as she stepped into the bathtub. Helen saw the darkened bruise that had formed on her right leg where she had fallen trying to escape the speeding car.

Lexi continued to push her way into the bathtub, pressing their bodies together as she backed Helen into the spray from the shower. Arms circled Helen's waist. Warm lips travelled up her neck, capturing Helen's lips in a hungry kiss. Her weary body came to life under Lexi's touch.

"I missed you today," Lexi whispered barely loud enough over the noise of the shower. "I saw you strutting around outside a couple of times, but you never came to see me. I'll have to hook you up to a pedometer if you keep that up."

Strutting. She had a point, though, Helen had been observing her from a distance all week. "I was trying to give you some space. Maybe I'll stop by and see you next time." She let her arms drape over Lexi's hips, trailing lower to cup her buttocks, pulling their bodies tighter.

Their bodies brushed, and a groan escaped Lexi's lips. "Maybe you should."

Did she really want to leave Lexi on her own? She had no idea how long she'd be, and after recent events, surely Lexi was safest where she could keep an eye on her. "Okay," she relented. "But you have to stay in the car."

"Of course, no problem." Lexi's arms moved higher, circling her neck, pulling their lips together again. There was no mistaking the direction this was taking. Warm water trickled down Helen's back as their lips parted. Lexi's soft lips were working her up into a frenzy as their bodies moved slowly against each other, stoking Helen's building desire.

Helen had never been keen on sex in the shower; it all seemed a bit too precarious to her. Lexi knew this, but it never stopped her trying any chance she got. Helen backed Lexi towards the end of the bath, away from the water. She had no intention of this playing out here. She released Lexi to grab two towels from the shelf next to the bath, handing one to her before stepping out with the other.

"I'll get you one day, Helen Taylor." Lexi followed Helen out of the bathtub.

Once she was roughly towelled off, Lexi immediately reached for Helen again, pulling her body tightly as their lips crushed together. They stumbled the short distance to the bedroom. Helen backed Lexi onto the bed before climbing on top of her. They were sideways on the mattress, but there was no time to adjust. Their lips locked together. Luckily, the bed was so big, it was almost square.

Helen cupped Lexi's warm breasts, teasing one hardened nipple before moving to the next. She slipped her hand lower, skimming over Lexi's torso to grasp the outside of her thigh. She sat upright, straddling Lexi's left thigh, her hand moving lower down to nudge Lexi's legs further apart. Adjusting her hand, Helen's middle finger easily moved between slippery lips. Her eyes never strayed from Lexi's as she pushed inside Lexi as far as she could. She groaned at the wet heat that greeted her and the gasp that left Lexi's mouth.

Lexi pushed her head back against the bed as she pushed her hips forward. Helen acknowledged her encouragement. She removed her finger, adding a second before slowly pushing them both inside. The muscles adapted to her intrusion. Their gazes bored into each other as Helen began a steady pace. Lexi rocked her hips in time.

Lexi sat up, clutching onto Helen as she pushed her hand between Helen's thighs, quickly finding her now-throbbing clit. Lexi drew slow circles, sending shockwaves through Helen's body. The white heat building between her thighs was almost too much as she tried to focus on Lexi's needs. She glanced down at her thrusting hand, watching the tension in Lexi's stomach as her gaze travelled up Lexi's body. The incredible waves of sensation flowing through Helen's body forced her to stutter as she pressed herself harder against Lexi's fingers, enjoying the tension growing in her body. "Come with me." Helen whispered.

Helen extended her thumb to circle Lexi's hardened clit. The muscles around her fingers began to spark. She knew Lexi was close to orgasm; the groan Lexi released confirmed it. "I'm so close." Helen offered, receiving a brief nod from Lexi, whose breathing remained heavy.

She leant into Lexi, forcing more contact with her clit. Helen locked eyes with her once more as she continued her thrusting actions.

Their hips rocked furiously. They both panted. Lexi came first, her whole body jerking as Helen's fingers became locked in a vice-like grip. She stilled her fingers, but her thumb continued to gently circle Lexi's clit, bringing her down slowly as her own orgasm ripped through her body and pressed her against Lexi. She buried her face in Lexi's shoulder as she caught her breath. When Helen slowly removed her fingers. Lexi moved her body, pulling her down into her arms as Helen snuggled closer to her warm, familiar skin. She had no idea how long they had been lying there when their earlier conversation flashed through her mind. She poked Lexi in the ribs. "I don't strut!"

Lexi jumped, making the bed jiggle. She laughed. "Yes, you do."

More movement caught Helen's attention as Lexi pounced, straddling her hips. She looked down at Helen, a wide smile stretching across her face. "And I love it."

The drive from Bristol to Bath had been relatively quick despite the rush-hour traffic. Without knowing exactly what to expect, it was hard to put a solid plan together. Helen needed a way of getting North's room number; then she had to wait to see whom he met, and if he was up to anything. She was genuinely not looking forward to it. She had no idea how he would react if he spotted her taking photos. She imagined Hillary North was the type who needed visual evidence, even though her mind had already done a pretty good job on its own.

Helen stared at the front of the revolving door of the Kettler Hotel, waiting for Jack North to arrive. She'd already checked the parking situation and knew that he would have to enter through the front. She'd managed to secure a spot on the opposite side of the street not far from the entrance.

It was an odd choice of hotel. Most conferences in her experience were either on a shoestring budget at a Travelodge out of town or, if they were trying to make an impression, maybe at a high class, all-the-bells-and-whistles-of- city-centre hotel. The Kettler didn't fit into either of those categories. On paper you would never know the difference, but scanning the street at either side of the hotel entrance, she noted the run-down takeaways and rough-looking pub at one end. It certainly wasn't the type of area you wandered around at night.

"Okay." Helen took a long breath. "This could take some time when he actually gets here."

Lexi turned to look at her. "I realise I'm no expert in these matters, but from what I know, if he is having an affair, it should only take a few minutes tops."

"Is that the voice of experience talking?" Helen asked before she could stop herself.

"Would that surprise you?" As a grin stretched across Lexi's face as Helen tried to think of a reply.

"Not at all," she bluffed, not wanting to reveal any resentment at Lexi's past. "We all stray from the path from time to time." To give herself something else to focus on, Helen quickly picked up her phone, bringing up the photo of Jack North that Hillary had provided.

She had never considered herself a possessive person, but the thought of someone other than herself being intimate with Lexi did not sit well. She needed to take her mind off it. "Want to play the alphabet game to pass the time?"

"Are you kidding me? After last time? Anyway, we need to be ready to catch him at it."

"*We're* not going anywhere." Helen released her seatbelt to get more comfortable. "*I'll* check it out when he gets here, give him some time to settle in first." She twisted in her seat to face Lexi. "Come on, don't be a sore loser." She tried to keep the annoyance from her voice.

"No, thank you."

"Okay. What about a different game?" Helen relaxed when Lexi twisted around to study her back; she'd clearly piqued her interest. "Do you know what a portmanteau is?"

"Like *par cark* instead of car park."

Helen shook her head. "That's a spoonerism. A portmanteau is where you join two words together to make a new word. I had a sergeant once who thought he was a master of it."

Lexi blew out a breath. "Okay, I'll bite. Give me an example."

"Like, smog is a mix of smoke and fog squashed up to make smog. Or glamping is glamorous and camping."

"So we take it in turns to think of a new word."

"Yes. You can go first if you like." Helen kept an eye on the front of the hotel.

"Phablet, a mix of phone and tablet."

She turned back to glance at Lexi, eyeing her suspiciously. She'd expected Lexi to take a little longer. Something didn't seem right here. She wasn't sure if it was Lexi's eagerness to play or the fact that in the time they'd been sat there she'd seen only individual men entering the hotel. Lexi didn't exactly have a good track record when it came to playing her games, and Helen didn't want a repeat of the A to Z chocolate bar fiasco. It turned out Lexi could be a very sore loser.

"What. That's not already a word, is it?"

"Nope don't think so, not yet. That's the point, isn't it? It could be."

Helen raised an eyebrow in Lexi's direction, letting her know she wasn't convinced. "I guess I'll have to give you the benefit of the doubt, won't I?" She knew she was being taken advantage of, but she let it go.

"Guess you will. Your turn, I believe."

"Umm, I thought of one the other day while I was listening to the radio. *Fooligan* as in football and hooligan."

Lexi snorted. "Sounds about right for some of them."

Helen picked up one of the bottles of water they'd brought with them. Taking a long drink, she offered it to Lexi before returning it back to its holder.

"Favicon, favourite and icon," Lexi offered.

"What! No way. That's way too geeky."

Lexi sat back in her seat. "Why not? You can have *fooligan*, but I can't have *favicon*!"

She glanced across to Lexi. "I know what you're doing."

"What?" But Lexi wouldn't meet her eyes.

"Pretending to make up nerd words that probably already exist." Helen arched her eyebrow to add weight to her statement. Not that it made any difference: Lexi wasn't even looking at her.

"Are you accusing me of cheating?" Lexi finally spun around to look in her direction.

"Possibly."

"Okay, what about *unkeyboardinated*, uncoordinated keyboarding. That's *typing* to you." Lexi said with a grin.

Helen snorted. "I like it." She poked Lexi in the thigh with her index finger. "Hey, is that aimed at me, by any chance?"

"No, you're just a bit computerphobic." Lexi's grin widened. "Oh my God, that's another one. I'm practically on fire here."

Helen fidgeted in her seat, trying to think of her next offering, but her mind kept going back to the image of Lexi with another person. "Who was it?" The words were out of her mouth before she could stop them.

"Who was what?"

"The man you dallied with?"

Lexi smiled at her. "There wasn't one."

"Really? I know we haven't really talked about our pasts. Obviously we both—"

Lexi's hand appeared on her thigh, halting her reply.

"There wasn't one. I was messing with you." Lexi stretched an arm towards her, their hands softly entwined. "Sorry."

"Good." Helen struggled to keep the satisfaction from her voice.

"No dick has breached these shores. Well, not a real one."

"What?" Helen was about to launch into another round of questions when movement past Lexi's profile caught her eye. North wheeled his small suitcase into the hotel. "Okay." Helen grabbed her phone from the console where she'd left it charging. "Our man has arrived. I'm going to pop inside, see if I can find out which room he's in."

"How exactly are you going to do that?"

"Not sure yet."

"Okay. Sounds like a plan."

Helen closed the car door before dashing across the road towards the hotel entrance. She entered the hotel. Scanning the foyer, she found Jack North standing at the reception desk, checking in. A bank of lifts were located at the back of the room. She slowly walked towards them, pulling out her phone as she walked. She fiddled with it as she waited next to the call button.

She texted Lexi, informing her that she was trying to look busy. She asked her to send her back several texts to give that appearance.

Helen then scanned the immediate area around her, noticing there was only one lift available. The other one was out of action, thank God. She sensed a presence next to her and turned her head, catching North's profile out of the corner of her eye. Turning away, she avoided any kind of scrutiny in her direction as he pressed the call button several times.

Her phone beeped as she waited for the lift to arrive. She tried not to smile at Lexi's further attempts at portmanteaus: *Mcfatty*.

As the doors opened, Helen waited for North to step onto the lift first and press the floor button. She joined him at the last second before the doors closed.

Helen had never really liked small spaces, and this lift was suddenly very tiny, considering she was trying to avoid the only other occupant. The lift pinged as the doors opened. They were on the third floor. North stepped off. She waited a few seconds before following him, careful to keep her distance.

A phone rang close by. It took her a moment to realise it was North's. He answered it on the third ring, juggling his bag as he pulled the phone from what looked like the breast pocket of his suit. Luckily, he was verbally exuberant as he answered. Helen figured it wasn't Hillary on the other end. She heard him arrange to meet someone in the bar as soon as he'd dropped his case off.

North walked down a hallway on the left. She followed. She could see the end of the corridor and pulled out her phone, pretending to make a phone call as she hovered outside a room a distance away. She fumbled in her pockets for her key card as she discreetly observed North enter his hotel room.

His door closed. She quickly walked closer, taking note of the room number before heading back to the lift. She then found the bar North was hopefully heading for as she walked back through the foyer. Helen zig-zagged around the tables, picking up a discarded newspaper from the arm of a recliner in an effort to look occupied. At the bar, she ordered a soft drink. Luckily, the bar was already busy. Maybe there was a conference here after all. She scanned the occupants as Jack North entered and joined a group of suited men on the far side.

She took a seat at a table a suitable distance from her quarry and pretended to scan through her phone as she switched on the camera app. She ended up taking several photos and tapping the screen numerous times before it started to record video. She was technophobic, not just computerphobic. She discreetly panned across the group of suited men before concentrating her focus on North. He was already on the hard stuff, ice clinking in his glass as he threw back the amber liquid. They were a rowdy bunch, on a jolly boys outing.

A few moments later, a conga line of identical women entered the bar. Helen observed them as they disappeared behind a pair of large double doors on the far side of the room. Their appearance reminded Helen of the Robert Palmer music video where all the band members were dressed in little black dresses, their dark hair slicked back so that they all looked alike. The room was silent for a few moments as the group of men all stared at the door the women had disappeared through.

Before the doors swung shut, Helen got a peek inside the room beyond. Her gaze landed on what appeared to be several covered tables. Something about the sturdy style of them said "casino". That put a slightly different spin on things. Okay, so maybe gambling was North's failing. Helen spotted the small *Private* sign on the door. Getting access might be difficult, especially if it was illegal. Any gaming establishment worth its salt, legal or otherwise, would have some kind of security system in place. Helen was annoyed with herself for the second time that night as she accepted that she needed Lexi's help. She dialled her phone as she braced herself for the humble pie she was about to eat.

"Hey. I think I might need your help with something."

"I see. Does that make me your partner again?"

"Maybe, for tonight," Helen relented.

"What do you need, Guv?"

Helen smiled to herself. There didn't even seem to be a question as to whether Lexi would help her. Simply what do you need. Not that Lexi wasn't above breaking the law; she'd seen that first-hand. "Well, I can see our man. He's booked into Room 412. Right now, he's throwing back a couple of drinks with his buddies, not a woman amongst them. But I think there might be something else happening here tonight."

"Like what?"

Helen kept her voice low. "Maybe a little gambling, legal or otherwise."

"Let me see what I can find out, I didn't see anything on their website about a casino on the premises."

"You've already checked the hotel website." Why was she surprised by this—she'd left Lexi alone for more than five minutes. Helen let out a deep breath. "Got anything in mind?"

"Umm, not sure. Maybe an impromptu security check-up."

"What?" Helen tried to keep her voice even. "Are you sure that's a good idea?"

"Absolutely. It's kind of my day job, remember."

Lexi hung up before she could reply.

CHAPTER 10

LEXI HAD BEEN PREPARED FOR this despite Helen's reluctance. She'd brought her messenger bag and laptop for a reason. First, she logged back onto the Wi-Fi for the hotel. She quickly found the security provider, or providers in their case. IFSEC was their main security provider, but there was also a second smaller system—Prism Secure. After a bit of research, she found they were a London-based company specialising in closed-circuit systems. Prism seemed to work on regional representation for the company. With a little more digging, she found that a Ross Davis covered this particular client.

She grabbed her mini printer from her bag and produced a makeshift ID badge with the Prism logo on it. It wasn't great, but it would have to do. She slipped it into a plastic pouch attached to an old plain lanyard she found in a zipper pocket. Loading her laptop into her messenger bag, she checked that she still had the gadgets she'd had the foresight to pack earlier. Her main fear was finding an air-gapped computer system. If it was, she hoped only a software firewall separated it from the internet. If she had to use a Wi-Fi dongle to breach the security, it would leave valuable evidence behind.

She stepped out of the car, grabbing Helen's black cap from the back seat. Although she already had plans to erase herself and Helen from the hotel security footage as soon as practically possible, she didn't want to let anyone get a good enough look at her to make a decent description.

Lexi made her way to the hotel. Once inside, she took a moment to get her bearings. She walked over to the reception desk, pulling her cap a little lower. She inwardly groaned as she stood in front of the unnecessarily tall check-in desk, instantly making her feel like a child in the headmaster's office.

"Hi, I'm from Prism." Lexi waved her lanyard, hoping the man on Reception wouldn't look too closely. "I'm here to do a quick check on your security system."

"I don't know anything about a security check. We're not expecting you."

Lexi swallowed hard. "Sorry. We've had a few glitches in the system, issues with video feed getting scrambled, so we're doing some quick checks with our special clients to make sure we iron out any potential issues." She hoped the buttering up would terminate his curiosity.

He picked up a phone, announcing her arrival to an unknown person at the other end. She stood back slightly to avoid his full-on scrutiny. He merely pointed in her direction when a large man appeared next to him behind the reception desk. Head of security, she presumed.

Lexi stepped closer to the desk as she attempted to address him. "Hi, sorry about the late visit. Got stuck in traffic. Bit of a pile-up on the M4."

The large man simply stared back at her as if he were some kind of human lie detector. She swallowed hard before continuing. "Your regional technician—umm." She attempted to fiddle with some paperwork she had tucked in the back pocket of her bag, as if clarifying the name. "Ross Davis, is on holiday this week, so they drafted me in from greater London. Only got the call at lunchtime, hence the lateness…" Lexi adjusted her grip on the strap of her laptop bag, hoping she'd given him enough information.

He simply grunted in her direction before checking his watch. With his cropped dark hair and beard, he looked like a gorilla in a suit. She imagined he'd been hired more for his brawn than his brains.

"I won't take up any more time than I have to. I've got to drive back tonight," she assured him. He simply nodded towards the back of the hotel. Lexi took it as a cue to follow him. She was surprised to see his height barely changed when he came out from behind the reception area. His name tag was at her eye level when he stopped to stand toe to toe with her. Red Garston was a large man. He wouldn't have been out of place in the ring with Big Daddy.

"I'm not familiar with your system. Could you talk me through the layout you have here?" She mentally prepared herself for a backlash.

Red sucked in a deep breath before checking his watch again. "Sure, follow me." His voice was suitably deep. "It's a separate system to the hotel security."

Lexi hoped they were heading towards it. She wanted to get out of here as soon as possible. If Red found out her true intentions, he could make mincemeat of her without breaking a sweat. They made their way through the foyer, cutting across a corner of the bar. She managed to spot Helen scanning through a newspaper on the far side of the room. Lexi had to do the quick step to stay on Red's heels as they disappeared down a dim corridor. Rounding a corner, she pulled up quickly as Red blocked the way, his thick fingers sorting through a wad of keys.

She stood to his side, watching as he unlocked a door that seemed to blend into the wall. A secret room. She'd always wanted one of those, like all the best James Bond villains. The room beyond was disappointingly small. Institutional grey breeze blocks lined the walls. She caught Red checking his watch for the third time since her arrival as she scanned the collection of screens attached to the wall at one end of the room. The cameras only seemed to cover one room. A keyboard, joystick, and separate screen were the only things occupying the small black Formica desk in front of the screens. The low hum of a server to the side of the desk provided the only noise in the room. *Not air-gapped, thank God.* The air smelt electrical and stale with no obvious ventilation.

Lexi made a grab for the only seat available as she attempted to log into the system. Dust on the keyboard; they obviously relied on the threat of being watched rather than actively observing their customers. "Okay. So it automatically backs up to the cloud every day, right?" she asked, trying to sound like she knew the network protocols. She'd already tried to access it from outside but couldn't find a back door. She'd need to crack the system from inside first.

Red's phone began to ring behind her before she could hit *return* and get her first login attempt rejected. She turned to see him looming over her as he frowned at the screen on his phone. He obviously had somewhere to be. "Take it, if you need to. I just need to run a few diagnostics before I check the cameras. Then I'm done."

Lexi breathed a sigh of relief when Red left the room to get some privacy on his call. She didn't need a witness to her brute-force attack.

The dull thunder of Red's voice echoing in the corridor made her fingers shake as they fluttered across the keyboard. She tried a few generic security passwords. Red's voice seemed to get louder. He sounded angry. She prayed he hadn't contacted the security firm.

The door behind her swung open, almost giving her air turbulence as her third login was finally accepted. She turned again, glancing up at Red's lumbering figure, fully expecting to be removed by the scruff of her neck.

He simply nodded at her before his eyes were drawn to the video feed screens on the wall. She returned her focus to the computer and blinked several times to regain her focus. *Set up a link and get out*, she told herself over and over in her head.

She quickly tapped the keys to ascertain the layout of the system before establishing the computer's IP address via the network. She prayed Red was as unfamiliar with computers as Helen. Checking for wireless ports, she found a suitable option. She needed to bypass the firewall.

"Just need to run a few diagnostics," she said, breaking the unbearable silence in the small room.

She grabbed her laptop bag from the floor. Fishing in the side pocket, she found the memory stick she was looking for. She risked another glance at Red. He was still fixated on the four large wall screens. With Red's focus engaged elsewhere, she took the opportunity. Reaching down, she inserted the memory stick into the server and opened the rootkit malware programme, adding a few extra lines of code to prevent anyone tracing her intrusion. As she waited for the malware RAT programme to upload, she studied the screens to see what Red found so interesting. There were four cameras in what looked like the casino Helen had mentioned on the phone. They covered several card tables, half of which appeared like they were being set up, nearly ready for business. Someone on the bottom left screen caught her eye. Karl Nesbitt, the caretaker from her apartment building. She was sure it was him. *Shit*. What the hell was he doing there in a bloody illegal casino she was trying to hack?

What if he saw her? How would she explain that to Red? A cold sweat covered her skin as she watched Karl make a nuisance of himself teasing a woman with a crate of chips, which unceremoniously landed on the floor. She glanced back at Red. His eyes had narrowed to lasers under his heavy brow.

Lexi raised her hand pointing to the screen. "Do you need to?" was all she needed to say as Red released a low growl. He left the room remarkably quickly for such a large man.

She swallowed hard, feeling bad for Karl, but saving her own skin was far more important. She needed to finish. Maybe she could slip out before Red came back. Her heart raced as she prayed Karl would be removed before she left the premises. She glanced back at the computer screen. She now had access through the identified port, bypassing the firewall and any encryption.

Lexi pulled her laptop from her bag and secured her remote access to the system. She uploaded the live feed from the cameras to an anonymous cloud account. Red passed through one of the screens, talking to several weirdly identical women who were organising chips and cards. Karl was swiftly dragged from the room. Red's figure looked even larger on screen, as none of the women dared smile as he barked orders. She didn't want to get on the wrong side of Red Garston anytime soon.

Her hands shook as she secured the laptop back in her bag, noticing that the system appeared too makeshift—cables unsecured, the screens a little wonky—to have been professionally installed. She stood to peek behind the bank of screens, finding a length of timber screwed to the wall at an angle. That explained the wonky screens; definitely not a professional installation, as she'd suspected. She retook her seat.

Underneath the table, her knee bashed against something. Ducking her head to see what the obstacle was, she found a small drawer set back from the front edge. Lexi glanced at the screens in search of Red. Nothing. She pulled the drawer open, revealing a black A5 notebook held together with an elastic band. Lexi held her breath as she pulled the book out. She knew she shouldn't be doing this; it was too risky. Still, she slipped off the elastic band. It fell open to where the silky marker split the pages. Someone had crudely drawn lines down the pages—dates, names on one side, figures on the other.

Lexi flicked through the rest of the pages. It was full of names. A tally of gambling debts and payments, she figured. Nothing for Jack North, but another name caught her eye—Karl Nesbitt. She pulled out her phone, taking pictures of as many pages as she dared. Heavy footsteps in the corridor flustered her movements as she quickly closed the book. She dropped it in the drawer, slamming it closed as she moved closer to the desk.

Red hastily entered the room behind Lexi, making her leap out of her skin. "Jesus, you made me jump." Her hand went to her chest as her heart almost pounded out of her chest. She needed to get out of here. "Looks good here. I just need to do a quick check on the cameras, and we're good to go."

Sweat pooled at the base of her spine as she tapped on the keyboard. Selecting each camera, she used the joystick to manoeuvre it before returning it back to its original position. "Okay. We're done." After she locked the keyboard, she surreptitiously wiped it down with her sleeve, removing any traces of her fingerprints. The elastic band from the book poked out from the side of the keyboard. Discreetly pulling it into her hand, she slipped it onto her wrist as she held it under the table.

Lexi got to her feet, drawing her bag back onto her shoulder. At the last minute, she remembered the memory stick was still in the server. She bent down to scratch her leg and plucked it from its slot, palming it till they left the room.

"If you have somewhere you need to be, I can find my own way out," Lexi offered, trailing behind him again as she slipped the memory stick into her pocket. She was desperate now.

Red stopped to check his watch again before glancing round to her. "Okay. You know the way, right?"

"Sure no problem. Have a good night." Relief filtered through her as she spied the exit across the foyer. As her left foot stepped onto the glossy floor, a male voice to her right made her flinch.

"Red!" The voice called from her right. "Red!" They quickly called again, this time more insistent. Karl Nesbitt was heading straight for her.

Lexi heard Red's grumble of annoyance behind her. Pulling her cap lower, she rapidly diverted her path, heading for the bar area, away from Nesbitt. Helen glanced up, meeting her eye for a second as she frantically scanned the room for an exit.

"I thought I told you to leave." Red began, his firm voice easily carrying across the room.

Lexi pushed on the door labelled *Toilets*, preventing her hearing any more of the conversation. She entered a small corridor leading to the male and female toilets, praying Helen would follow her.

A door opened next to her. Jack North was coming towards her. He offered her a wide smile as he passed her on his way back to the bar. Jesus, she couldn't believe her luck today: first she bumped into Nesbitt, then North.

Lexi's heart pounded in her chest again as she gripped her bag tighter. She shuffled further along the corridor until she entered the ladies' toilets and leaned against the far wall, out of sight of the door. She pulled out her phone to type Helen a message when the door opened sharply. She held her breath as her hand shook.

"Lex?" Helen's voice was barely above a whisper.

Lexi gasped for breath as she stepped forward towards Helen's voice. "Thank fuck for that."

"What's going on?" Her voice was full of concern.

Lexi stepped closer. "That guy out there was Karl, the bloody caretaker from our flats."

"The balding guy." Helen asked.

Lexi nodded as she slipped her phone back into her pocket. She moved towards the sink, and her bag collided with the unit as she splashed water over her face. She needed to calm down, catch her breath for a moment.

"Are you okay?" Helen's arm wrapped around her shoulder.

Now upright, she caught Helen's eye in the mirror. A slight frown covered her brow. "I'm okay. I was just worried he'd recognise me."

"Did he?"

"I don't think so. I walked away before he got close." Lexi pulled a paper towel from the stack next to the sink. "I've only met him a couple of times. He was too focused on Red to see me." She hoped that was the case, anyway.

Helen let out a breath. "Okay. Well, he's either brave or stupid. The gorilla out there just dragged him outside by his neck."

"What was he doing here?" Lexi tried to recall any of the conversation she had overheard.

"He owes the house, apparently. He was trying to get in so he could make some money to pay off his debts. He's not very good at taking no for an answer."

The ridiculous justifications of an addict. Lexi had heard them first-hand from her mother, with alcohol. "Has he gone?" she asked as she dried her face on the paper towel. "I can't leave until he's gone."

"I'll go and check. Stay here. I'll call you to let you know when it's clear."

Lexi went back to her hiding place, phone in hand. Her phone vibrated only moments later, and she answered it on the first ring.

"All clear, Mr Orange," Helen said by way of greeting.

Lexi moved towards the door. "Okay. I'm on my way. Err, who exactly is Mr Orange?"

"Are you serious? Mr Orange is the undercover cop in *Reservoir Dogs*."

Lexi entered the bar. Glancing around, Helen was nowhere in sight. "Wow. And how do you know that?"

"Does it matter? Aren't you even a little bit impressed?"

She was about to ask where Helen was when she came into view through the glass front of the hotel. Helen turned her back to the entrance as Lexi moved through the revolving door. "I'm always impressed. But I think I'm more of a Rachel Bailey from *Scott and Bailey*."

"Who?"

Lexi smiled as she stepped out onto the street. "It doesn't matter." She hadn't expected Helen to know the reference. "I'm out." She carefully scanned the street, finding no sign of Nesbitt.

"Okay. I'll meet you at the car in a few minutes. I want to make sure the coast is clear first."

Out in the fresh air, Lexi filled her lungs as she made her way across the road, passing Helen's car. She stopped on the corner at the end of the street, figuring it was far enough away from the hotel if anyone was watching. *Jesus, fresh air tastes good.*

Relieved Red hadn't questioned her, she wondered if he would even mention her visit when the real tech showed up again. Either way, she knew she had to delete the footage from the hotel security cameras. She didn't want there to be any evidence of their visit.

CHAPTER 11

HELEN HUNG AROUND THE FRONT of the hotel for a few moments, still pretending to be on the phone. Satisfied Lexi wasn't followed, she dropped her phone into her pocket. As she walked towards her car, she searched the street for Lexi but came up empty. Her phone buzzed. Helen answered it without even looking, fully expecting it to be her. "Hey, are you back at the car?"

"Nope. I'm sat at my desk in the office."

The deep, dulcet tones of her ex-colleague echoed in her ear. "Pete, sorry I was expecting someone else."

"Sorry to disappoint. I thought you'd want to know we've found a burnt-out Volkswagen Polo. Apparently it was dark blue before it was dark roasted."

Helen smiled at the initial amusement in his voice before it changed to business. "Can you send me through details of the dump location and where it was stolen from?" She wanted to be able to plot the scene in relation to Lexi's flat. It might also give her an idea of the area where the car thief was located.

"Sure. No number plates, though. I'm waiting for info from the cremated remains' VIN number to confirm the owner, but it matches one reported stolen from the Kingswood area. That's a good four or five miles from where your friend was."

His words grated on her nerves. She had initially used *friend* to describe Lexi to him, but now she regretted it. It was wrong. She swallowed back her annoyance with herself. "Where was it dumped?"

"On a patch of waste ground near Cadbury Heath. No witnesses; found by a dog walker this morning."

The locations meant nothing to her yet. She needed to get a map of the area. "Was there a wing mirror missing?" She figured it was worth checking, on the off chance he would know. She heard the rustling of paper down the phone.

"Err—yeah. Driver's side."

We have a winner. Helen half smiled to herself. Give it to dog walkers and joggers to find dead bodies and burnt-out cars every time. "Okay, thanks, Pete, I appreciate your help. Let me know when the owner is confirmed."

"Sure. Don't forget I need to sort out a statement for this to be official. Can you bring your friend to the station so we can write it up?"

"I'll ask her." Helen knew what the answer to that question would be. She hung up before she crossed the road to head towards her car. Lexi was nowhere in sight. A cold chill slipped over Helen. As she scanned the surrounding area, she finally spotted Lexi loitering at the end of the road, even though she had the keys to her car. The sight of her safe and sound brought a lightness to her limbs as she moved. Helen had been expecting the VW to be found burnt out. It could just be joyriders. It didn't necessarily mean anything more, but she still couldn't shake the disquiet in her gut.

As soon as Lexi unlocked the car, they both got in. Helen hoped they were far enough away from the entrance to not draw attention from any of the hotel employees. She waited for Lexi to stow her bag in the foot well.

"So?" She braced herself for what she was about to hear, or, rather, what laws Lexi had broken. She noticed Lexi's hands shook as she placed them in her lap and so held them in her own. "Shit—are you okay?" They were cold to the touch. "I'm sorry. I shouldn't have got you involved in this. We should go home, call it a night." She could tell Hillary it was a bust, try again next time. Lexi was her priority, not Jack bloody North.

"No." Lexi placed one hand on top of hers. "It's fine. I wanted to help, like I said earlier."

"That secret casino thing took me by surprise," she admitted. And now Karl the caretaker could be involved.

"It's fine." Lexi let out a long breath. "Shall I talk you through it?"

Helen nodded as guilt settled upon her shoulders. Was it a coincidence that Karl the caretaker turned up at the same illegal casino they found when following Jack North? Surely not. But what the fuck did it all mean?

"Well, the Kettler Hotel has two separate security systems. The first deals with the day-to-day stuff—door security, CCTV, and that kind of thing. The second one, which looks like it's probably off the books, covers only the casino room. They must have some kind of deal with the tech from Prism."

"Prism?" Helen queried.

"It's the second security system they have."

"Okay." Helen picked up the opened water bottle, taking a drink. "What did you find out?"

"Now, don't freak out. I…"

Panic started to rise in Helen's stomach. "Why would I freak out? What did you do?" She finished the dregs from the bottle.

"I've installed a RAT—remote access tool—on the computer. It will send us the feed from the cameras in the casino. It should show if North is canoodling with another woman, or simply frittering all his money away. Or both, if you're lucky."

Lexi's words filtered through Helen's brain as she swallowed the last of the water, except this time it didn't stay down. The words "send feed from the cameras" stuck in her head. Lexi had hacked into their security system. Helen clutched at her chest, trying to stop any water from exiting through her nose at the same time as she gasped for breath. A strange sense of clarity came over her as she sat staring out of the windscreen, her vision blurring as she struggled to breathe. She'd sent her in there to do a job, and she'd done it. She couldn't complain about it now.

"Shit!" Lexi reached for her. "Arms up. Arms up!"

"What?" Helen gurgled between coughs. She looked to her left to see Lexi with her arms above her head. She tried to do the same and was grateful when Lexi stretched across to assist her.

The obstruction began to clear. The fire in Helen's chest reduced to a smoulder. Her mind came back online and filled with a backlog of questions. "What? How did you…?" Helen took another calming breath. "Please don't say 'More hidden depths.'" Her voice was hoarse from coughing.

"I read it in a book."

"You read first-aid manuals now?" Helen's breathing slowly resumed its usual rhythm.

"Not exactly."

She saw Lexi's lips fold into a straight line as she sat back in her seat. "What does that mean?"

"I *did* read it in a book." Lexi sighed. "But it was a novel where the main character was a doctor."

"What?" Helen could feel her pulse rising again.

"It worked, didn't it?"

Helen wiped at her watery eyes. "How did you know it would work?"

"It worked on someone at my job who was choking on their coffee—opens up the airway or something."

"Thanks," Helen relented, relieved.

"I practically saved your life."

And not for the first time. This woman could infuriate her sometimes, but she always, always had her back, and Helen knew that. "Will they know we have it?" Helen closed her eyes in frustration. Lexi was a risk taker. That was exactly why she hadn't wanted her to get involved. *Stupid.* This was her fault, not Lexi's.

"Of course not, trust me. It's being uploaded to an anonymous cloud account. It's untraceable."

"Really?" Helen knew Lexi's prowess with technology. She had to trust her conviction.

"Really."

"Okay." She placed her hand on Lexi's thigh.

"Speaking of books. I found a notebook in the CCTV room." Lexi pulled out her phone. "It's got names, dates, and figures in it." She offered Helen her phone. "I took a few pictures while Red was out of the room."

Helen felt her annoyance surface again as she took the offered phone. She scanned the screen, flicking through the pictures. The long list of names and numbers blurred. Some people were in serious trouble with the Kettler casino. Karl owed almost seventeen thousand pounds. It started out with a modest four grand a few months ago then grew exponentially. "Karl's in serious debt."

"I know. I couldn't see anything for North in it. Red came back, so I didn't get a chance to get a good look through it."

Helen handed the phone back. Leaning across the console, she pressed her lips to Lexi's. "Thank you. I promise I won't put you in that position again."

Lexi smiled as she settled back in her seat. "So—what's next?"

"I'm going back to check up on North. You'll need to stay here, especially if Karl's still around." She fully expected Lexi to fight her, but a cool hand clutched hers a little tighter.

"Be careful, and stay out of Red's way."

"Always." Helen rested her hand on top of Lexi's. She turned her body and started to get out of the car. She stopped when her feet hit the pavement and twisted back to face her. "Oh, by the way, I've thought of another one—cremated remains, *cremains*."

"Nice." Lexi smiled back at her. "I hope you're not referring to the pizza I cooked the other night, because that was all down to you distracting the cook."

Entering the hotel bar lounge, Helen scanned the room for North. He was exactly where she'd left him, chugging down drinks with his buddies. She headed for the bar to order another soft drink in an effort to fit in, then took a seat with a good view of North and the door to the casino. Fortunately there was no sign of Karl; she didn't need that added complication.

She pulled out her phone as a text message from Lexi arrived. She opened it immediately, hoping there weren't any more unexpected developments. This was, after all, meant to be a straightforward task.

Hackintosh—a mix of hack and Macintosh

Helen grinned. How appropriate for Lexi. The bar was getting busy with more punters for the casino. She had to wait another forty minutes before North and his buddies disappeared through the private door. She called Lexi to make sure he was on camera before returning to her car to watch the live video feed.

───── •••• ─────

"He's leaving." Lexi's hand rested on Helen's thigh.

Helen stretched in the confines of her seat, suppressing a yawn. "Any women?" She glanced at the screen on Lexi's laptop. She could barely make out the image Lexi was watching.

Helen rubbed at her eyes before glancing at the dashboard. Nearly four hours had passed since Jack North had entered the casino.

"Nope. He's pawed a couple of the waitresses but not hooked up with anyone." Lexi tilted the screen in her direction.

By the looks of things, alcohol had certainly taken its toll. He was being assisted out of the room by one of the Robert Palmer women. "Lost much?" Helen asked as her hand landed on the door release.

"He was doing all right till about an hour ago."

"Okay. I'll follow him back to his room to make sure he's alone." Helen extracted herself from her car. The air was cool against her skin as she jogged across the road. A couple of people clustered outside the takeaway next door.

The hotel was bright inside. She crossed the foyer and found Jack North and a male employee waiting for a lift. As she moved towards them, she removed her phone, taking a quick snap for Hillary. The lift arrived almost immediately. North was piloted inside. A sated expression covered his face as he slumped against the wall of the lift.

The young employee rolled his eyes in Helen's direction.

She smiled in reply. "Someone's had a good night."

The lift pinged, and Helen indicated for them to leave first. She watched as North was steered down the hallway towards Room 412. Helen videoed the event from a distance as she watched them both enter North's room. She needed to make sure the employee left. Not that North was in any condition to seduce anyone right now. She retraced her steps to the lifts. Room 412 was just in sight. She waited several minutes before the door opened again, then turned her back as she pressed the lift call button several times.

"Forgot something," she offered by way of explanation as the employee joined her. As they travelled back down, she speculated how many times North had been here. How much he'd lost. A certain somebody would, of course, be able to find that out for her.

Helen headed straight for the exit. She noticed Big Red hovering by the door. *Shit.* She secured her phone and continued avoiding any eye contact he sent in her direction. Had he been watching her?

"Can I help you?" Red's voice echoed in the now empty foyer. His tone was more accusing than helpful.

Helen reluctantly met Red's glare. "Uh, no. I was just getting some air." Her hand instinctively dug into her pocket, searching for her gas batten. It wasn't there. She had nothing as she came face to face with the large man.

Red stepped closer, blocking her way, getting in her face. "Keep it that way. We don't want your type round here—understand?"

Helen nodded, confusion clouding her mind. He thought she was a prostitute? Not too much of a stretch, considering she'd hung out in the bar and ventured upstairs a couple of times. Maybe Red wasn't as dumb as he looked. She wasn't about to set him straight, despite wanting to use him as a punchbag. Instead, she quickly moved around him, slipping out onto the street.

Lexi was half-asleep by the time she returned. Helen started her car. She pulled out a little more quickly than usual, heading back home. Home was what it was now. She knew she should be looking for her own place, but she struggled to see herself without Lexi by her side.

Helen guided her car into a space outside Lexi's flat, glad to be home after what had seemed like an extremely long night, let alone week. Lexi was rubbing her eyes, obviously equally as tired. She saw no need to mention her run-in with Red. Besides, she'd never hear the end of it, knowing Lexi.

Neither of them had slept well since Lexi's hit-and-run experience. Helen realised she'd barely scratched the surface on that particular problem. She placed her hand on Lexi's thigh. "Come on. Let's get inside. We're both knackered."

The air was cool as she walked around and waited on the pavement for Lexi to shoulder her bag before closing the passenger door. She took Lexi's hand as she pressed the key fob. The last few days had made her a little clingy, fearful of leaving Lexi alone. Scared of losing her altogether. Lexi's hand quickly gripped hers, telling her she wasn't the only one.

A phone buzzed nearby, distracting them both. Lexi reached into her pocket for her phone with her free hand.

"Shit!" Lexi let out a frustrated-sounding breath.

"What's up? Is it the cloud stuff?" Helen tightened her fingers around the keys in her other hand.

"No, it's my mother reminding me I said I'd go over on Sunday to sort out her computer."

"Oh." Helen held her tongue, unsure of the current status of Lexi's relationship with her mother. "Everything okay?" It was after two a.m.—late for a text reminder.

"Would you come with me? It should only take a couple of hours, and I'd really like you to meet her."

"On Sunday?" It was the least Helen could do, considering what Lexi had done for her. "Where does she live?"

"Near Slough."

"Sure. I'd like to finally meet the woman responsible for your attitude towards food."

CHAPTER 12

HELEN DROVE TO THE MCDONALDS in Barrs Court to meet Hilary North. She wasn't looking forward to it, considering she was her new boss—for now anyway.

Hilary's car was already there when Helen pulled into a space. She must have been looking out for her arrival because she was walking towards her passenger door before she'd even switched off her engine.

"I'm guessing it's not good news." Hilary slumped in the passenger seat.

She had black smudges under her eyes. Business-wear people always seemed awkward in casual clothes, and Hillary was no exception. After having seen her in her power suits, leggings and a T-shirt just didn't seem to cut it. She wondered if Lexi thought the same of her, although she'd never mentioned anything.

"It's not, I'm afraid."

Hillary twisted her body slightly to face Helen. "Okay."

She had intended on meeting in Hillary's car to give herself an escape route, but the woman's keenness had put pay to that. She took a breath before delivering the bad news. "I went to the Kettler Hotel. Your husband arrived around seven thirty. He checked in, then went straight back down to the bar."

Hillary nodded. "Was it another woman?"

The words stopped Helen's train of thought. She'd wanted to outline the events first. "Uh, no. Well, not exactly."

"What does that mean?" Hillary pulled a balled-up tissue from her sleeve.

"He met up with some friends in the bar for a while. Around nine, they all went through to a private room hidden at the back of the hotel." She caught the frown on Hillary's face. She was clearly fearing the worst. "It's being used as an illegal casino—roulette, cards…"

"Jesus," Hillary whispered as she swept the tissue across her right eye.

"He did get friendly with some of the waitresses, but he didn't leave with anyone. He had to be helped back to his room at the end of the night, but there was no evidence of any affair that I could see."

Helen pulled out from her pocket the piece of paper Lexi had given her. "He's been to that hotel four times in the last six months. Room service doesn't show any sign that he had company during his visits."

Hillary let out a long breath. "I should be thankful for small mercies, I guess."

"I'm sorry," Helen offered. Her past job, had given her ample experience in delivering bad news. But somehow it was more difficult when the individual was still alive and totally unaware that his indiscretions were being aired to his nearest and dearest.

"I'm guessing I shouldn't ask exactly how you came across this information." Hillary began shredding the tissue in her hand.

"Probably best," Helen replied. "I'm sorry it's not better news."

Hilary continued to fiddle with the dismembered tissue. "To be forewarned is to be forearmed."

"You know you can't tell anyone about this, right?" The last thing Helen needed was the story of an illegal casino getting out. Especially if it was traced back to her and Lexi.

"Of course." Hilary got out of the car.

At least Hillary could make contingency plans regarding their finances to prevent any further losses on her part. Helen certainly wouldn't want to be in Jack North's shoes when the shit hit the fan.

Helen prepared to drive off but stopped short of pulling out of her parking space. She pulled her phone from her pocket and dialled an old friend, hoping she could help with Lexi's protection. Especially if it was someone from Helen's past, someone who was trying to dish out a bit of revenge for being caught.

"Hey, stranger." Chief Superintendent Grace Scott sounded relaxed, no doubt the benefit of rank giving her the weekend off.

"Hi." Helen wasn't sure Grace would help, but she had to give it a try.

"So, what are you doing with your newly found freedom?"

"This and that. The house is on the market. I'm staying with a friend in Bristol at the moment." *Friend again. God, when was she going to learn?*

"Sounds like you're actually surviving away from the job."

"That's sort of why I'm calling." Helen heard a flutter of voices in the background before they were silenced.

"Okay, what's up?"

"I, err…" Helen cleared her throat. She hated laying this on Grace, asking for help to do what had been her job for years. "I think I might need your help with something."

"What's going on? You're being weird."

Helen sighed. "A friend of mine is being threatened or stalked or something. She was almost run over, her flat and mailbox broken into."

"Okay, and what do the locals say?"

"She doesn't want to report it." Helen flinched as she prepared for the backlash.

"What? Why?"

What could she say to that? *Well, the problem is she impersonated a police officer for a couple of months after accidentally killing the paedophile that abused her younger sister.* "The thing is…it only started after I got here. I'm worried som—"

"Someone's after you. Why would you think that?" Grace was quiet for a moment. "Come on, Helen, it could be anyone—someone she works with, an ex, anything."

Helen closed her eyes. Maybe she was being too panicky. But there was definitely something going on here. She needed to stop it before it got out of hand. "I know that, but I need to be sure it's not someone I helped put away." Not to mention the criminals she didn't catch; there were always the ones that slipped through the net.

"What do you expect *me* to do exactly?"

"I need to know if anyone has recently got out." If Grace was in her position, Helen liked to think she would do the same for an ex-colleague.

"Anyone. Like who?"

"You know, most of my cases from Manchester. Three names immediately come to mind." Just saying those names brought a cramp to Helen's chest.

The thought of any one of them getting within touching distance of Lexi made her sick to her stomach. "Paulson, the serial rapist." *Serial* although he was only convicted of one rape due to a lack of evidence. "Collins, the kidnapper's accomplice. And Snell, the stalker of several young men in Manchester."

"Jesus. Are you serious?"

"Trust me. I hope it's the most ridiculous idea I've ever had."

He watched her walking around her flat as he bagged up the last of his stuff. Miss L. Ryan. Her hair was up. She hardly ever wore it up, unlike her friend. He stared as she rolled her head to the side to look at something. Her ponytail was short, like a badger's. Was it wet? She must have washed it.

The heat inside the face mask was almost unbearable. A sheen of sweat covered his enclosed skin. He was breathing too hard. He needed to calm down. He moved across the room, flashing his torch in the air vent. Everything was still in place. He glanced around the rest of the flat. It had barely been touched since Morris had moved in. He'd filled it to the brim when he finally closed his stupid shop, the one he'd visited many times as a child with his mother before they moved away.

He stepped back to the window. She was in the kitchen now. He couldn't tell what she was doing—cleaning, maybe? Was she alone? It had been spotless when he'd been in there. He dropped the flashlight in his bag, he saw the unregistered phone. He couldn't resist it. He wanted to tell her how nice she looked with her hair up, how it showed off the shape of her face.

He turned on the phone, blocking his number before dialling. His latex gloves stuck to the rubber keys as he pressed them. He wanted to see the shock on her face when she realised she was being watched. It rang three times before it was picked up. He pulled his top lip into his mouth, sucking the condensation off his own skin. He thought for a moment she would ignore it, let the answerphone kick in.

"Hello."

A small voice sounded in his ear. She wasn't local, barely an accent at all. *London, maybe.* The words died in his throat.

"Hello," she repeated.

He pictured her standing in the dim hallway, holding the phone. He smiled, wondering if she could hear him breathing through the mask he was wearing. What would she do if she knew he was there on the other end and wasn't some call centre multidialling random numbers.

"Hello!" A more frustrated-sounding tone now.

He ended the call. Morris's weak wheezing coming from the other room, reminding him why he was there. After he placed the phone in his pocket, he moved to the bedroom and removed the two items he'd come for. He sealed them in bags before installing replacements.

He probably didn't even need these last two doses, but he couldn't stand the thought of Morris making a recovery after everything Morris had put him through. He studied the figure emitting the wheeze. His chest barely moved, only a slight rise and fall. It would be over soon. He was sure Morris could hear him still. He didn't move around much, but he still grunted every so often.

"You see what you made me do, Morris." His voice was muffled below the mask. "All because you couldn't keep your dick in your pants." He kept his voice low. His breathing increased as his jaw clenched.

"I'm killing you Morris. Me. With every breath you take, you're dying. I hate you—I hate everything about you. Do you know how hard it was for me, trying to get to know you—spending time with you—knowing exactly who you are?"

"I'm killing you. Then I'm taking everything you have. It's mine. All of it." He closed his eyes as he left the room, elation running through his veins. He felt good, so fucking good.

He moved to the window, looking for her again. She'd returned to the kitchen. The light was on now, making it easier for him. He thought for a moment she was looking straight at him as she blankly stared out. Her arm movements told him she was washing up. Relieved, he moved to the shadows in case she was tempted to look across. Was this what it was like for her that night—obsessing, fixating on every subtle movement? He liked watching her, spying. He was an unknown quantity; it was easy. He didn't even exist in her world… yet.

He knew they were going somewhere tomorrow. Overhearing that snippet of information in the car park had become invaluable. Now he had a perfect window of opportunity to end this. He dialled her number again. She picked up after two rings this time.

"Hello?"

She appeared in the kitchen with the phone in her hand. His heart pounded at the thought of being caught. What if she glanced across and saw him right now? He moved the phone away from his mouth. He tried to steady his breathing, hoping she wouldn't hear how frantic it was. She pulled the phone away from her face, muffled words travelling down the line before she ended the call. She looked angry as she sharply moved her arm, slamming the phone down. Her frustration brought a smile to his lips. He wanted more.

With the scrambler already on, he could move freely between the buildings without being recorded. He didn't even worry about being spotted anymore. He could easily silence them.

Outside her flat in the hallway, the crowbar slipped from his sleeve as he waited for any sound in the building. Loud music started in one of the flats below. Taking the opportunity, he swiped at the light, crushing the shade and the bulb. Fragments fell with a musical ring as they sprayed across the floor.

He stepped out of the mess, quickly walking back to the stairwell. He wondered if she would link it all together—every little move he'd made. He reached the ground floor and moved to the back of the building, leaving via the fire exit in case he crossed paths with any residents, especially her friend with the ponytail.

CHAPTER 13

HELEN PARKED UP OUTSIDE THE flat. She looked up at the lit windows, wondering what Lexi was up to. Was someone watching her right now? She wasn't looking forward to meeting Lexi's mother the following day, considering the stories Lexi had shared about her alcoholism. Helen knew she needed to have a conversation with Lexi about the events in Warner, and about exactly how much her mother knew about Helen's involvement in the case.

She entered the building. Her eyes scanned the mailboxes. She noticed the slightly discoloured metal doors, grateful that they had already been fixed. Helen felt quite sprightly after her first few days at work. She declined the lift in favour of the stairs, hoping she wouldn't regret it when she got to the fourth floor.

Out of breath when she finally got to the top floor, she left the stairwell, frowning when the security light failed to turn on despite her lingering to catch her breath.

Instead of turning left towards Lexi's flat, she went right, finding a long corridor on her left that led to the back of the building. Daylight shone through a small square window high up, creating a glare on the shiny industrial flooring. The outline of a fire exit sign glowed below the window. She'd seen the metal stairs that were on the other side of the door the other day when she was taking out some rubbish; at least now she knew how to access them.

She returned to the stairwell, ascending the next flight. A small skylight offered some additional light, muted due to the outer surface being encrusted with dirt. A cage door padlocked to the wall prevented any further access as she rounded the corner. Pressing her face against the obstacle, she could see there was a padlocked door further beyond.

It raised more questions for her curious brain. If the two buildings were identical in layout, how did the other guy get on the roof, past two padlocks? Unless it was the caretaker, although Lilly had said how little time he spent here. And, of course, the question of why still annoyed her. She hated not knowing things. Maybe Lexi was right. Maybe she should become a PI; at least then she'd get paid for being nosey.

She jogged back down the stairs and walked back along the corridor to the flat. A loud crunch under her right foot made her stop abruptly, and she scanned the flooring. Unable to see anything clearly with no light, she crouched down closer to inspect the floor. Jagged shapes came into view. She stood there a moment, taking in the scene. Glancing around, she searched for the broken light. She found the remnants a few feet farther along. It was a distance from the floor, and certainly not at a height that could be damaged easily. She stepped close enough to see that the outer casing for the light had been obliterated with something substantial. A gouge in the wall next to the light fitting was testament to that.

What was the endgame here, intimidation? Forcing Lexi out of the flat? Again she came back to her original question: was Lexi the real target, or was it her? Was Lexi just collateral damage along the way? That thought alone made her chest ache. But the harassment had only started after she came here to be with Lexi; surely that wasn't a coincidence. With her phone she took a few pictures of the damage in case she needed them at a later stage. *Document everything.*

Using her feet, she tried to gather up the glass as much as possible, not that anyone came along this part of the corridor unless they were actually going to 4A.

Helen unlocked the front door, checking around her once more before leaving it on the latch. She entered the kitchen, opened the cupboard below the sink and grabbed the dustpan and brush before heading back to the communal corridor.

Helen blindly swept at the floor. Her mind ran through the long list of possible criminals she'd upset along the way. She felt a little more justified in calling Grace earlier. The three names she'd given Grace were the only ones that immediately came to the front of the line. She couldn't think of anyone from her last few years in Warner. Maybe she should ask Mike about recently released prisoners they'd put away, to cover all bases.

"What are you up to?"

Helen jumped a little at the echoey words. "I'm being community spirited."

A beam of light fell across her hands as she swept up the last of the debris. She looked up and realised it was from the phone in Lexi's hand. "Thanks." She placed the brush in the pan to prevent the glass from freely escaping.

"Did you do that?"

It took a second for Helen to register the sarcasm in Lexi's question. "No. I didn't."

"Umm, I'll believe you. Did you try and call me earlier?"

The glare of the light made it difficult to read the expression on her face. "No. Why?"

"Someone called, twice, but they hung up each time I picked up. I think they were there but didn't speak."

Was this a continuation of Lexi's persecution or hers? "How do you know they were there?"

"I heard noises, breathing, I think."

Shit. Helen got to her feet. "On your mobile?"

"No, the landline."

No caller ID. Helen tried to keep her tone casual. "Did you try and check the number? Maybe it was your mum again." She hoped that it could be dismissed so easily.

"Number was withheld."

Shit. Helen was torn between telling the truth, laying it all out for Lexi to pick through, or continuing her ruse to protect her. She knew what she'd want if she was in Lexi's position. Maybe she *was* in Lexi's position. She took Lexi's free hand and led them back inside the flat. She placed the dustpan carefully on the kitchen worktop and spun around to face her, all too aware that last time she'd gone all cop-and-victim on her she'd done a pretty crappy job. "Okay. We need to talk about what's going on here."

Worry lines immediately appeared on Lexi's forehead. "I knew this was coming sooner or later."

"Good." At least they were on the same page. "What do you think we should do?" Helen hoped it would involve going to the police.

Lexi released her hand in favour of folding her arms in front of her chest. "Well, I think it's too early to make any rash decisions. I mean, it's only been a week or so."

Helen flinched at Lexi's defensive stance, but she ploughed on. "But we both agree there is some weird shit happening around here."

"What?" Lexi let her arms drop.

Helen saw confusion in Lexi's eyes. She leant against the worktop next to her. "I think we're having two different conversations."

"Oh, so you're not telling me you're going to look for your own place."

"What? No. Do you want me to?" Helen tried to hide her surprise. She had no intention of leaving Lexi on her own. She'd moved down here to be with her.

Lexi stepped closer. "No. God, no. I thought you might want your own space or something."

Helen wrapped an arm around Lexi's waist. "No. I'm good, thanks. But now that you come to mention it, I will be paying half the rent and bills from now on." She'd been meaning to bring up the subject of rent since taking the security job.

"You don't need to do that." Lexi placed a sweeping hand on the worktop, stopping short of the dustpan.

"Yes I do. I'm not a freeloader." Helen was annoyed she'd been side tracked from her task. She let out a frustrated breath. "Anyway, that's not what we're talking about right now." Her tone was harsher than she'd intended; she needed to dial it back. "Sorry." She edged closer, draping an arm around Lexi's waist. "I'm worried about you. Someone tried to run you over the other day—"

"We don't know that for sure."

Helen hesitated. There was no real proof to the contrary besides the car being found burnt out. "You thought someone had been in here before that." She tilted her head towards the interior of the flat. "Then the phone calls today, the light outside, other stuff."

"Like the mailboxes the other day."

Shit. Had she actually checked? Helen moved a little closer. "I'm sorry. I was…" There was no suitable excuse. "I was trying to protect you."

"From what?" Lexi pushed.

"I don't know." *Yet.* "But it only started after I came here, unless there's other stuff you haven't told me about?"

"No." Lexi shook her head. There was no hesitation in her reply.

Guilt settled heavily on Helen's shoulders. Lexi seemed to stand taller, her body rigid under her hand. *Was this really all her fault again?* "What if someone's trying to get to me through you?"

"You think they're after you?" There was a sceptical edge to Lexi's words.

In truth, there was no good answer to that question. "Maybe."

"Who the hell have you upset lately?"

"I don't know. But I plan on finding out." She pulled Lexi into her arms. "I'm sorry for not telling you earlier. I wasn't sure about any of it; I'm still not." The stiffness in Lexi's body slowly relaxed in her arms. Despite the risk of bringing it up again, curiosity got the better of her: "How did you find out about the mailbox?"

Lexi pulled back. "Guy from downstairs in 2B told me they'd been fixed when I was coming back from the shop earlier."

Damn the apartment-building grapevine. Maybe she should enlist their help to find this idiot causing so much trouble.

"So, does that make me your next client?"

"I guess it does."

Helen sighed in relief. Now she just had to tackle the delicate matter of Lexi's mother.

CHAPTER 14

"I'll drive if you like," Helen offered as they exited the building. At ten a.m., it was still relatively early for a Sunday in this neighbourhood. Neither of them had slept well after recent events. The only difference was that Helen was used to getting by on minimal sleep, unlike Lexi, who supressed a yawn.

"Are you sure you don't mind?" she asked.

Despite her hesitation about going in the first place, Helen wanted to get there in one piece. After all, Lexi could do with a break from here for the day to take her mind off things.

"Of course not." She reached for Lexi's arm. The warmth of her skin filtered through the thin shirt she wore. "Type the address in the sat-nav."

Lexi pursed her lips. "I'll drive back, then."

Helen ignored her statement as they got into her car.

An arrival time of 11:40 a.m. appeared on the bottom of the screen as Helen pulled out of the car park. As soon as they got on the M4, Lexi dropped off. Helen turned down the sat-nav and let Lexi sleep while she could. Her brain was still turning over the mental list of potential suspects she had tried to make last night. She needed Pete to get back to her with details of the car; then, at least she'd have a starting point to work from.

Her mind drifted back to Valeri Ryan, to all the stories Lexi had shared. She was pretty curious to meet the woman, especially as Lexi had confirmed that she knew nothing of Helen's involvement in the events in Warner. Helen couldn't remember the last time she'd been formally introduced to a girlfriend's parent. Christ, was she nervous.

Lexi relaxed against the seat. Helen's BMW was certainly a more comfortable ride than her Mini, and her mind wasn't filled with the usual dread when she visited her mother. Instead, all she could think of was who was trying to hurt, kill, or simply threaten her. Could it really be someone from Helen's past? It would almost be a relief, but then again, the people she'd pissed off probably weren't the kind to walk away without finishing the job. Not the best thought to drift off to, but exhaustion had taken over her body; her limbs began to float with the subtle vibrations of the car's movements.

She stretched those limbs in the confined space as she looked out the windscreen. She glanced over at Helen, who seemed relaxed. The only indication of her vexed demeanour was the white-knuckle grip she had on the steering wheel.

"I think I've got carcolepsy!" she offered, breaking the silence.

"What?" Helen's head spun quickly to glance at her.

"*Carcolepsy*. Like narcolepsy, but in a car."

"Another new word. I've created a portmanteau monster."

Lexi heard the amusement in Helen's voice as she caught sight of a road sign. They were almost there. Another fifteen minutes or so. "Yep. I think I'm getting a real taste for it now." A familiar anxiety began to surface. She settled her hand on Helen's thigh. "Thanks for driving."

"No problem. Did you have a good nap?"

"Umm," she mumbled through another stretch. Although it had taken her some time to finally drop off, she was grateful for it. "Sorry I haven't been much company." She continued to poke at an idea that had settled in her head some time ago. There hadn't been a good time to bring it up lately, mainly due to recent events and her concern for the reaction it would bring. The last thing she wanted to do was hurt Helen.

"You okay?" Helen queried.

Helen's hand settled on hers in her lap. "Fine," Lexi replied. Keeping hold of her, she turned slightly to face her; there was no time like the present. "I was wondering if…you've ever thought about finding your birth mother."

Wide eyes flashed in her direction. "What? No. I mean, I don't even know if she's…"

Helen's voice seemed to die in her throat.

Lexi gripped the hand that she still held. "I'm sorry. I shouldn't have brought it up." But she pressed a little harder. "You never talk about it—her."

"I shut the door on that a long time ago, and I've moved on. Please don't search for her, Lex. Promise me."

Helen replaced her hand on the wheel, obviously agitated at the prospect. The eagerness for Helen to close the door on it so quickly worried Lexi. "Okay. I promise." Reaching across the seat, she placed her hand on Helen's thigh. "I'm sorry. I didn't mean to upset you." From the little Helen had shared, she knew her mother had been a drug addict when Helen was a toddler. Eventually Helen was removed from her charge and placed in foster care, which probably turned out to be a godsend as Julia proved to be exactly what she needed—a loving mother. Her death from dementia complicated by breast cancer had been difficult for Helen.

It took a couple of weighty seconds for Helen to reply. Even as Helen placed her hand on top of hers, Lexi could tell Helen was far from happy about the situation.

"You didn't. Forget about it." She slowed the car down a little. "Is this it?"

There was no more time to discuss it as Lexi's eyes scanned the large brick building in front of them. "Yeah. The car park's just there." She pointed towards a brick pillared gateway.

Helen pulled into the small car park for residents and visitors. Lexi realised that it had been nearly three years since Val Ryan had downsized here. It had been a good idea; the family home had become too much for her to maintain in her current state, and there was more of a support system for her here, so why was Lexi's need to separate herself from her mother's tangled downfall still a continued source of guilt? Although it was nothing compared to the weight of blame her mother carried, she supposed: she had been the one to introduce the paedophile into their lives, after all. If only Leah hadn't wanted a guitar tutor.

In the end, it didn't matter that the abuse hadn't lasted long before Leah had confided in Lexi, did it? The damage had already been done—years of mental health issues before she took her own life at just twenty-eight.

Shutting off the ignition, Helen turned to her, a slightly nervous-looking expression covering her face. It appeared out of place on this usually unflappable woman.

Lexi couldn't resist a little needle before they went in. "We need to play it by ear. If I give the signal, we should make an excuse and go, okay?"

"Lex, it's going to be fine. Don't worry."

Lexi looked at the clock on the dashboard, not that it mattered what time it was. "She's probably been drinking." Alcohol had been her mother's only partner after the family imploded. She'd managed to bring up two kids on her own only to be floored by her own guilt.

Helen rested her hand on Lexi's. "I promise it'll be fine."

The words were not particularly convincing, despite Helen's mock enthusiasm. As she took off her seatbelt, Lexi outlined their escape plan. These visits had to be cut very short on occasion. "If I start itching my right ear, then we're going. Grab what you came with, and get to the door."

"Are you serious?"

Lexi refused to answer Helen's question, testing her unflappability once more. "Let's get this over with."

When she got out of the car, the cool breeze was a shock to her car-warmed skin. She shivered as she made her way around the car to Helen before heading towards the external stairwell. They were silent as they approached the flat.

The door opened with a flourish. The floral-scented air swept over her. Lexi held her breath to stop it from completely engulfing her.

"Darling. I thought you were never going to get here."

Lexi was quickly wrapped in her mother's arms. She imagined toothpaste being squeezed from a tube. "Mum, it's barely even lunchtime yet." As they separated, she eyed the glass of wine gripped in her mother's right hand. Would she understand her statement's double meaning?

"But I thought you said you were coming earlier for brunch?"

"No, Mum, I didn't say that." Lexi was immediately annoyed that she'd failed to keep her tone neutral. She gave Helen a sideways glance. "Mum, this is Helen. Helen this is my mum, Val."

To her credit, her mother seemed like she'd actually made an effort. She looked clean and tidy. Her shorter hair was no doubt easier to manage. The style seemed to make her look younger, more vibrant despite her attempts to put on eyeshadow with what appeared to be a two-inch brush. Val Ryan would have made a perfect beautician for an undertaker.

"Well, it's lovely to meet you. Lexi's told me so little about you."

At least her mother still had her sense of humour. "I've told you plenty." Lexi stepped inside past her mother. "We can't stay too long. We've both got work tomorrow." She set the boundary early. She was always more comfortable with it set out in front of her.

"Oh. I see. Well, you can at least stay for lunch, can't you?"

Her mother's plea followed her as she entered the main room of the flat. Again, it looked pretty tidy. She felt a little bad for all the negative thoughts she'd had about their visit. Gone were the endless empty bottles clogging up the kitchen surfaces at the far end of the room. The small wooden dining table was free of debris. "Sure. How have you been?" She was actually curious about the apparent changes in her mother's life.

Her mother stopped next to her, a sly smile on her face as she reached for Lexi's arm. "Good."

Lexi had the feeling her mother was saying so much more, but she couldn't quite put her finger on exactly what yet.

She scrutinised the mature woman in front of her. There was definitely something different about her. She seemed…okay. She looked past her mother as the figure of Helen came into view behind. Her two raised eyebrows posed the question that was already forming in Lexi's own brain. *What the fuck!*

In some of Lexi's past visits, her mother had barely been able to dress herself or speak without slurring her words, evidence of a three-day bender. The one time she brought someone else to witness it, she'd somehow morphed into Beverly bloody Goldberg by the look of her gaudy jumper, minus the pre-noon glass of wine, of course. "So, what have you been up to?"

"Well, I joined a new club with Maggie from downstairs."

"Who's Maggie-from-downstairs?" *A fellow imbiber.*

"She's new. Scottish. Moved in a few months ago."

"I see." *A friend. That's good, right?* Lexi told herself despite her own inability to fulfil that role herself. "What sort of club is it?" Her curiosity was rising.

"It's a social club. We go out and about. We went to a show in London the other week. *Blood Brothers*—the matinee show. It was amazing. I haven't been to a show in years."

Guilt squeezed her insides as Lexi fought to find her voice.

"I saw that a few years ago. Took my stepmother. She loved it."

They both turned to look at Helen. Once again, Lexi was grateful for her presence and her knack at always knowing what to say.

"That's great, Mum. I'm glad you're out enjoying yourself for once."

"Sit down. I'll make some tea."

Still a little shell-shocked, Lexi moved towards the sofa. A warm hand slipping inside her own made her look up into bright blue eyes. A slight nod of the head asked if she was okay.

Was she okay? A bit of normality wasn't a lot to ask for considering the last few days she'd had. Obviously that wasn't going to happen here anytime soon. Pursing her lips, she nodded, offering Helen a weak smile as her mother filled the kettle in the kitchen.

CHAPTER 15

HE'D MANAGED TO KEEP HIS distance the whole way. Luckily, the motorway was a pretty good place to follow someone, with people travelling in the same direction for hours on end without even noticing who was behind them. He didn't know exactly where they were going, only that it was near Slough. They didn't have any bags when they left, so he figured they weren't planning on staying the night. He hoped he had the time he needed to do what he had to do. Time was running out. That only gave him a few options.

He came to a stop a short distance behind them. He watched as they walked up the stairs to the flats beyond the car park. Once he was satisfied they were safely inside, he slipped the can of expanding foam into his jacket and got out of the car. He needed to be back at Morris's flat in a couple of hours. He knew the boy would be hanging around in there for a while; he always did. Morris had suffered enough now. So he was an absent father—big deal. Not everyone had a fucking choice. His hands tightened to fists as he approached the BMW.

———————

Lexi sat at the small dining table as she scanned through the internet history of her mother's laptop. She was YouTube crazy—not to mention the dodgy online dating sites she still visited. No doubt one of them was to blame for this particular malfunction.

Shit. Was that it? Had the online dating worked? Had she found a man? Or was she maybe dating Maggie-from-downstairs? A grin crossed her lips at that thought. Something or someone had obviously filled a hole in Val's life. She should be grateful for that alone.

Lexi listened to Helen chatting to her mother about *Blood Brothers,* giving her recommendations for other shows she'd seen. She'd had no idea Helen was such a musical buff.

The distant ring of a phone drew her attention away from the computer screen. Helen glared at her phone before moving to the doorway. "Sorry. I need to take this."

Lexi caught Helen's eye as she moved to the hallway to accept her phone call. She vigorously rubbed at her right ear, hoping Helen had got the message. They'd stayed longer than she'd intended. Her mother seemed to be making a real effort with a new guest to entertain. Still, she'd rather be back at home with Helen all to herself.

The mumbling continued from the hallway. Lexi was curious as to who was on the other end. Maybe Hillary North had another job for Helen. *Get in line, North. I'm her client now.* She finished scanning the hard drive of her mother's laptop. "We need to get going soon. Are you all sorted for food for a while?"

"Yes. Maggie from downstairs took me the other day."

Maggie-from-downstairs again. She wondered if that was her actual name. "Good." Lexi didn't need to ask about alcohol. She'd refused to purchase any ever since it became a problem.

Helen came back into the room, a slight frown stretched across her forehead. *A conversation for the journey home.* "Okay. Your laptop is now working again. You need to be careful which sites you go on. I've put some new antivirus on it, which will stop you accessing any dodgy sites, so it should be okay for a while."

"Thank you, darling. You're so good at this stuff. I don't understand a word of it."

Her mother still had no idea what she did for a job.

Helen remained on her feet. She'd obviously taken Lexi's rather blunt hint.

"Well," Lexi rubbed her ear again just in case, "we should probably get going." She glanced over to Helen, who nodded. Helen still had a slightly pensive look. The phone call had obviously affected her, which worried Lexi.

Helen stepped closer to her mother. "It was lovely to meet you, Val. And thank you for lunch."

Lexi got to her feet the same time as her mother. She crossed the room to pull her mother into her arms. "Thanks, Mum. I'll call you in a few days to check on the laptop, make sure it's okay." She still couldn't bring herself to say "To check on *you*"; to admit aloud that she would concern herself with her mother's wellbeing. Maybe she didn't need to anymore with Maggie-from-downstairs stepping in. A slither of jealousy rose to the surface as she walked behind Helen out of the room.

"Keep an eye out for *Funny Girl*. I think you'll like it," Helen said as they made their way to the front door.

"I will. Thanks for the suggestion. It was very nice to meet you at last, Helen."

Lexi ignored the dig as they said their goodbyes. She took Helen's hand and started to move towards the steps, waiting for the click of the door closing before speaking. As soon as they were out of earshot, she let rip. "Holy fucking shit!"

"I told you there was nothing to worry about."

Lexi saw the wide grin on Helen's face as she forced a shoulder bump between them as they made their way down the steps. "You have no idea how fucking weird that was. I haven't seen her like that in years."

"Well, maybe musicals have healing powers."

"Funny." She bumped shoulders with Helen again. "Who knew you were such a musical aficionado."

"You're not the only one with hidden depths."

God, there was definitely a catalyst at work here somewhere. But did it really matter what it was? "I'm driving, remember?" Lexi held out her hand for the keys. "I promise no *Banana Splits* driving in your car. I know how attached you are to it."

The offered keys were snatched back before Lexi could get them. She was about to voice her frustrations when Helen took the words right out of her mouth.

"What the fuck!" Helen stood looking down at the back of her car.

"What's up?" Lexi moved to stand next to her, where the issue of Helen's annoyance became clear.

Helen stood to look at the back of the car. "What is that stuff?" She bent to get a closer look. Her fingers prodded the substance that protruded out of her exhaust pipe.

Squatting, Lexi pressed the surprisingly hard foamy material. "I think its expanding foam or something."

"We won't be going anywhere. The exhaust is totally blocked. We can't drive it."

"Shit." Lexi stood, unsure what to do. "Fuck." She glanced back at her mother's flat. Did they really have to go back in there?

Why the fuck would somebody do this?

CHAPTER 16

HELEN IMMEDIATELY TOOK OUT HER phone, dialling her breakdown service. It was a slim chance, but she had to ask the question. She visually checked the doors and fuel flap for damage as she gave the operator the required information. It looked untouched except for the exhaust. The modern version of the potato in the exhaust pipe. It was the simplest form of damage. No alarm had been triggered, and they got away scot-free. Even with her basic knowledge of the combustion engine, she knew the car sucked in air through the exhaust. There was also the possible leakage of carbon monoxide into the car to consider.

The phone conversation dashed her hopes only moments later. They were stuck there.

"I'm sorry, madam. Your membership doesn't cover that kind of damage."

Helen closed her eyes in frustration. She checked the time on her watch; it was after three on a Sunday. "Can you recommend a local garage that will be open today, now?"

Shit! They'd only been there three hours. How the fuck could this happen in the middle of the day… and why? Had they been followed all the way from Bristol? How did this person even know where they were going? Was it another coincidence? Helen knew better than to just accept it. It was still no clearer as to who the target was or why. She caught sight of Lexi rubbing her arms. Unlocking the car, she pulled a jacket from the boot, offering it to her. She seemed a little lost as she accepted the offering. They needed to talk about this latest episode.

Thankfully, the operator offered to put her straight through. After several minutes of sweet talking and bribery, the garage owner finally agreed to pick up the car and repair it and deliver it back in the morning.

Helen moved closer, pulling Lexi into her arms. "Hey. You okay? I'll sort this out, I promise."

Lexi's arms wrapped around her waist as if in reply to her words. "I know you will." The words were muffled as Lexi pressed herself into Helen's frame. "When are they coming for the car?"

Helen rested her chin on the top of Lexi's head as she burrowed closer. "Soon. I offered to pay double if they drop it off before eight in the morning."

"I'm sorry."

"Why? It's not your fault." None of it was Lexi's fault, yet she was bearing the brunt of it, especially right now, standing in front of her mother's flat. "Where do you want to stay tonight? We don't have to stay here if you don't want to. We could find a hotel."

"And miss the biggest change I've seen in my mother in years? Maybe we'll even get to meet Maggie-from-downstairs. Do you think she might be her lesbian lover?"

Helen chuckled. Whatever the situation Lexi could always make her laugh.

"Who was on the phone earlier? You looked worried after you'd taken the call."

"An ex-colleague. They've found the car that tried to run you over, burnt out. He's traced the owners. It was stolen the same day. He's sending me some info on where it was stolen from—might help narrow down who took it at some point."

"I'm glad you're on the case."

Helen took a breath. She hoped she could find the culprit before anything more serious befell Lexi. This new development had only increased her unease. Someone wanted them trapped here overnight, but why? What did they want? Why did they want them out of the way?

Lexi pulled back to look at her. "How do you know it's the same car?"

Shit! She hadn't told her this yet. She hoped Lexi wasn't going to get angry with her again. Not that she didn't have a right to, but there was never any malice involved. "Lilly managed to get part of the registration when she saw it drive away—a dark blue VW Polo, which is a match to the car…and the wing mirror is missing. I'm guessing the one in the boot of my car is a match." Helen saw no reason to add the detail of switched number plates to avoid detection—or the fact that they had probably stolen that car for a reason, that it was an easy take, no modern alarms to deal with. The perpetrator had skills but obviously wasn't an experienced car thief. Was that a good thing or bad thing? She really couldn't say at this point.

Lexi made no reply, but simply burrowed back into position.

"How about we go shopping, pick up some food, and I'll cook us all a meal? You can spend a bit more time with your mum, or with me in the kitchen as my sous chef, depending on how you feel."

Lexi made no reply for several minutes. Helen figured she was either annoyed with the news about the car or was mulling over the pros and cons of their evening plans. Either way, she didn't like the silence.

"Okay. But can we stay here for a bit like this?"

Helen kissed the side of Lexi's face. "Sure."

The sound of a tow truck arriving broke them apart. They both stood there, watching the vehicle pull into the car park and reverse in their direction. Lexi grabbed her hand, giving it a squeeze to get her attention. "I'd better go and see if we actually *can* stay. She might have big plans with Maggie-from-downstairs tonight."

Lexi finally pushed away her empty plate. She always felt a little better with a full stomach. Two helpings of chocolate gateau and spaghetti and meatballs tended to have that effect on her. Her mother had been entertaining them, or embarrassing Lexi mostly, with stories of her geeky childhood. Thankfully she was too tipsy to remember where the photo albums were kept, saving her the supreme humiliation of Helen seeing her baby pictures.

Photo albums hadn't been a talking point in their family for some time, with too many bad memories outweighing the good ones. It was weird and even a little uncomfortable to have it now be an acceptable topic of conversation. Leah's life had been tormented by her abuse, yet somehow her mother had managed to capture moments of happiness. She'd never seen these photos before. Too painful, Lexi figured. She was grateful to finally see them now.

Lexi stifled a yawn as Helen took her plate to the kitchen. The events of the day were catching up with her. She was exhausted. "I'll wash up," she offered as she got to her feet.

"No need. All done," Helen replied, drying her hands on the tea towel.

Lexi glared across at her mother. Her hand still gripped the stem of an empty wine glass. Her head was slumped on her other hand, and her eyes starting to droop as she struggled against alcohol-induced fatigue. Choosing to ignore the spectacle, Lexi stealthily walked over to Helen in the kitchen. "We can sleep in the spare room." It was an offhanded statement, almost too casual. She could hear the tension in her own voice as she delivered the words. Her mother no doubt heard it without needing any visual clues.

"No you won't. One on the sofa and one in the spare bed," her mother ordered from the table.

Her ears still worked like a drunk listening for the last-orders bell. "What? Mum, you do realise I'm a grown-up?"

"I know, but you're not married, are you?"

There was amusement in her mother's voice as she delivered the rhetorical statement.

"No, but—" Lexi spluttered.

"Then you don't sleep in the same bed. It's a single anyway, too small for the two of you."

Now she's saying we're fat. She was about launch into another tirade when Helen stepped in.

"The sofa will be fine. Thank you, Val."

"What? No." Lexi aimed her gaze at Helen, hoping she could read the frustration she was sure showed on her brow.

"Lex, you have your old room. I'll take the sofa."

She usually avoided that room when she visited. "It's not my old room; it's just a spare room with some of my stuff in it."

Helen placed her hand on Lexi's arm. "It's only one night. I'll be fine on the sofa."

She was too tired to argue. "Fine. I'll get the sheets." She stomped off, annoyed at Helen's levelheadedness.

He let himself into the flat. Waiting in the hallway, he heard no sound. No wheezing, nothing. He pulled the mask over his face, resisting the urge to turn on the light. He stood there, taking in the ambience of the flat. The last couple of weeks he'd come around he'd been welcomed by the sound of laboured breathing, usually finding Morris hunched over in his armchair, watching his tiny TV. Was he too late? Had he missed his opportunity to see the light fade from Morris's eyes?

He moved through the flat. Diffused light provided enough guidance for him to step over the piles of newspapers and boxes as he made his way to the bedroom. The interior was darker, the thick curtains preventing any light from the streetlights below entering the room. There would be no onlookers today.

His eyes quickly accepted the darkness as he scanned the room. A large lump occupied the bed. He tilted his head as he listened for any sign of life. A gentle rasp erupted. He was still breathing. Still occupying the earth.

Morris had grown more delirious over the last day or two. According to all the articles and books he'd read, it was a good sign—for him. Keeping the light off, he moved to the side of the bed.

He reached out a gloved hand over the face in the bed. He held it hovering several inches above, waiting to swoop down. Morris wasn't even aware of his presence anymore. Yet, he still hesitated.

He was a pathetic human being. His opportunity was right there in front of him, and he still couldn't grab it. Steeling himself, he dropped his hand. He smothered the faint wheeze, restricting its flow. He let the weight of his hand do the work, testing the reaction. Morris barely responded. A twitch lower down the bed caught his eye as a noise emanated from below the covers. A leg moved, forcing him to put a little more pressure onto the features below his hand. His heart thudded uncontrollably as he held his breath, like he was in sympathy with the figure lying in the bed next to him. It seemed to take forever as his chest began to burn under the pressure.

He released his hand, pulling it to his side as he backed away. The figure in the bed released a shallow breath. He left the room as silently as he came. He didn't want any question over the manner of Morris's death. He needed to be patient; it would be over soon enough. He slipped out of the flat, closing the door softly behind him. He stood for a moment in the corridor, a shuffling sound nearby making him freeze. He waited several minutes before walking to the stairwell, leaving the building behind him.

CHAPTER 17

LEXI TOSSED AND TURNED. THE mattress was too soft, making it impossible to get comfortable. It was like lying on an enormous marshmallow.

She opened her eyes. Even in the gloom from the streetlights beyond the window she could see the shrine her mother had put together. The silhouette of the guitar came into view, an odd choice of object, considering the part it played in Leah's short life. Lexi wondered what would have been chosen for her shrine if it'd been her instead. A computer. *A Commodore or Spectrum*, she thought, reminiscing back to the first computers she'd wrangled her mother into buying before she cannibalised them and added new parts to improve their capability and speed.

Lexi switched on the small desk light next to the bed before kicking off the covers. She got to her feet, trying not to look around the room as she made her way to the door. She grabbed an old dressing gown from the hook, tying it loosely. She remembered the squeak of the door handle just in time as she slowly depressed the lever until it released the catch and freed the door. She held her position for a moment, listening for any sound or movement—nothing. Moving to the open doorway leading to the sitting room, she could see there was a glow of light. She moved closer. She could see Helen's face lit by her tablet as she stretched out on the sofa.

"What are you doing?" Helen hissed from across the room.

"I couldn't sleep...not on my own." She moved closer and straddled Helen's stretched-out figure. "What are *you* doing?"

"Nothing." Helen quickly switched off the tablet, setting it on the floor. Bringing her hands to Lexi's exposed thighs, Helen met her eyes in the near darkness. "Don't you think it's weird that the exhaust was damaged here?"

"I don't know. What time are they coming in the morning?" Lexi had been so caught up in the fact that they'd actually stayed over, alongside the changes in her mother's behaviour that she hadn't really given it much thought beyond her initial concern that trouble had followed them.

Helen kept her voice low. "Around eight, hopefully. Have you contacted your boss to let him know you'll be late?"

Lexi nodded. She bent down to kiss Helen, brushing their lips together. "Sorry about today." Finding the hem of Helen's T-shirt, she slid her hand inside and touched soft skin that she caressed with the pads of her fingers. She bent closer again and captured Helen's lips. There was something inherently naughty about making out with your girlfriend on your parent's sofa while they slept only metres away.

Helen pulled back, tilting her head to one side. "What for?"

"Dragging you here, having to stay over, asking about your mum—everything." Her hand travelled higher, cupping a round breast. In the near dark, she guessed that the arch of Helen's eyebrow carried a coming admonishment, but she pressed on regardless.

"Your mum will hear us…" Helen tried to prevent her other hand from venturing under the waistband of her shorts.

"She won't. She's probably crashed out already." Lexi knew from bitter experience that her mother could be dead to the world before her head even hit the pillow—or floor, depending on how much she'd had to drink that particular night.

Lexi sat up, preparing to remove her dressing gown. She wanted to feel Helen next to her. They had only been together a short time, but she always slept better when she was touching Helen's bare skin. Movement on the far side of the room caught her attention, halting her movement. The presence was on her in a flash.

Lexi tried to shield her face, but the stream of liquid continued. "What the fuck!" She blurted between gulps of what she quickly realised was soda water.

"I told you. Not under my roof." Her mother's voice held a hint of gratification.

"Mum…! Stop, stop!" Lexi struggled to get to her feet, the flow of liquid finally abating. "Okay, okay." She separated herself from Helen. "I'm going." Glancing back, she saw the look of amusement on Helen's face. She'd never hear the end of this.

Lexi reluctantly returned to her room, drying her face with the towel she'd used earlier. She draped it over the back of the small chair pushed under the wooden desk, then pulled the chair out, taking a seat at the desk that had been in her childhood bedroom. Maybe it wasn't only a shrine to her sister. Lexi pulled at the large drawer that spanned the length of the desk. Inside were instant reminders of her youth. Bits of computer and various pieces of stationery littered the front of the drawer. Metallic marker pens were Leah's favourite; she'd constantly been tagging her schoolbooks with hearts and stars. There was a choice of several silver or gold pens, none of which probably worked after so many years; but that wasn't the point.

She searched further back and found a pack of what felt like playing cards. She pulled them out into the light, recognising the *Top Trumps* game immediately. *Deadliest Predators*. They'd spent hours playing this game, usually on long car journeys to break up the monotony.

Tears welled in her eyes. Leah had never had the chance of a normal life. She'd spent so many years in institutional care after being sectioned that her life never even began. Leah had never had a first love, a first job, nothing. Suicide was her only way of escaping the pain. An image of Richard Jarvis's dishevelled body flashed through her mind. Somehow he never quite got what he deserved for the pain he'd caused. This was the other reason she stayed away. There were too many reminders of her failure to protect her own sister.

Lexi opened the plastic cover, releasing the cards into her waiting hand. She moved to the bed and stretched out on the small mattress. She flicked through the cards, remembering the categories. *Killer Rating*—that was the best one. Or *Weight*—that came a close second.

The Komodo dragon card appeared in front of her. Its continued appearance had fuelled her irrational childhood fear of them after her sister made her watch a nature documentary one Sunday night. Maybe Leah would have become a vet or zoologist had she had the chance. She closed her eyes, drifting off as she remembered the times she'd played *Top Trumps* with her little sister.

With a cup of tea in hand, Helen carefully opened the bedroom door. To her surprise, the lamp was on. Lexi was still asleep, her exposed body partially covered with a combination of a dressing gown and duvet. Helen had taken the time to appreciate Lexi's firm body largely due to the fact that most mornings at home she was naked or, at best, scantily clad. This time, there were a number of playing cards of some kind covering both the bed and Lexi.

Helen placed the cup on the side before carefully sitting on the edge of the bed. It was narrow; how Lexi thought they would both sleep on there, she would never know. She drew a stray lock of wayward hair behind Lexi's ear. "Morning," She kept her voice soft.

She watched as Lexi began to stir, rubbing her face against the pillow as her hand reached out for Helen.

"What time is it?" Lexi's voice was croaky from sleep. Her hand landed on Helen's thigh.

"Half seven." Helen picked up one of the cards. "What are these?"

Lexi sat up a little, her heavy-lidded eyes looking down at herself. "*Top Trumps.*" She locked eyes with Helen, a slight grin on her lips. "Don't tell me you never played."

"Umm, I think so." Helen picked up the next-closest card. It was mildly familiar. "*Deadliest Predators.*" When she turned the card over, Helen faced a piranha with its rows of razor teeth. "Gruesome."

The sound of a truck pulling up outside drew Helen's attention to the window. "That sounds promising." The offer of extra money had obviously been too good to refuse. She looked out of the window as the flatbed lorry came to a stop. Most importantly, her car was on the back.

CHAPTER 18

He sat in his car, watching the fallout in front of him. It was finally over. Morris had died in the night. He hadn't even had the chance to witness Morris's last gasp for breath. The man had cheated him out of even that little pleasure. He only got to observe the aftermath. The body had been removed over an hour ago. Two officers had made several trips to their car with brown bags. Surely it was cut and dried.

He nervously stared at his clenched hands. Why were they looking through the things of an old man, dead from ill health?

The clattering of a door drew his attention as another uniformed officer carrying more evidence bags exited Gallagher House. His breathing increased as a familiar black BMW pulled up near the police car. What the fuck were they doing back here? Hadn't they already left for work? He watched the ponytailed sidekick get out of the car and head straight for the uniformed officer. Her stride was confident, practised even, as she approached. She waited for the officer by his car.

He was transfixed as he watched their interaction. Although she was calm and in control, he could sense her almost demanding answers from the officer. His hands began to sweat as they gripped the steering wheel. Was she a copper or something? *Shit. How does this shit keep getting so fucked up?* Anger boiled up inside as he pounded the steering wheel. What if she did know something? Had they talked about the other night? Dropping his right hand, he pressed at the wound on his leg, waiting for clarity. His mind traced the misshapen letters as they stretched across his thigh. *FAILURE*.

Focus. He still couldn't be sure what she had actually seen, but he couldn't take any more risks. He'd show her. She'd regret spying on him once and for all. She needed to suffer like Morris. Put the fear of God into her. Maybe she'd disappear for a while at least.

―――――― •••• ――――――

"Excuse me, Officer!" Helen shouted as she made her way to the uniformed man. His hands were full of what she knew all too well were evidence bags. She watched as he deposited the bags into his car boot. His head then popped up, flashing her a suitably fake smile as he finally made eye contact with her.

"Hi, I live in Longwell House." Helen waved in the direction of the flat. "There's nothing to worry about is there, officer?"

"No, madam. No reason for alarm." He closed the boot of his car, preventing her from seeing anything that lay inside. "Elderly gentleman from the top floor of Gallagher House."

Gallagher House, thank God. The car park was shared between both blocks of flats. It was impossible to tell which block the police had come from. Helen's mind had raced to Lilly. She'd been the only witness to Lexi's so-called accident. She hated the thought of anything happening to that sweet old lady because of what she'd seen.

Helen considered revealing she was ex-job, but she knew from experience how annoying ex-coppers could be when they got involved. Besides, Pete was her best hope at finding out any information right now. She made a mental note to call him.

"Passed away sometime in the night. Natural causes. He'd been ill for some time," the officer continued.

He seemed to emphasise his last words. She realised there was no more to be gained from this man. "Thanks for letting me know." She was about to turn and leave when another vehicle arrived. A white van parked in the empty space next to them. The driver got out, nodding to the uniformed officer before heading towards Gallagher House. More reinforcements. Maybe things weren't okay after all. She gave the officer a dubious look.

"Nothing to worry about, just routine. Were you home last night?" the officer questioned.

"No. We were in Slough visiting friends. Got back a few minutes ago."

The officer raised his eyebrows. "Which flat do you live in?" He checked his watch.

"4A." Helen realised she'd put herself right in the middle of an inquiry if there actually was one. Getting involved, asking questions before ruling yourself out entirely. Ordinarily it would have raised a flag for her if she were in charge. She hoped that wouldn't be the case on this occasion.

Helen saw the look of concern on Lexi's face through the windscreen as she walked back to her car. Coming face to face with police officers after having her car sabotaged probably wasn't the best way to start the day. *Shit*. That had to be what this was all about, getting her and Lexi out of the way, trapping them in Slough so they wouldn't see this play out. That night on the roof—there had to be a connection. She'd known it from the start. Unfortunately, she couldn't figure out what they were doing up there. Whoever they were, they'd seen Lexi when the kitchen light had flashed on, making her a perfect target. Yet ironically, she'd seen nothing.

"Well, what's going on?" Lexi's voice was firm as she extracted herself from the car to join her.

"Just being a concerned resident," Helen bluffed, not wanting to reveal her worrying thoughts.

"And?"

"These police officers are not very community minded." Helen caught the grin on Lexi's face as she moved toward their building. She chose instead to redact the information she had gained, providing Lexi with only the basic facts. "A resident in Gallagher House died of natural causes last night."

"Did he say who, which flat?" Lexi queried.

"No. As I said, not that helpful."

Helen waited for the sound of Lexi in the shower before walking to the kitchen to grab the binoculars off the worktop. She moved towards the window, training them on the top-floor flat opposite. The visible rooms were well-lit, considering it was a bright summer's day. Helen could see several figures moving around, checking the place out. It seemed a bit overkill for a natural death.

The rooms appeared very full, reminding her of Lilly's flat. Helen planned to check on her on her way out. Glancing at the clock on the wall, she groaned. There was no time for this now; she had to get to work. With the police still around, it seemed safe to leave Lexi on her own. Whoever they were, surely they wouldn't try anything with patrol cars parked out front. She stuck her head into the bathroom to kiss Lexi goodbye, saying she would stop by and see her at work.

On her way across the foyer, Helen stopped by Lilly's flat. She wanted to make sure she was okay, and maybe ask her a few questions about last night. Lilly opened the door on the second knock.

"Helen." Lilly seemed pleasantly surprised to see her. Her eyes travelled down her uniform.

"Hi, Lilly. I just wanted to make sure you were okay. I saw the police outside this morning—"

"You better come in." Lilly stepped aside.

Helen waited in the narrow hallway for Lilly to lead the way. "Do you know what happened last night?" Helen launched straight into it as they moved towards the kitchen. She didn't have a lot of time.

"Something in Gallagher House, I think. Looks like a death of some kind. Saw them taking out the body earlier," Lilly said over her shoulder.

She smiled to herself, Lilly could prove very useful indeed. "Do you know anyone in the next block?"

"Well, not anymore." Lilly said sadly.

For a moment, Helen thought Lilly meant the deceased man.

"She moved out last year after a fall. Lives in a home in Bracknell now."

"Oh. I'm sorry."

Lilly offered a brief smile. "The police arrived early this morning."

Helen nodded. "No idea who lives in the top-floor flats, then?"

Lilly shook her head. "No, sorry. But I'm sure I can find out for you."

"No. Thank you. I'd rather not risk any more accidents."

"You weren't here last night?"

"No. We were unavoidably detained." Helen saw no reason to lay out all the details.

"Sounds interesting."

"Umm, something like that." Helen checked the time on her phone. She was going to be later than late.

Lilly grinned. "New job?" She waved a teaspoon in Helen's direction.

Helen regarded her attire. "Umm." Returning to her days in uniform was not something she cared to do but needs must.

Arriving at work, Helen took a couple of minutes to call Pete. It went straight to answerphone. He was obviously busy, but that didn't solve her problem. She'd tried to keep Lexi out of this, but maybe it was the only way to resolve recent events. Lexi was more than capable of digging up information. Maybe it was time to let her help. Helen could ask her to find out the names of the residents in Gallagher House, do a bit of background on them. She still wanted to check out the location of the car theft and dumping.

Rubbing her tired eyes, she realised, not for the first time lately, how frustrating and horrible it was being out of the loop.

It was fair enough when she'd been on the force, when she'd been racing around trying to help people after the event, but at least she'd had access to information and manpower to try and prevent these things from happening again. Right now she had nothing. She was just waiting for the next terrible event, all the while hoping that for once it wouldn't involve Lexi. But maybe it had already happened. An old man was dead, natural causes or not.

CHAPTER 19

Lexi arrived home, starving as usual. She moved through the flat, depositing her bag on the table in the kitchen. She pulled the bread from the cupboard, slicing off a sizeable chunk before buttering it generously. As she took a satisfying bite, she realised she still had on her lanyard and quickly dropped it into her bag before Helen arrived. She didn't want to be reprimanded again, especially after recent events.

With her snack finished, she grabbed the large bottle of water from the fridge to wash it down. She drained and crushed it with her hands, adding it to the overflowing pile in the recycling box. She blew out a breath, resigned to the fact that she would have to empty it. She'd been putting it off since before the weekend.

Lexi grabbed her keys, pulled the door closed behind her, and headed for the stairs, passing the rubbish chute, a remnant of the old building before it was modernised. Unfortunately, they hadn't catered for recycling back then, so walking the box down to the bin was her only choice.

She heard a noise farther down as she entered the stairwell. A glance over the railing below revealed no one, and so she shrugged off her unease. Simply another resident returning home from work. She continued her journey to the back of the building. The box was getting heavier. She needed to get to the bin before she covered the floor in recyclables.

Leaving the stairwell, Lexi walked down the short corridor. She'd developed irrational fears of late, her mind filled with worst-case scenarios. Even in this small space with no one else in sight, she sensed scrutiny. The last week was definitely getting to her despite her best efforts to ignore it.

At the end of the corridor, she could see that the door had been left ajar, propped open with something. Unsure, she glanced around, but again she saw and heard nothing. She considered dumping the box on the floor, leaving it in the hope that another resident would complete the job for her. Maybe she could ask Helen when she got back. No. She didn't want to put Helen in any more danger than she already was, especially if some nutcase was after her for simply doing her job.

Lexi peeked through the gap, between the door and the frame. She could see the large recycle bins beyond; they were only a few feet away. She pushed the door with her shoulder, scanning the area. The brightness of the day had clouded over. The back of the building was in shadow, making it feel gloomier than it was. She moved towards the bin, lifting the box higher to deposit its contents successfully. She rested the box on the bin's corner. Using her free hand, she flipped back the lid. The loud echo made her jump. As she dumped the contents, she told herself she would be back inside in only a few seconds.

Contents unloaded, she stepped to one side grabbing at the lid again to close it. Movement behind her made her flinch.

Hands pulled at her, dragging her behind the collection of bins. Panic shot through every limb, and she managed a small scream as she dropped the box in favour of struggling against the figure behind her. A strong arm wrapped around her torso, trapping her arms, forcing the air from her lungs, rendering her mute. The box had tumbled and clattered to the floor, hitting her bruised knee on the way.

She struggled to twist her head around, only to catch a glimpse of a masked face that made it impossible to see any features. Something was pulled over her head to prevent any further observations. A damp smell filled her lungs. Her senses heightened as darkness filled her sight and she considered the very real fear of being kidnapped. She could feel herself being tugged to one side, her leg hitting against something hard. The arm loosened a little, giving her an opportunity she wasn't about to pass up.

She blindly directed a sharp elbow behind her, failing to make any contact. She almost fell with the force of her momentum. Strong arms held her upright. She struck out with the other elbow and was rewarded with a groan of pain from her assailant. *Male.*

The arm tightened again, tipping her backwards as something was sprayed over her face under her hood. Cold, damp material pressed against her mouth as she gasped for air. It was fluid of some kind, tepid. Whatever it was, there was no chance to taste it in the confusion. Was it meant to knock her out? Was there more than one person? They could carry her off without a trace. She needed to scream, make a noise. But the force of more fluid made her splutter. Choking, she tried to turn her face away, but a strong hand held her in place to face the onslaught. Her mind wandered back to the soda syphon her mother used on her only days ago. What the fuck was going on here? As she continued to gag, she desperately wanted to hold her arms above her head to be able to take a breath. The darkness was claiming her, fear leaving her body. She had taken a life. Maybe this was justice, regardless of her intentions that night. Closing her mind, her body went limp.

⬥

Helen walked out of Shield Securities, taking a moment to scan the car park in search of Lexi's Mini. The space it had occupied earlier was now empty. She'd planned on cooking tonight but wanted to check with Lexi before going shopping. Unfortunately, Lexi had been locked in some weird "Red Team/Blue Team" meeting, unreachable all day. She unlocked her car, slipping her keys into the ignition as she dialled Lexi's mobile. She waited till the answerphone message kicked in before hanging up. Sitting back in her seat, she waited a moment to see if Lexi would call her back. Out of the corner of her eye, she saw a figure passing, and glanced up. It was Shelby passing by the end of the row of cars further down. Lexi had said there was something off about her. She'd even caught her going through someone's desk. Now, Helen scrutinised the woman on her walk towards the riverbank that edged the car park. Some of her co-workers used the bench that had been installed to have their lunch.

Helen knew from getting acquainted with the area that the footpath was a shortcut to a bus stop on this side of the technology park. A beech hedge provided some shelter, or maybe a place to hide from the boss. Helen's position to one side of an opening in the hedge gave her a clear view of the bench. As Shelby approached the footpath, she pulled out an envelope from her backpack, dropping it in the waste bin next to the bench. *Interesting.*

Why would Shelby suddenly decide to throw something away after leaving an office with a perfectly good waste bin?

Helen pulled the keys back out of the ignition, intrigued. She was about to check out what Shelby had thrown away when she saw another figure approaching from the opposite direction. Helen could only see his head due to the height of the hedge. She quickly pulled out her phone, switching from camera mode in order to film whoever appeared in the hedge gap. A small white dog appeared first, then the figure of a man in his thirties. He was dark haired and smartly dressed. He hesitated as he passed the bin. *Bingo.* Helen waited patiently, trying to focus the camera a little more sharply on his actions as he scoped the area before pulling the envelope from the bin. He slipped it inside his jacket and turned around to walk back the way he came.

Helen clicked off the camera. So maybe young Shelby was passing on trade secrets to competitors. Why else would she conduct such an elaborate drop right outside her workplace? She needed to talk to Lexi before passing the information higher up. It's not like they could retrieve the information now, but maybe they could prevent it from happening again.

Helen took a gamble and stopped off at the supermarket anyway. As she parked up outside the flat, she noticed Lexi's car on the far side of the car park. Great, she was home safe. She certainly had a story to tell her when she got in.

Her eyes were drawn to the entrance of Gallagher House next door. She pulled out her phone to call Pete again, hoping he wasn't going to start avoiding her calls.

"Helen Taylor," he said, "what can I do for you?"

He didn't sound pissed off yet. "Hi, Pete. I was wondering if you heard anything about a death at Gallagher House."

"A death. Gallagher House?"

Helen tried to keep the frustration from her voice. "Yeah. Old guy was found early this morning in the top-floor flat. I spoke to Uniform. They said it was natural causes."

"Okay. And?"

"And I'm not sure I believe them. I think it's connected to what happened with the attempted hit-and-run the other week." Leaving the shopping in the car, Helen couldn't resist a quick look inside the adjacent building.

"What? Why?"

Helen heard the scepticism in Pete's tone. Ignoring his question, she preferred to ask one of her own. "Any more news about the car?"

She waited for his reply as another resident headed towards the Gallagher House entrance, a woman pushing a buggy. Helen did the same making sure she wouldn't arrive first. The click-clack of computer keys being tapped sounded in her ear. Pete was a one-finger typist like herself by the sound of it.

"I still need to get a statement ASAP for this to be official, you know."

Helen sighed. "I know, I know. I'm working on it." Getting Lexi to report anything was going to be impossible, but Pete didn't need to know that yet.

"Okay. I'm still looking for any CCTV along the route. The Polo pinged a few times on ANPR, but no clear picture of the driver. They've got a hat on and sunglasses, whoever they are. It…" He hesitated, the sound on the phone muffled.

"It what?" A familiar sickness bubbled in her gut.

"It just looks odd. The plates were changed after it was stolen. First time it's caught, it has the original plates near Millsbridge. Then what looks like the same car pulls out of a car park in Millsbridge with new plates on it, ones that match your witness's description with *ABL* at the end of the plate. But…"

Pete took a breath, blowing it out down the phone line. Helen resisted the urge to snap at him as she let the information sink in. *Planned* was the only word that came to mind as she waited patiently for him to continue.

"Whoever it was, they were smart enough to make a new prefix number plate that fit with the age of the car so it didn't stand out. They obviously stole the car because it was an easy take. Then it's used to try and run someone down, and then burnt out. So maybe they panicked, or maybe you were right. But why do you think it's connected to Gallagher House? Don't answer that. Either way, we need to make this official."

Shit. It sounded so much worse hearing someone else say it out loud. "I know. I'm trying. I really need to know how the old man died. If you hear anything, I'd really appreciate it if you let me know."

The woman approached the glass door. Helen kept her voice low, turning her back to make herself seem indifferent to the woman's actions. She waited for her to key in her code to enter the foyer. Stepping up, she pulled the door fully open, allowing the woman to enter unhindered. Helen released the handle, letting the door almost close, catching it with her foot before it shut against the frame. She looked through the glass, waiting to go inside until the woman entered the lift. The layout appeared exactly the same as the block next door, minus the extra storey.

"Okay. I'll see what I can find out about Gallagher House."

"Thanks, Pete." She dabbled with the idea of letting him in on her theory. He'd been trustworthy so far. "I'm worried it might be connected to someone from a job in the past."

"Someone you've had dealings with?" He sounded doubtful again.

"Yeah."

"Has anything else happened?" Pete asked.

Helen pondered her options for a moment, quickly deciding against a full confession. "A couple of weird things, nothing major."

"Okay. Keep a record and let me know if anything else happens."

Helen hung up as she walked over to the mailboxes and scanned for any names, but they were mainly identified by flat numbers. Using her phone, she recorded what she saw. Three of the six flats had names slotted into the name holders—two from the second floor and one from the third. Flat 3B was occupied by a *M. Ryder.* It wasn't handwritten like the other two, it was typed. Times New Roman font. *Old school.*

Helen needed to make sure that was the recently deceased occupant. She entered the stairwell, sprinting up the steps, her adrenaline quickly taking her to the third floor. She moved to the corridor, grateful when the light immediately clicked on. The space was again an exact replica of the Longwell block. A door appeared on the right. She could easily see the brass number identifying it as 3B. The blue and white remains of crime-scene tape on the door handle was the only indication of the events that had happened inside.

As she turned to leave, the door to 3A opened. An elderly woman appeared in the gap, her frail hand gripping onto the door.

"Hello, I was just…" Helen searched for words to put the old lady at ease. She hoped her uniform might assist her. Old people always seemed to feel at ease with a uniform. "I wanted to pay my respects to Mr Ryder's family."

"Oh." Her hand shook a little as she removed it from the door. She opened it a few inches more. "I thought you were his nephew. He visits sometimes. Did you know him well?"

Helen took a gamble. "Only from Meals on Wheels. I delivered to him a couple of times."

The old woman glanced towards the empty flat. "Morris didn't really have any family except his nephew. No one will be there now."

Morris, Morris Ryder. "Thank you. I'm sorry to have disturbed you." The door started to close, and she quickly spoke up. "Oh, sorry. You wouldn't know how I could contact his nephew, would you?"

The woman's eyes narrowed as they glared at her. The door stopped for a moment, long enough for her to say "No." Helen watched the door softly close.

With no more information to be gained, she made a move to leave. Returning to the stairwell, Helen saw the short flight that led up to the roof area. Except there was no cage door preventing access this time. Another question for Lilly when she saw her again. As she approached the door, she pulled out her phone, flicking on its torch. There was a padlock dangling from a clasp. Upon closer inspection, she could see the lock had been cut and carefully placed back in position to look untouched.

Helen pulled the sleeves of her jumper over her hands. She separated the two parts of metal, released the hasp, and opened the door, then stepped out onto the roof. The breeze was cool on her face, the earlier heat of the day long gone. From her position she could see straight into Lexi's flat, the thirty-foot distance between the blocks creating a feeble modesty barrier. Lexi really needed to get some net curtains.

She walked around the perimeter of the roof, scanning for any obvious tampering—not that she even knew what she was looking for.

She tried to think back to that night, to the figure moving around. What exactly had she seen? The torch on the floor, she tried to picture where it had been—in the middle somewhere, more towards the right-hand side, maybe. The only thing there was a metal ventilation turbine spinning in the breeze. Was that the squealing she'd heard that night? Had someone taken the top off? As she looked more closely, she noticed one of the fins had been bent out of shape, creating a gap of a couple of inches. She held the cone still while she tried to look down, but the angle and darkness below obscured her view. She tilted her head to one side. She could make out something below. It was white-ish. Squinting, she could see something else shiny as it caught a glimpse of light, but it was too far away to see clearly.

Helen released the cone. She moved to the roof's edge again. The low railing that surrounded it seemed woefully inadequate the closer she got to the edge. She noted that the metal fire exit stairwell didn't stretch to the roof.

A bang emanating from the back of the adjacent block drew her attention. She moved towards the back corner of the building, trying to follow the continuing thuds. It sounded like they were coming from the bin area.

Helen squinted against the dim light. She could just make out the vague outline of a dark figure struggling with something, but she couldn't see what it was. The figure was blocking her view. A shrill voice that sent a chill down her spine broke through the silence.

Lexi. Lexi was what the figure was struggling with. *Shit. Shit. Shit.* What the fuck was she doing down there, and what could she do from up here?

"Hey!" She bellowed. Taking out her phone, she began filming—she hoped. "Hey, you, by the bins. Leave that woman alone. Police. My colleagues are coming through the front door right now. I'm filming your every move."

It was worth a try. From that distance, she figured they wouldn't be able to tell if she was telling the truth or not. To her annoyance, the figure seemed to disappear around the side of the bin, taking Lexi with them. She needed to get down there, now. She bolted back to the stairwell.

Fuck! She took the steps as fast as she could. Her haste was slowing her down like a lanky teenager. Her limbs jarred as they moved in the panic that engulfed her. Taking a breath as she rounded a corner on the stairwell, she tried to coordinate her body to move more efficiently. Helen crashed out of the stairwell like a bullet, heading straight for the back door, dodging several bags of rubbish that had fallen from an overflowing bin. She headed straight for where she'd last seen Lexi, stepping over a low wall that separated the two blocks of flats.

Fear gathered at the back of her throat as she hoped against the odds that Lexi would still be there. "Lex!" She shouted as she made her way closer to the bins. "Lex!" *Abducted from her home* was all she could see, as if reading it in an incident report.

"I'm here!"

A weak voice greeted her as she assisted her body in rounding the tight corner by grabbing onto the edge of the wooden fence that shielded the bins. Helen was faced with the sight of Lexi bending down and dusting off her trousers with one hand while the other grasped at a blue plastic box sitting on the floor, a box that Helen realised had contained the overflowing recyclables from the flat. She'd meant to empty it when they got back from visiting Lexi's mother. "Jesus! Are you okay. I saw—"

"I'm fine."

Lexi cut her off. Her voice was flat, almost disjointed. She was dishevelled, her hair wet in places. Her white shirt was soaked tight to her skin around her shoulders. Helen could see the outline of her bra straps below. She could tell by the set of Lexi's jaw that she was pissed off.

"Hey. Come here." Helen resisted the urge to bend double and assist in catching her breath in favour of pulling Lexi into her arms. "What the fuck happened? Did they hurt you? Did you see who it was?"

Lexi reluctantly let go of the box under her insistence. Helen's chest was on fire as she struggled to restrain her breathing. Clutching Lexi to her, she feared letting her out of her sight ever again.

"No. I couldn't see anything." Her body was still rigid with obvious anger. A sob escaped her chest as she finally relaxed against Helen. "He put a bag on my head."

He, she noted. Helen scanned the floor, looking for it, but there was nothing. "What—What kind of bag?" Her mind raced to plastic bags—suffocation. She really didn't want to go there now.

"Material. It was wet." Lexi offered between small gasps.

"Did he take it with him?" Helen immediately regretted her continued questions as Lexi's body shuddered with emotion. She instinctively held her tighter.

"It was like he was waterboarding me for information, but he didn't ask me any questions. He didn't say anything."

Lexi's muffled words froze her heart. This had gone way too far now, beyond intimidation. It was time to act, to fight back. The woman in her arms was just the person she needed to do that.

"Let's go inside." Helen wanted to tell her it was okay, that she was safe, but the words sounded hollow even to her. Lexi's damp hair brushed against her cheek.

The brazen actions of the man irked her. Why throw water over someone—more intimidation? "Was it water he poured over you?"

Lexi didn't seem to be suffering any ill effects beyond anger and shock, but she had to ask the question.

"I think so. It didn't taste of anything. He poured it over my face. I think he must have heard you, and ran away."

He again. "You're sure it was a he?" Helen wanted her to be sure.

"I elbowed him when he grabbed me. It was definitely a man."

Helen flexed her jaw at the thought of someone manhandling Lexi, the woman who currently gripped her waist, fingers digging into her flesh. She pulled back to look into Lexi's eyes and saw the same fear that she had felt as she had helplessly watched from the rooftop. "We should call the police. This is getting out of hand."

"And tell them what? I don't know who it was or what they want."

"He assaulted you." Helen tried to keep her voice even.

"Don't you think I know that?" Lexi's voice flared as she pressed her head against Helen's shoulder. "I can't take the risk. What if he knows what I did?" she continued in a calmer voice.

"You didn't kill him, Lex; it was an accident. He fell," Helen pleaded softly.

"You and I are the only ones who know that. I think it should stay that way for now."

Aware that this wasn't a discussion to be had in public, Helen relented for the moment. "Come on. Let's go back inside." Helen paused to pick up the box before she led them back to Lexi's flat. They were both silent the entire way as they clung together, lost in their thoughts. Helen's were firmly on finding out exactly what was going on.

She closed the door to the flat before beginning her plea, hoping that the latest development would make Lexi see her point of view. She held on to Lexi's hand as she spoke. "Lex, I think we should move out, for a while at least. I hate to think what might have happened with that car…" She didn't want to finish the sentence. There only needed to be a slight change of circumstance for it to have ended very differently… if Lexi had been a little slower.

"No fucking way. I'm not being forced out of my own flat because of some fucking freak."

The anger was back, surprising Helen again. She replied with equal annoyance before she could stop herself. "Lex, it's not about being forced out. This is not some kind of penance for what happened in Warner. I'm scared. I don't want anything *else* to happen to you." She instantly regretted her raised voice, but it felt like the only way to get Lexi to listen to her concerns.

"I need a shower."

Helen could only watch as Lexi walked off towards the bathroom. Irritated, she pulled off her now damp jumper and threw it onto the kitchen table as she walked towards the fridge. "Shit."

She hadn't known Lexi that long, but having worked together for a few months, the one thing she did know was how infuriatingly stubborn she could be. Helen pulled open the freezer. She rummaged around as ice crystals fell onto the back of her hand, making her flinch. She grabbed onto the stash of vodka, freeing it from the ice at the back. Pouring a generous amount, the smell emanating from the glass was enough to put Helen off taking a drink. She leant back against the worktop giving Lexi a moment to calm down and take stock. Hearing the shower turn off down the hall she went back in search of Lexi.

Helen sat on the edge of the bath, waiting as Lexi towelled off from her shower. Her clothes were piled up on the floor. She made a note to bag them up for trace evidence.

"Is that for me or you?" Lexi queried without making eye contact.

Helen looked down at the drink in her hand. "Both." When she glanced up, she saw the weariness in Lexi's face. She walked over, offering her the drink. "I'm sorry I shouted."

Lexi took a quick swig before placing it on the side of the sink. "I'm sorry too. I'm just *so* tired of feeling angry and scared."

Helen stepped even closer, reaching for Lexi's hips. "I know. I'm trying, I really am." She felt useless as Lexi rested her head on her shoulder. All the strength was leaving her character. She needed to get a grip on this before it slipped any further away. The escalation was undeniable; someone had just had their hands on Lexi. What would have happened if she hadn't interrupted him? Why hadn't she come straight home and emptied the bloody bin herself? None of this had to happen.

"I know you are."

Lexi gripped her a little tighter. Helen did the same. "I'll find them, I promise." But Helen felt helpless all over again. She needed to stop sitting on the side lines and start acting before this bastard tried anything else.

CHAPTER 20

Lexi struggled to catch her breath as she reached the top of the stairs. The last couple of days, she'd felt progressively crappier, weaker and achier. The attack had set her on edge, yet she still refused to be budged from her work routine. It was the only thing keeping her sane—that and Helen's support, of course. God knew what would have happened if she hadn't appeared.

The burning in her chest continued as she grasped for the door handle. She was definitely under the weather, run-down, maybe. It wasn't like she'd been sleeping well lately. Skipping lunch probably wasn't the best idea either, but she had no appetite. That in itself should have been a warning sign.

Lexi's hand missed the handle on her first attempt; her fingers just grazed the metal. On the second attempt, she managed to pull the door open, but even that was a struggle. Her arms felt pathetically weak as she fought against the door closer.

She slumped at her desk, hugging the water bottle to her forehead. The slight sheen of condensation on the bottle cooled her head a little. The tap-tapping of keys around her echoed the throbbing pain in her head. She opened her drawer to rummage around for some pain killers. A half-full blister pack appeared from the back. She pushed two out, downing them with a chug of her water. Her throat felt raw as the pills slipped down.

In her haste, the water went down the wrong pipe. The cough that rumbled in her chest and raised her arms involuntarily was a shock. Lexi quickly pulled them down. One hand went to steady her chest, while the other covered her mouth. The bellowing cough only brought further scorching pain in her chest. She closed her eyes, waiting for the pain to ease before daring to move.

She opened her eyes when she felt the presence of someone next to her, a presence that made her jump. "Shit," she murmured as another cough overcame her. Helen was looking down at her, a small grin on her face.

"Catnapping?"

"I wish." Lexi wheezed.

"Are you busy right now?"

Intriguing. "I'm sure I can fit you in," Lexi replied.

"I think I might need your help with something."

"Sure." Lexi was even more curious now. Helen rarely visited her in her office, preferring to keep her distance.

Helen nodded towards the corridor behind them. Getting to her feet, Lexi inwardly groaned at the ache in her body as she followed Helen out of the office.

"I think we need to start playing a little dirty. I've got the name of the guy that died in the flat next door. Can you see what you can find out about him?"

"Are you asking me to hack for you?" Despite the ache all over her body, Lexi struggled to hide the grin on her face.

Helen pursed her lips as she stared back at her. The bright light of the corridor made her squint as they made their way to the end where the stairwell was housed. "Yes."

Lexi felt Helen's gaze on her as they ambled along.

"Are you all right? You don't look too good."

"Just a headache." Lexi wheezed as they continued along the corridor.

Helen's gentle hand gripped her arm, stopping her in her tracks. She twisted to look at Lexi, and a slight frown knitted her brow. "You don't sound good either. You've been like this a couple of days. You're getting worse, Lex."

"I'm just tired." Lexi was exhausted, with little sleep after the events of the other night.

Helen placed a raised hand across Lexi's brow. It felt cool and refreshing against her skin.

"You're boiling. You should go home. We can do this another time. I'll drive you."

Lexi's raised eyebrows had no effect. "Are you kidding? The sooner we find this prick, the sooner I'll feel better." She noticed a scrap of paper in Helen's hand. Holding out her own hand, she waited for the name of her target. "What's his name?"

"Morris Ryder. Aged seventy-one. I don't have a date of birth." Helen held out the piece of paper.

"No problem. I'll let you know what I find out." Lexi placed it in her pocket without even looking at it. "And how exactly did you come across this information?"

"I asked one of his neighbours and called in a favour from an old colleague."

"I see." Helen had obviously been busy working the case behind the scenes.

Lexi returned to the office, avoiding the looks of her colleagues and taking her seat. She grabbed her laptop from her bag, preferring not to use the work computer. She opened the usual search engines. Pulling the scrap of paper from her pocket, she keyed in the name, checking the spelling. She used the calculator on her phone to work out the year of birth. Ideally, she would have wanted a middle name. Luckily, Morris wasn't too popular for a first name. Due to his age, she didn't expect to find much of a social media digital footprint for Morris Ryder.

Lexi searched the UK electoral roll first and found his missing details. Date of birth the second of November 1946. His address for Flat 3B, Gallagher House in Bristol was also listed, as was his old address in Redlands, a more affluent area towards the centre of Bristol. A Maureen Ryder was also listed at the Redlands address. His wife, she presumed. Deceased, according to the information in front of her.

Her next stop was Companies House in case he was a business owner. There she discovered Ryder ran an antique shop for many years, Ryder Antiques and Collectables, until around ten years ago, after his wife passed away.

With the basic questions answered, Lexi printed out the information she had so far to give to Helen later. She checked the clock, deciding to call it a day. She stopped by Roman's desk and informed him she was going home sick.

She sent Helen a quick text as she sat in her car, letting her know she was going home to bed and that she would talk to her about the info she'd found on Ryder when Helen got home.

———— ·•· ————

Helen unlocked the door. It was eerily quiet inside. She moved through the flat in search of Lexi. She'd managed to escape work without finishing her shift. Hilary North would no doubt be on her case about it tomorrow.

The bedroom was dark, curtains pulled across to block out the light. A figure lay prone in the bed. The duvet covered Lexi entirely. Helen stood still near the end of the bed, appraising the situation. She couldn't be sure if Lexi was awake. The sound of raspy laboured breathing made its way through the duvet. She sounded terrible. An arm moved under the duvet as Helen stepped closer. Placing her hand on the resting figure, she felt the warmth from the body beneath.

Helen kept her voice low. "Hey. I got your message. How are you feeling? Can I get you anything?" There was no reply. The stress of the last week or two had obviously had an effect, draining Lexi mentally and physically.

Her phone buzzing in her pocket drew her attention. With no reply from Lexi, she figured she should let her sleep. Helen backed out of the room, pulled the door closed behind her, and walked towards the kitchen.

She scanned her buzzing phone, saw the number. "Hi, Pete. Is there any news?"

"Some. Gallagher House."

"Yeah, what have you got for me?"

"Morris Ryder, seventy-one, flat 3B. Found by his nephew. Died of pneumonia, but—"

Helen knew all this already from their earlier conversation. The *but* made it a little more interesting, though. "But what?"

"Environmental Health are involved."

"Why would…?" Helen eyed the bedroom door that Lexi lay behind. She recalled seeing a van in the car park yesterday.

"Looks like there might be something in the flat."

Something. "Like what?"

143

"Could be a couple of things. They're doing tests on one of the cleaners they got in to clear it out; he's been taken ill." Pete spoke quickly.

"What kind of ill?" Helen's heart pumped double time as she continued to glare at the plain white door.

"Not sure. Could be Legionella. It's something that affects the respiratory system."

"What?" Helen grabbed Lexi's laptop from the kitchen table, clicking on the Google icon.

"Are you okay? Helen."

Her fingers fumbled across the keys as she hoped she was wrong. The search came back as she had feared: symptoms included fever, loss of appetite, headache, and lethargy. "Fuck. I have to go, Pete. I'll call you later."

"Helen, what's go—"

She cut him off as she closed the laptop and headed for the bedroom. She pushed open the door, her eyes focused on the slow rise and fall of Lexi's chest. A gentle wheeze sounded in time with the movement.

"Lex, we have to go. I'm taking you to the hospital." There was no movement, only a slight groan of what she took as disapproval.

When Helen pulled back the duvet, Lexi was dressed in only her underwear. Her skin felt clammy, feverish to the touch. Raiding the drawers turned up a long sleeve T-shirt and tracksuit bottoms. She struggled to dress Lexi's limp figure. Even as Lexi tried to assist, their lack of synchronised movement made the job physically taxing.

They took the lift to the ground floor, shuffling together to her car. Lexi barely said a word, her breathing laboured the entire way. Helen strapped her in and drove with purpose to the nearest hospital, grateful to find St Michaels had a large A and E department. She parked as close as she could, hoisted Lexi to her feet, and headed for the entrance.

"Help!" Helen struggled further inside through the sliding doors. Thankfully, a nurse came forward with a wheelchair.

"What happened?" Her tone was firm but kind.

Fear gripped her as she reeled off information. "She's been poisoned with something. Someone threw a substance in her face a couple of days ago. She swallowed some. It's made her ill."

Another nurse arrived, attempting to take Lexi's vitals. "When did she become ill?"

"She came home sick today from work," Lexi's eyes seemed to glaze over, "but she's been getting worse over the last couple of days."

"Any medication or allergies?"

Shit. "No. Not that I know of." *How did we not talk about this stuff?*

"Family member?"

It was a question that sounded like a statement. Lexi managed to cough up something into her hand, preventing Helen from having to answer the question.

"Take her through." The nurse communicated to her colleague.

Helen watched helplessly as Lexi was carted off through double doors. She waited till the gurney was out of sight and the doors swung closed before she could move.

"Can you book her in at Reception?" a shrill voice sounded behind her.

Helen reluctantly walked back to the reception area. Her attempt to provide the receptionist with the details that she could was a washout as she realised that she knew very little. The basics weren't a problem. When it came to date of birth, she racked her brain, recalling a conversation they'd had one weekend. But the name of Lexi's registered GP was a step too far.

The process of detailing the presenting complaint and where it happened was equally as tricky even though she had witnessed it, albeit from a distance. The only easy question was giving her own name. The receptionist dismissed her in a snippy tone as more patients arrived. The new arrivals huddled as a family group around the reception area. Helen wondered if she had time to go back to the flat to get Val Ryan's number from Lexi's phone.

Helen stepped out through the sliding doors to find some privacy and pulled out her phone, selecting a familiar number. She needed to do something productive. She needed information if she was going to find the person who attacked Lexi.

"Helen Taylor, how goes it in the big, wide world?"

Grace's familiar voice was reassuring after the day she'd had. "Not great. Have you managed to get any info on those names for me?"

"What's happened? Are you okay?" Grace's tone cooled considerably.

Helen needed to be straight with Grace if she wanted her help. "Someone was attacked the other day, someone I care about."

"Shit. What happened? You know you can call her your girlfriend—or partner. Isn't that what people say these days?"

"What?" Helen took a moment to catch up. This wasn't the conversation she'd been expecting.

"I take it from your response that someone has actually managed to pin you down, then."

"Y–yes. I guess they have."

"Thank God for that. Are you still in Bristol? Who's the lead on the case?"

"No one yet. She's scared. She doesn't want me to make it official. It's complicated."

Grace released an audible sigh down the phone. "Tell me what happened."

"He waited for her behind her flat, then attacked her when she went outside to the bin. He sprayed something in her face—it's made her sick." Helen took a breath to slow her breathing. "I had to bring her to the hospital."

"Jesus, Helen. You need to report it."

"I know. I need to talk to her first. I'm at the hospital waiting to see her now."

"Who is she? Is it serious between you two?"

Helen was limited in what she could say. She didn't want to compromise Lexi's trust in her. "She's someone I met before I left Warner. Yes, it's serious."

"Okay. I've still got one more name to check up on the database. I'll get back to you. Call me if you need anything."

There was silence for a moment. Helen thought she'd hung up.

"And, Helen, please call it in. Don't try and do it all on your own."

"Okay." Helen hung up. She returned to the waiting room, taking a seat in one of the plastic chairs placed in rows to create a makeshift waiting area. Despite the fresh air coming through the sliding doors on a regular basis, the large room smelt of stale food and sanitiser. A low table wedged between two chairs held the remains of someone's lunch. The thought of food curdled her stomach. After what she felt was a suitable time, she approached the receptionist again, only to be told Lexi was still being assessed. Grudgingly, Helen walked back to the waiting area.

CHAPTER 21

A DIN ECHOING IN THE corridor roused Helen. Her shoulders and neck ached from the ridiculous angle she had slept in. She rolled her neck, grimacing as she stretched her muscles as best she could. She was alone in a small waiting room off a corridor. She'd tried to escape the late-night mayhem of drunken idiots that had appeared in the main waiting area a few hours after bringing Lexi in.

In search of a drinks machine, Helen retraced her steps from last night. She found Reception and a row of vending machines. Selecting a couple of bottles of water, she bypassed the food option. She still had no appetite despite not eating for almost twenty-four hours. Her mouth, however, was as dry as the desert.

She sipped what passed as tea without sugar from another vending machine, scowling at how it was hot and wet and little else. Helen snuck a look at reception before approaching the desk. She hoped the new nurse on shift would be amiable. "Hi, I'm trying to find out about someone I brought in last night, Lexi Ryan."

The nurse wasn't even looking at her as she spoke. Helen wished she still had her warrant card to shove in her face right about now. She hated being out of control and helpless; it felt so alien to her. She was used to being in charge and having authority.

"Are you family?"

Honesty had always been Helen's worst fault. "I'm her partner. We live together." She knew she should have lied the instant the words left her mouth.

"I'm sorry. Family only right now."

The nurse didn't even make eye contact as she filled in some paperwork. She must have taken her cue from her colleague who had blanked Helen. "Is it serious? Have you contacted her mother?" Helen continued.

The nurse tapped away at her keyboard. "We haven't been able to contact her yet. Would you be able to get in touch with her?"

Fuck! She didn't have Val Ryan's number. "Sorry, I don't have her number in my phone."

The nurse eyed her, a frown creasing her forehead.

Helen needed fresh air before she said something she would regret. The early-morning air was chilled. She was left with little choice as she pressed her phone to her ear. "Pete, I need your help!"

"What's up? You sound—"

"Can you come to St Michaels A and E now?"

"Now? What's going on?"

"Just get here, please." Helen hung up.

Fifteen minutes later, Pete's unkempt figure appeared in the doorway. He looked older than she remembered. It had been almost ten years since they had worked together. Although they had spoken on the phone in that time, it had mostly been about work—cases or suspects that crossed regional boundaries. By the look of him now, he was approaching retirement. His face looked as dishevelled as his clothing. His suit trousers were wrinkled, his shirt untucked.

Helen saw his eyes travel the length of her body as he approached. She was still in her work uniform. Bringing Lexi to hospital had taken priority yesterday. *Yesterday, already.* She needed to know how Lexi was.

"Helen, what's going on?" He sounded as tired as she felt.

She kept her voice firm, demanding almost. "I need you to find out the status of a patient I brought in last night."

"Jesus. You got me all the way down here for that?"

"I'm sorry, it's a bit more than that." Helen prepared to plead her case. "I'll explain later, but right now I need to know how *she* is. It's really important. I wouldn't bother you at…" she glanced at her watch—*shit!* "… five o'clock in the morning if it wasn't." Her effort to keep her voice even was failing her.

He rested a hand on her shoulder. "Okay, okay. Who is it? What's wrong with them?"

"My girlfriend." She saw Pete's eyebrows flicker; it was brief, but she saw it. "She was the one who was almost run over." Helen swallowed hard before continuing. "She was attacked two nights ago behind the flat where we live, next to Gallagher House."

"What happened? Did you call it in?"

Helen shook her head, hoping she wasn't making a terrible mistake in trusting Pete. "Someone grabbed her. They threw something in her face. I think it's made her sick." She nodded towards the nurses' station. "They won't tell me anything."

"Okay. What's her name?"

"Lexi Ryan."

"*Then* will you tell me what the fuck's going on? Including your new line of employment?"

Helen nodded. "Find out how she is, and I'll tell you what I know."

A small grin appeared on his lips. He knew her too well. She stood back, waiting as he flashed his warrant card to the same nurse that had refused her. Their conversation was brief, and the nurse eyed her suspiciously as Pete returned to her side.

"She's been transferred to a ward upstairs on the third floor." Pete scanned the map on the wall next to them. "This way."

They headed toward the lifts. She needed Pete on her side. He had always been a loyal colleague. "They need to do a test to see if it's Legionella."

"What—why? You think it's connected to the old guy from Gallagher House?"

"I do." Helen considered how much she could tell him without compromising Lexi.

"You think the old guy was murdered?"

"I do." It was the only thing the made sense to Helen right now.

Pete stopped abruptly in front of her. "Look, I'm glad you actually have somebody in your life. But, please, tell me what's going on."

"Okay." Helen took a deep breath. "Two weeks ago, I saw a man on the roof of Gallagher House in the middle of the night. Ever since, someone has been gunning for Lexi."

"Gunning, how?"

Helen used her fingers as she listed the incidents that had occurred. "She thinks someone broke into the flat. He tried to run her over. Broke into the mailbox. Made weird phone calls. Then he attacked her the other night."

"*He?*" Pete repeated.

She frowned at him confused.

"You said *he?*"

Helen blinked for a moment. "Lex thought it was a man driving, and she thought it was a man that attacked her."

"Same man?"

"Don't know. The driver wore a hat and stuff, as you know, and the man who attacked her wore some kind of mask."

"Okay." Pete stepped aside. They walked the short distance to the lift.

Pete pressed the call button for the third floor. "What does she do? Is she involved in anything?"

Typical. Suspect the victim. "She works in IT." Helen tried to keep her voice even.

"She's clean?"

"Yes." The doors to the lift opened. Before she could step in, several people filed out. *Shift change.*

"You're sure she's not involved in anything."

Helen let out a long breath. "I'm sure." With the lift empty, she stepped in. Pete followed, pressing the button for the third floor.

"How long have you known her?"

"A few months." This was getting into sticky territory. Why hadn't she gone through her story before calling Pete?

"Has she been in Ryder's flat?"

"No." Tiredness was the only thing keeping the frustration from her tone. "The guy who attacked her sprayed her in the face or poured something down her throat. I think that's how she got ill."

He nodded, watching her closely. "So you're a security guard now?"

"No. Well, temporarily. I was trying to keep an eye on Lexi while she was at work. I was trying to keep her safe." Helen heard the ridiculousness of her own words.

"Where were you when she was—?"

"On the roof of Gallagher House. I saw it happen, I shouted at him. If I hadn't been there, he could have taken her."

"It's not your fault." Pete placed a hand on her shoulder.

"Yes, it is." She rubbed both her hands over her face. "I'm the reason she's in here."

"What do you mean?"

"I saw something on the roof that night. Lex switched on the light, and whoever it was, they saw her, not me." It was time to be straight with Pete, even if she still didn't know what she'd seen that night.

The lift pinged their arrival on floor three. The vacant look on Pete's face worried her as she got off the lift. Helen hesitated and scanned the corridor for a nurse.

Pete quickly accosted a member of staff coming from the other direction and flashed his warrant card. Helen held her tongue, happy to let Pete do the questioning, considering he had the ID.

The nurse was a little snippy, voicing her reluctance to let anyone see Lexi. Thankfully, Pete persisted, and she pointed in the direction of the ward.

Helen's boots squeaked on the shiny floor as she entered the room. She tensed her legs, trying to reduce the noise as she approached the propped-up hospital bed. An oxygen mask partially obscured Lexi's face. Her hair was swept off her forehead.

She stepped closer. A drip was attached to Lexi's left hand, neatly tucked by the side of her body. Helen swallowed her fear as she walked around the bed. She took Lexi's right hand. It was warm and soft in her own cool hands, but there was no reaction. A tear slipped down her cheek at the relief of being able to see her at last. She hastily wiped it away as Pete appeared next to her.

He placed a hand on her shoulder. "I'll see what else I can find out."

His footsteps trailed off out of the room. Helen didn't take her eyes off Lexi. Fear and guilt threatened to overtake her as she stood there. Why did it always have to be Lexi who got hurt, just like before when it was Helen's fault? Another lapse in judgement. Helen was pretty sure it only ever happened when she was in this particular woman's vicinity, and unfortunately it usually ended up with hospital treatment on Lexi's side.

Helen adjusted her feet. She felt something brush against the back of her leg and turned to see a plastic chair. She blinked, realising Pete must have placed it there for her. She pulled it closer, taking a seat. She picked up Lexi's hand once more. The warm fingers moved against hers. She gripped them a little more, letting Lexi know she was there. Lexi's eyes fluttered for a moment before opening, and her free hand moved slowly as if to remove the oxygen mask. Relief filled Helen's chest, bringing her heart back to life. The tears flowed freely now.

She placed her hand over Lexi's. "I think you might need that for now."

The grunt that followed made Helen's smile widen as Lexi slowly lowered her hand. Lexi rolled her head as she gazed back at Helen, bleary eyed, but there. Still clasping Lexi's hand, Helen pulled it to her face, pressing her lips against the knuckles. "God, I was so worried." More tears slipped down Helen's cheeks as a lightness settled in her chest. Behind the mask, a ghost of a smile appeared as warm fingers gripped hers again.

"I should call your mum, let her know what's happened." She had a pretty good idea of Lexi's view on this topic, but she wanted to give her the option anyway. As expected, a frown appeared on Lexi's brow along with a fierce squeeze of her hand.

"Okay, okay," Helen soothed reluctantly. "I'll leave it for now."

A nurse appeared on the other side of the bed, clipboard in hand. Helen sat back and watched as the nurse took Lexi's temperature, noting it on the clipboard. She nodded at Helen. Nonverbal communication must be part of their training now. Helen waited for her to leave.

"I should let you rest." Helen kissed her knuckles again. She stood but was reluctant to leave. She knew she had to make a start on finding the bastard that put Lexi in here. "I'll come back later." She placed a kiss on Lexi's forehead. "I love you."

Before she could stop her, Lexi's hand was on the mask, again pushing it aside. "Don't do anything stupid. Promise." Her words were barely above a whisper.

"I promise." Turning to walk away, Helen wiped at her eyes, removing any evidence of her tears.

She entered the corridor and found Pete checking his phone. He looked up as she approached.

"They're monitoring her. She's on a couple of different antibiotics to fight the infection. Too early to say if they're working or not. If they do, she should only be in for a couple of days, or as soon as her temperature goes down and her breathing improves."

Although satisfied for now, Helen still wanted to get her point across. She couldn't take the risk of more people becoming ill. "They still need to check for Legionella."

Pete pointed an aimless finger back down the corridor. "She's getting someone to talk to us."

A man in scrubs appeared around the corner in the distance. He stopped next to the nurse, who nodded in their direction as she spoke to him, then took the clipboard from her and ambled towards them. When she saw the large bags hanging under his eyes, Helen wondered how long he had been on shift.

"Dr Avery." He offered his hand in greeting. "You're with the police. What can I help you with?"

"We have concerns that Miss Ryan's illness is connected to two other people that have suffered similar conditions." Pete lowered his tone as he glanced at Helen. "One of which has died."

"Okay." Dr Avery studied the chart in his hands.

"We think they're connected to a residence, a flat in Hanham," Pete continued.

Dr Avery made no reply, his eyes still fixed on the notes.

Frustration mounted in Helen's chest. "You need to test for Legionella," she blurted out, getting his attention at last.

"And why would we do that?" Avery glanced up at her, eyes wide, eyebrows raised.

"Because I think that's what she was infected with." This guy was an arrogant moron.

Avery hugged the chart to his chest, folding his arms in front of it. "An outbreak of Legionella is very rare, and Miss Ryan is not a typical case—wrong age, wrong sex, and in good health, according to her notes. Listen, right now she's on antibiotics. They seem to be slowly reducing her temperature."

"Can you do the test anyway to make sure?" Pete countered. "Crime-scene techs are currently combing the flat to find the source of the illness."

Helen could feel herself getting worked up. Seeing Lexi had given her the strength she needed. "One man has already died. We're trying to prevent any more." Pete shifted uncomfortably beside her as her voice climbed.

"Okay, okay." Avery held a hand up. "We'll do a urine test to be *sure*."

Helen caught the sarcasm in his tone but didn't rise to it.

"We'll need to contact the National Scheme if it tests positive," he informed them.

Before Helen could fire back a reply about doing his fucking job, Pete's hand appeared on her arm, steering her away. "Thank you, Doctor. Someone will be in touch if we find anything at the flat in the meantime," he said over his shoulder.

Helen allowed him to steer her around the corner towards the lift. As they approached the doors, he turned to look at her.

"Do you still have the clothes she was wearing when she was attacked?"

Helen allowed a small smile to cross her lips. "Of course."

"Good." Pete pressed the lift call button.

CHAPTER 22

HELEN UNFOLDED THE MAP SHE'D purchased on the way home from the hospital, placing it on the kitchen table. Not being familiar with the area or the people in it, she was way out of her usual comfort zone. She needed to get a feel for the other locations in relation to the flat. From talking to Pete and Lilly, she'd decided the Hanham area wasn't exactly a criminal hotspot. She needed to plot Lexi's workplace, the shops she used, and her routes regularly taken. Maybe that would help her figure out how and why Lexi was being victimised.

She was pretty sure the offender would live or work within a short distance of either the VW's home location or where it was stolen from. It had caught the culprit's eye somehow. Then there were the types of crime that had been inflicted on Lexi: lock picking, the car theft for a hit-and-run, the preparation of the number plates. This offender had some skills and was a planner; it wasn't only about violence and persecution. He was organised, which meant he would travel further afield to complete his crimes.

She recalled a conference she'd attended on crime pattern theory. Adult offenders usually travelled greater distances compared to juveniles. Disposal sites were generally farther away from where the offender lived than the victim.

Helen rubbed her face as she stared straight out the kitchen window. Why was she even bothering with this? Didn't she already have a working theory? Why was she still kidding herself with this two-pronged attack?

It wasn't like she'd seen anyone from her past over the last couple of weeks. Not that she was looking for anyone, but a familiar face rarely escaped her notice. Right now, she felt pretty sure she'd sparked both attacks on Lexi. She thought back to the night of the roof incident. Clearly, Lexi had been seen when the light flashed on. Whoever was on the roof, they knew exactly what she looked like after that. They could have been following her ever since, could have waited for her to come home that day. Had they meant to kill her, or just scare the life out of her? The flat and mailbox break-ins had obviously been designed to highlight Lexi's sense of oppression.

Then there was the incident that had put Lexi in hospital. Had the same man spotted Helen on the roof before the attack? Was he warning *her* off now by striking out at Lexi right before her eyes, knowing full well she was too far away to stop it? She clenched her jaw as she thought of how that event could have escalated.

Helen knew she was in danger of confirmation bias, but her gut told her there would be a way of proving it to be true. It was up to her to find it. Lexi was lying in a hospital bed, and still she had nothing. Her eyes were drawn to the window. The tops of the trees were swaying in the breeze. She stood to look across at Morris Ryder's flat. There was movement inside, lights flashing. Pete had said they were searching it again, but she hadn't seen the tech van when she'd parked up. Looking at the front of the building, she saw that the car park was full. They must have parked around the back.

She spun around, placing her back to the window. Her gaze fell on a stack of papers on the far side of the kitchen. She picked them up, scanning the printed information. The addition of Lexi's handwritten notes told her exactly what it was. Morris Peter Ryder, born 2/11/46. Widowed ten years ago. She scanned the next page, Morris owned and ran an antiques shop for many years until his retirement seven years ago. He moved soon after to Gallagher House. The next page showed the address for Ryder Antiques and Collectables, 12 Pershaw Road, Redlands. The residential address was 12A—the flat above, she presumed. According to Lexi's information, Ryder and his wife had had no children to pass the business on to. Morris Ryder had to be the first victim. He was her way in.

Helen's phone chimed as she located Pershaw Road on the stretched-out map. She snatched it up. Grace had finally got back to her with some addresses. She scanned through the information. None of the shady characters of her past lived within a hundred and fifty miles of Bristol. Not that it meant anything right now, but she wanted to cover all bases. Helen couldn't afford to leave the area to check up on them right now, in case Lexi took a turn for the worst. She racked her brain for any colleagues that she could request a favour from. Of course, with two of them still in the Manchester area, one name came to mind. Her ex-DS, now DI, in Warner, would be a perfect choice. She called, unsure if Mike would be free to answer. Surprisingly, he was. Helen spent a few minutes catching up before laying out the story, giving only as few details as necessary. DI Richards was thankfully receptive, simply requiring a few days to get back to her. As she hung up, it comforted her to know she'd achieved at least some progress that day.

Tired of the empty flat, she made her way to her car, planning to look around the area where the car was stolen. The retail park was just over five miles from Hanham. It took only fourteen minutes to arrive and park up. The retail park itself was sizeable, housing a number of out-of-town facilities, including bed and carpet outlets alongside DIY megastores. What she did pick up on, however, was how exposed the area was—with several routes in and out of the car park. And despite its location, there were a sufficient number of footpaths and enough foot traffic to not look out of place. A perfect location to steal a car.

She'd seen enough. Pulling out of the car park, she headed for Redlands. She wanted to find out more about Morris Ryder.

She walked along Pershaw Road. A symbol on a hanging sign told Helen that Morris's shop was still an antique shop… and a pawnbrokers. She got her story straight in her head before pushing open the door.

The bell chimed to indicate her arrival. Helen scanned the double-fronted shop. Stock obviously wasn't an issue. Display cases on either side held several precious and delicate items, while pieces of heavy, dark furniture took up the floor space. Before she could look around in more detail, a man appeared behind the counter at the back. Slim and tall, in his forties, she thought. He smiled as she caught his eye.

Helen moved towards the counter. "Hi there. I wonder if you could help me at all."

"I'll certainly try. What are you looking to buy… or sell, maybe?" His eyes seemed to glow with anticipation.

She sized him up. He was a possible for the attack on Lexi. "It's a bit delicate, really." She'd already decided while on the drive to the shop that due to her lack of warrant card it was now okay to tell a few white lies to get the information she needed. She didn't want another situation like what had happened at the hospital.

"Oh." He scanned her from head to toe as if guesstimating how much she was going to spend. He was going to be disappointed.

"I'm a neighbour of Morris Ryder. I think he used to own this shop. I wondered if you knew him at all."

He placed his hands flat on the counter as he studied her, a slight frown on his face.

"Why do you want to know?"

"He died a few days ago. I don't think he had any family. At least, he didn't mention any. And, well, I'm trying to get a bit of background on him for the eulogy. I didn't want it to be impersonal." She studied his reaction to hearing Morris had died. He seemed genuine.

"Oh, right. Sorry. You need to speak to my dad. He's the one who bought the shop off Morris." With that, he ducked through a doorway to the left of the counter. She heard muffled voices but couldn't make out what they were saying.

A door opened and closed. Another man appeared behind the counter moments later. Older by some twenty years, the shape of his nose and eyes showed familiar characteristics to the younger man. The father, she presumed.

"Steve Chadwick." He held out his hand towards her.

She shook it, feeling a chill from his cool skin. Bad circulation, she speculated. "Helen."

"Sorry to hear about Morris. What happened?"

She needed to be tactful. "Pneumonia."

Chadwick nodded. "Morris was a good guy. I knew him for a couple of years before he sold up. Did me a good deal on the stock he still had when I bought him out." He rubbed his hands together in front of him. "Kept some of the good stuff, though." His mouth twisted slightly as the words came out. "Bent your ear about the shop, did he?"

"He did." Helen smiled. "He didn't have any other family?" she questioned as she pulled a pad and pen from her pocket. "He never mentioned anyone when we spoke. I just don't want to miss anyone."

He shook his head "His wife died years ago. No kids." Chadwick rubbed the back of his thick neck. "He had a nephew, I think, on his wife's side. Not involved in the business. He didn't have much to do with Morris from what I can remember. He popped by the shop every now and then."

Helen nodded. Another dead end. "His shop—Ryder Antiques and Collectables, wasn't it?"

"Yeah, that's right. Ran it for some twenty odd years before he sold up. We went on the odd buying trip, to auctions, together."

Helen nodded, making a few notes for show. "You wouldn't know the name of the nephew, would you? I'd like to try and get in touch with him."

He blew out a breath as he rubbed the side of his face. "Now you're asking—it was something shortened, I think. Ben, no Dan—that's it. Dan. Daniel."

"Good memory." She offered another small smile.

"Don't remember his surname. It wasn't Ryder; I know that."

"Okay. Thanks for your help, Mr Chadwick. I appreciate it."

"No problem. Will you let me know when the funeral is? I'd like to pay my respects." Chadwick pulled a card from the stack displayed next to the till.

"Sure." Helen tucked the card into her pocket. It was the least she could do. Leaving the shop, she headed towards her car. She needed the surname of Morris's nephew. Maybe he was the key to all of it. She checked her watch as she approached her car. She had time to visit Lexi before heading back to the flat.

———————◆•◆————————

Helen looked out the window. The police were long gone from Gallagher House. The forty-eight hours she'd spent dealing with the consequences of Lexi's attack had also given them ample time to do what they needed to do. What she really wanted was to get into Morris's flat, but she knew that was out of the question. She could, however, get another look around on the roof, if only to satisfy her own curiosity again. This time she wanted answers.

She needed to enlist the help of the illusive caretaker, Karl. Helen knew exactly who she needed to see. She tucked her phone into her pocket before heading out the door.

"Hi, Lilly. Sorry to bother you. Do you have a minute?"

Lilly stepped to one side. "Sure. Come on in. Would you like some tea?"

"No thanks." Helen closed the door before following Lilly into the lounge.

"Lexi fully recovered now, has she?"

"Umm, not exactly. She…she's in hospital." Helen felt guilty burdening Lilly with this information, but she didn't want to lie to her either. She was grateful for the help she'd given Lexi.

"What happened?"

Lilly appeared visibly shocked as her hand reached for the back of an armchair to steady herself. Helen resisted the urge to reach out to her as she took a seat on the edge of the sofa. "She was attacked the other night, outside."

"Outside. Where?" Lilly plonked down in her armchair.

Helen nodded towards the exterior of the building. "The back, near the bins."

"Jesus!" Lilly gripped onto the chair's arms. "Please tell me you called the police this time?"

Helen shook her head. "No. She wouldn't let me. Although I don't think she'll have a choice now. I had to call in a few favours when I took her to the hospital." She saw no point in worrying Lilly with all the details, as she wasn't in danger of being targeted—at least she hoped she wasn't.

"Good." Lilly relaxed her grip on the upholstery.

"I know." A warmth filled Helen at the thought of Lexi coming home soon. During her visit to the hospital earlier, Lexi seemed to be responding well to treatment. She would need to take antibiotics for a few weeks, but there wouldn't be any lasting physical effects from her attack.

Helen's mind flicked back to the reason for paying Lilly a visit. "I was looking around the entrance to the roof in both buildings the other day," she motioned to the building next door with her hand, aware that Lilly's eyebrows rose at her words, "and I noticed that there is an additional gate in this building preventing people from getting on the roof?"

"Yeah. It was put in a couple of years ago," Lilly offered, her brow still furrowed. "A child fell off the roof. They had to put it in to prevent it happening again."

Helen remembered the low railing when she was up there the other day. *Makes sense.* "I see. They didn't put one in the building next door, though." Surely they should have, if they were really in the business of prevention.

"That's Karl for you. He's had it all on sorting out the CCTV, and that's still not working properly. He was fixing the mailboxes the other day, so..."

Helen held up a hand in a relenting gesture. "I get it. He's a busy man." She smiled as she waited for Lilly to take a drink from her tea before asking her next question. "Do you have a number I can contact him on?"

"Karl, the caretaker?"

Helen nodded. "I just want to ask him a couple of things."

"Sure." Lilly got to her feet. Moving behind her armchair, she shuffled around in the drawer of the large unit lining the wall. She bent slightly, writing something on a pad before returning to her chair. She took her seat, then offered a piece of paper across to Helen. "Not sure if you'll get hold of him. He was looking for another job when I saw him last week."

"Really." Helen stared at the piece of paper. Karl Nesbitt's name was written in block capitals, followed by a mobile number. At the bottom of the page was another number, a landline with the name *Lilly* written next to it.

"I've put my number at the bottom, in case you need it."

"Thanks." Helen smiled. This woman was fast becoming indispensable.

"Will she be in hospital long?"

"A day or two more, I think."

"She's lucky to have you looking out for her."

Helen didn't have the heart to tell her exactly how badly she done at that particular task lately, or how many times Lexi had saved her ass. She could only offer a weak smile.

Helen waved the piece of paper, hoping to change the subject. "Thanks for this."

"No problem. You'll let me know if you need anything else."

Helen glanced over at Lilly. The implication under her words hadn't escaped her notice. But the last thing she wanted was to get someone else hurt. She felt bad enough as it was. "I'll be fine, thanks."

Leaving Lilly's flat, Helen called Karl Nesbitt. He reluctantly agreed to pay her a visit when he did his so-called "rounds of the flats" in the morning. He sounded dismissive and curt. If he was looking for another job, as Lilly suggested, she was about to add to his frustrations.

CHAPTER 23

HELEN WATCHED FROM THE KITCHEN window, her gaze firmly fixed on the car park below. She hoped to spot Karl's arrival. She had a picture of him in her head from the casino, although she couldn't recall seeing him around the flats at all. She figured he hadn't given her an exact time so that he could brush her off if he wanted to. Helen wasn't about to let that happen.

A knock at the door made her jump, bringing an involuntary chuckle as she headed for the front door. The elusive Karl, she hoped.

Karl Nesbitt almost filled the doorway. He seemed a little older close up, at least middle-aged. His receding greying hair was wispy on the top of his head. Stubble covered most of his face. The knees of his work trousers were wet as if he'd been kneeling in something. A bundle of keys hung from a wide, black leather belt. His shirt sleeves were rolled up, exposing thick arms and hands. She tried to mentally compare Karl to the man Lexi had struggled with. Karl was a bigger build. Lexi might not have got away from Karl as easily.

"Karl?" She held out her hand in greeting, the same way she had hundreds of times on the job. "Helen Taylor." He looked at her hand for a few beats before taking it. "Hi. I'm sorry to call you out, but I really needed your help with a couple of things, and I figured that as the caretaker, you were the best person to ask." Maybe a little flattery would have the desired effect.

"Is that a new lock?" Karl asked, nodding towards the door, his voice matching his crusty demeanour.

Not this time, obviously. "Ahh, yeah. We think we may have been broken into, so it was just a precaution." Helen hoped he wouldn't press her on the issue of giving him a key.

"You *think*?" Karl twisted his neck to look back at the lock. "Taylor, you say. Your name's not on the rental agreement." He glared at her, deep lines creasing his brow.

There was the surly attitude she'd encountered on the phone yesterday. At least he was consistent.

"No." Helen took a breath as she decided to answer his second question. She was fast losing her patience with this idiot. "I moved in a couple of weeks ago, while I'm looking for my own place." Karl didn't need to know the intimate details. She doubted they would stay there after this business was settled anyway.

He adjusted his feet on the mat. "I see."

"Are we meant to give you a copy of the new key or something?" Helen asked, scrutinising his face.

"I'm meant to have a copy in case of emergencies—gas, water leaks. Not everyone does, though."

He sounded irritated, although she wondered exactly how many flats he had access to in the two blocks he supposedly took care of. "I'll try and get one cut for you," she said.

"Thanks." He placed his hands back in his pockets. "So, what can I help you with?"

Now comes the tricky bit. He could quite easily walk away. She had to tread carefully. "I know you've probably been questioned over Morris Ryder's recent death, and I wanted to ask you about something I saw on the roof of Gallagher House."

"You've been on the roof?" Karl's voice remained irritated as his thick hand tried to tame the wispy hair on his head. Helen wondered if he was always like this or just with her. Although she was pleased that was the only thing he'd taken on board, she continued. "The door was open, and I sort of went up there."

"What? The padlock wasn't *on*?" Karl's hand returned to his side, his fingers splayed in frustration as he spoke.

"It was there on the staple, but it had been cut and put back to look like it was still doing its job." Helen hoped it sounded suspicious enough to pique his interest.

"When was this?" His thick hand flew from his side, gesturing in front of him. "The police will need to know. I didn't even know it'd been damaged. They don't give me time to do anything around here."

He must mean his employers. "Two days ago. After Morris was…" she had been about to say *killed*; she was at least certain of that, "…discovered." But how much did Karl actually know?

"Shit!" Karl wiped his big hand over his stubble. It was a strangely comforting sound. She'd had an old DCI that used to rub his stubble when he was thinking.

"The thing is, I saw someone messing around on the roof during the night a few weeks ago. I went to take a look and saw something I think I should show you. To be honest, I wasn't sure if it was normal or not."

"Jesus. Who did you say you were again?"

He's got the mind of a sieve. "Helen Taylor."

"And why are you telling me and not the police?"

Helen was tempted to say she used to be the police, but she couldn't be sure of his reaction. It was better he thought of her as simply a resident. "Well, to be honest, I didn't want to bother the police in case it wasn't anything important. I thought I could show you and—" She let the words hang.

"Okay." He held his hands up in submission. "What do you think you saw?"

"It looked like one of the ventilation shafts had been damaged, but maybe you already know about it?" Helen studied his face for a reaction. Nothing.

"No, I didn't know. I haven't been on the roof in a while. I usually check it out in a month or so to make sure there aren't any issues to fix before the winter." Karl blew out a long breath.

"I can show you, if you like," Helen offered again, unsure if he took in her earlier attempt.

Karl nodded and moved towards the door, the cuffs of his work gloves poking out of his back pocket. They'd been stood in the hallway for the entire conversation. Helen firmly closed the door behind them as they left.

"Did you know Morris Ryder?" Helen asked, trying to keep the conversation going as they made their way up to the roof of Gallagher House.

"A bit. I used to visit him when I was on shift. We played cards in the evenings sometimes, but not for a while."

Helen laid it on thick, hoping for a reaction. "It's sad to think he died alone in that flat without someone finding him till it was too late."

Karl simply grunted his reply.

"Did he have much family?" Helen persisted.

His keys jangled as they took the stairs to the roof. "A nephew, I think. He never talked about anyone else."

That nephew again. "Oh, do you know his nephew's name? I know my flatmate wanted to send her condolences."

"Err, Daniel something. Daniel. He works at a school in Brislington, I think. I can't remember his surname. It's not Ryder, it's something different that Morris told me." Karl's breath came thick and fast, cutting off his voice as they reached the top. "Hickman, maybe." He panted as they approached the roof door.

A faint buzzing sound echoed in the stairwell. Helen instinctively checked her phone, hoping it wasn't from the hospital. That was unlikely, considering the hostility at her initial visit, but Helen's phone was silent as her hand grasped it in her pocket. It must be Karl's phone. She decided to say nothing, not wanting to distract him from their task. He was obviously ignoring it.

Daniel Hickman. At least she finally had a name to follow up now.

Helen scanned the hasp and staple. The padlock was still in place, the same as she'd found it before. Someone else had obviously replaced it after her swift departure the other day. Someone knew she'd been up there. She pulled at her sleeve to cover her fingers. Stepping forward out of habit, she got ready to remove the lock.

"I should do that." Karl stepped up behind her, cramming his body into the tight space between Helen and the door.

She watched his big hands move towards the lock. "You might want to put your gloves on," she advised, unsure if he was being deliberately stupid.

His hands froze in the air. "Yeah, right." Gloves on, he twisted the lock free. He took a moment to inspect the ends of the cut metal before awkwardly slipping it through the staple of the padlock catch.

Helen followed him out onto the roof. His hand indicated for her to lead the way.

"It was over here." Helen walked towards the ventilation hub. As it slowly spun in the wind, she could see the misshapen spokes. Reaching out a covered hand, she stopped the cone from moving. Standing close, she tried to peer down through the darkness. Her eyes found nothing but blackness. "There was something down there at the bottom. It's gone!"

"What?" Karl stepped closer. "What was it?"

"I don't know. It was hard to see clearly." It was gone, all of it. The empty shaft was cavernous and dark below. Shit. Why hadn't she tried harder to take a photo if it, whatever *it* was? Had Lexi not been attacked moments after finding it, maybe she would have been able to get a better look. She hoped the police had recovered it as evidence rather than the mystery man she was seeking.

"Are you sure there was something down there?"

Karl's sceptical tone made her more frustrated. "Do you know where these vents go?" she retorted.

Karl stood back. "They go down into the flats, ventilating them. It's an old system original to the building."

In other words, right down into Morris Ryder's flat. "Did you know this vent was bent?" Helen asked, instantly regretting her tone. She was, after all, on a three-storey roof with a complete stranger.

Karl shook his head. "I need to tell the police about all this."

Now she had to be careful. "I won't tell them if you don't. I'm not here to blame *you*. I only want some information." She lied again. If Pete didn't know already, she would certainly pass on the information.

Karl stared back at her for several seconds, obviously unsure of her motives. "Morris was your friend, wasn't he?" she continued, hoping to break his sense of duty.

Karl studied his feet for a moment. "He put me in touch with one of his old contacts, gave me a good deal on some stuff I was selling after my mum died, saved me getting ripped off."

"He sounds like a good guy."

Karl pursed his lips as he continued to stare at her. "He was. What do you want to know?"

"I know there's CCTV in the flats, and I know it's a bit temperamental."

"It's the bloody building. They never renovated it right. Too many bloody shortcuts."

Pot and kettle came to mind, but Helen bit her lip. "I've heard you're having a tough time with it. I just want to get a look at some of the footage over the last couple of weeks."

"Why?"

"A friend of mine was almost hit by a car out the front last week, and there were no witnesses. I need to check there's nothing on the cameras."

"Haven't you been to the police?" Karl asked, sounding surprised.

"No." She'd been expecting this. "I think I know who did it. I'd rather resolve it privately if I could for now. With your help, of course."

Karl frowned at her. "If you know who did it, shouldn't you go to the police?"

Helen shrugged dramatically. "I can't be sure without seeing the footage. He's an unwanted admirer—a work colleague, you see." Helen played her trump card. "His brother's a copper, covers for him. It's a real mess."

Karl's eyebrows travelled a good inch up his head. "I see."

She could see him breaking. It never surprised Helen how many people were anti-police. "You'd be doing me a really big favour. I promised I'd try and help in return for her letting me stay."

"Okay." Karl nodded. "I'll see if anything recorded that day. Follow me."

Was it really going to be that easy? Helen had been prepared to share a little more information. "Thank you."

She followed him back to the ground floor. They walked in silence down the corridor that led to the back of the building. Karl pulled up next to a door on the left, jiggling his keys until he found the one he was looking for.

With the door unlocked, she followed right behind him. The small windowless room that doubled as Karl's office housed a desk with two computer screens, both blank. The other two walls were filled with metal shelving full of paint tins and tools of various kinds.

A small camp bed was folded against the far wall. This was obviously his little hideaway. Helen said nothing, preferring to keep him onside.

"How long do you keep the footage for?" she asked, trying to keep the conversation going.

"Six months or so. Then it automatically reformats the disks."

Maybe there was more to be found on these recordings—the comings and goings to Morris's flat, for a start.

Helen stood behind Karl as he took his seat in front of the screens.

His thick hands hung over the keyboard. "Maybe you should wait outside."

"Sorry." Helen stepped back a little. "I won't look, promise." She offered a small grin as she twisted her body away and heard Karl tapping on the keys. She scanned the shelving again. The jaws of a pair of bolt croppers poked out from under a rag. The ends had been sprayed bright green, no doubt to prevent them from being left behind on a job.

"What was the date and rough time?" Karl asked.

Helen resumed her attention on the computer screens. "Around five in the afternoon on August the sixth."

Karl pulled up a menu on the left-hand screen. He began scrolling through the files, clicking on the date she'd given him. "This is the view from the front cameras. It's a fixed view of the entrance. There's another one that covers the rest of the car park."

The screen next door flickered to life, giving Helen a fish-eye black-and-white view of the pedestrian and car entrance all the way to the front door. The large tree that Lexi had sheltered behind was clearly visible. "Okay, that view looks good. Can you fast forward to 4:45ish?"

The timestamp blurred as it moved forward along with the image on the screen, cars breaking the sound barrier as they moved across from one side of the screen to the other. Then there was nothing but static, no image, only a blur of monotone particles.

"What's happened?" Although Helen had her own sneaking suspicion, she wanted Karl's opinion. His phone buzzed again, breaking their stunned silence. Helen wondered who was so desperate to get hold of him. She hoped it wasn't a resident expecting some actual help.

"It's that bloody interference again. I'm fucked if I know what's causing it."

"It hasn't always been like this?" she questioned. Karl avoided her eyes as he attempted to reshuffle some of the paperwork poking out of his desk drawer.

"Well, no. I've had an engineer in. He thought that the CCTV cables might be too close to a power source. But he couldn't find anything when he looked. Eventually he said we needed to install some ground loop isolators."

"Okay," she replied, hoping he would pick up on the questioning lilt in her voice. He didn't, or didn't want to. "And have you done that?"

"I passed it on up the chain. I'm still waiting for a reply."

Helen nodded, reluctantly letting him off the hook. She couldn't afford to make him hostile now. "What about the mailbox damage. Any footage of who did it?"

Karl eyed her with a little more scrutiny. "Same, already looked." He pulled his hands away from the keyboard. "Who are you again?"

"Just a concerned citizen who wants to feel safe in her temporary home." She laid it on thick, hoping he wouldn't question her on it.

"Umm." He pursed his lips again.

The other camera footage Karl offered didn't show enough of the car park, forcing her to question him more. "Don't know anything about car park spaces being coned off, do you, on the day my friend was almost run over?" He seemed genuinely surprised by the question.

"Not me. I normally get stuff delivered around the back. Could be another resident. They're pretty territorial."

Another plausible explanation. "Have the police asked for any of the footage yet?" Helen wanted to know how much the police knew about this so-called interference.

Karl glared at her sharply. "Why would they? Morris died of pneumonia?"

Helen studied his face. He seemed clueless and confident in his reply. It wasn't the right time to inform him of her suspicions—best to leave that to Pete.

She heard his phone buzz again. Speak of the Devil. Maybe Pete was trying to get in touch with him already. "Right. Thanks for your help, Karl. I'll let you get on."

Helen's phone rang as she returned to the flat. "Hi, Pete."

"It looks like you might have been right about Morris's flat."

"Why's that?"

"The Environmental Health worker that was taken ill after being in the flat has died. He had a compromised immune system apparently. Bit of a drinker."

Shit. Thank God Lexi was responding to treatment. "And the flat? Did they find Legionella?"

"Yeah. This is one sick fuck! They found Legionella in a plug-in air freshener. The old guy could have been breathing it in for weeks."

The spray in Lexi's face. "Jesus. Any more cases reported?" Maybe the perpetrator had been sloppy, especially if it was over a long timeframe. That still didn't explain the stuff on the roof. A two-pronged attack, maybe?

"Not that we know of. You have to breathe it in first-hand, apparently. We're trying to track down anyone that went to the flat in the last six months. He was a bit of a hermit, so the list shouldn't be too long."

"What about the other residents?" Helen questioned. Lexi's test had come back positive, but with her good health and early treatment she would be fine. Other residents might not be so lucky. "What about the caretaker, Karl Nesbitt. I think they were friends."

"We're screening them all in case. They found something in the air vent—rubbish, rusty metal, and possibly contaminated water."

Helen sighed with relief. At least that explained why it wasn't still there. "Suspicious, or conveniently accidental?"

"No idea. We're trying to get hold of the caretaker, see when he last went up there. He's not answering his phone, so I've sent Uniform to try and round him up. We're looking into Morris's family at the moment."

Helen allowed a brief smile. For once, she knew more than Pete. She also had the name of a prime suspect. Her amusement was short-lived as her gaze landed on the wall vent. She recalled Lexi's fear that someone had been in the flat. "Okay. Thanks, Pete. I've got to go. Oh, and you might want to look into Morris's nephew, Daniel Hickman."

"Wha—?" was all she heard as she hung up.

Helen immediately walked to the ventilation grate farther along the hallway. Its location high up the wall surface prevented her from getting a clear view. She grabbed a chair from the kitchen to inspect the fixings. They looked like they'd been untouched for some time. Paint still covered the slotted heads, along with some of the vent's gaps. She knew she couldn't take the risk.

She moved to the kitchen, grabbing a knife from the cutlery drawer. Returning to the grate, she set about removing the screws. Out of the four screws, she could only remove three. In her haste, she'd managed to mash up the head of the last one. Forcing the grate down, she exposed the hidden shaft.

Helen flicked on the torch, peering into the darkness. She estimated it to be around a metre long and thankfully empty besides a bit of debris. Satisfied, she replaced the grate. Next she searched every plug socket in the flat. Lexi didn't use plug-in air fresheners, and she was pretty sure she would have noticed if one had appeared since moving in. But she still needed to ease her mind.

With the last outlet checked, Helen leant back against the kitchen worktop. She remembered she still had one more thing to do before Lexi's arrival home tomorrow.

CHAPTER 24

HELEN OPENED THE FRONT DOOR, fumbling as she carried the plastic bag containing Lexi's medication and belongings. Her other hand still held on to Lexi's as she led the way into the kitchen.

"Are you hungry? Thirsty?" Helen dropped the bag on the table.

"What's all this?"

Helen didn't need to look at what Lexi was referring to. Her addition of net curtains and blinds to the flat's side windows was to prevent anything like this from happening again, at least while they lived there. She hated to think the attack on Lexi had provided the first real concrete evidence for her theory. Even so, Lexi had made it perfectly clear that she intended to stick it out in the flat. Her stint in hospital may have changed that, but she still needed to do something in the meantime.

"I thought I'd give you back your privacy. That way you can go back to walking around in the nude, which is much better for me, obviously."

"I see." Lexi stepped closer. "You didn't need to do that, but thank you." She pressed her lips against Helen's before pulling back to look at her. "Don't worry. The doc says I'm not contagious." She raised a hand to cup the side of Helen's face. "I love you."

The dark circles under Lexi's eyes had faded over the last couple of days. She appeared almost well. Helen quirked a smile. "I love you too."

"Your friend stopped by earlier to take my statement."

The words hung in the air for a moment before Helen replied. In the chaos of the last couple of days, she'd forgotten all about making it official, let alone softening the blow. "Pete?"

Lexi nodded. "DS Laker. When you said 'old colleague', I thought you meant you'd worked with him a while ago, not that he was an old man."

"He was my sergeant for a while when I was promoted to inspector." Helen often wondered why Pete had never chased promotion like she had. He'd probably happily retire a DS.

"I knew there was a reason I felt sorry for him."

The corners of Lexi's lips twitched upwards, relaxing Helen a little. "Sorry. I couldn't keep him out of it any longer, especially after the other night at the hospital." Lexi's gaze stretched to the other side of the room. Helen wondered if she realised what a difficult position keeping quiet had put them in. Now wasn't the time to press the issue.

"He told me about the Legionella in Morris's flat," Lexi said. "He thinks it might be connected to what happened to me."

Helen pursed her lips and raised an eyebrow. "He does." She raised her hand to cup Lexi's cheek. The warm skin was soft on her fingers. She worried if Lexi should be that warm. Did she still have a temperature? "Well, I think he might be right. They're looking into Morris's family."

"And did you have anything to do with that?"

"Who, me?"

Lexi grinned, copying Helen's arched eyebrow for a second before stepping closer and wrapping arms around her waist. She nestled close enough for Helen to feel Lexi's breath on her neck as she spoke. "This is exactly why you should be a private investigator."

Helen draped her arms around Lexi's shoulders. She didn't have the heart to tell Lexi exactly how much she'd fucked up right now. Her main focus was to keep her safe going forward. "Umm." She certainly wasn't about to let Lexi know how much she'd thought about it in the last couple of days.

"So it's nothing to do with your past life, then?"

Helen rested her chin on Lexi's head. Her gaze fell across to the flats opposite. The net obscured some of the detail, but she couldn't remove it from her mind. "I won't know for sure till Pete finds out more information." Holding Lexi close, she thought about the two deaths related to Morris's flat, all too aware of how close Lexi had come to being the third. Her eyes darted from the window to the clock on the wall. "Hungry?" she asked, trying to shake the image of an almost-unconscious Lexi from her mind.

"Starving."

Helen smiled. If there was one thing she could rely on, it was Lexi's appetite. "Why don't you have a lie-down while I put some lunch together?"

"I can help."

"You should be resting. When do you need to take your next lot of pills?"

"With lunch."

The skin on Helen's neck shivered with the heat from Lexi's breath. "I'm so glad you're okay." Helen buried her head in the hollow of Lexi's neck, grateful for the familiar scent of her skin once more. She placed several kisses up the length of Lexi's exposed flesh, stopping just below her ear.

"Me too."

Lexi's words were husky as she spoke, sending another shiver down her spine. "I'm sorry." Helen hadn't meant to spill yet. She'd intended on letting her settle in a little first.

Lexi pulled back to look at her. "What for? You know none of this is your fault, right?"

"Yes, it is." *Or at least I think it is.*

Lexi narrowed her eyes. "You know who it is?

"Maybe."

"Who. Is it to do with Jarvis?"

Helen hated to think that that was immediately where Lexi's mind went. "No, it's a bit simpler than that. Well it *might* be." There was a flicker of something in Lexi's eyes as she stepped back out of Helen's embrace—relief. No. Excitement, maybe.

"Okay, I'm listening."

"I think it's all to do with the guy on the roof."

"The other week."

Helen nodded. "When you switched on the light, he saw you, not me. He must have thought you saw something that you weren't meant to, something that could incriminate him."

Lexi ran her hand across her forehead. "All this because of that night."

"The man that died in the top flat, Morris Ryder, I think it could be his nephew, Daniel Hickman. Unfortunately, I haven't figured out why—yet."

Helen reached out for Lexi's free hand. "Money was my first guess, but the method's a bit too sadistic for that, don't you think?"

Lexi raised her eyebrows as she nodded. "What does Pete think?"

"I'm not sure. His boss is a real glory seeker. I don't think he's taking it seriously, not high-profile enough for him."

"Can I help with anything?"

"*Seriously?* I think you've been through enough. You've only just got out of hospital."

———

Lexi chewed the last of her bacon and cheese toasted sandwich. She pushed her plate away as she washed the last bites down with her cup of tea, then placed the empty cup on top of the plate.

"Another round?" Helen asked.

Lexi shook her head. "I think two is my limit."

Helen smiled, relieved that Lexi had her appetite back. She placed her hand over Lexi's. "You should probably go and lie down."

Lexi turned over her hand, letting their fingers intertwine. "I want to take a bath first."

"Okay." Helen picked up their plates, depositing them in the sink. Stepping close to Lexi, she kissed the top of her head. "Stay right there. I'll run you a bath."

With Lexi settled in the tub, Helen wanted to do a bit more investigating. "Lex, can I use your laptop?"

"Sure." A voice echoed from the direction of the bathroom.

The screen was laid out differently to what she was used to seeing. "How do I find a site I was looking at the other day?"

"Click on the three dots on the far right of the search bar, click on *history*. It should list all the searches you've made."

"Thanks." Helen leant against the doorway of the bathroom, laptop in hand. Her eyes found Lexi with a full beard of bubbles, her head resting back against the end of the bathtub. "Nice," Helen offered with raised eyebrows.

"Thanks." Lexi carefully added more bubbles, checking her profile in the glazed tiles that lined the walls. Lexi's rosy cheeks shone through the thin layer of bubbles. "You look a little poached. Would you like a cold drink?" Looking back at the screen, she clicked on the Legionella search she'd made the other day.

"No thanks." A flurry of bubbles and water fluttered along the surface of the millpond Lexi had been lying in. "Time I got out, I think."

Helen glanced up to see Lexi hastily stand up in the bath. She looked a little unsteady as she grabbed a towel and pulled it around her before bending to pull out the drain plug.

At the sound of her phone vibrating across the kitchen table. Helen took the laptop with her and grabbed the phone before it slipped from the edge of the table. Pete's name flashed up on the screen. She quickly accepted the call.

"Helen, we need to talk."

The tone in Pete's normally relaxed voice instantly set her on edge. "What's happened?" She instinctively glanced around for her keys as if she were still on duty, ready to run to her car.

"They took another look at Morris Ryder's body."

"And?" Helen couldn't think where this was going. Wasn't this cut and dried already?

Pete let out a long breath. "Turns out he was asphyxiated. They found fibres in his nose and throat. Some slight bruising on his face."

Fuck. Had she got it wrong again? "What made them take another look?"

"They needed to confirm how Morris ingested the Legionella."

Helen paced around the small kitchen. "Shit. How did they miss that last time?"

"Who fucking knows? The fibres might be a match for a cushion in the flat. They're checking into it now."

"So now it's a murder inquiry? Brooks must be loving this." *Total arsehole that he is.* "What does Hickman say about it?"

"We're trying to track him down now. No one's seen him for at least twenty-four hours. Brooks is doing a press conference later."

"Already? Jesus!" She could imagine Brooks preening himself, ready for the cameras. "He's releasing the information about it being a murder?" She knew it could make Hickman volatile; he could go after Lexi again.

"He's backpedalling. Thought it was cut and dried, didn't he? He's looking for another promotion, so he's got some ground to make up," Pete said as if it explained everything.

"Arsehole." Helen took a seat at the kitchen table. "Thanks for letting me know." She needed to be on alert. He'd got to Lexi before, and she wasn't about to let that happen again. They couldn't go back to Warner, but they were sitting ducks in the flat. Which left only one possibility.

"There's something else." The sound muffled down the line as if he were manhandling his phone.

"What's going on?" Helen feared the worst. Her eyes were immediately drawn to the bathroom. Lexi's shadow moved beyond the door.

"I just spoke to Hickman's mother and Morris's sister-in-law, Margret Hickman, in Spalding. She hasn't seen or heard from her son since they had a bust-up almost seven years ago. His father's not seen him either—parents are divorced. The mother had an affair with Morris when they lived in Bristol. They moved to Spalding when Daniel was a little kid."

"Moved away for a fresh start." *Was that Daniel Hickman's motive—revenge for Morris's indiscretion with his mother?*

Pete continued. "Went tits up when they moved. Daniel got bullied at school, his dad couldn't keep a job—it all turned to shite."

She'd always admired Pete's turn of phrase. "Is that what caused the rift between Daniel and his parents?"

"Not exactly. During the bust-up, his mother let it slip that his dad wasn't his dad, that Morris was his real dad."

"Shit. Did Morris know?" *That his own son was trying to kill him?*

"She says Morris knew. She told Morris he was Daniel's father when she was pregnant with Daniel."

"Is that a good enough motive to kill? I know seven years is ample time to plan it out, but—"

"We've both seen it committed for less." Pete cut her off. "Looks like Daniel came back here to take his revenge. We're going to take another look at his home and work as he's still MIA."

Helen ended the call. Placing her phone back on the table, she mulled over the latest news. Daniel Hickman had certainly gone to town on his plan. But something still niggled at her gut. She couldn't quite put her finger on it.

"What's happened?" Lexi slumped into the seat next to Helen. Now dressed in jogging bottoms and a T-shirt, her ruddy cheeks were still flushed from the bath.

Helen avoided the question, posing one of her own instead. "Lex, I need to ask you something." Helen rested her hands flat on the map that still covered the table. "We need to eliminate anyone else we haven't talked about yet." The slight frown on Lexi's brow made her nervous. She didn't want to open up old wounds, but she needed to be sure of her theory. Despite the new information, she still wasn't one hundred per cent sure it was Hickman she was after in relation to the attacks on Lexi. Without the results from Lexi's clothing, she still had nothing solid.

"Okay."

"When you looked into Jarvis before," she waited for her words to sink in as Lexi's eyebrows lifted a little on her forehead, "did he have any close family or friends apart from his mother?"

Lexi took in a long breath, her lips pursed. "No, not that I found. I didn't want to delve too deep into his contacts for obvious reasons."

People like Jarvis had connections all over, but rarely would they risk exposing themselves to take revenge. Officially he was still missing anyway. "And work. I know you haven't been there that long, but there's no one you can think of who could have it in for you or who has stalker potential?"

Lexi burst out laughing. "You've met them, right? I've tracked down and killed a paedophile, and I'm still the most normal one there."

Helen bristled at her words. "You didn't kill him, he fell." Her frustrated tone was involuntarily sharp. She saw the guilt that Lexi carried around with her; it was understandable but maddening at the same time. Helen had never knowingly taken a life, so it was hardly her place to judge. Still, in her eyes, Richard Jarvis was a disgusting human being that deserved everything he got. "You cornered him, and he panicked. He was going to attack you. If he hadn't fallen, we don't know what could have happened."

Lexi placed her hand over hers, forcing the fight out of her voice.

"Sorry." Helen relented.

"No, I can't think of anyone." Lexi used her thumb to caress the back of Helen's hand. "As Roman would say, it's Occam's razor: the simplest solution tends to be the correct one."

Helen sat back in her seat, amazed by Lexi's statement. "You spend far too much time with that weirdo." The mention of Lexi's colleagues brought something to the front of her mind, something she had yet to deal with. Could it be Shelby, fearful that she'd been spotted stealing information? But every incidence had involved a male. Of course, that didn't rule out a partner—Shelby and Hickman working together.

"I know. But I sort of like him, though." Lexi pulled the laptop closer. "So, shall we see what we can find on Mr Daniel Hickman?"

"Actually, there's something I need to tell you about one of your colleagues first." With all that had happened since that night, she'd had little time to think about Shelby. "I think Shelby might be passing on company information to someone."

Lexi's hands hovered above her laptop keyboard. "Information? What sort of information?"

"I don't know." Helen hadn't had much time to think about it beyond the obvious spying-on-a-competitor scenario, often classed as competitive intelligence or intellectual property theft, if the perpetrators were unlucky enough to get charged. The lack of privacy laws in the UK left plenty of room for exploitation, especially when companies preferred to handle the issue themselves rather than publicise the breach.

"How do you know about it, then?" Lexi questioned.

"The night you were attacked, I was leaving work. I was just getting in my car, and I saw Shelby drop a package of some kind in the bin by the river as she left. Then someone else came along a minute later, picked it out of the bin, and walked off."

Lexi sat back in her seat. "Are you serious? Why are you only telling me this now?"

"Well, I've been pretty busy the last few days." Helen picked up her phone. "I did get a video of the man and his dog."

"His dog?" Lexi's face squashed up for a second before a frown joined her eyebrows together. "What did they say at work?"

"Err—actually I haven't told anyone yet. I wanted to run it past you first, but…" Helen didn't need to finish that sentence. "I mean, I don't know what she has access to. It might be nothing." Helen pulled up the video on her phone before showing it to Lexi.

"*Or* she might be working for a rival, or even some hacking group." Lexi scrutinised the tiny screen.

"Do you recognise him?"

Lexi squinted at the phone. "No. I don't think so." She handed it back. "I knew there was something weird about her. Roman's gonna go fucking nuts." She rubbed her face as she sat forward again. "Okay. We'll deal with that later." Tapping a key woke up her laptop. "Right. Mr Daniel Hickman first, Shelby Larson later."

Helen placed her hand over Lexi's. "Are you sure you want to do this?"

"Definitely. The sooner this is over the better."

Helen relented. "Okay. I don't have his home address, but I know he works for a school in Brislington."

"We'll start with the electoral roll, then." Lexi tapped away at the keys.

The screen flashed up with several boxes as Lexi scrolled through information. It took her a few minutes for her to find what she was looking for. "Hickman, like Ryder, is not a very common name. I've got two Daniel Hickmans—one born in 1968, too old. Next one's born November 1987." Lexi blew out a breath. "That makes him thirty-two."

"Sounds about right."

"He's got an address listed in Soundwell."

Helen pulled the map closer, scanning the areas around the circles she'd already made. "Found it. It's a bit further out than Kingswood, where the owner of the VW lives." Helen noted Lexi's raised eyebrows.

"That's convenient, Guv." Lexi smirked.

Helen marked it on the map. "It certainly is."

"Let's try social networks."

Lexi blew out a breath. A light wheeze sounded as she bottomed out, reminding Helen how sick she'd been. "Can't see him on there. Obviously not a social butterfly. Westbrook Academy's the only school in Brislington. I'll try the staff portal."

"Lex." Fear crept up Helen's back.

"Don't worry. I've blocked our IP address." Lexi tapped on the keys again. "Most educational institutions have a student and staff portal. Here we go: staff search. Daniel Hickman, Science and Technology Technician."

"Technician." Perfect situation to brew up what he needed to kill Morris.

"His email isn't very interesting. Mostly orders for the department, staff memos. He's sent a few snotty emails, though."

"Who to?" She wanted a tone for the man she was after.

"Err, other staff—teaching staff by the look of them—for not making their students tidy up after themselves, that kind of thing."

Helen looked down at the map with this new information. She studied the rough circles she'd drawn around the final location of the car, its registered address, and the location from which it was stolen. Daniel Hickman lived in Soundwell, less than two miles from the home address of the registered owner. From the road layout, he could have driven past it on his way to work at the Brislington Academy. It was stolen from the West Retail Park in Brislington, less than a mile from Hickman's place of work—again, on the way to and from home if he went via the most direct route. It had to be him. There were too many coincidences.

"Was that any use?" Lexi queried.

As for the car dump location, there was nothing there. But surely that was the point. It should be randomly picked, suitably deserted, and far enough away from home. How did he even get back home after he dumped the car? Public transport?

"Maybe. There's something else you need to know." Helen felt guilty for not leading with this piece of information earlier as she reached for Lexi's hand.

Lexi's eyebrows raised. "Please don't say we're going to look for Daniel Hickman."

"God no—quite the opposite, actually. He's missing." Helen clarified.

"Missing, as in on the run or something?" Lexi seemed genuinely surprised.

"Exactly." *Or something.*

"So you're not going to look for him?"

Helen smiled at Lexi's surprise. "My priorities have changed. But if they don't find him in the next twelve hours or so, I think we should consider leaving—at least until he's caught."

The frown appeared on Lexi's forehead again. "Leaving. You think he'll come back for me."

Helen tightened her grip. *Not this time.* "It's a possibility. He's missing for a reason." Helen prepared for her next bombshell. "Pete's done some background on Hickman. Apparently, Morris was his father. His mother and Morris had an affair before they moved up north."

"Jesus. It's all going on, isn't it?" Lexi pushed her laptop away. "Where would we go—if we leave?"

Helen brightened a little. It wasn't an outright lie, not like before. She had only one place in mind, somewhere nobody knew about. "I've got somewhere where we'll be safe. And…" Helen hesitated for a moment. "…Pete's just told me Morris's death is being classed as murder. They're launching an inquiry."

"Why?"

"They found some fibres in his nose and bruising around his face. He was smothered with something."

Lexi rubbed at her forehead as her eyes slipped closed. "So it wasn't Legionella?"

Helen moved her chair closer, pulling Lexi into her arms. "Maybe not." It didn't change a whole lot in Helen's eyes. She'd suspected Morris had died at the hands of someone from the start; only the method had changed. This information raised another question she couldn't answer yet. Why the two-pronged attack?

"That's good, right?" Lexi gripped her firmly, burying her face in Helen's shoulder. "When is all this shit going to start making sense?"

"I don't know."

CHAPTER 25

HELEN'S PHONE RANG FOR THE second time that day. This so-called closed case was proving pretty hot right now. "Pete, did you find anything at his home?" She paced the small kitchen space.

"Nothing in his flat. Not found his car yet; nothing on ANPR since yesterday at—"

"Where was it last seen?" Helen interrupted. She hoped it would indicate where he was heading, at least—out of the city, with any luck. She heard paper being rustled down the line.

"Picked up out towards some heathlands near Fishponds. Uniform are on the lookout for it across the city."

Helen released a frustrated sigh as she scanned the map for Fishponds. Despite what she thought she knew, there was still no smoking gun. "Shit. I was sure you'd find something at his place."

"Well, if you'll let me finish."

"Sorry." A sliver of hope grew inside her.

"We're at Westbrook Academy in Brislington now. He couldn't hack it as a teacher, so he works here in the science labs. Came to talk to a few colleagues, get a bit of background. Hickman's got his own little secret grotto set up over here. He's been growing all sorts of shit over the years apparently."

"What's the address?" Helen knew perfectly well where Pete was, but she needed him to invite her, willing or otherwise.

"No way, Helen. Can't do it."

Pete sounded firm, but she wasn't about to give in. "Come on. I can help. Please. I need to find him for Lexi's sake."

Helen dropped Lexi off at Lilly's flat on her way out, convincing her that Lilly had been concerned about her wellbeing after hearing she'd been in hospital. Fifteen minutes later, Helen pulled up behind Pete's car. Westbrook Academy was a modern building trying to be anything but a traditional school. Its sign proudly announced it was a STEM school. She squinted while reading the sign's fine print: *Science, technology, English and maths.*

Pete's lumbering figure appeared from his car. Slipping off her seatbelt, she got out to meet him. His white Tyvek oversuit was pushed off his shoulders and tied around his middle like a workman. His face mask clung to his thick neck.

"Thanks for this, Pete." He barely acknowledged her words. She was definitely outstaying her welcome. "Where's Brooks?"

"He's already left." Pete walked to the boot of his car.

Typical Ian Brooks, the glory hunter. He wasn't bothered about the detail, especially as he'd got it so wrong with this case. Brooks probably thought it wasn't big enough for him to ride on the back of into his next high-flying job.

"Put this on."

Helen took the familiar white forensics suit and mask from Pete. Hopefully she would be just another white-clad figure amongst many.

She held her nerve as she watched Pete sign them in at the scene and kept her hood and face mask firmly in place. She followed him as they moved around to the back of the building. Several crime-scene tech vans were scattered around the staff car park.

"Down here," Pete offered, leading the way as they entered the back of the building. The interior was clinical in style, not a glossy, easy, clean wall in sight like she remembered from her own secondary school. Their journey took them to what felt like the far corner of the building, down several corridors to the science labs, if the signs were to be believed. Pete gave her the silent treatment the entire way. The rustle of their suits provided the only sound. Helen wanted desperately to break the silence but feared that she might say the wrong thing and make him change his mind about her presence.

They finally entered the labs. Pete continued straight past the workstations to the back of the room. She followed through an open doorway, catching sight of the storeroom sign screwed to a wedged-open door.

Helen made her way past shelving that held various sets of lab equipment. Some she recognised from her own school days; others appeared almost alien to her. The end of the room was sectioned off with hanging plastic sheeting. Open boxes of latex gloves and masks were stacked on the shelf next to the plastic barrier.

"Through there." Pete's tone was ominously muffled.

Helen stepped between the suspended sheets. The makeshift lab was around ten to twelve feet square. It looked like it had been set up with precision. Hickman obviously had in-depth knowledge of what he was doing. Despite his lack of teaching ability, his practical skills seemed more than competent.

A white-clad figure stood from a crouched stance. From Helen's position, it was impossible to make out if it was a man or a woman. She watched as they removed a stack of circular dish samples from a shelf at the far end of the room. The items were sealed in an airtight container, labelled, and placed in an additional container before being removed from the room. They were taking no chances. Helen stood aside as the tech left, leaving her alone with Pete.

She glanced around the confined space. She could see additional lighting had been set up, yet it failed to reach the dark corners of the dingy space. A microscope took up most of the work surface, on a steel trolley that doubled as a workbench. The wall behind held a whiteboard covered with dates and sample numbers, Hickman was very thorough, methodical.

"What's that?" Helen asked, pointing to an off-white small fridge with a glass door. The panel on the front indicated the temperature to be thirty-five degrees.

Pete stepped closer, no doubt to keep his voice low. "An incubator. He's been culturing specimens for some time by the look of the samples we've found so far."

"The rusty metal—he used it to grow the bacteria?" Helen asked seeking confirmation. A frown crossed his brow before a brief nod of agreement. *Shit.* She hadn't told him about what she'd seen on the roof yet.

"We found these earlier," Pete told her with an outstretched hand.

Helen spun around to see a sealed bag of electrical plugs. "What are they?" They were vaguely familiar. The large label blocked her view of the contents.

"Plug-in air fresheners like the ones we found in Morris's flat. Modified, maybe. Looks like he was filling them with the cultured bacteria. The lab is checking to see if it's the same Legionella strain as we found in Morris's flat. Poor bastard. He didn't have a clue."

Jesus. Lexi had been lucky. Helen thought about the cleaner getting sick. "Why didn't he remove all the evidence from Morris's flat? No offence, but we would have been pretty clueless without it." Helen was glad she'd kept Lexi's clothes from the night she was attacked. Hopefully they could match the strain or something.

"Maybe it was too risky to go back for it."

Helen stared at the air-freshener units. The irony would have been almost funny had two people not died. Something stopped him from tidying up. Did he want to get caught? Or did someone stop him?

"These were in the drawer over there." Pete nodded to the small set of drawers next to the trolley.

Helen picked up two more evidence bags. The first held a key in the bottom corner, Yale in style. It wasn't a regular key, though. It had been modified, altered into what she knew was a bump key. The normal undulating shape individual to each particular lock had been replaced by a regular and repeated pattern of points. *A perfect way to get into Lexi's flat.*

The second bag contained another key, this one was smaller, more flimsy, and homemade, by the look of it. The big irregularly shaped head had a corner bent over. It looked like it was made out of thin metal. By the size of it, she figured it was for a padlock of some kind. The one on the door to the roof of Gallagher House had been cut. Why have a key and cut it anyway?

"It's made it from a tin can lid." Incredulity crept into Pete's tone.

Helen glanced up at the voice interrupting her thoughts. "Clever bastard." Considering what she'd seen so far, she wasn't surprised. Hickman had certainly honed some skills—that was for sure. "The question is, what does it open and what did he copy it from?"

Pete shrugged. "Don't know yet."

"No one here knew about all this?"

"They thought he was setting up experiments for the labs. It was part of his job. According to some of them, they thought he was a bit weird—their words not mine. But not like this." Pete waved his hand around the room.

Helen shook her head. *Unbelievable.* Stacks of bottled fluid littered one side of the room, some partly used, others still in sealed packs. Stepping closer, she read the labels. *Deionised Water.*

"It's used in the culturing process, along with charcoal and yeast extract."

A small extraction system led to a fanlight window near the ceiling. Hickman had planned every last detail. Which begged the question, why rush it? He was in it for the long game. All he had to do was wait for his plan to take effect. Smothering Morris to death only drew attention to his plans.

She'd seen enough, and she didn't want to put Pete in the firing line. She caught his eye, nodding in the direction of the way they came.

They left the labs, walking in silence as they retraced their steps out of the building. Helen waited till they were stood next to Pete's car before pulling off her mask and hood. She took a long breath of fresh air into her lungs. She'd never liked wearing face masks on the job. She sucked in another long breath as she took a seat in the passenger side of Pete's car. Unfortunately, his car was far from fresh. Her feet landed on several takeaway cartons in the foot well.

"Where is everyone?" Helen nodded towards the school. She realised she hadn't seen anyone who wasn't investigating the scene. Pete was using his hand to slick back his thinning hair. The hood had made him perspire.

"They finish at three-thirty."

Helen eyed the time on the dash. It was after four. She should get back to Lexi. First, she needed to talk to Pete. "I don't think Hickman killed Morris."

"What. After all that in there?"

"I know but—he's too much of a planner. He's methodical. Some of those dates on that board in there go back years. Why would he leave the evidence behind? If he was there that night and killed Morris, then surely he would have taken the contaminated air freshener. He wouldn't leave evidence that points directly at him." Who else wanted Morris Ryder dead?

"He made a mistake, got frustrated that it was taking too long. Helen, there's no evidence of anyone else even being there."

She glared out of the windscreen. "That doesn't mean anything; you know that."

Pete made no effort to reply, so she continued. "Can you ask the techs to see if the bump key was used in a particular lock, if it leaves any traces inside?"

Pete leant back against his seat. "What are you thinking?"

"Someone got into Lexi's flat; I think it was Hickman with the bump key." She swallowed back her amusement at what she'd said. If Lexi were here, she'd no doubt make a quip about *Cluedo*. "I got the lock changed but kept the old one."

Pete nodded. "I can ask. Where is it?"

"It's bagged up, safe in my car."

Pete glanced back towards the school. "They think the other key is for a padlock."

Helen nodded. "Just out of curiosity, I'd check it against the padlock to the roof of Gallagher House."

Pete twisted towards her, frowning. "That lock was cut through."

"I know." But Helen suspected that was a recent development. "Any news on Hickman yet?"

"Got a call a few seconds before you got here. They found his van on a side street not far from the railway station."

"Convenient. But it wasn't picked up on any ANPR cameras in the area?"

"Nope." Pete sounded as frustrated as she'd felt the last couple of days. Except maybe things were getting a little clearer for her now.

"So the plates were probably changed to move it there undetected, like with the stolen Polo." Preparation was everything to Daniel Hickman, which was exactly why this clumsy act made no sense, just like Morris's cause of death. "Anything in the car?"

"Techs found a box of tricks, some kind of jammer."

Helen quirked an eyebrow. "Signal jammer. Could it interfere with the wireless CCTV at Gallagher House?"

"Maybe. I don't know. They think it's been modified or something. They're looking into it."

Helen smiled. Pete was about as technological as she was. That would explain all the bad CCTV footage and, of course, how Hickman came and went without being seen.

"Found some small bolt croppers hidden in the boot."

Bolt croppers. She'd seen a pair of those recently. "What colour were they?" she asked out of curiosity.

"I don't know. I haven't seen them myself yet. Why?" Pete frowned.

"I'm not sure yet." Helen replied honestly, although her mind was already making connections.

"Could be how he got on the roof," Pete replied, throwing his mask in the back of his car. "His mother certainly won't win any awards, kept saying shit about rotten fruit not being able to ripen again. I got the feeling she wasn't too happy with how her life had panned out. She blamed Daniel for most of it."

Helen removed her gloves to rub her face with her hands. She'd seen enough shitty parenting to last a lifetime. Right now she needed to focus on persuading Lexi to leave town for a while, especially after what she'd seen in that lab.

"We're tracking his phone and bank cards, waiting to see if he uses them." Pete struggled to pull his arms out of his white suit. "We've already got his car, so public transport hubs out of Bristol are on alert for him. I've got someone keeping an eye on stolen vehicles, considering he's done it before."

"Or he's already dead."

"What?" Pete raised his voice.

"If Hickman *didn't* actually kill Morris, someone else did, and thanks to Brooks's little press conference, Hickman knows it. Makes sense he'd need to be removed from the situation—permanently, make it look like he's on the run. Meanwhile, you stop looking for anyone else."

Pete simply stared back at her, his lips making a thin line.

"What?" Helen wondered what she'd said that had offended him.

"Nothing. I'd forgotten how annoying you can be, especially if you think you're right."

Helen relaxed a little. "Well, we don't know that, do we?" *Yet.* "Have you got the CCTV from the night Morris was killed?"

"Yeah. Nothing but fuzz."

"Which means that the jammer or *a* jammer could have been used, linking Hickman to being there that night. How full was the air freshener you got from the flat?" She continued without waiting for Pete to catch up. "He could have been changing it or checking up on Morris. What if someone was watching Hickman and knew what he was doing and waited for him to leave? He slips into Morris's flat after Hickman leaves, kills Morris, then leaves before the CCTV is back up and running."

Helen glanced across at Pete, waiting for a reaction to her speculation. Nothing. He simply stared straight out the windscreen.

Taking advantage of the silence, Helen continued to question him. "What else did you remove from Morris's flat when he was found?"

Pete turned to her, a look of confusion on his face. "The uniforms bagged up some stuff."

"Ah, you mean eager beaver PC Woodward. He collected Morris's medication in case it contributed to his death."

"He didn't wait?"

"As I said, eager beaver. I don't think Morris threw much away. That flat is packed to the gills."

Pete pulled the car keys from his pocket. "We need more evidence." He mumbled so faintly that it seemed as if it was for his ears only. Pete twisted his head to look at her. "Listen, I have something I'd like you to take a look at."

Helen grinned. "I thought I'd made it pretty clear which team I bat for."

"Don't get excited. It's a case I worked last year. Murder. We got someone for it, but something's not right with it. Brooks wasn't interested. As soon as CPS signed off on it, he didn't look any further."

Story of Brooks's life. Helen hoped she'd made a more positive impact when she was a copper. "Okay. And you think he made a mistake?"

Pete shrugged. "He told me to drop it, but I think I've found a pattern. A similar murder was committed earlier this year."

"You think there's a link."

"Maybe. It's hard to tell. I'd really like your opinion on it. Fresh eyes." He smiled.

"That's the least I can do after what you've done for me. Get me a copy of your case files, and I'll look it over."

Helen glanced at the clock again before getting out of the car. She then turned, bent down, and eyed Pete through the passenger side window. "I'll get you that lock." She walked back to her car, pulling off the protective suit, then unlocked her car before throwing the balled-up Tyvek into the boot. She ducked down to pull out the bagged-up door lock from Lexi's flat, handing it to Pete when he appeared next to her.

"Thanks." Pete took the bag. "I'll let you know what they find."

"Any news on the clothing I gave you?" Helen asked, hoping for something to positively link Hickman to Lexi's attack.

"Not yet. Lab's pretty backed up." Pete sighed as he twisted the bag between his fingers. "I swear I'm just your bitch. One boss was bad enough. Now I've got fucking two."

"Thanks, Pete. The difference is I'm grateful." Helen closed the boot.

Helen's phone chimed as she got into her car. The text was from Mike Richards. She'd been expecting news on the three names she'd given him. She scanned the information, surprised to find two of the three men had confirmed alibis for the last two weeks or so, all except Stuart Snell, the stalker. Released three years ago, he'd done a midnight flit from Bolton over a month ago after his probation ended. No one seemed to know why or where to.

She sat back in her seat, considering her next move. She thought she'd been clutching at straws when she called in the favour, but now...who knew? Before heading home, she sent a quick thank-you text to Mike, asking him to send her Snell's latest mugshot to put in front of Lexi.

———————————

Lexi sat back in the armchair opposite Lilly as the woman poured the tea. Lilly's flat was warm and homely, if a little overstuffed. It suited her remarkably well. A side table next to Lexi's chair held a silver framed photograph of a middle-aged man. "Is this your husband?"

"That's Eddie. Still talk to him every day."

Lilly didn't even look up from her task. Lexi wondered if it was positioned opposite her chair for that very reason.

"So where was Helen rushing off to?" Lilly added milk to the cups on the coffee table between them.

Lexi thought for a moment. Surely there was no harm in telling Lilly. "She's gone off to meet an old colleague." Lexi smiled at that thought, remembering her conversation with Helen about Pete.

"I'm glad you're feeling better. Helen said you'd been in the wars." Lilly rotated the handle of one of the cups in Lexi's direction before picking up her own and sitting back in her chair. "Help yourself to biscuits."

Lexi eyed the custard creams in the tin. She couldn't remember the last time she'd had one. Leaning forward, she snagged one before sitting back in her chair. She was wondering whether it would be bad etiquette to dunk it when Lilly distracted her with another question.

"How long have you two been together?"

It must have been obvious from Helen's reaction after Lilly helped her back to the flat. "Not that long." Lexi counted the time since she'd first met Helen in Warner. "Almost six months." Had it really been that long?

"She obviously loves you." Lilly grinned.

"I hope so." The creamy custard filling melted in Lexi's mouth. She made a mental note to buy some the next time she went shopping.

Lilly sipped her tea. "She was working pretty hard to find out what happened to you when you were in hospital. Even came to get Karl's number."

Lexi raised her eyebrows although she wasn't surprised at all from what Helen had shared with her earlier. Although she didn't recognise the name. "Karl?"

"The caretaker for the flats," Lilly supplied between sips. "Now, eat some more biscuits. You need building up after being sick."

"Thanks." Lexi pulled another biscuit from the tin.

"She's out looking for the man that hurt you, isn't she?"

"I think so, yes."

"Love will always have you at a disadvantage." Lilly picked up a biscuit.

A sudden tightness gripped her chest at the thought of Helen getting hurt in the process. She felt pretty sure Pete wouldn't let that happen; but whoever they were, they'd done a pretty good job at not getting caught so far.

"Are you okay, dear?"

Lexi suddenly felt exhausted. She gazed up from the biscuit still clutched in her hand, Lilly was sat forward, staring straight at her. "Sorry. Just tired."

"Of course, dear. You should be resting up."

CHAPTER 26

LEXI HEARD THE FRONT DOOR close. Turning over, she watched the bedroom doorway, expecting to see Helen appear at any moment. She sat up and leant back against the headboard, hoping Helen wouldn't be angry for returning to the flat without her.

"Hey." Helen leant against the door frame. "Weren't you meant to wait for me?"

Lexi was relieved Helen didn't sound mad. Being poorly had its benefits. "Sorry. I was tired."

Helen stood next to the bed. "How do you feel now?"

Lexi smiled at the concern in her words. "I'm fine, I took a little nap." She saw the worry still evident on Helen's tired face. "What's happened?"

"Hickman's van was found near the train station. He could be miles away now. But—"

"But you don't think so." Lexi knew Helen's need for closure.

"No. I get the feeling he hasn't quite finished. He needs to be drawn out of his hidey-hole. I've seen Hickman's makeshift lab at the school he works at. He could have been doing all sorts there. I don't want to take any more risks. I think we should leave tomorrow."

The fear was evident in Helen's tone. "So, where are we going to go?" The thought of leaving made Lexi feel tired all over again. She hated the thought of being chased from her home, but she had to agree with Helen that they had little choice right now. She didn't want either of them to get hurt.

"I was thinking we could go to the flat I have in Scarborough. It belonged to Ellen, Julia's sister. It passed on to Julia, then me. I brought the details and keys with me when I moved down from Warner the other week."

Lexi reached out to take Helen's hand. "Okay. Sounds like a plan. I'll start packing. I need to do one thing before we leave, though."

Helen frowned. "What's that?"

"Talk to Roman about Shelby." She was pretty sure Roman would know how to deal with their leak. She'd feel more comfortable going away knowing it was being dealt with.

"Right." Helen nodded. She pulled out her phone and unlocked it before offering it to her. "Do you recognise this guy from anywhere?"

Lexi took the phone from her, scrutinising the image. "No. I don't think so. Should I? Who is it?"

"Nobody, hopefully."

Helen relented under her glare.

"It's a guy called Stuart Snell. He's got form for stalking. I put him away a few years ago. He did a runner as soon as his probation was up a few weeks ago."

Although the timeline was a fit, Lexi didn't recognise him at all. She handed back the phone, wondering exactly how many others would crawl out of the woodwork from Helen's past.

"I'm just trying to cover all bases. I'm sure it's nothing. He wouldn't be that stupid."

Lexi knew exactly where Roman Prescott lived. The small estate near Willsbridge seemed perfect for him and his mother. She knew where all her colleagues lived; it was all part of their unspoken rule of spying/not spying on each other.

She also knew he would be in. Roman rarely went out. Socialising wasn't high on his list of things to do when there were crushing online gaming victories to be carried out. As much as she liked Roman, she knew he'd find some way to persecute her about what she was going to tell him.

Lexi stepped up to the front door to ring the bell with her usual gusto. Helen's snigger rang in her ear as they waited on the doorstep.

A mature woman opened the door. Her large, stiff plastic apron covered a flowery blue dress peeking out below. Piercing blue eyes matching her dress stared back at Lexi, eyebrows raised.

"Hi, Mrs Prescott. We work with Roman at Shield Securities. Is he in?"

The woman's mouth twitched. Upon closer inspection, Lexi noticed that the woman wore an earpiece, a hearing aid maybe. She saw the thin cable running down the side of her apron to a walky-talky dangling from her apron strings.

"He's in his fortress." The woman used a stained wooden spoon to point backwards up the stairs. "I'm making a new batch of jam," she offered as suddenly conscious of what was in her hand. "Blackcurrant is Roman's favourite. I'm making raspberry. It doesn't always pay to give him exactly what he wants. Come in."

She led the way to the bottom of the stairs. "Top floor. I'll make some tea." She waved her spoon above her head again before disappearing towards the back of the house.

Lexi smiled as she led the way to the top floor up a second narrow flight of stairs. She hesitated a moment to catch her breath before knocking. The sooner she got this done, the sooner they could leave Bristol. She heard movement beyond the door.

"Ryan?" Roman leant to one side looking around her. "And the new security guard."

"Hi, Roman. Sorry to turn up like this, but I need to talk to you about something. Work related," she added to confirm the parameters of their conversation.

He said nothing as he stepped to one side for them to enter. "Tea!" Roman shouted down the stairwell before closing the door behind them.

Roman's room was cavernous. No wonder he didn't want to move out. He had the whole of the attic space. There were three separate computer stations. Blackboards and wipe boards covered with snippets of code lined the walls. Roman was a grown man still living in his teenage fantasy.

"You look like shit, Ryan. Lingard said you were ill. It's not contagious, is it?"

If he only knew. Lexi chose to ignore his question. They didn't have time for this. "This is Helen. Helen Taylor. She moved in with me a couple of weeks ago."

"Don't you think I know that already? Ex-DCI Taylor." He attempted a clicked heel salute, but with socked feet it had little effect.

"Roman." Helen stepped in. "I think one of your colleagues is passing on company information."

Roman sighed as he walked away. He fell into an office chair. "Lewis talks to his dog about all of us. I'd hardly say that warrants an evening visit."

Lexi leant against one of the desks, aware that there were no other seats on offer apart from Roman's bed on the far side of the room. That was not an option. Roman appeared bored as he stared at one of his computer screens, although the twitching of his hand made her think he was far from that. She knew his mind was whirling.

"It's Shelby." Lexi provided, putting him out of his misery.

"I fucking knew it. Arsegard recruited her. He's bound to be part of it." Roman sat up straighter, turning his chair to face them.

Lexi released a sigh. In her absence, they'd found yet another new name for their boss. Nevertheless, Roman did raise a sensible question. Did Lingard know? She hadn't even considered that facet, focusing instead on staying alive.

"Did you check her out like you did me?" Lexi wondered what Roman had missed.

Roman was clearly affronted by her words. "Of course I did." He directed his gaze to Helen. "What did you see?"

The main thing Lexi liked about Roman was that she didn't need to explain everything in detail to him. If only Roman were to follow the same policy, he'd be an almost palatable human being.

Helen seemed to weigh him up for a second. "I recorded it." She pulled her phone from her pocket, unlocked it, and offered it to Roman. "Shelby put something in the bin by the stream. I only got footage of the man picking the package out of the bin."

Lexi stifled a grin as Helen only travelled half the distance between her and Roman, forcing him to do the same. She knew his desire to see the video would be too great.

Roman got to his feet. He snagged the phone from her, pressing the screen frantically before handing it back. When he took his seat again, he was soon tapping at the keyboard in front of him. The video appeared on the large screen, and they both moved closer as Shelby's indiscretion played out on the screen.

A light knock at the door broke the silence after Helen's damning evidence ended.

"Leave it out there," Roman bellowed from his seated position. "Fucking snitch."

"Roman. That's your mother. Show some respect." Lexi couldn't help herself. She had problems with her own mother, but he was being plain rude right now.

"Not her. *Shelby*," Roman hissed under his breath. "I'd love to see her Johari window."

"Oh. Anyway." Lexi stumbled, confused for a moment. *Johari window.* "We need to go away for a few days. I thought you should see it before we left." She adjusted her feet, hoping Roman wouldn't question her urgent departure. "I thought that, of all people, you'd have a suitable solution."

Roman played the video again. He glared at the screen, unblinking. "Oh, I'll catch the fucking betrayers."

"Do you think it's got something to do with Bitblocker?"

"Could be." Roman turned to look at her.

She knew he wouldn't say more in front of Helen. "I thought you could set up some of your little cameras, catch her at it."

Roman pulled at the top drawer of a metal filing cabinet set under his desk. "I have a drawer full at my disposal. I'll fucking catch them both."

Lexi frowned. *Lingard, really? He's an idiot, but a corporate spy?* "You really think he's involved?"

"Only one way to find out."

Helen stepped forward. "Roman, you wouldn't happen to have a couple of those I could borrow, would you?"

Lexi snapped her head around to look across at her. She wanted to question her need for them, but not in front of Roman. She needed to wait till they were alone.

"Uh, sure." He rummaged in another drawer, pulling out two small black boxes with trailing cables, and offered them to her.

"Thanks." Helen tucked them into her jacket pocket. "I'll get these back to you as soon as I can."

"No problem. I have shitloads."

Lexi rolled her eyes. She was fully aware of Roman's penchant to record his mother's every movement inside his man cave. Paranoia flowed through his veins. He didn't even trust family.

"You'll need to charge them for a couple of hours, till the blue light flicks off, or keep them plugged in while you're using them. They're motion sensitive, so they'll only turn on when something triggers them."

"Okay, thanks." Helen stepped back to Lexi's side.

"When you set it up, avoid backlighting, or you'll lose detail in the image. And make sure you have some form of ambient light in the room too. Point it towards a chokepoint, a doorway, a hallway. And do a test run to check the location—"

"Okay! Jesus, I have used these before, you know." Lexi broke up Roman's techno rant. "Now that we've had sufficient mansplaining, I think it's time we left."

"Mansplaining—exactly." Roman sniggered.

Okay, enough was enough. "You know," Lexi wandered to one of his whiteboards and picked up a marker. "I only have to change one letter of your name to make you an honorary female." She glanced back to see all eyes were on her as she pulled off the pen cap. She turned back to the board, finding a suitable space to write his name in block capitals. She spun around to see the knitted brow on Roman's face. She used her hand to rub out the *R*, replacing it with a 'W' creating *WOMAN*. "Maybe we should make that your new name at work."

"Funny."

Lexi was being childish, but she didn't care. It was the only thing that worked with him. She caught the slight flick of an eyebrow from Helen as she replaced the pen on the desk. If they'd still been in Warner, she could have expected a rocketing for her behaviour.

Roman eyed Helen as she made a move to leave. "Are you sure you want those? What are you even hoping to catch?"

"A murderer hopefully." Helen's expression was deadpan.

Lexi tried not to snigger at the look on Roman's face. *She*, on the other hand, was all too aware Helen would have a plan. She was resolute in her determination to get this guy; it was personal for her. "Let me know what you find on Shelby," she said before leaving his room.

"I'll send you a link to the feed."

"Thanks." Lexi descended the stairs behind Helen.

She waited till they were back on the pavement before speaking. "How come he calls me Ryan, but he calls you Helen?"

Helen bumped her shoulder. "What can I say? He obviously recognises my authority?"

Lexi poked out her tongue as she got in the car. "Who knew Roman had such a passion for preserves? I liked his mum. And what the fuck is a Johari window?" She caught the grin as Helen put her key in the ignition.

"Who knows? It's Roman, for God's sake."

Lexi clicked her seatbelt in place. "So, when are you going to fill me in on your plan?"

"Right now." Helen started the car, pulling away from the kerb. "I want to catch this bastard. I just don't think Brooks is up to it. What he did to you... I think I can find him first before anyone else gets hurt."

Anyone. As in me again. "Okay. Let's hear it."

"I want to set a little trap for him, something he won't be able to resist." Helen placed her hand on Lexi's thigh. "And the best thing about it is, we don't need to be anywhere near it."

Hence the cameras. "So, we're still going away?"

"Definitely." Helen gently squeezed her thigh. "We just need to bait the trap before we go."

"Not with me, I hope." The thought of meeting her nemesis for a third time filled her with fear. Third time was a charm; maybe he'd succeed this time.

"No. Well, not you per se. More the thought of you." Helen took her hand, rubbing the back of her fingers with her thumb.

Unease rose in Lexi's chest. "I'm not sure I like the sound of that bit."

"Trust me. We'll be miles away when he's caught on camera."

Helen's tone was reassuring. The one thing Lexi could be sure of was her safety in Helen's presence. "That sounds better."

"We'll be in Scarborough, which will give us over four hours before he's even able to get there. We could be out of the flat with the police waiting for him. They nab him; it's all over."

"Sounds good. What do we need to do to set it up?" Lexi was actually beginning to feel like they had a solution to this situation at last.

"I need to talk to Lilly, ask a favour."

Helen parked up outside the flats, then dialled the number Lilly had given her the other day. She picked up on the second ring.

"Hi Lilly. It's Helen from 4A. I need to ask you a favour." She glanced across to the passenger seat. The uncertainty on Lexi's face concerned her. Was she pushing this all too far? Should she leave it to the police? No, she needed to see it through to the end. "Would you like to come round for a late supper?" Helen released her seatbelt as she hung up. "She'll be round in thirty minutes," she told Lexi.

She was pulling the homemade pizza from the oven when there was a knock at the door.

"I'll get it," Lexi said from the hallway.

Helen glanced at the clock as she threw down the oven gloves. Lilly was a very punctual dinner guest. She placed the pizza on the cutting board to take it to the table, slicing it up into large triangles as she waited for Lilly and Lexi to take their seats. She offered it around, and they ate in virtual silence, with only the odd comment of appreciation to the cook. As Lilly finished the last bite of her pizza, Helen waited patiently, her mind constantly rewording what she needed to ask of her hoping it wouldn't be too much. After all, she'd need Lilly to fit the camera tonight so it was in place.

"So…" Lilly clasped her hands together on the edge of the table. "What can I do to help?"

"I need your help to set a trap, to catch the person who's been after Lex." Helen said.

Unsurprisingly, Lilly didn't seem shocked at all.

"First I need you to put a small camera in your mailbox downstairs," Helen continued.

Lilly frowned, clearly surprised by that part. "I see. And why's that?"

"We're going away," Lexi offered.

"Yes." Helen nodded. "Lex will drop a key to our flat in your mailbox. If we plan it right, the person that I'm expecting won't be able to resist getting near her again. But…" Helen raised a finger to emphasise her point. She knew Lilly wouldn't want Lexi in any more danger than she already was. "She won't be alone, and, of course, we'll have several hours to leave where we are before this person arrives."

"But how will he know all that?"

"Good question." Helen didn't want to say how often she'd heard shuffling feet whenever they left the flat, or the times she'd felt someone outside watching them come and go. "We'll need to do a bit of playacting, put on a show in the foyer downstairs. Lex will tell you she's going away alone. She'll say I'm going away for work purposes too, hence the empty flat. We want him to think Lexi will be alone where she's going. She'll give you a spare key to our flat, ask you to look after the plants or something. She'll tell you that the contact details of where she'll be will be on the fridge in case you need to get in touch with her."

"Isn't that a bit dangerous?" Lilly asked.

Helen toyed with the stem of her wine glass. "As soon as the camera is triggered, we'll know he's on his way. And we'll have time to get out and call the police."

Lilly wiped her fingers on the napkin next to her plate. "What if he's not working alone?"

Lilly was shrewd, but Helen was pretty sure Hickman was a loner. "Well, that doesn't really matter. He or they won't be able to get there any quicker, and we won't even be in the flat around the time he or *they* arrive."

"I see." Lilly nodded.

"Okay." Helen stood, grabbing an item from the worktop. "So what I'd need you to do first is put this small camera in your mailbox." She saw the confusion on Lilly's face quickly turn to interest as she eyed the small black box Helen had placed on the table in front of her.

But as she picked it up, Lilly appeared concerned. "I'm not sure that's a good idea. I'm not very technology minded."

Helen ignored Lexi's snigger.

"It will look suspicious if one of us does it. He could be watching the block. There isn't really anywhere else in the foyer to put it without him spotting it. We need to catch him in the act of taking the key, and as you know, the CCTV in the building is not reliable." A guy like Hickman could easily have another jammer in his possession.

"I see." Lilly took a sip of her wine.

"We'll plan it so Lex doesn't actually get to see you to hand over the key. To make sure you get it, she'll leave it in your mailbox with a note."

"And you want to catch him taking it."

"Exactly."

"I see, dear. Well, this is all very exciting."

"Let me give you a demo using this cupboard." Helen casually gripped the small black box. Using her sleeve to conceal it, she made sure the sticky side of the tape was on the outside. She approached the cabinet. Reaching her hand a couple of inches inside, she attached the box to the side wall. She slowly withdrew her hand, pulling out the takeaway menu she'd planted earlier before walking away.

"Very good, dear." Lilly beamed.

Helen smiled at Lilly's obvious fascination. "There's a very good chance no one will even be watching you do this, but I want to be sure that nothing will be seen as suspicious." She knew the camera she planned to put in their flat was fully legal, but the one in the mailbox was definitely not. It was a public space. "As soon as you notice the mailbox has been tampered with, you'll need to remove the camera and plug it into this laptop."

Lexi stepped in. "I'll leave it all set up for you, so all you'll need to do is plug it into the side here." Lexi pointed to the USB drive. "It will load automatically, and we'll be able to access it in Scarborough. I'll get a notification to say it's been activated, but I won't be able to access the footage till you put the stick in the computer."

Lilly nodded. "So this little thing will take a picture of the man when he breaks in to get your key?"

"Yes." Lexi verified. "It's activated by movement, so when I put the key in, it will record for a short time, then shut off. If he tries to break in and get it out, it will record what happens, capturing him on the footage. You'll need to fit it on your way back to your flat tonight."

Helen was grateful for Lexi's simple explanation. She hoped it reassured Lilly, who rotated the little box over in her hand, looking at it in awe. "Amazing."

She remained content to watch Lilly practice a couple more times at placing the small box inside the cupboard. To her satisfaction, it was paying off: Lilly's movements had become slick and efficient.

"Here." Lexi offered Lilly a now fully charged camera. "I've stuck a magnetic strip on the back so it will stick to the inside of your mailbox." Lexi turned it over in her hand to show her. "Just attach it to the inside of the box with this end facing forward."

Lilly nodded. "Right." There was a glint of excitement in her eyes as she handled it.

With the plan finalised, Helen walked Lilly out, hoping to give her a final pep talk before she left. "Thank you for doing this, Lilly." Unlocking the door, she cursed the fact that she'd installed such an unpickable lock.

"Don't be silly. I wanted to help."

That was at least true. Helen smiled to herself. Lilly had wanted to help from the start. "I'll call you in twenty minutes to see how you've got on."

"Okay, dear." Lilly smiled. "Do you know why he's doing all this yet?"

Helen glanced back to see Lilly was rooted to the floor in the hallway, making no effort to pass through the open door. Relenting, she pushed the door too. "I have an idea, but the main thing to know is he seems to be infatuated with Lexi." Helen wanted to put Lilly's mind at ease regarding her own safety. "He's developed some kind of dyadic relationship with her. He's had two opportunities to…" Helen's mouth went dry at the thought of saying the words.

"But he hasn't."

Helen nodded, grateful that Lilly had finished her sentence. "From what I've seen, it's not from the lack of means either." She thought back to the scene she'd visited at the school where Hickman worked. If he was responsible for the attack by the bins, then he could have easily cooked up something far more sinister than Legionnaires' disease or bronchitis. "He's toying with her. I need to stop him before he goes too far."

CHAPTER 27

Lexi walked across the foyer, straight to Lilly's door. She knocked three times, making a show of tapping the envelope to her thigh as she waited several seconds. The weight of the key inside made the envelope sag to one side. Lexi glanced outside the entrance. She continued to playact. Maybe Lilly was an early riser. She could have been up and out already. Her gaze travelled over the CCTV camera for a split second. She couldn't help thinking about who was watching.

She moved back towards Lilly's door. Bending down, she pressed the envelope to the floor, trying to slip it underneath. The threshold at the bottom of the door prevented it from getting any further than a couple of centimetres. Lexi got to her feet to knock again. Nothing, as expected. She scanned the stack of mailboxes; it was her only option if she wanted Lilly to have the key. She pulled a pen from her back pocket to scribble a note on the envelope, then leant on Lilly's door, hoping someone was watching it all play out. Satisfied she'd taken long enough, Lexi moved over to the back wall, slipping the envelope into Lilly's mailbox.

She walked back to the stairwell. Right on cue, Lilly's door opened. She twisted to see a phone pressed to Lilly's ear. Lexi immediately suspected Helen was giving Lilly some last-minute coaching.

"Lexi." Lilly placed her hand over the mouthpiece of the phone. "Was that you knocking, dear?"

"Hi, Lilly. Yes." Lexi moved back into the foyer, but no closer. She needed their voices to be heard. "Sorry it's so early. I wanted to ask if you'd look after my flat, water a few plants while I'm away."

"You're going away?" Lilly pulled the phone away from her ear.

Lexi smiled briefly. "Uh, yeah. Only for a few days, maybe longer. I don't know yet."

"Nothing serious, I hope."

"No, just wanted to get away for a while. House-sitting for a friend. Helen's going on a training course in London, and she'll kill me if her herbs die while she's away. I've put a spare key in your mailbox."

Lilly briefly glanced across to the mailbox and nodded. "Of course, dear. Don't worry. I'll keep an eye on the place."

"Thanks. I'll let you know when I'm coming back. I've left some contact details on the fridge, if you need to get in touch with me before."

"Okay. Have a good time." Lilly waved from her doorway before closing it.

Lexi spun to leave. Making her way back to the flat, she hoped they'd put on a suitable show. She entered the flat to find Helen in the kitchen with her bags ready to go. They'd arranged to leave separately to up the ante a little. "Was that you on the phone to Lilly?"

"Giving her a bit of moral support."

Lexi smiled at her attention to detail. "So I guess you should see me off next."

Helen carried the bags as they made their way out to the front of the building. As they crossed the foyer, a shuffling sound in the corridor leading to the back of the building drew Lexi's attention. She glanced behind them but saw nothing except an empty corridor. The door at the end was propped open again. Helen gripped her hand for a second, getting her attention. She turned back as they continued out into the car park.

Lexi unlocked the car, allowing Helen to deposit the bags in the boot. Helen stepped closer, pulling their bodies together.

"I'll see you in about ten minutes," Helen whispered as she planted a final kiss on her cheek before opening the driver's door.

Lexi drove out of the carpark, watching Helen in her rear-view mirror as she waved her off. She drove to the agreed meeting point three streets away to wait for Helen's arrival.

───────── ·•·· ─────────

Helen dumped the recycling in the bin before slipping around the side of the building, ironically, following in the footsteps of the man that had attacked Lexi. She quickly crossed several streets before she spotted the red Mini Cooper on a side street. Getting in the passenger seat, she eyed Lexi, who looked exhausted.

"I'll drive. You look like you could use a nap."

"Thanks." Lexi extracted herself from the driver's seat, allowing Helen to slide across.

As they made their way past Gossington, Helen glanced over to see Lexi was fast asleep. Another case of carcolepsy. She reached across to turn down the radio as the eight o'clock news began. Her mind drifted through the usual crap until an item caught her attention:

"Police in Bristol have launched a murder investigation after a man was found dead in his flat six days ago. It was initially thought that the man, from the Hanham area of Bristol, had died of natural causes, but further medical tests have revealed—" Annoyed at the prospect of hearing Brooks at the press conference, Helen reached across to switch it off.

Helen meticulously followed the sat-nav and pulled up outside the flat at just after twelve thirty. She stretched her neck and shoulders as she glanced across to see if the lack of movement had finally woken her passenger. "Hey," she greeted a sleepy-looking Lexi, who squinted at her new surroundings.

"God, sorry. Did I sleep the whole way?"

"No problem." Helen grinned. Lexi was beginning to look more like her old self. "I think you needed it."

"So this is Scarborough. Have you been before?" Lexi turned in her seat to glance around.

"Nope. Never." Helen stretched her back against the driver's seat.

"Not with Julia?"

"No. Ellen didn't live here when I was a kid. She only moved here a few years before she died." Helen recalled the summer holidays she'd spent with Julia. If they did actually go away, it was never further north than Blackpool.

"Which flat is it?"

"15A." Helen scanned the street, looking for the flat numbers on the doors. Most of the three-storey townhouses on the street appeared to have been renovated into flats, based on the number of buzzers near the entrances. "That one." Helen pointed to the flat just to their right. The large black door had no numbers, but one of the pillars lining the steps leading to the door held a plaque with the number fifteen on it.

"Let's take a look, shall we?" Lexi asked.

Helen grabbed the bags from the boot. She dug out the keys from her pocket as she moved. "I should warn you, I don't know what state it's in. No one's lived here since Ellen died."

"Now she tells me." Lexi bumped Helen's shoulder as she joined her on the pavement in front of the flat.

It was true Helen had held back some of the details, mainly out of fear that Lexi wouldn't agree to leave Bristol. "It's the ground floor flat, I think," Helen said, glossing over the situation as she led the way up the concrete steps. She glanced at the keys in her hand. Selecting the first Yale key, she slipped it into the lock on the front door. It slipped home straight away.

Lexi pushed the door open. The tiled hallway ahead was large with a white painted staircase on the right leading to the next floor. On the left was another wooden door, a large metal "A" screwed to it.

"This is us." Helen selected the second Yale key from the bunch.

The door was heavy, a fire door, she figured. The closer at the top was loose, allowing the door to swing fully open. Helen stepped inside. She could immediately see that the flat was pretty much empty. A large bay window at the front elevated from the street brought lots of light into the room. She frowned. No nets again. Was she cursed with this shit?

Their feet echoed on the wooden flooring as they moved farther into the room. A large table near the bay window was the only furniture. Dropping the bag on the floor, Helen turned to her left, spotting a small kitchen area. Units lined the wall with an oven but no fridge, only a gaping hole where one had previously lived.

"It's a little....sparse in the furniture department," Lexi said as she closed the door.

"It certainly is." Helen hadn't known what to expect, but it was definitely more than this. She'd have to do some serious shopping, considering she was the one who had brought Lexi here. "I'll start making a list of stuff to get. Could you find out where the closest retail park is?"

"On it."

Helen picked up a bag as she moved towards the back of the large room, searching for the bedroom. Finding a thin corridor, she saw a bathroom lurking at the end. That left only one other door. She frowned at the key sitting in the lock, hoping it wasn't a cupboard. When she pushed open the door, the size of the space surprised her. It was a generous double at least.

A mattress-less bed frame was the only furniture occupying the room. Helen noticed another door on the far wall. She walked over to peek inside. She turned the handle, but the door didn't budge. A glance down at the lock revealed the large head of another key sticking out of the lock. Her fingers twisted the key. The door gave immediately.

A quick look behind the door revealed a large walk-in cupboard with shelving and hanging rails. At the sound of footsteps behind her, Helen turned around to see Lexi scrutinising the back garden. "There's plenty of room in here for our stuff."

"Looks big enough for a panic room in there," Lexi replied as she sat on the bed frame. Her eyes were glued to her phone as Helen unpacked their clothes from the bags.

"There's a retail park a couple of miles away. The good news is it's got a mattress place too."

"Perfect." Helen glanced towards the back garden. She didn't want to say it, but being on the ground floor was good for them, easy for a man of Hickman's capabilities to break into. She'd created the perfect opportunity to catch him in the act and end this once and for all. She turned back. Lexi's attention was locked on something. "What's up?" she enquired, hoping she hadn't pushed her too far by bringing her here.

"Is that a fire extinguisher?"

Helen followed Lexi's line of sight, finding the object leaning against the wall behind the bedroom door. "It is. But purely ornamental, by the look of it." The red cone-shaped object appeared ancient.

Helen pulled the last of the clothing from the bag, snagging the pair of handcuffs she'd managed to keep hold of after leaving Warner.

"What are those for?"

"In case I need to make a citizen's arrest." Helen stepped a little closer. "Or...maybe I'll use them on you. Although," she considered what Lexi was sat on, "I'm not sure that the bed frame will take it."

Lexi raised her eyebrows. "Really? You choose this particular minute to say that to me?"

Helen grinned at her. "Come on. We've got shopping to do." She took Lexi's hand, leading her back to the main room.

"The key to the lock is on the outside of the bedroom door. That's a bit weird, isn't it?" Lexi asked as they passed through the doorway.

"It is." Helen made a mental note to move it to the inside on their return.

"We're getting a mattress, right?"

"If you're good." Helen closed the door as they left the flat.

CHAPTER 28

LEXI UNFOLDED THE STRIPY GARDEN chairs they had purchased to sit in around the large wooden table. She smiled at the mismatched nature of the room. It reminded her of her student days.

She spun around to see the empty space of the remainder of the room. No sofa or TV, just bare walls, except for a small wooden shelf on the far wall. Lexi wondered if Helen had plans to keep this place as a bolt hole. She moved to the curve of the large bay window looking out the front of the flat. The street was relatively quiet, although the flood of parked cars told a different story. She could imagine them all wedged on the beach, enjoying the August sunshine.

The sound of Helen crashing around behind her filled the empty room. She glanced over her shoulder. Lexi could only see Helen's lower half as she stacked the new pans in the kitchen cupboards. "So, if this is Seaview Terrace, where exactly is the sea view?" she asked as the din died down.

Helen stepped behind her, wrapping arms around her waist. "Umm." She placed a kiss on the side of Lexi's head and then loosened her grip to manoeuvre Lexi's body around to the left.

"There." Helen pointed with a finger.

"What, that little bit?" It was stunning that the postage-stamp-sized blue square counted as a sea view. Lexi would have purchased some black paint to update the street sign if she were that way inclined. But come to think of it, Lexi *was* that way inclined. How hard could it be to hack into Google Maps? Seaview Terrace could easily become Barely Partial Seaview Terrace. Soon her mind buzzed with the possibilities of all the other street names she could alter for greater accuracy.

Helen sniggered. "Well, I'm guessing those buildings are newer. We'll have to wait for a few more years of climate change to get the sea view back."

"Oh my God." Lexi twisted in Helen's arms. The worry she saw on Helen's face concerned her for a second. "Are you finally catching up with the world around you?" Lexi scrutinised her for a moment. "You've been watching TV again, haven't you?"

"No." Helen seemed to shrink an inch or two. "Well, I might have caught a few bits."

Lexi grinned at Helen's admission. "A few bits." She pulled a hand in front of her to use as a makeshift microphone. "What can I tell you, we have a sea view where we barely had one before. This is Helen Taylor reporting for the BBC. Back to you in the studio."

Helen's eyes widened. "Why are you so mean to me?"

"Because you have amazingly soft but thick skin, and you love it." Although it had been a while since she'd had chance to explore that fact.

"I love you." Helen moved forward and pressed their lips together.

The kiss was soft, undemanding. Instead of pulling all the way back, Helen hovered in front of her. Lexi felt Helen's breath graze her cheek and guided their mouths back together. As they made contact, Lexi parted her lips, welcoming Helen's warmth as she reciprocated and slowly slipped her tongue inside Lexi's mouth. The gentle movement alongside the certainty of what was to follow, the anticipation, elicited from Lexi a low moan. She'd missed the passion and need that Helen could always rouse within her. A gentle throb began to emanate below her stomach.

Lexi was breathing hard as she took a small step back to catch her breath. "I haven't had one of those for a few days."

"The oxygen mask tends to get in the way." Helen kissed the side of her neck.

That's when Lexi caught sight over Helen's shoulder of the large box containing the mattress. "Let's get this new-fangled thing sorted, shall we? At least we'll have a bed to sleep in." *And possibly more.*

"We can go to a hotel if you'd rather—"

"No, it's fine. I like it." Lexi surveyed the room again. She imagined many of the hotels and B&Bs would be booked up solid this time of year; it would be a pointless task. "Do you think you'll keep this place?"

"I don't know. I haven't really thought about it. Selling my own house was bad enough." Helen glanced around before focusing back on Lexi. "I can't really see myself living here, but I'm not sure I'm ready to get rid of it yet."

Releasing her, Helen headed for the bedroom, picking up the mattress box on the way.

"There's no rush." Lexi followed behind, unsure if she should have broached the sensitive subject. She grabbed the box top as Helen placed it on its end and undid the flap to expose the shrink-wrapped plastic-covered mattress.

Helen heaved the plastic lump onto the bed. With a pair of scissors from her back pocket she sliced through the plastic in one long stroke.

Lexi watched in amazement as the mattress sprang into action, righting itself, forcing her to stand back. Her phone buzzed in her back pocket, and she pulled it out. She scanned the message from Roman. "Fuck. Shelby's connected to Epoch."

"What's that when it's at home?" Helen asked as she laid out the mattress onto the bed frame.

"It's a bit like OneLife or a kind of Scientology group. Basically, they're brainwashing financial scammers."

"Like a cult or something?" Helen asked as she turned to face her.

Lexi nodded. "He needs to take a step back." She quickly texted her warning back to Roman before it went any further.

"Are you serious?"

"Yeah. They launched their own fake cryptocurrency a few years ago and pocketed about eleven billion quid from investors, disappeared without a trace."

"Shit." Helen scrunched up the plastic from the mattress. "But what was in that envelope? Does Roman know what it was?"

"I don't know, and I don't care. We can't get involved with these people. Lingard needs to sack her and get her out of there." Some people were not worth fucking with. She'd read enough horror stories about Epoch. "They're not your regular black hats. Epoch are connected to all sorts of organised crime groups." With Shelby excluded from the danger area, the immediate threat should be over, or at least delayed.

Helen took a step closer. "Should we be worried?"

"No. Well, I don't think so. They weren't targeting staff. I think they wanted information from Shield Securities, and they used Shelby to get it." Lexi studied her phone, hoping for a reply.

"He still needs to find out what that information was?"

Lexi glanced up, meeting Helen's gaze. "One case at a time. Besides, she'll be miles away as soon as she realises we're on to her."

"You're right. Sorry."

"I knew there was something off about her." She caught the hint of a grin on Helen's lips. "What?"

"Once a copper, always a copper."

Lexi's phone buzzed in her hand, stunting what would have been a curt reply. "Roman's going to talk to Lingard now." Relieved, Lexi put her phone away. The mattress still looked pretty thin compared to the one she had left behind in Bristol. "Is that thing going to be comfortable to sleep on?"

"We need to leave it for a while to acclimatise. It'll thicken up." Helen began unpacking the bedding, putting it together.

Lexi took a pillowcase and slipped a new pillow inside. A rumble radiated from her stomach. What with sleeping and shopping, she hadn't eaten for hours. She left Helen to finish making the bed as she slipped out to the kitchen area. All she could think about were the biscuits she'd bought earlier.

"What you got there?"

Lexi jumped, shoving the rest of her biscuit into her mouth to prevent having to share. "Nothing," she mumbled, wiping her mouth before turning her back to hide the packet she'd opened.

Helen quickly closed the distance between them, leaning to one side to look behind Lexi.

"Are those custard creams?"

"Maybe."

"*The* most dangerous biscuit in the world," Helen announced, placing the scissors in the drawer next to Lexi.

"I'm sorry, what?"

"It's a well-known fact that they cause the most biscuit-related injuries."

"It is?" Lexi picked up another from the pack, inspecting it in detail. "And is this something you, as a police officer, have investigated?"

Helen leant back against the worktop. "Dunking and scalding injuries. Not to mention choking."

Lexi took a generous bite of the biscuit in her hand. "I see. And the safest being?" She was curious as to where this was going. She could imagine this being another game Helen played while on surveillance: *The A to Z of Biscuits*.

"Jaffas, obviously. Not really dunkable, so they reduce a lot of the risks."

"Of course." Lexi smiled. "Then I probably shouldn't offer you one, should I?"

Helen shook her head. "Too risky."

Lexi decided to change the subject. She wanted to know if Helen's thoughts mirrored hers. "I'm guessing that with Hickman avoiding the police, he probably won't go for the key until it's quiet."

"Overnight, I expect." Helen unpacked the remaining shopping bags on the worktop.

"I expect Lilly will keep conk all night despite what I said," Lexi said out loud. She could easily picture Lilly parking herself behind her front door and looking through her spyhole for any suspicious behaviour.

Helen stopped what she was doing and stared at her. "What?"

"Keep a look out. You must have heard that one before?"

Helen shook her head. "How about I cook us some real food?" she asked, visibly eyeing the biscuit Lexi had picked up.

The material that Helen had pinned to the bedroom window did little to restrain the bright August morning. Lexi turned over to see that Helen was still fast asleep. The long drive had obviously taken it out of her. But when Helen's phone buzzed next to the bed, Lexi nudged her awake.

Helen groggily made a grasp for her phone. "Taylor."

Lexi hid a grin at the way Helen still answered her phone when she was caught off guard.

"Lilly?" Helen questioned.

Lexi scrambled to her feet. Helen was still rubbing her eyes as Lexi booted up her laptop.

"Okay, calm down." Helen glanced across the room in Lexi's direction, her eyebrow arched. "We'll check the camera. Okay, so it was after one o'clock." Helen pulled the phone away from her face. "We need to go." Helen's voice was firm. "Lilly, did you remember to remove the camera and plug it into the—?"

Lexi caught Helen's nod as she fastened her jeans. As she pulled a jumper over her head, she spotted the notification window on the screen. Signing in, it took only a few seconds for the triangle tab to appear. She tapped it, watching as the video played. The dark image showed a little movement, then nothing. The timestamp fitted with when she had posted the key early yesterday morning. Fast-forwarding the footage, she watched as the dark image was quickly drenched in light as the door to the mailbox was prised open. There, in the centre of the white square, was a silhouetted image of a man. Before playing anymore, she checked the timestamp: 2:17 a.m. It was gone six a.m. now. They didn't have much time, if Helen's predictions were correct.

Lexi grabbed her bag as they left the flat, slipping her laptop inside to show Helen the camera footage while they waited for Hickman to appear.

Helen had already moved the Mini to a residential car park opposite the row of townhouses. They both settled in, waiting for their target as they slumped down in their seats. Helen watched the video several times, mostly to pass the time and confirm her suspicions, Lexi thought.

Slamming the laptop shut, Lexi then dropped it into her bag. "I can't get the footage from our flat. There's something interfering with the signal."

Helen shrugged. "We know he's got the key. It's just a waiting game now."

Lexi mainly prayed there would be no more word games to keep them amused while they waited. It seemed to be taking an age for Hickman to appear. She had never been great at waiting. Her stomach was rumbling and her mouth was dry without a cup of tea to keep it lubricated. She turned in her seat to look out the rear window and spotted a possible out. "That café's open now. How 'bout we get some breakfast while we wait?"

Helen appeared sceptical as she twisted around to look at the café behind them.

"We could get a seat near the window," Lexi pleaded. "And I need to take my pills." She aimed right at Helen's heartstrings.

A cooked breakfast was exactly what the doctor ordered, at least in Lexi's eyes. Once replete, Lexi blew over her second cup of tea as Helen's phone flittered to life.

———————

Helen almost spilled her tea as she grabbed up her phone. "Pete?"

"We've found Hickman."

"What? That's good news." Helen caught Lexi's eye and reached for her free hand. "What's he saying about Morris?"

"Not a lot. He was found dead in a stolen car, looks like suicide. Doc's taking him back for the autopsy now."

"Shit." Maybe he'd realised there was no way out after the evidence from the school. But Helen still didn't believe Hickman had killed Morris. She barely heard Pete's next question.

"Where are you? I went round the flat. No one's there?"

"No. We decided to get away for a few days. I've got a place in Scarborough." Helen took a breath; she wanted more on Hickman. "So, how did he do it?"

"Car exhaust. Locked himself in, jogger found him. Smashed a window to pull him out, but it was too late."

Hickman hadn't actually killed anyone yet, except for the incidental death of the environmental health worker of course. So why had he killed himself? Had he found out he was responsible? "Thanks for letting me know." Helen pulled the phone away from her ear, about to hang up when a thought hit her. "Oh. Pete, did you find a key in his possession? It's really distinctive—has little black magnets on the shaft, E-V-V-A written on the key head." Muffled silence came through the phone. "Pete?"

"What's the key for?"

Helen avoided his question. "Did you find it?"

"Hang on. I'm checking his personal possessions."

Helen was all too aware she was quickly wearing out her welcome with Pete. She hoped she could repay him when she looked at the case file he talked about the other day.

"Labelled as a door key. Silver with black disks. Got it. What's it for?"

Again she avoided his question. She knew full well that telling him now would only make him mad. "Thanks." Helen felt a sigh of relief filter through her body as she glanced across to Lexi. She ended the call, letting out a long breath.

"So it's over. He's dead?" Lexi whispered.

"Umm. Looks like it."

Lexi had visibly perked up at the news. Helen didn't have the heart to voice her concerns. Something didn't quite sit right with this new development.

"Why don't we stay a couple of days, enjoy the sun while it's here?"

Lexi asked no questions regarding Hickman's suicide, but Helen still had so many. "You don't want to get back home?" Maybe keeping her distance from Pete would be a good thing for a few days. By the time they get back, he might have all the answers she wanted.

"Nope. I'd rather spend some time with you." Lexi smiled broadly. "We could do with a bit of a break."

"Okay." Helen agreed. Lexi had certainly been through the wringer of late. "What would you like to do now?"

"Let's go for a walk on the beach. Then we can get something to eat."

"Already?" Helen frowned. "You've only just had breakfast."

"That was nearly an hour ago. The sea air always gives me an appetite."

"As long as it's not custard creams," Helen replied with a raise of her eyebrows.

"I thought you liked living on the edge."

"Not that close." Helen pulled out some cash to pay for breakfast.

Helen placed a bottle of wine and a stack of plastic cups on the worktop. Somehow, she couldn't face drinking wine from a mug. In their haste earlier with the shopping, they'd forgotten to get a couple of glasses, but at least they remembered a corkscrew. She washed her hands to remove the aroma of fish and chips from her fingers.

The bathroom door opened as she pulled the cork from the bottle. Lexi's arms wrapped around her while she poured them both a drink. "Only a small one for you. You're still under the doctor." She offered Lexi her reduced measure, ignoring Lexi's pout as she sipped her own wine.

"Maybe we should invest in some proper furniture, if we're staying a bit longer."

Helen sniggered. "You're a fast mover. I've just took you out to lunch, and now we're buying furniture."

"And by lunch you mean eating fish and chips along the sea front." Lexi settled next to Helen, who was leaning against the kitchen units.

"Did you or did you not eat lunch?"

"I did," Lexi relented with a grin.

"You want the moon on a stick, don't you?" Helen moved to rest her hip against the worktop as she faced Lexi. She used her free hand to tuck some strands of wind-struck hair behind Lexi's ear as she bent forward to kiss her neck. The familiar scent of Lexi's skin was intoxicating.

Lexi leaned closer. "I do, and I'll start with you first." She downed the last of her wine, placed her cup to the side, and took Helen's hand, pulling her towards the bedroom.

Helen tugged her phone from her back pocket to check it one last time. Something about the door key still niggled at her. Why had he taken it if he didn't intend on using it?

"No more phones today." Lexi took it from her and placed it on the small shelf before they entered the bedroom.

"Are you sure you're up to this?" Deep down, she hoped that Lexi wasn't going to back out now.

"I've been manhandled and prodded by everyone except you lately."

"I see." Helen grinned. "Let me see what I can do about that." She pressed their lips together, tasting Lexi's salty skin.

Lexi's fingers worked quickly at the buttons on Helen's shirt while Helen concentrated on Lexi's jeans, pushing them down her thighs as far as she could. She stepped closer, capturing Lexi's lips in a firm, demanding kiss. She'd missed the intimacy they usually shared so freely.

She wasted no time, slipping her hand under the waistband of Lexi's underwear. She cupped Lexi fully. Moisture seeped through onto her fingers as she gently pressed her hand in place. She suppressed a growl as Lexi groaned at the contact. Helen moved her first two fingers between Lexi's wet lips, separating them. Urged on by another groan, Helen separated her fingers placing one on either side of Lexi's clit, slowly drawing them up and down, teasing Lexi's clit with each pass.

The reaction was instant. Lexi gripped at her flesh as she craved more contact.

"Lie down," Helen whispered as she released Lexi's lips.

Lexi quickly obeyed. Helen bent to tug off Lexi's jeans and underwear.

"Now you," Lexi demanded from her prone position on the bed.

Helen complied, shedding her clothes to the floor before climbing onto the bed. She settled on her right side, not wanting to crush Lexi in her weakened state. Her left hand roamed over warm skin as Lexi quickly pulled their lips together again. Helen leaned forward and trailed her hand between Lexi's thighs in order to resume her actions. She purposely avoided Lexi's clit; she wanted to take her time. Lexi's searching hands urged her on top. Helen dropped her hand lower between Lexi's thighs. She was quickly rewarded with pure liquid heat coating her fingers.

Helen circled Lexi's entrance before pushing a finger deep into the white-hot inferno that was Lexi's centre. She gradually withdrew, then slowly pushed back inside as Lexi's hips thrust forward to meet her actions. This time, Helen added a second finger. Lexi's response as she writhed below her stoked her own needs. She adjusted her position, pressing her hot centre against Lexi's hip. She groaned at the pleasure that rippled through her body as she continued to thrust her fingers into Lexi.

"Are you clit-blocking me?" Lexi pulled back, her voice tinged with mild annoyance.

"I don't know what you're talking about." Helen captured Lexi's lips again, stifling her next words. Ignoring her desires, she slowly kissed her way down Lexi's body towards her centre and that heady scent.

She used her fingers to spread Lexi's lips, exposing the glistening nub below. Unable to wait any longer, she sucked it between her lips. She was quickly forced to grip Lexi's hips when they began to buck with her relentless contact. Lexi's hand on the back of her head held her in place as escalating groans filled the room and Helen used her tongue to stroke and circle the hardened nub. She released a hand from Lexi's hip, returning it between those moist lips.

Lexi adjusted her position as Helen eased two fingers inside, allowing the soft muscles to accommodate her intrusion. Helen began a slow and steady tempo, her fingers working in time with her tongue. Lexi's fingers dug into her hair and scalp. She was getting closer to the edge. Helen held on through the thrust from Lexi's hips. The orgasm that ripped through her forced them both from the surface of the bed.

Helen stilled her fingers amidst throbbing muscles. She continued to caress Lexi's delicate skin, easing her down gently as she rode out her orgasm. Once Lexi's hips stilled, Helen slowly removed her fingers and adjusted her body to cover Lexi once more, focusing on each breast before capturing Lexi's lips.

"You make me so wet when you come," Helen whispered. Her teeth grazed Lexi's neck.

"I know." Lexi reacted immediately. Lowering her right thigh, she slipped it between Helen's. An orchestra of need drummed out of her clit at the contact. Bracing herself, Helen ground down hard against Lexi. The pooled moisture immediately eased her movement. Lexi slipped a hand between them, providing more friction for her to press against. She could feel her orgasm building already. She knew it wouldn't take long.

"Come for me."

Lexi's whispered words had their desired effect. They sent Helen over the edge. She buried her face in Lexi's shoulder, releasing a muffled moan as she came. Helen held her position, gently rocking her hips against Lexi's firm body and enjoying the aftershocks as she caught her breath. Lexi's hand drew wide circles on her back as she lay there. Helen could have stayed like that forever, as the tension in her body slowly ebbed away.

"Have you recovered yet?" Lexi asked as she kissed the side of her face.

Unable to hide her giddy grin, Helen glanced up, meeting her gaze. "Maybe."

Lexi used her foot as leverage to turn them both over. "Good. Because I'm getting my second wind, and I have to taste you right now."

CHAPTER 29

THE SOUND OF HER PHONE drew Helen from her slumber. Years of waking to the sound of a phone had her well-trained. She raised her head to confirm her fears before gently extracting herself from Lexi's embrace. It had been several hours since Hickman had been discovered. Pete would have more information for her now. The chill in the flat made her slip on her jeans and T-shirt as she made way to her phone in the main room.

By the time she got there, her phone was quiet. She touched Pete's name on the screen to return his call. He picked up on the first ring.

"Pete, what's up?"

"The doc's just confirmed: looks like Hickman was murdered. He had a head wound, and restraints were used in the car. Pretty stupid. Hickman must have come round, realised what was going on."

"What?" Helen felt it even before she twisted around—a cold chill on her arm. A figure came into her peripheral vision. "He's here now." She quickly twisted her neck to see if Lexi was still asleep, praying she would've heard something. A crack on the side of her head forced her to the floor. The pulsing pain shocked her for a moment, then she rolled onto her side, scanning for her phone. It was nowhere to be seen.

"I heard you two in there, screwing away."

The voice was vaguely familiar. Dazed, it took her a moment to place it, but she didn't need to look up. She glimpsed past him to see that the bedroom door was still ajar. The bathroom window down the hallway hung open, the blind blowing in the breeze. "Pervert as well as a murderer, then, Karl?"

In her confusion, Helen couldn't be sure if the open window was how Lexi had gotten out or how Karl had gotten in. If Lexi was calling for help, she needed to keep Karl here till they arrived. "Don't come in here, Lex. Stay where you are till the police get here."

Karl moved to the other side of the room, rummaging through the bags they had left on the table. Helen assumed he was looking for the laptop that wasn't there. Realising she had an opportunity, she lunged the short distance to the bedroom door, turning the key and swiftly pulling it out as the bolt slipped home.

"Daniel didn't have a fucking clue about you two, the dumb fuck!" Karl spat in her direction as he faced her again. "Till I told him."

"Is that when you killed him?" The words were out of Helen's mouth before she knew it. She desperately wanted answers, but she also needed to keep him away from Lexi.

Karl rushed towards her, forcing her to cower on the floor. Laughter echoed above her head. "She's next unless I get what I want." He jabbed the lump of wood in his hand towards the locked door.

That thought alone drove her on. Not this time. Helen eyed him, making an effort to shrug off her injury. She spotted the bottle of wine on the bathroom floor. He must have finished the bottle they'd opened earlier. It could work in her favour, slow him down.

"Did I give it away? Or was it your endless bloody snooping around? Once a copper, always a fucking copper."

Helen frowned. Was it really that obvious? Or did somebody tell him?

Karl was already wound up. It wouldn't take much to send him over the edge. "How did you get that fucking car fixed so fast, anyway?" he growled.

Helen glanced up as if studying him for the first time. It took a second for his words to sink in. He'd been the one to trash her car, not Hickman. Her mind worked overtime as Karl adjusted the grip he had on the thick length of wood.

"You killed Morris?" Helen stated, hoping to get him to spill his guts.

"Someone had to put him out of his misery." He glared at her as he spoke. "I watched him sneaking into his flat, torturing him for weeks."

Karl jammed his free hand into his pocket, pulling out a trailing cable with a small black box attached. He flashed her a satisfied grin as the camera clattered to the floor.

Shit. He'd found the camera from the flat. If they'd been able to download the footage, they could have avoided all this.

"Daniel had a thing for her." He poked his lump of wood at the closed bedroom door. "Couldn't leave her alone after she saw him on the roof." Karl stamped on the camera, punctuating his words as he shattered the plastic casing across the floor. "Obsessed, he was. Watching her in her flat, following her around. Till I told him he didn't stand a chance. Had no idea I was watching him the whole time."

Helen got to her knees. Her mind was fuzzy as she placed her hand to the side of her head. Her fingers came away bathed in blood. She needed to keep him talking.

"Little wooden tops on their way, are they?" Karl snarled. "Give me the footage, and I'm gone. I won't touch her." He moved around, circling her.

"Really, you expect me to believe that?" she managed to throw back at him. She gripped the door key, knowing it was going to get a lot worse for her.

"Well, it was worth a try." Karl rushed forward as if taking a penalty kick. "Your loss."

Helen was unable to prevent the cry that left her chest as Karl's boot made contact with her stomach, pushing out every ounce of air. Despite the pain, a wave of clarity came over her, flipping a switch in her head. Karl was desperate for money. She slumped against the wall, gritting her teeth at the wave of pain from the movement. "St–still on a losing streak at the Kettler casino?" she said as she slipped the key to the bedroom door into her back pocket.

Karl turned, glaring at her. Helen could have smiled at his anger. She gambled some more. "Run out of things to steal from Morris to pay your gambling debts? Or did Daniel finally catch you in the act of stealing his inheritance? Is that why you killed him?"

Her words sparked a fresh wave of anger. He dropped the wood and grabbed at her arms, throwing her against the adjacent wall. The fresh pain in her shoulder and chest took the breath from her lungs once more as she slipped down to the floor.

An earthy series of thumps echoed in the empty room. The vibrations hummed along the wooden floor up through Helen's limbs as she lay slumped against the wall. She struggled to catch her breath, but pain radiated through her body. The struggle with Karl had wiped her out. She gave in to it, closing her eyes for a second to rally herself.

CHAPTER 30

A HEAVY THUD WOKE LEXI from her slumber. Turning her head, she realised Helen was gone. She was about to call out to make sure Helen was okay when a muffled male voice came from the next room. There was no TV or radio in the flat.

She sat up in bed and pulled the duvet over her shoulders as she listened for more. She hoped to hear Pete Laker's dulcet tones, but the sound of a scuffle pulled Lexi from the bed. She sucked in a breath as she moved towards the door. The stifled conversation continued. The male voice sounded angry and familiar. The casino. That was where she'd heard it before. Karl bloody Nesbitt.

Helen's plea for her to stay put till the police arrived filtered through the gap in the door. How could she even consider that? God knew what was happening to Helen in the next room. Was there more than one of them? Before she could act, the door was shut in her face. Shit, the key was still on the outside. It was promptly locked as her hand gripped the handle.

She moved back to the bed. Rummaging through her discarded clothes, she found her phone. Her hands shook as she unlocked it and made the call. Informing the operator that someone had broken into her flat and was attacking her girlfriend, she refused to stay on the line, in the hope that they would arrive more quickly.

More talking erupted from the next room. She couldn't make out what Karl was saying. A series of stamps vibrated along the floor. Lexi threw on her clothes, slipping the phone into her pocket. She spotted Helen's handcuffs and pocketed those too. Her eyes moved frantically around the room in search of a weapon. She rushed to the cupboard in hopes of finding a hanging rail. Only a flimsy rod spanned the gap, not the substantial weapon she was looking for. Stepping back, her eyes fell on the old fire extinguisher. Perfect.

But what good was a weapon if she couldn't get out of the bloody room? The window was her only option. The front door keys were on Helen's makeshift bedside table. If she could get out the window, she could get back in through the front door and surprise him. She slipped across the latch of the sash window. With her palms, she pushed at the bottom frame. It didn't budge. She tried again till she noticed the screws poking through the sides of the sash. Fuck.

Lexi was about to use the extinguisher to smash the window when her eyes landed on the door to the built-in cupboard: there was a key in the lock. It was worth a try. She yanked the key from the cupboard door. Carefully she slipped it into the bedroom door's lock.

It fitted. She twisted it, slowly easing the bolt across. She wasn't sure what to expect on the other side of the door, but surprise was going to be her best weapon.

The next room had gone silent. Grabbing the extinguisher in one hand, she eased the door open. Karl was only a few feet away, with his back to her. He loomed over Helen as she lay slumped against the wall. She didn't have time to worry about him being armed.

With the fire extinguisher aloft, she rushed across the room. Karl half turned at her footsteps. A look of shock registered on his face before the base of the extinguisher collided with the side of his head. The momentum knocked him to the floor. He was motionless.

Lexi dropped the extinguisher, hastily pulling the cuffs from her pocket. Karl was on his side. Lexi quickly grabbed his arm, dragging him onto his front. Sitting on his back, Lexi struggled to secure his thick hands with the cuffs.

With Karl secured, Lexi's attention moved to Helen. Blood ran down the side of her face from a head wound. "Helen. Helen, are you okay?" She noticed Helen's chest rise and fall with shallow breaths. She was battered but breathing. Lexi held her position on Karl, fearful he would escape. She touched Helen's leg. "Helen, are you okay? The police are on their way."

Helen's eyes flickered open for a moment. "I'm okay." Her words were barely above a whisper.

Karl began to moan and squirm beneath Lexi. His legs flailed against the floor.

"Ucking itch," Karl spat in her direction. His words were slurred as he tried to turn onto his side.

Lexi stood, abruptly moving out of Karl's kicking perimeter as he tried to get to his feet. His movements were lumbering, but she feared the cuffs wouldn't be enough to keep him secure till the police arrived.

The sight of Helen's battered body enraged her once again. Lexi grabbed the extinguisher again. Pulling it back, she launched in against Karl's knee, hoping it would hinder him. The whine that spilled from Karl's mouth was piercing as he tried to curl into a ball, the cuffs hindering his movement.

"No, Lex," Helen began as she tried to sit up higher against the wall, only to slip down seconds later, breathless.

"Okay." Lexi reluctantly dropped the extinguisher again. She still needed to detain him till the cavalry arrived. The large table was the only option. She checked the cupboards on the far side of the room. The only likely candidate was a retractable washing line. Grabbing it, she placed it on the table. She pushed the table closer to Karl's writhing body. Lexi took a breath as she pulled at him, sitting him upright next to a table leg. His garbled words continued as she wrapped the washing line around him, securing him to the table leg. She must have got too close as the next thing she knew he head-butted her on the side of her face, knocking her backwards. Lexi tasted blood in her mouth. Any guilt she'd felt at hitting him evaporated.

Lexi resisted any further retaliation, sure that Helen would scold her again. She extracted more line, securing Karl's upper body by wrapping a few loops around his chest and tying him firmly to the table. Finally, she wrapped the line around his legs and ankles preventing any chance of him being able to make a run for it.

Lexi left Karl to his own devices. Stepping closer to Helen, she cradled her cheek. "Hey, are you back with us?"

Helen sprang to life immediately, trying to get up. "Where's…?" Hair fell across her face as she jerked upright. The deep groan told Lexi she was regretting the sharp movement.

"It's okay. It's over. Stay where you are. You're safe." Lexi placed her other hand on Helen's knee to prevent her from trying to right herself.

With a shaky breath as she leant back against the wall, Lexi pushed the hair away from Helen's eyes.

"You're bleeding." Helen reached out a hand, releasing it from the firm grip she had on her upper arm.

Pain etched itself on Helen's face at the movement. Helen's shoulder didn't look good, from the way she was holding it. "It's nothing. You look much worse," she said.

"Thanks." A wry grin flashed across Helen's face. "What happened?"

Lexi smiled down at her. "I tied him up." A groan from across the room accompanied her proud statement. "It's not easy tying up a semiconscious lump of a man." Another moan echoed behind her.

"What did you do?"

"Well, I had to improvise. There's not a lot to tie him to or with." Lexi tried not to sound too proud of herself.

"Okay." Helen tilted her head to one side to look past her shoulder.

"I hit him with the fire extinguisher, then used your cuffs on him. The police are on their way." Lexi repeated the last part in case Helen hadn't heard her the first time.

"Good. I'm not sure I could take another round with him right now."

Karl obviously had other ideas as he struggled against his restraints. Lexi could see the dark stain of blood on the side of his head where she'd stunned him. He leant back, using his feet to propel himself forward like a drunken caterpillar. From the look of it, the pain in his knee was hindering him as he slowly dragged the table behind him.

Lexi dearly wanted to give him another clout, but she knew Helen wouldn't approve. "We should wait in the hallway."

"Umm," Helen said through a grimace, "I can't move my arm."

They both eyed Karl as he slumped back against the table from the effort of his movement.

Lexi returned her attention to Helen. "Shit." She'd seen that injury before. "Your shoulder looks pretty bad." Lexi got to her feet. "Right, don't move. I'll be back in a sec." She ran back to the bedroom to grab a pillow from the bed. Pulling off the pillowcase, she ripped it down one of the side seams to form a large square piece of material.

Lexi returned to Helen crouching down next to her. "Okay. We need to support that arm." She folded the ripped pillowcase into a triangle, laying it on the floor. She flattened the pillow with her arms before slipping it between Helen's upper arm and chest.

"Please tell me you read this in a first-aid book," Helen said with another grimace.

Lexi caught her eye for a moment before focusing on her task. "You might have dislocated your shoulder. It's lower than the other one."

"It fucking hurts. I know that," Helen said through gritted teeth.

Lexi chuckled for the first time that morning. With Helen's focus on her, she carefully slipped the pillowcase material between Helen's body and the pillow. "You need to let go for a second so I can tie this off."

"Okay." Helen gasped as she released her arm.

Lexi quickly tied the two ends of the triangle around the side of Helen's neck, strapping her arm tight to her body. "Right. Let's get you up." Lexi shuffled on her knees. Getting behind Helen, she urged her up.

Helen released another yelp as Lexi's hands made contact with her body, wobbling as she finally got to her feet.

Karl must have sensed his chance. He tried to move towards them, again dragging the table in their direction.

Lexi stood between Karl, the human slug, and Helen as she supported her awkward stagger towards the flat entrance. They both slipped through the front door. Lexi quickly closed it behind them, trapping Karl in the room.

"Please tell me that table won't fit through the doorway?" Helen asked as she gingerly took a seat on the stairs to the upper flats. Karl's thudding feet echoed in the hallway.

"You'd think he eats Duracell batteries the way he goes on. I'm a bit worried I might have given him brain damage," Lexi replied as she bent to look at Helen's head wound.

"Good. He clouted me with that bloody great lump of wood." She flinched at Lexi's inspection of the wound.

The sound of distant sirens finally made Lexi breathe a little easier. Moments later, two uniformed officers thundered through the large front door.

"He's in there," Lexi told them as she pulled Helen's set of keys from her pocket.

CHAPTER 31

LEXI PEERED ROUND THE SIDE of the curtain. "Hey. *This* is where you're hiding, is it?"

Dark circles hung under Helen's eyes. She sat on the edge of the hospital bed. A black Velcro sling held her left arm. The other hand pressed a blue ice pack to the side of her head.

Lexi stepped through the curtains, carefully balancing the tray of cups and snacks as she pulled them closed behind her. Moving the short distance to Helen, she placed her handful of goodies on the bed, then took the ice pack from her and inspected the lump that had formed. She forced a smile despite her frustration at Helen's bashed-up appearance. Using her free hand, she cupped Helen's face, placing a soft kiss on her lips. She lingered long enough to breathe in her familiar scent.

Helen's arm wrapped around her back, drawing her in, pressing their bodies together. Lexi urged Helen closer, resting her chin atop Helen's head. She smiled to herself. Only a couple of days ago, their positions had been reversed, when Helen comforted her upon her return home from hospital. Now they were back in a different hospital because of another selfish bastard.

Lexi felt Helen's frame shudder. Instinctively, she tightened her grip as she moved her hand in slow circles down Helen's back to comfort her. "It's okay," she whispered as she kissed the top of Helen's head.

The yell of another patient nearby made them both jump. Lexi stepped back as Helen loosened her grip. She'd never seen Helen look quite so regretful and broken. It didn't suit her. As much as she wanted to grill Helen, for now she tried to lighten the mood. "It wasn't you I heard screaming earlier, then?" Lexi nodded in the direction of the sound.

Helen shook her head. Then immediately regretted it by the look on her face. "They gave me a stick to bite on when they forced the bone back in."

Lexi's body shivered at the very thought of it, making Helen's smile a bit wider.

"What's all this?" Helen gestured to the takeaway cups and bag on the bed.

Lexi had already forgotten all about the refreshments. "Oh. I got you a tea."

"Thanks." Helen attempted to sit up a little more, her strapped shoulder hindering her movement.

"I got you some biscuits too, in case you're hungry." Lexi pulled the small pack of custard creams from her pocket, placing them next to the cardboard drinks tray. She took off her shoulder bag and let it drop to the floor as she selected one of the cups from the tray. She pulled off the lid to take a sip. It didn't matter which one she took as they drank it the same way.

"Custard creams. Really?"

The arched eyebrow aimed at her instantly made Lexi smile as she blew on her tea. "What does the doc say?" she asked over the brim of her cup as she studied Helen.

"They need to check the X-rays to make sure it's okay, then I can go."

"Pete's lurking around out there." Lexi indicated towards the waiting room. From the choice words he'd fired in Helen's direction over the phone earlier, Lexi thought it best to prepare her before they met again.

Helen closed her eyes, rubbing her face with her free hand.

She placed her hand on Helen's thigh. "He just wants to make sure you're okay." She unfolded the bag she'd placed on the bed earlier and pulled out a chocolate muffin. The wide-eyed look on Helen's face told her she'd made the right choice. Well, sweet things were meant to be good for shock.

"What's that?" Helen enquired.

Lexi placed her tea on the small side table, then turned back to Helen. "*This* is a chocolate muffin." Pulling off a small chunk, she placed it in her mouth. "Umm." She pointed to the biscuits. "I got you biscuits," she said, tearing off another small chunk of sponge.

"You mean the most dangerous biscuit in the world. I'd rather have some of that, I think. I've used up enough luck for one day."

Lexi chose to ignore the last of Helen's words. "Oh, you would, would you?" She handed over the muffin, watching exactly what Helen planned to do with it in her incapacitated state. She released a small snigger as Helen frowned at her prize.

"Here, let me help you." Taking back the muffin, Lexi pulled off a chunk and offered it to Helen.

Helen dodged her approaching fingers. "You're loving this, aren't you?"

Lexi smiled. "I have to admit it feels weird not to be the one on the hospital bed for a change."

Helen took the offered sponge. "How did you make it past Nurse Ratched anyway?" she asked around the muffin chunk.

"I told her I was your wife." The words seemed to tumble from Lexi's mouth before she could stop them. Besides, it was true. She'd managed to reel off all the required information, minus the name of the GP as they were only visiting the area and in the process of moving.

"You did?" Helen sounded only a little surprised as she chewed her next bit of muffin. "I guess if you keep saving me, I'll have to come good on that, won't I?"

"Yes, *Rocky*, you will."

Helen frowned. "I don't—what?"

"I thought that was the tactic you were going for—wear him out by letting him batter you to a pulp. Then you'd take him out right at the end."

Helen opened her mouth, but no words came out. Her body seemed to droop towards the floor.

Lexi pressed on. She needed to get this off her chest now that she'd started. "You should have let me help you." Her tone was harsher than she meant it to be.

The colour drained from Helen's face. She reached out to Lexi with her free hand. "Lex, I'm sorry. I was trying to protect you. You've been through enough lately." Helen's voice was wavering, far from her usual confident self.

Although what Helen had said was true, Lexi still needed to get her point across. "I don't need that kind of protection if it means you get beaten to death while I'm somewhere else twiddling my thumbs."

Lexi let her words sink in for a moment. "None of this was your fault. You happened to see something that you weren't meant to, that's all."

"Exactly. *I did*—not you. But you're the one that got hurt." Helen almost choked on her words. "You could have died."

Lexi relented. Dropping the muffin onto the bed, she stepped into Helen, embracing her again. The strange thing was that Lexi felt more comfortable being a victim than a perpetrator, but now wasn't the time to discuss that—if ever. How could she explain that the weight she'd carried around since Warner had lightened after almost being run over? She thought at first it was simply a distraction. But since being attacked and hospitalised, she felt more balanced, normal. A spot of counselling might be in order after this was over.

Regardless of what Richard Jarvis was, she'd still ended his life, accidentally or otherwise. Now it was almost like she'd suffered for her crime, making it a little more palatable—to her, at least. Is that what this was for Helen, a penance for not neutralising the threat that had boiled over against her for the last couple of weeks?

"I'm sorry."

Helen's muffled words reached Lexi's ears, pulling her back into the present. "No, I'm sorry. I know you were trying to do the right thing in your mind."

Lexi pressed her lips onto the top of Helen's head. She felt the warmth from her body. "I love you. I don't like seeing you being used as a human punch bag."

Helen pulled back at her words. They were almost at eye level. "I love you too." Helen's voice was a little more familiar now.

Lexi cupped the side of Helen's face, bringing their lips together. The kiss was soft and warm. "Well, as a wise woman once said to me, 'Love will always have you at a disadvantage.'" She picked up the ice pack, gently putting it back in place. At the blank look on Helen's face, she added, "Lilly said it the other day."

"I've never been to so many hospitals since I met you."

232

Lexi grinned as she kissed the side of Helen's face. "Me neither." She kissed Helen one more time, closing her eyes in gratitude that this time; thankful that it was only relatively minor injuries that had brought them there.

"I'm glad it's finally over." Helen blew out a breath.

"And you caught the murderer," Lexi added, trying to add a bit of shine to the events.

"You mean *you* did—just before he killed me too!"

Lexi's grin faltered as images of Helen slumped against a wall floated through her head. "Well, I did say you needed a sidekick."

"How exactly did you get out of the bedroom, anyway?"

Grateful for the change of subject, Lexi rested her hand on Helen's thigh. "I tried the key to the big cupboard. Turns out all the door locks work off the same key."

"Lucky."

They both knew it was more than lucky. If Lexi had waited for the police to arrive, they could have both been killed.

Helen's hand covered hers, breaking her train of thought. "The nurse was very impressed with your first aid."

"She was." Lexi shrugged. "My mum dislocated her shoulder falling over pissed a few years ago. I copied what the paramedic did to her."

"Lex, did you say anything to anyone about me being an ex-copper?"

"No." Lexi frowned. "Why, did Karl say something?"

Heavy footsteps headed in their direction. Helen's eyes darted towards the curtains. "I'll tell you later."

The curtains were ripped back sharply, making them both jump despite the warning.

Pete joined them in the confined space. Closing the curtains, he spun around and nodded to Lexi, offering a small smile.

"How are you doing?" Pete directed his gaze to Helen.

"I'll recover."

Pete sighed. "Good. You-know-who's on his way."

Helen nodded. "So tell me about Hickman?"

"He suffered a head wound, could have knocked him out. He was restrained in the car—marks around the neck, wrists, and ankles. The red skin from the carbon monoxide covered up the bruising for a while. Doc noticed it when he eventually got around to the autopsy."

Helen nodded. "He wasn't taking any chances."

Lexi frowned, trying to piece it together in her head. So Karl made Hickman get the key from Lilly's mailbox first before getting rid of him, making the footage from the flat priceless. It certainly explained Karl's motivation.

"Has Nesbitt said anything yet?" Helen asked.

"Doc won't let me interview him yet—concussion."

Lexi's gaze went straight to the floor. She didn't feel guilty, not considering what he'd done to Helen. Then there was the trail of destruction he'd left behind him in Bristol.

"I know how he feels," Helen offered, holding up her ice pack.

Pete nodded, taking out his notebook. "So he broke into your flat, made threats, and attacked you both."

Lexi caught Helen's eye. Pete was virtually repeating her statement word for word.

Helen nodded. "He must have got into Lexi's flat in Bristol to get the Scarborough address."

Lexi interrupted, filling in the gaps. "I've managed to get the footage from the camera in my flat. Karl looks pretty pissed when he spots it."

"Yeah, he brought the camera with him to show me exactly how angry he was," Helen added.

"And you put the camera up because you were concerned for your safety after recent events." Pete wrote notes as he spoke.

"Yes," Helen confirmed. "Lex has been attacked twice in the last couple of weeks. Lilly said the CCTV wasn't working very well in the building, so we wanted a bit of extra security."

"Lilly Murdoch, your neighbour?" Pete confirmed.

Lexi placed her laptop on the bed, turning it to allow them both to see the screen. "It's motion activated, so it only starts when he enters the space."

The image was a little gloomy. Karl Nesbitt had waited until it was dark before going to the flat. Leaving the lamp on in the kitchen had given enough light in the hallway to catch the figure moving through the frame, triggering the camera.

The figure passed by the kitchen archway, heading farther into the flat, then disappeared out of sight. He was dressed in black, moving too quickly to see any detail at this speed. With a bit more time, she could have cleaned up the image, but that wasn't down to her anymore.

Lexi had positioned the camera on a shelf facing the archway, which also gave a good view of the area around the fridge where Helen had placed the Scarborough address. The figure appeared back in the hallway moments later, hesitating in the archway long enough to clearly see his face.

The wispy hair of Karl Nesbitt appeared on the screen. He reached an arm around the wall to turn off the lamp. As the light dimmed, it was hard to see any detail with only streetlights on below. A flash of light shone on the screen, obliterating the dark image for a few moments. A hand holding a phone slowly came into focus. He'd taken a picture of the address.

"This is where he gets mad," Lexi said. "Looks like something outside makes him look around." Nesbitt moved sharply towards the window. "He must have seen the red light on the camera in the dark. The tape must have fallen off."

They continued to watch as the camera was ripped from the shelf. Lexi glanced up, eyebrows raised. "That's it."

Pete spoke up. "What were you thinking? You set him up with that key."

"I…" Helen avoided his question. "When was it recorded?"

Lexi clicked on the timestamp. "Two fifty-three this morning. Yesterday morning," she corrected as it was now after midnight. She took a breath. This was all going far too easily, considering what they'd done to reel Nesbitt in. A second later, Pete turned to scrutinise her.

"I'll need a copy of that footage." His eyebrows raised.

"Sure." Lexi placed her messenger bag on the bed. "I'll put it on a memory stick for you now." She caught Helen's eye as she rummaged in her bag. She wasn't about to offer up her laptop; God knew what they'd find on it.

She quickly transferred the footage, offering the stick to Pete. "He must have overheard the conversation I had with Lilly about going away."

Pete glared at her, frowning before turning to Helen. He was getting suspicious. She was overcooking it.

"We searched Nesbitt's office at the flats, found a few choice items that looked like they might have come from Morris's flat, including a bronze statue that has blood on it. Could be what he used to crack Hickman on the head."

All heads twisted around as the curtains were sharply separated again.

"Well, this is a nice little conclave, isn't it?"

Lexi regarded the man with confusion. He was sharply dressed. She thought for a moment he was a doctor or consultant, but his overcoat indicated that he was a visitor of some kind.

"Sir, this is Lexi Ryan and Helen Taylor."

The man stepped into the cubicle. His gaze moved like a laser pointer straight towards Helen. Pete shoved his notebook into his pocket. The movement caught the man's attention, drawing his gaze away from Helen.

"DCI Brooks." He offered his hand to Lexi. "*I'm* in charge of this investigation."

Lexi picked up on the inflection as she saw the slightest flinch register on Helen's otherwise blank face.

Pete started to make his way out of the cubicle. "Thank you for the footage. We'll need to see you in a couple of days for your full statements."

DCI Brooks held his ground for a moment before following Pete down the corridor.

"He seems *nice*," Lexi offered as she closed the curtains again.

Helen waited till Pete was out of earshot. "Hickman must have caught Karl stealing stuff from Morris's flat, confronted him."

"But why isn't Karl sick? If he'd been in Morris's flat regularly lately, surely he would be."

"He said he'd been watching Hickman for a while, knew what he was doing all along. He said *he* put Morris out of his misery. Karl must have cut the padlock to the roof of Gallagher House. He did it even though he had a key. He wanted to see what Hickman was up to, and he wanted it to look like it had been tampered with."

"But Karl Nesbitt didn't do all that other stuff in Morris's flat."

Helen rested her hand on the bed to steady herself. "No. I think he's more of an opportunist than a planner."

"Then he makes it look like suicide—badly," Lexi finished for her.

Helen nodded. "Nesbitt could have gone back and checked the CCTV, seen me leaving out the back after you left. With my car still in the car park, he must have put two and two together."

Lexi let out a long breath. "We were waiting for the wrong man."

Helen fiddled with the ice pack on the bed. "Someone told Karl I was an ex-copper."

Lexi frowned. "Did he say that?" She hadn't heard much of the conversation at the flat.

Helen nodded. "Apart from your geeky friend, there's only one other person that knew."

CHAPTER 32

HELEN KNOCKED ON THE DOOR. The sequence of events seemed pretty straight in her head now. All except for one thing.

"Hi, Lilly," Helen said as the door pulled open.

"Helen. Wow, he really put you through the mangle, didn't he? Come on in."

"Thanks." Helen glimpsed into the small spare room as she followed Lilly along the hallway. They moved through the flat towards the kitchen. Several framed prints were leaning against the wall. Entering the sitting room, she scrutinised every piece of furniture and ornament in Lilly's flat. There was definitely at least one new addition on the sideboard, a small colourful vase.

"Tea?" Lilly asked, her back to Helen. "I was just making some."

"Please." Helen manoeuvred her strapped arm through the kitchen doorway. She watched as Lilly set about tea-making preparations.

"How's Lexi?" Lilly asked, her back still to Helen.

"She's good, really good. Thank you." She waited for Lilly to finally turn and face her. "I wanted to thank you for all your help with the camera stuff, and thanks for not telling the police."

Lilly leaned back against the kitchen units as the kettle shut itself off. "No need for that. I wanted to help."

Helen held Lilly's gaze. She definitely seemed a little worried. "I didn't want to put you in an awkward position with the police. Sorry about that."

"No problem." Lilly opened a drawer along the line of units. "Here's your little gadget. They were none the wiser."

I bet it wasn't the only thing you kept back from the police. Helen took the offered pen drive camera. "Thanks."

Lilly poured water in their mugs, seeming to avoid her scrutiny.

"You didn't happen to mention to Karl that I was an ex-copper, did you?"

Lilly hesitated as she got to the second mug. "I—I don't know. I might have said it in passing." Lilly glanced back to look at her. "Why?"

"I didn't think you had much to do with him," Helen pressed, "with him being pretty elusive around here."

Lilly added milk to the mugs. "Well, I bump into him from time to time."

"Like when he's selling you stuff from Morris's flat?"

Lilly avoided looking at her. "What? I—I don't know what you're—"

Helen cut her off. "Really?" She waved her hand in the direction of the corridor she'd walked down. "So, if I go into that spare room down there, I won't find anything? Or maybe check the CCTV for the last few months, see if Karl's visited you with various items?"

"You won't find anything on there." Lilly let out a long breath. "We always met away from here for that reason."

"Smart." Helen was genuinely disappointed her theory appeared to be true. She, like Lexi, had grown fond of Lilly. Now it turned out she was Karl's fence for the stolen goods, and part of this whole mess.

"I was just trying to make a little money. Things have been so tight since my husband died. I had to move out of our home. His pension isn't worth the paper it's written on."

Helen nodded. "I see. I'm sorry to hear that."

"I promise I didn't know what Karl was up to, or the other one, with Morris." Lilly's voice was strained.

Helen studied the worry lines on Lilly's face. She had to take Lilly at face value, after all. She'd seemed genuinely upset by Lexi's scrapes. She'd even attempted to help solve the case, even though she'd been caught in the middle of it. Helen nodded again, not wanting to verbally confirm her belief in Lilly's words.

"Are you going to tell the police?"

Helen hesitated as she moved to leave, then stopped in the doorway. "No. Your secret's safe with me."

She might never know if it was Lilly's guilt that had motivated her to help, or a genuine affection for Lexi. But she didn't have it in her to send a desperate old lady to jail for a few bad decisions. Besides, Lilly might make a good informant in the future, if they decided to stick around.

Helen led the way out of the interview room, their statements completed for the events in Bristol and Scarborough. Pete met them in the corridor, a vending-machine cup of coffee in his hand.

"Hi. On the mend?" Pete nudged his cup in the direction of her arm, still in its protective sling.

Helen smiled. "I think so." The pain in her arm had subsided a little with the help of the painkillers. She waited for the uniformed officer to leave before launching into her questions. She had spent the last two days trying to piece everything together with what felt like only half of the information.

"So, do you know what actually happened yet?" She was desperate to know the chain of events. What had Nesbitt said since his arrest? She'd reluctantly held back the footage from the mailbox and the casino. She didn't want to have to explain her illegal methods of acquiring them. She prayed they had enough evidence without it, or she'd have to come up with a convincing story. There was no way she was letting this murderer get away.

"Most of it." Pete drank the last of his coffee, then edged to the side of the corridor to let a uniformed officer pass. They both huddled around Pete conspiratorially, waiting for him to start.

"We're holding Nesbitt on the ABH while we investigate the other charges. Daniel Hickman moved down here from Spalding a little over six years ago." Pete kept his voice low. "A month later, he started working at the school in Brislington. Soon after that, he got in touch with Morris. The van Hickman was driving was previously registered to Morris when he owned his antique business."

"Morris gave him the van?" Helen queried.

"Possibly. There's no sign of any payment in Hickman's finances. The registered owner changed two months after Hickman moved down here."

Helen raised her eyebrows. *Maybe Morris was trying to build bridges.*

"We don't know exact details yet, but Hickman started using his lab to grow the Legionella to harm or kill Morris. Some of the samples we found are over two years old. We already know Hickman blamed Morris for imploding his family after the affair Morris had with his mother. Hickman didn't have any financial problems, so we're still digging around for any other possible motives."

Helen let out a breath, pushing out her words. "Hate is a pretty strong motive."

"He had the word failure carved in his thigh. Doc thinks it might have been self-inflicted so I don't think he liked himself much either."

"Jesus," Lexi mumbled.

Pete nodded before continuing. "From what we've gathered so far, it looks like Nesbitt knew what Hickman was doing to Morris."

"He told me he'd been watching Hickman for a while," Helen added, recalling Karl's words from the flat in Scarborough. "I think he felt sorry for Morris. He wanted to put him out of his misery—his words not mine."

Pete nodded. "Neighbours say Nesbitt had stopped going round to visit Morris in the last couple of months. According to Nesbitt's financials, he's broke—credit cards, loans, you name it."

"Gambling?" Helen offered, knowing full well it was the truth.

Pete raised his eyebrows. "We searched Nesbitt's office at Gallagher House. Found a collection of valuables." He used his thumbs and forefingers to make an oval shape in front of him. "Little paintings, and quite a few coins, stamps and watches. We're also checking the blood we found on the bronze statue for DNA to see if it's a match for Hickman."

"They fought. He hit him on the head with the statue, knocked him out."

"No blood at the office, so we checked Morris's flat again—found blood and signs of a struggle. Someone tried to clean it up, covered it with a rug and other crap."

"I'd talk to the guy that bought Morris's shop off him. He said something about Morris keeping the best stuff for himself when he sold up," Helen said, hoping Pete wouldn't question how she knew that information.

Pete twisted his lips. "Good to know. I'll check it out."

Helen glanced at Lexi. "Nesbitt trashed my car, stranding us in Slough the night Morris was killed. He didn't want any onlookers."

"When were you going to tell me this?" Pete asked.

"Sorry. I did put it in my statement, if that helps," Helen relented. "It made perfect sense for it to be Nesbitt. Hickman was happy to wait it out, but obviously Nesbitt had other ideas."

Pete nodded. "We checked the CCTV for both buildings. Some bits have been wiped." Pete lifted his free hand, making one set of air quotes with his fingers. "Not the so-called 'interference–wiped.' Techs found records of it being deleted."

Nesbitt had scrambled to cover his tracks. Apparently he wasn't very good at it. He should have taken a page out of Hickman's book.

"There *is* footage of Hickman stealing your key from the mailbox in Longwell House. Then he disappears out the back of the building. Nothing after that anywhere. The cameras in Gallagher House weren't working at the time."

"Bit convenient" Lexi offered.

"Exactly," Helen agreed.

"Also, with Hickman being restrained over his clothing, it raises suspicions. The markings left on the skin are unclear. Especially around his neck, where he might have used a scarf or something. Techs are checking several items found in the car for a fibre match. *But* we did find a cut cable tie near the car where Hickman was found. It's the same type and brand that we found in Nesbitt's office. Could be what he used on his wrists."

That sounded more solid. "So Nesbitt knocks him out, ties him up in the stolen car, and then sets it running till he's dead. Cuts the ties and leaves him to be found, making everyone think suicide—at least for a while."

"Yeah," Pete confirmed with a nod.

"Anything on the stolen car Hickman was found in?" Helen asked. Loose ends were her kryptonite.

Pete sighed. "Stolen from a side street, not far from the station. Nothing more than that yet. Techs are still going over it."

Handy. Perfect place to make it look like Hickman stole it after dumping his van. "Where does Nesbitt live?"

"Out past Oldland."

Oldland. Helen made a mental note to check her map later. "Does he have any family?"

Pete adjusted his feet. "Wife and daughter. Left him a couple of years ago. He lives alone."

Had his gambling driven them away? "Is Nesbitt talking?" At this point, Helen would probably give her only working arm to be the one doing the interview. She had so many questions and still so few answers.

"Not much. Brooks is interviewing him again now. Mostly 'No comment' so far."

"Could we…?" Helen raised her eyebrows hopefully.

Pete blew out a breath. "Five minutes, that's it. Brooks is already pissed with you for solving his case and making him look like a dick."

He led them farther down the corridor to a darkened room. A desktop computer with a large monitor occupied the opposite side of the room. The back of what she figured was Brooks's head filled part of the screen. Karl Nesbitt sat the other side of a table, leaning back in his chair. A bandage covered the left side of his head. His solicitor sat next to him, making notes on a legal pad.

Pete threw his empty cup in the bin before tapping a few keys on the keyboard. The rustling of paper from the speakers filled the room.

"I have some video footage I want to show you, Mr Nesbitt." Brooks opened a laptop, tapping several keys before turning it to face Nesbitt. After a few seconds, he tapped the keys again. "Is that you in the footage?"

"No comment."

"Mr Nesbitt, can you tell me where you were between the hours of two-thirty and three-thirty on the morning of the twentieth of August?"

"Is that Daniel Hickman's time of death?" Helen aimed her question at Pete, waiting for his nod of confirmation.

That was after the mailbox footage was recorded. Thank God Nesbitt had kept the CCTV footage, no doubt with the idea of incriminating Hickman.

"Do you know a Mr Daniel Hickman?" Brooks continued.

Helen sighed in frustration, Nesbitt knew he was in deep trouble, but his "No comment" answers would go against him in the end. He might not be adding strength to the case against him, but she knew it would weaken his defence in court, if it got that far. Nesbitt was dodging the inevitable.

"His brief's just scoping out the evidence. He'll give a prepared statement by the end of the day," Pete said with confidence.

Helen studied him for a moment. "You think?"

"Okay, let's try something else." Brooks was obviously getting irritated. "Mr Nesbitt, we're here to get your version of events, to get your side of the story, if you like. We're not trying to trip you up."

Nesbitt made no reply. He simply stared at his thick hands.

Brooks shuffled his papers before addressing Nesbit again. "You were arrested after an altercation two days ago at Flat 15A, Seaview Terrace in Scarborough. You have since been charged under section 47 of the Offences Against the Person Act. What brought you to that flat, Mr Nesbitt?"

"No comment."

"The woman that you attacked, Helen Taylor, do you know her?"

"Fucking bitch! One of yours, was she? Sticking her nose into everything."

Everyone stood a little straighter as Karl Nesbitt finally broke his "No comment" rule.

"Is that why you attacked her, Karl?"

"She couldn't fucking leave it alone—"

Pete switched off the sound. "That's enough of that." He stood to look at Helen. "We'll get a statement pretty soon I'd say."

Helen stared at the screen. Nesbitt was discreetly talking to his solicitor. Maybe Pete had called it correctly after all. She prayed he was right. She didn't fancy either herself or Lexi being called as a witness if he didn't admit his guilt.

Helen leant against the wall to her right. "He was after me. He thought I knew he was involved—thought I'd seen something." She racked her brain, trying to picture the inside of Karl's office. She'd seen the bolt croppers, but what else? The stolen items could have been there, but she couldn't recall seeing them.

"Shit." She'd been so sure after seeing the camera footage from the mailbox. She caught Lexi's eye. She'd been so intent on protecting her, she hadn't realised she could be the target.

"I was wrong." Helen mumbled. *Fuck.* She did the mental maths. "Hickman must have fought with Nesbitt right after the key was taken from the mailbox. Karl was obviously watching him that night too."

Helen glanced at Pete, then Lexi before continuing. "They fight. Nesbitt ends up with the key. He goes to our flat and looks for me, realises he's been tricked when he sees the camera. He deals with Hickman, then heads up to Scarborough to—"

Lexi grabbed her hand, silencing the words in her throat.

Helen pulled away. She rubbed her eyes in frustration. It was all becoming clear now. Just as she'd suspected, Nesbitt had cut the lock to the roof of Gallagher House with the purpose of leading a trail up to the roof and the evidence against Hickman.

Finding that makeshift key in Hickman's lab had been niggling at her for days. There had been no reason for Hickman to cut the lock. He'd been meticulous in his planning; the lab was proof of that. Nesbitt, on the other hand, was a very different animal. "Did you check out those keys from the lab?" she asked.

"What?" Pete took a moment to slip back into the conversation. "You were right. The homemade key fitted the roof padlock."

"And the door lock?" Helen persisted.

"They couldn't be definitive, but there were shavings in the lock and some marks on the pins inside."

Helen had played right into Nesbitt's hands. She'd practically made the case against Daniel Hickman when she showed him the damage on the roof. The way he reluctantly let her look at the CCTV footage confirmed her theory. With Lexi away and her car still in the car park, he'd checked the CCTV footage and saw her leaving out the back door. He'd been one step ahead every time.

Lexi took her hand again. "Come on. We should go."

———

Lexi led the way back to her car. She stopped next to the passenger door, ready to open it for Helen. She hesitated as she twisted to look at her. There were still tell-tale flinches in Helen's movement indicating that she was still in pain from her beating.

With travelling back to Bristol and catching up on sleep, they hadn't had much time to talk over the last two days. Helen's morose mood hadn't helped. Still, Lexi needed to clear the air.

"I know the last few weeks have been a whirlwind with everything that's happened. I hope it hasn't put you off moving in with me."

"Are you kidding me? I can't leave you alone. God knows what you'll get yourself into if I'm not there."

Lexi grinned, considering Helen was the one with her arm in a sling. She couldn't resist the customary raised eyebrow as she eyed her injury.

"This," Helen raised her arm for a second, "this is a blip; that's all. It's the first time I've actually needed hospital treatment when making an arrest."

Typical. Nearly twenty years in the police force without a scratch. Less than a month with me and she needs hospital treatment. "I hope you're right." Lexi grasped the door handle to open it again but stopped. "Listen. I know you think this is all your fault, but you could never have known what Daniel Hickman was up to. We don't even know if he was really trying to kill Morris or merely punish him." She took a quick breath, not wanting Helen to interrupt her. Reaching out, she seized Helen's free hand.

"If he'd wanted to kill me, he could have. We both know that. The truth is, without Hickman around, we may never know what he was thinking or what he was really up to."

Helen hung her head. This was not going well. She was meant to be pepping her up, not bringing Helen down even more. "I know how frustrated that makes you. How neat and tidy you like it all to be at the end. But the important thing to remember is you ferreted out the real murderer and he's in police custody. That's got to be a win."

"It is."

Lexi smiled.

"Maybe that private investigator's course I'm booked on will give me a few pointers for the future."

Lexi's move to grab the door handle stilled again. "What? Really? You're doing it?" She very much doubted a week's training course could teach Helen anything that being a police officer hadn't already taught her. It was merely a formality, a hoop to jump through before getting licenced.

"I am. You wore me down. Now, are you taking me to lunch?"

"Absolutely." Lexi finally pulled open the passenger door, guiding Helen to her seat. "Okay. I guess being the one-armed bandit, you'll be stuck with the soup today." Lexi swiftly closed the door. Helen was already glaring at her when she got in the driver's seat.

"You're not going to help me?" Helen's tone held some mock hurt that felt more familiar than her mood over the last couple of days. "Think of it like when the oxygen masks drop down in an aeroplane. They always say to look after yourself first, then look after those around you." Lexi clicked her seatbelt into place before starting the car. "And, well, you know how I feel about food, so if you're hungry, you should probably choose the soup."

"You *are* a food monster." Helen sighed as if considering her options. "Maybe the waitress will take pity on me."

"Good luck with that." Lexi laughed.

"Shit!" Helen huffed as she pulled away.

EPILOGUE

Three weeks later

WITH THEIR BAGS UNPACKED, HELEN gathered the last of their clothes, ready to put them in the washing machine. A knock at the door halted her progress. She dumped them on the bedroom floor and headed for the door. She'd been expecting a certain visitor for the last hour. Lexi had made herself scarce to give her some space.

Pete Laker stood on the other side, carrier bag in hand. "Hi." She stood to one side as he passed, allowing her to shut the door.

"Hi." He twisted his Tesco carrier bag between his fingers.

"Tea?" Helen offered as she led the way into the kitchen. When Pete didn't reply straight away, she spun around to look at him and found him peering into the lounge.

"She's out," Helen told him, wondering why there was a sudden need for secrecy. Was he really that freaked about handing over a case file for her to look over?

"Tea would be great," he replied sheepishly and followed her into the kitchen.

Helen flipped on the kettle before she turned to look at him. He appeared awkward in the small space. She took pity on him as she took a seat at the table, indicating for him to do the same.

Pete settled into the seat opposite. "Okay. So, as I said last week when you were in..." He let his words hang in the air between them.

Helen rolled her eyes. "London."

"London!" Pete repeated with raised eyebrows. "New job?"

"I was on a training course," was all Helen gave him. She figured he might not be over the moon with her choice of employment. She didn't want him to think of her as a permanent thorn in his side.

"Training? For what?"

"Don't laugh." Helen gave him a stern look. "It's a private investigator course. I need to do it before I can get officially licenced."

Pete sniggered. "I knew you wouldn't be able to give it up."

"Well, I figured this way I can be my own boss. No red tape. It gives me options."

"Yeah, yeah, whatever you say." Pete rested his hands on the table in front of him.

The kettle clicked off behind Helen, bringing silence to the small kitchen.

"Anyway." Pete let out a breath. "Nesbitt changed his plea. He finally decided it was a waste of time, considering the evidence we'd gathered. He pleaded guilty. The CPS have offered him eighteen years."

"Is that it? He'll only do nine or ten." For murder times two, he'd got off easy.

Pete raised his hand from the table. "I know it's not ideal, but we could only get him for Daniel Hickman, not Morris Ryder."

"What?" Although she already knew the reasons, in Helen's mind there was no way Hickman killed Morris.

"We couldn't place him at the flat on the night Morris died. No one saw him in the area. His phone puts him at home, and neighbours saw his car in his driveway all night. We couldn't find him on CCTV or public transport, no taxi firms—nothing."

"Shit. You couldn't find anything to link him at all?" It seemed impossible to Helen that such a klutz could get away with murder.

"Well, Nesbitt's fingerprints were in the flat, but he admitted visiting Morris in the past and stealing the stuff before and after Morris was dead. None of Nesbitt's DNA was found on the cushion that was actually used to smother Morris."

Gloves. "Lucky bastard." It wasn't the first time she'd had to accept that the evidence just wasn't there, but it didn't make it any easier to swallow.

Pete nodded. "I know."

"What about my car?" Helen wondered what story he'd spun to get out of that.

"He admitted that, said Hickman told him to do it in exchange for items from Morris's flat. He didn't question it at the time. He needed the payoff to sort out some debts."

Bullshit. Karl Nesbitt was one cocky bastard. Helen stood to make the tea as Pete continued. "He did it off his own back so he wouldn't risk being seen when he topped Morris. We both know it."

"ANPR cameras found Nesbitt's car following you on your trip to Slough on the twelfth, so, like you said, he trashes your car. Twenty minutes later, he travels back to his home in Bristol."

Helen tossed the used teabags into the bin. "How did he explain Hickman's death?"

"He says he fought with Hickman over the stuff he stole from Morris Ryder's flat."

Helen placed the milk back in the fridge. In her frustration, she tossed the teaspoon in the sink. "About the only honest thing he did say."

Pete leaned back in his chair, folding his arms in front of him as she placed a cup of tea in front of him. "Claims he thought he'd killed him, panicked, and tried to make it look like suicide."

"Crazy. How did he expect to get away with that?" Helen said incredulously. *Money-saving at its best. Why go to the expense of a court case you don't have a guarantee of winning?* Helen slumped in her seat.

"Total bollocks, I know, considering he had to restrain him in the car. But he doesn't exactly have an exclusive relationship with the truth."

Helen arched an eyebrow, sensing there was more to Pete's words. "What?"

"He said that Hickman started moving stuff around Morris's flat—for him to fall over—isolating him, making him scared to go out."

Not surprising with the plans Hickman had in the pipeline. Helen toyed with her mug handle. Did he really deserve to die for it? "He knew Hickman wasn't dead when he put him in that car. He only wanted to stop him talking about Morris."

Pete sat back, chewing his lip as she vented.

"I know," Pete placated her, "but we couldn't find the evidence. The CPS refuse to take it further. Unfortunately, when we talked to Hickman, he was nothing more than a witness. Had we got to talk to him after we found out Morris was killed, then it might have been different."

"You mean if Brooks hadn't spouted off about it, announcing to the world." Helen blew vigorously on her tea as she seethed.

"Yeah that. Hickman might have been willing to talk, come clean maybe."

A silence settled between them as they drank their tea.

"We did find Hickman's blood in Nesbitt's car boot," Pete said. "He must have kept Hickman in there before putting him in the stolen car to kill him."

"Makes sense." Helen nodded as she took a tentative sip of her tea. Over the last couple of weeks, she'd contemplated Hickman's part in the events. She'd started to see him as another victim. It was easy to forget he'd been responsible for the death of an environmental health worker in the process, and not just a pawn in Nesbitt's nasty game to get himself out of debt.

"He planted our flat key on Hickman to tie up the loose ends. If he'd had a better plan to get rid of Hickman, he could have got away with all of it," Helen thought aloud.

"Until the next time," Pete replied. "People like Nesbitt don't change. He'd have got himself in another pickle soon enough."

Helen nodded, concurring with Pete's statement. "Can we have our door key back? They're a nightmare to get cut."

"Uh, sure. I'll sort that out for you."

"Thanks." Helen took a sip from her tea. "I think Hickman freaked when he thought he'd actually succeeded in killing Morris." Helen waited for Pete to meet her eye. "Why else would he attack Lexi with the same stuff? He knew we'd link the two incidents."

"You think he wanted to be caught?" Pete questioned.

"Maybe. I mean Hickman found Morris. Why not get rid of the plug-in air-freshener thing before calling it in?" Helen let him weigh up her words as she drank her tea. The rustle of the bag on the floor reminded her that Pete wasn't there to fill her in on Nesbitt.

"He could have panicked. But who knows?"

"Anyway." Helen let it drop. She could have speculated for hours on this particular subject. "What have you got for me?"

251

Pete placed the carrier bag he'd brought with him on the table and set it between the two of them. He rested his hand on top, rustling the plastic. "This is the case I was telling you about. It's a copy of both case files—ours and the later one in Preston. No rush. Let me know what you think."

"Okay. No problem. I owe you big time." Helen fingered the front cover through the plastic. "I'll get back to you if anything pops out at me." In truth, after recent events, she was hoping for something a little lighter than a possible double murder. She slipped the thick folder out onto the table.

"It's a bit of a weird one. Apart from blood on the murder weapon, which was found in the perpetrator's home, there were no links between the victim and murderer. Same in Preston. Both perpetrators claimed to not know the victims at all."

"There was enough forensic evidence to convict them?" Helen asked with a frown.

Pete nodded. "One even took a plea." He tapped the file with his free hand as he drank his tea. "I'd better get off."

Shit. Helen regarded the mass of papers sticking out of the brown folder. She didn't even have her licence yet and she already had another case lined up.

OTHER BOOKS FROM YLVA PUBLISHING

www.ylva-publishing.com

BODY OF WORK
Charlotte Mills

ISBN: 978-3-96324-308-0
Length: 231 pages (81,000 words)

Artist Noa has hidden herself away after losing her wife and brother. Her worried agent sends her to rural England for a break and fresh inspiration. District nurse Paige is intrigued by the stubborn out-of-towner and romance flares. Noa's torn between protecting her heart and trusting it, just as ghosts from her past surface.

A lesbian romantic suspense about taking a chance on love after loss.

PAYBACK
Charlotte Mills

ISBN: 978-3-96324-125-3
Length: 219 pages (76,000 words)

Det. Constable Kate Wolfe is sent to a small backwater, but before she can settle in, something catastrophic happens. There's an arson attack, a dead body, and a missing man to investigate. Not to mention the new boss to stare down. But her growing attraction to Det. Chief Inspector Helen Taylor is the least of her problems when a dumped vehicle in a lake changes their lives forever.

A CURIOUS WOMAN

Jess Lea

ISBN: 978-3-96324-160-4
Length: 283 pages (100,000 words)

Bess has moved to a coastal town where she has a job at a hip gallery, some territorial chickens, and a lot of self-help books. She's also at war with Margaret, who runs the local museum with an iron fist. When they're both implicated in a senseless murder, can they work together to expose the truth?

A funny, fabulous, cozy mystery filled with quirkiness and a sweet serve of lesbian romance.

MEANT TO BE ME

Wendy Hudson

ISBN: 978-3-96324-164-2
Length: 283 pages (94,000 words)

A chance meeting in Scotland binds two friends and a stranger together. Engineer Darcy faces the world with a smile, despite having a shadowy stalker. Her best friend, Anja, has a dark past but a new chance for love. Stranger Eilidh's instinct is to run toward the chaos, but will she be burned?

The women's lives intertwine in a love triangle in this romantic suspense that will keep you guessing.

ABOUT CHARLOTTE MILLS

Charlotte Mills was born and bred in the south of England, after studying Fine Art at Loughborough University she has made the Midlands her home for the last twenty years where she lives with her long term partner.

Her career has bridged several different fields including the arts, education and construction.

She began creative writing in 2013, taking the plunge with self-publishing in 2014 with her first book *Unlikely Places*. This was followed up with *Out of The Blue* and its sequel *Latent Memories* in 2016 for which she won a gold medal at the Global EBook Awards for LGBT fiction in 2017.

When she is not writing she enjoys watching films and day dreaming about living in the middle of nowhere without any neighbors in earshot.

CONNECT WITH CHARLOTTE
E-Mail: charlottemills863@gmail.com

Fair Game
© 2020 by Charlotte Mills

ISBN: 978-3-96324-397-4

Also available as e-book.

Published by Ylva Publishing, legal entity of Ylva Verlag, e.Kfr.

Ylva Verlag, e.Kfr.
Owner: Astrid Ohletz
Am Kirschgarten 2
65830 Kriftel
Germany

www.ylva-publishing.com

First edition: 2020

Credits
Edited by Miranda Miller and Michelle Aguilar
Cover Design and Print Layout by Streetlight Graphics

Lightning Source UK Ltd.
Milton Keynes UK
UKHW010202250820
368747UK00001B/1